BANGERS AND MASH

BANGERS AND MASH

Graham Scholey

The Book Guild Ltd
Sussex, England

This book is a work of fiction. The characters and situations in this story are imaginary. No resemblance is intended between these characters and any real persons, either living or dead.

This book is sold subject to the condition that it shall not, by way of trade or otherwise, be lent, re-sold, hired out, photocopied or held in any retrieval system or otherwise circulated without the publisher's prior consent in any form of binding or cover other than that in which this is published and without a similar condition including this condition being imposed on the subsequent purchaser.

The Book Guild Ltd.
25 High Street,
Lewes, Sussex

First published 1996
© Graham Scholey 1996

Set in Baskerville

Typesetting by Wordset
Hassocks, West Sussex

Printed in Great Britain by
Anthony Rowe Ltd.
Chippenham, Wiltshire.

A catalogue record for this book is available from the British Library

ISBN 1 85776 074 3

CONTENTS

The Boys in Blue		vii
1	The Decision	9
2	The Shape of Things to Come	16
3	Introducing Bob	22
4	The Interview	34
5	*Docendo Discimus*	44
6	Jimmy Settles in	57
7	Politics at Garnstone	65
8	Service with a Smile	74
9	Who is Sylvia?	80
10	Out of the Frying Pan	92
11	At Home with Principal Ness	101
12	Partners in Arms	108
13	Back to Garnstone	117
14	The Christmas Party	131
15	I'm Dreaming of a White Christmas	146
16	Hi De Hi	160
17	Back to Dronsley	171
18	Hector Britain and Bob Malone Investigations	181
19	Nemesis	192
20	Things That go Bump in the Night	204

21	A Pressing Engagement	210
22	Those Wedding Bells	222
23	The Great Outdoors	234
24	Retribution	243
25	On the Move	254
26	Twilight Classes	266
27	The New Tribulations of Hector Britain	273
28	The Time for Change	281
29	Into the Future	291

THE BOYS IN BLUE

Many, many, years ago when I was in my prime,
I signed on in the RAF and there I served my time.
This little tale's about those days, to give a brief description:
All men were bold; and Britain great; and *all* youths did conscription.

I'd heard about the Army; but I thought that's not for me.
I didn't want the Navy, for I just don't like the sea.
I thought I'd be a man in blue, in aircraft in the sky,
But after I'd signed on the line – they would not let me fly.

They gave to me a little card – to take to doctor man.
He gave to me a bottle and said, 'Fill it if you can.'
Behind the screen I filled it up. He brewed it up like tea.
'You're fit,' he said. 'We'll take you on. An airman you will be.'
And when I told my mates at work, they laughed and thought it fun,
And so I duly took the train, and went to Cardington.

We got there in the afternoon, the nicest place you've seen:
The corporal so friendly; and the billet oh so clean.
'Go out tonight,' the corporal said. 'You'll really like it here.'
We did: we really lived it up, and drank a lot of beer.

The next day, he said, 'Come for a stroll, come sign the contract line.'
And when we'd done as he did wish, he changed into a swine.'
No longer were his tones so soft: he now did *roar* and *bellow*,
'You've signed on now, you bloody fools,' said that quite dreadful fellow.
He made us march; he *cursed* and *yelled*. 'Off to the stores,' he said.
They gave us misfit uniforms; and small hats for our heads,
Then to the barbers for a trim, with hair sheared off like sheep,
The lovely locks all hacked away, all laid on floor in heap.

Then back to billets once again, the corporal bawling loud.
'You see this floor', he said to us, 'Of it, I was once proud.
But you have scratched it with your boots; and this will just not do.
I want to see it gleam again, my face in it to view.'

They practised *bull* there such a lot; and *bull*, as you well know,
Means lot of polish everywhere; and brasses that do glow.
They made up bed packs every day; and these had to be square,
And though we knew that we'd been conned – Complain? We did not dare.

No flecks of dust were allowed there, and not a splash of mud.
To keep the place so sparkling clean, we all had to sweat blood.
They woke us up at crack of dawn, our lights went out at ten,
And everywhere we went we marched, up hills and down again.

The morning call at half past five was done with clanging bell.
We'd march to breakfast, half alive. They made our life like hell.
The porridge was a gooey mass to keep us warm in winter.
The eggs were plastic in their feel; and bacon burnt to cinder.

One lad who seemed to be well-born complained of awful tea.
'Excuse me corporal,' said the lad, 'it's not quite right for me.'
'The tea is stewed and in the urns is stain of dreadful brown.'
The corporal man was most upset, on face came nasty frown;
His neck went red, he puffed up large and then he 'went to town'.
And every night the innocent was marched all up and down.
And every evening after tea the innocent would suffer.
He had to polish all the urns. This lad he was a duffer.

And I was also sacrificed, for lack of crease in togs.
The corporal man was very brusque, he made me clean the *bogs*.
I had to swill out the latrines and wash and scrub the pan,
To think I'd thought that I would fly, not be a sanitary man.

And all too soon came happy day, when square-bashing was over.
I really felt so very grand, I really felt in clover,
And though I never flew the planes, I was a man in blue,
I helped to make those plastic eggs; and that strange porridge goo.

1

THE DECISION

It was a lovely spring afternoon in March. Taffy Owens the dour cynical woodwork teacher stared wistfully out of the windows at the host of golden daffodils fluttering and dancing in the light breeze. He thought of his own well-regimented garden, and dreamt of the new pond planned as an enhancement to the second lawn at the bottom of its far reaches. He would have liked to start operations this very afternoon before nightfall. Taffy had a nice timetable, with a 2.30 p.m finish on Fridays. This was a recompense for making old Millipede, the incumbent headmaster, a replacement 'Georgian' chair for the one given to the Scouts' bonfire by the headmaster's dotty sister-in-law. Now old Millipede was about to retire and escape from these horrible kids whose only culture was The Beatles and The Rolling Stones. Now he was to be replaced by this white-haired trendy from the Department of Education.

Miss Todd, the domestic science teacher also resented the delayed departure for the Easter vacation. Miss Todd was a large lady who was a walking advertisement for the culture of eating well. Unlike Taffy, Miss Todd lived for her work. She coached and encouraged her girls, she insisted on absolute cleanliness in thought and deed, and she had a thorough contempt for about 95 per cent of the male species. Old Millipede fell within the 5 per cent of the males falling within the Todd tolerance range. Every Friday she would leave a biscuit tin of her scrumptious sultana scones on old Millipede's desk. She paid for these out of her own pocket. Miss Todd was as scrupulously honest, as her kitchen was scrupulously clean. Miss Todd was of the 'old school'. Miss Todd was born a hundred years too late. She belonged in Edwardian times. Miss Todd had formed a quick impression of Mr Parable, and it was not good. It would seem that Mr Parable would probably not be on the receiving end of the weekly sultana scones food parcel. A sherry leaving-party for old Millipede had been arranged, until the untoward early arrival of this new interloper. Mr Parable had definitely put a further blight on the sad departure proceedings. Was this the shape of things to come? Unlike Taffy, Miss Todd taught until the last minute, the 'God Slot' from 3 p.m. until 4 p.m. so nicknamed by the irreverent Taffy. Taffy of course went to church for weddings, christenings, funerals and Remembrance Sundays. Miss Todd resented the cancellation of her class, but this new mountebank was intolerable.

Mr Etchells, the English teacher, sat next to Taffy. The two had served in the army together and shared a mutual bond in the realms of discipline. Mr Etchells was a marksman class one at throwing chalk at distracted pupils. He always caught the victim's earlobe with a resounding 'ping'. He was also in the Black Horse darts' team. It was only schoolboy lobes that received the Etchells chalk bombardment though. For schoolgirls Mr Etchells was unparalleled in the art of sarcasm. Several hard-bitten St Trinianish girls had broken down into waterfalls of tears, after one of his fierce diatribes. Miss Todd and he had clashed on several occasions, but even she had broken down on one occasion. It was noticeable that whereas Taffy would always be found adjacent to Mr Etchells, Miss Todd would migrate to the opposite end of the room so as to be as far away as possible.

Mr Foskett and Mr Johnson sat almost holding hands. There had never been proof but they were both repeatedly slandered for suspected homosexual leanings, even though Mr Johnson was married.

Mr Smythe Browne, the Deputy Headmaster of Fanshawe

Secondary School was trying to gain the attention of the motley group of teachers sprawled around the long committee table.

'Where's Miss Liberty?' he asked pompously.

Miss Liberty was the young delicious-natured biology teacher who had caught the eye of Mr Gordon the games master.

'Mr Gordon's probably taking liberties behind the tennis court,' said Taffy scandalously. At that moment Mr Gordon appeared through the door followed by the blushing Miss Liberty.

'Would you like to come outside and repeat that?' asked Mr Gordon aggressively.

Taffy hastily declined. 'Only joking, boyo, only joking,' he said retiringly.

'Come along now, let's get this meeting under way,' said Smythe Browne hopefully.

Old Millipede winced, whilst Mr Parable put on his bifocals to peer at Mr Gordon and Miss Liberty, rather in the manner of a biologist studying animal behaviour. Mr Parable had got first class honours in sociology and study of psychological behaviour. Miss Kippling and Mrs Cooper continued in deep conversation about the antics of the divorcée who lived on their street. Mr Best was engrossed in *The Times* crossword. Miss Giving was engrossed in her knitting. Mr Smythe Browne banged on the table for attention, and the proceedings at last began.

'Before we say our sad farewell to Mr Millipede, our headmaster for thirteen years and six months, I should like to disseminate some information, and then our new headmaster, Mr Parable, would like to say a few words,' said Mr Smythe Browne.

Mr Smythe Browne rambled on in his normal style. He had a somewhat monosyllabic style of delivery which would have made a best-selling record for insomniacs. Arthur Milne, the Latin teacher, had fallen asleep once during a Smythe Browne marathon, and had fallen off his chair and banged his head on the corner of the table leg. Taffy had claimed a £1 bet from Mr Etchells as a result. Mr Gordon had had to render first-aid. Taffy looked at Mr Milne speculatively, decided against his pecunious inclinations and muttered loudly under his breath, 'Get on with it.' Smythe Browne glared at him. Mr Etchells stared pointedly at the large grandfather clock bought by Freddy Fanshawe. Eventually Mr Smythe Browne released the centre of the stage to Mr Parable. The staff broke off from their distractions in an attempt to weigh up the newcomer.

Mr Parable was slim and a jogging freak. Not that they called it jogging in those days. Mr Parable was ahead of his time. He had long white hair like Jon Pertwee, the second Doctor Who. Mr Parable peered over the top of his bifocals at his new staff. It was difficult to imagine what he was thinking. He seemed to look down on them as lesser mortals. He was dressed in pinstripes with a cravat instead of a tie. His shoes were suede and scuffed. He had bright pink socks which were incongruous with the pinstripes. He wore a pink shirt. Miss Todd remarked, to no-one in particular, that dress sense he had not.

Mr Parable was a B.A. (*Hons*) Cantab and York. He had a vocabulary second to none, including the late William Shakespeare. Unfortunately, he was, to say the least, totally incomprehensible. He began by paying the usual tribute to his predecessor, Old Millipede, who looked on in embarrassment. He was rather sad to be leaving, but he was not at home with the new initiatives coming from the Department of Education.

'Think BIN,' said the professor-like Mr Parable. 'B for bounteous, I for innovative, N for novel.'

'Think *crap*,' muttered Taffy. 'Completely revolting and prattish.'

Mr Parable seemed not to notice whilst a few sniggers came from some of those who had.

Mr Parable had had two years at the Department of Education and had developed a special style of lecture delivery designed for large audiences at impressive educational conferences. The intellectuals who go to such conferences might have understood him, but more than likely had pretended to do so in the hopes of avoiding a loss of face. At such gatherings it is traditional for the speaker to be high up on a rostrum or stage with amplification loudspeaker. The lesser standing mortals sit in the sea of audience below and should one or two fall asleep it remains unnoticed. The question time given up at the end of session normally reveals one or two questions submitted by a few sycophants and are frequently obsequious or totally irrelevant. Mr Parable was by now engrossed in his favourite topic which was non-specific gender education. Taffy and Mr Etchells had a bet on about the potential nodding off of Arthur Milne who had made a cradle with his arms to support the slowly subsiding chin. The eyes kept slowly closing like shutters to the brain of the declining Mr Milne. Taffy was almost completely distracted from the murmuring of Mr Parable as he and Mr Etchells awaited the outcome of their latest bet. This was for £2 this time. Taffy also had a sweepstake running on how many 'ums' Mr Millipede would bring forth in the forthcoming farewell speech.

'I should like to change Friday afternoon's timetable for non-gender education,' expounded Mr Parable, 'with woodwork for the girls and cookery for the boys. This is an absolutely splendid opportunity for role reversal, don't you think, Mr Owens?'

At that moment Mr Milne's praying mantis style chin support capsized as Mr Milne hit the table with a resounding thump. Taffy let forth a joyous whoop.

'That's two pounds you owe me, boyo,' he said to visibly downcast Mr Etchells.

Mr Parable attributed the whoop of joy as a sign of significant approval. Miss Todd, however, was growing red in the face with explosive indignation. Mr Gordon rushed round the table to see if Mr Milne needed first-aid. Miss Liberty looked at Mr Gordon in sheer admiration. Mr Millipede pondered that perhaps it was time to retire. Mr Smythe Browne inwardly gloated. Mr Foskett and Mr

Johnson and Miss Kippling and Mrs Cooper resumed their deeply consuming shared conversations.

One might have expected Mr Parable, as the new school manager, to have been annoyed at an apparent lack of respect received from his audience. Mr Parable, however, seemed unaware as to why Mr Milne had fallen onto the table with a thump. He was also unaware of the £2 bet and, moreover, he had definitely not observed the obvious irritation of Miss Todd. He was also somewhat shocked when Miss Todd took centre stage by launching herself to her feet in an abject show of confrontation.

'This is absolutely preposterous, Mr Parable,' she began. 'I have no intention of accepting grubby little boys in my kitchen,' she continued. 'And to think of exposing young girls to that lecherous reprobate in charge of woodwork is absolutely outrageous.'

At this point Taffy was about to launch into a reciprocal attack but the retort from Mr Etchells, 'Serve you right,' made him pause in mid-sentence.

'What do you mean, serve me right?' he said.

He was soon put in the picture as regards girls in his woodwork shop. Taffy was not amused. Taffy regarded the female sex as lesser mortals in much the same way as Miss Todd regarded males as inferior to women. Mrs Owens was almost dominated by him but she had survived as Mrs Owens by skilful manipulation. Mr Owens was always having to demonstrate his cleverness around the house and never realized what a pawn he was in Mrs Owens' hands. Taffy did not at all relish the prospects of dozens of helpless females wandering around the woodwork classroom. Miss Todd continued in her tirade against the new non-gender reforms. Taffy became her ardent supporter. No one present could ever remember Miss Todd and Mr Owens ever agreeing on anything. They now launched out in a unison more like that of Mr Gordon and Miss Liberty than their normal cat and dog relationship.

Mr Parable, although somewhat taken aback by the turn of events, was not going to be thwarted. It was clear that old Millipede's departure could become second fiddle to the potential clash of wills over non-gender education. For once in his career Mr Smythe Browne demonstrated a hitherto latent potential for statesmanship. The issue would be sorted out after the Easter break. Mr Millipede was invited to give his farewell address. It was surprisingly short and melancholy. Only fifteen 'ums' and Mr Etchells won £3–15s–3d as the nearest with his estimate of forty-two 'ums'. The farewell tribulations were completed with Taffy fetching and pouring sherries for Miss Todd. An embryonic unholy alliance had been born.

Meanwhile a young freckle-faced boy who was a pupil at the Fanshawe Secondary School was unaware of how the concepts of Mr Parable would affect young Jimmy's lifestyle. Jimmy was reading comics, as usual. His favourite was *The Lion* and this was far more interesting than Mr Graham's enquiries as to what Jimmy would do when he left school that summer. Mrs Graham was busy preparing sausages and mashed potatoes with tinned peas. She was also making pancakes in lieu of the customary Yorkshire pudding which was served with everything when the oven was being used. Mr Graham had come home early and so the sausages and pancakes were a quick improvisation. Jimmy's careers advice to date had included a trip around the Sheffield Steelworks. He had been appalled at the dirt, the noise, smoke and smells of the foundry. Jimmy hated school but the prospects of work in the steel industry appeared to be significantly worse. Jimmy liked animals but his potential for being a vet was offset by lack of qualifications for acceptance on a veterinary course and Jimmy was paranoid about live blood. Mr Graham's suggestions usually met with rejection but today's conversation wasn't even as bilateral as that. Jimmy read his comic, Mr Graham swore under his breath and Mrs Graham acted as a peacemaker

'Perhaps the school will put forward some ideas next term,' she said optimistically.

2

THE SHAPE OF THINGS TO COME

It was 9 a.m. on Monday morning as the pupils of the Fanshawe Secondary School gathered for their customary beginning of the day.

'Cor, is that weirdo the new headmaster?' asked Jimmy of his friend Arthur Turner.

The object of their attention was in fierce debate with Mr Owens and Miss Todd.

'The Education Department are in favour of non-gender-specific education and I am firmly in agreement,' said Mr Parable with a steeliness incompatible with the trendy image. 'You can work with me, or you can leave,' continued Mr Parable. 'I am the new headmaster and I have been appointed with the intention of invoking new concepts and innovations compatible with the changing sociological trends of the sixties. Boys should be able to apply culinary expertise and they should be able to share matrimonial responsibilities. Girls should be liberated from domestic chores and they should be conversant with practical applications in simple mechanics and handicrafts. I cannot accept stereotyped gender typification endorsed by restrictive curricula.'

The discussion was adjourned for two separate meetings with Mr Owens and Miss Todd to take place at 4 p.m. on two separate sessions beginning with Miss Todd that very afternoon. Mr Parable had wisely determined that Miss Todd was the more formidable opponent and that Mr Owens could be vanquished at leisure.

'Now children,' began Mr Parable, 'I know you must all miss Mr Millipede and I would like to say that I hope that I can achieve a similar rapport with you as my protégés. I propose new innovations in the curricula and I should like your form masters and mistresses to implement liberal studies curricula options to take place in the Friday post-meridien session.'

Mr Parable continued in similar vein over the next half an hour with an increasing escalation of complex communications which left pupils and teachers in similar misunderstanding. At the end of the session, the total audience was grateful for relief. It was probably true to say that although Mr Parable might have understood the theme of the Mr Parable address, Mr Parable was singularly alone in this perception.

Miss Todd, however, was left in no doubt that the new headmaster was intent on introducing grubby little boys into her spotless female kitchen domain.

At her interview Mr Parable oozed charm.

'Do come in and sit down for a cup of tea,' he began. 'I'm afraid I only have biscuits, which are so uninteresting compared with those delicious sultana scones which Millipede used to drool about. Mr Millipede has spoken so well of you, that I do so hope that our little misunderstanding can be resolved. You know those ill-mannered boys need a firm ladylike resolve to shape them into gentlemen.'

Mr Parable flattered and then bribed his way through in order to coerce Miss Todd into non-gender teaching. The domestic science area could be supported in her campaign to obtain new stoves and equipment. The kitchen could be redecorated in the summer vacations. It would, of course, be necessary to inform the board of governors that the new facilities would be used by *all* the schoolchildren, not merely half the school potential. The combination of charm, bribes and coercion culminated in a bemused U-turn on the part of Miss Todd. The new schedule would begin this very Friday.

Although Mr Parable had had to use all of his skills in

the arts of persuasion to obtain Miss Todd's cooperation, he did not need half so much time or skill to deal with Mr Owens. Diplomacy for Miss Todd was replaced by gunboat diplomacy for Mr Owens.

There were two genuine recruits in the contingent which were scheduled to meet for the pilot class. Mr Etchells, the form master, tried to select lads who would not be too troublesome. He didn't want too much flak from Miss Todd. Jimmy was the first true volunteer. He was trying to avoid class contact with Mr Gordon because he did not like the macho Rugby class. In a recent Rugby scrum Jimmy was underneath the writhing mass of bodies and was being steadily and painfully crushed. Jimmy was most anxious to escape the tortuous effect. He lashed out blindly and then kicked out viciously at the Rugby ball in order to escape the crush of the scrum and Mr Gordon had received the kick as a direct hit on the shin. Mr Gordon howled in agony and had to be helped off the pitch. The Rugby match had ended half an hour early and the boys had been allowed to go home early. Jimmy had become an anti-hero. Mr Gordon was intent on retribution and Jimmy had become a dab hand at forging Mrs Graham's hand in a regular batch of sick notes. In those days telephones were not so common and two of Mr Gordon's letters to Mrs Graham had been intercepted. Mr Parable was an answer to Jimmy's prayer. He had only to get by for one more term before it was time to leave school.

At 1.25 p.m. precisely Miss Todd thundered down the corridor to her locked kitchen classroom. Jimmy had one accompanying boy with him and the two were stood at opposite sides of the door ignoring one another. Giles Smythe Browne, a bespectacled, spotty youth, was the deputy headmaster's son. There was a twin sister too, but neither was very popular, nor were they like one another in any discernible manner or appearance. Both were diligent in their studies but they rarely accompanied one another. The girl, Beverley, had some friends, though, whilst Giles did not.

'Where are the others?' asked Miss Todd imperiously.

'It's not quite half past yet, Miss,' said Jimmy apologetically.

'They're always late,' said Giles, who did not like his classmates. Giles did not like sports either, and even though his father's position protected him from the worst extremes of the macho Mr Gordon, it did not protect him from the sadistic ragging of his classmates in the changing room. These two boys were the only true refugees or volunteers, whichever you prefer to call them. The remaining eight, Miss Todd had extracted a ceiling of ten from Mr Parable, had been coerced, bribed and brainwashed. Miss Todd sent Jimmy to round up the others with dire threats of practical hygiene for any not present by 1.35 p.m. Only Giles was naive enough to ask what practical hygiene was.

At 1.35 p.m. Miss Todd had an 80 per cent attendance ratio. Fred Carruthers arrived breathlessly at 1.38 p.m. His practical hygiene consisted of washing up after Miss Todd and subsequently he was given the job of cleaning the dishes used for cream caramel which had been left in soak from the girls' class that morning. After that he had to scrub the pan rack. It wasn't very dirty really because Miss Todd had everything neatly lined up in pristine cleanliness. 'If cleanliness is next to Godliness' Miss Todd must be destined for a celestial afterlife.

Arthur Scargill arrived breathlessly at 1.45 p.m. and could hear Miss Todd laying down the law to the other boys. He decided to sneak off home with a headache. Miss Todd lined the boys up with hands outstretched as she inspected each boy's fingernails carefully. Jimmy had been warned by Rosemary Walsh what to expect. Even Giles Smythe Browne had to take his turn on the sink with the nailbrush and nailfile. Joe Hinchcliffe had been messing with his bicycle over the lunch period and he could not get his hands clean. He joined Fred Carruthers on practical hygiene. The 'volunteers' and coercees were not particularly happy.

At 2 p.m. Miss Todd announced her willingness to allow

the class to commence. Since it was half an hour behind schedule scones were out, pancakes were in. But first Miss Todd brought in the House rules:

'Clean hands are essential, with clean fingernails; There should be cleanliness of body and mind; Wash your hands after any visit to the lavatory; Clean down as you go; All equipment should be cleaned before putting it away in the place from whence it originated; Weigh carefully; Listen carefully; Watch carefully; Work carefully; Do not rush; Do not run; Do not guess; Do not act inconsiderately.'

Miss Todd finished by hinting that little boys had never been in her kitchen before. At fourteen years old plus they would normally have received such insults with great indignation. Miss Todd, however, had quite an imposing personality and the liberal 1960s had not to date begun to change adolescents into the rebels of today. The demonstration began. They were to make the batter in pairs and the crêpe pans were to be wiped carefully, no washing. This was good, they thought. No washing-up. Then Miss Todd did a clever thing. The pre-heated pan was lightly oiled and a small amount of batter ladled into the centre. The pan was tilted to and fro. The pancake set and Miss Todd tossed the pan deftly to turn the pancake over. Jimmy was not the only one to be impressed.

'That's how it should be done,' said Miss Todd, 'but you will use a palette knife.'

She then repeated the operation using a palette knife. Having demonstrated six pancakes, these were sugared, quartered and displayed on an oval plate. Lemon wedges were put on each.

'Could we try a piece of your lovely pancakes so that we know what to emulate?' said Jimmy hopefully. 'You do make it look so easy,' he added. In for a penny in for a pound.

Miss Todd almost melted. One pancake was chopped into ten. She wasn't completely gullible.

Whilst Miss Todd was busy supervising the pancake

cooking, the practical hygienist, i.e. Fred Carruthers, found his way into the food cupboard. The sultanas intended for the scones were washed and draining in a colander. Young boys do tend to have a ravenous temperament. Several sultanas were consumed but Miss Todd did not find out until after the boys had left. The pancake yield was in shortfall too but there weren't many rejects in the bin. The sponge intended for Monday's trifle 'shrank' and so did the glacé cherries intended for decoration. Miss Todd was too busy ensuring that the cookers were cleaned down properly to notice the effects of the schoolboy locusts. Her 4 p.m. finish was more than 30 minutes behind schedule in spite of her change of classroom objectives to save time.

When Miss Todd eventually arrived in the staffroom to close down for the day she was in a furious mood. She found Taffy Owens clutching at a hip-flask of something smelling like brandy. He was the worse for wear, although far from being drunk. They resolved to confront Mr Parable together on the coming Monday.

Meanwhile Jimmy had visions of himself dressed in a tall chef's toque meeting The Queen. Jimmy was going to be a chef.

3

INTRODUCING BOB

Bob Malone had just bought himself out of the RAF after ten years, three hundred and thirty three days. His marriage was another casualty of war, even though the only physical wounding that Bob had seen was one of the guards who had inadvertently shot himself in the foot. Since the magazine should not have been attached to the 303 rifle in the first place, the guard had also been discharged after court martial. A three-month sentence in the glasshouse had been suspended and the luckless guard had spent the time in hospital recovering. Bob reflected that the £150 fee to purchase the discharge was a better way of gaining release. He had seen an advertisement for trainee teachers in further education and had applied for interview at Garnstone College. Surprisingly, he had been accepted and was filling in time working for an agency which had sent him to Dronsley, in the very same region of Derbyshire as the Fanshawe Secondary School. It was Bob's first night out prior to starting work at the Southern Constellation Hotel and he thought that he would take a girl friend there to see what it was like from the front of the house.

The Southern Constellation had been built at the turn of the century. It was in an advanced state of dilapidation, even from the front of the house. The carpets were almost threadbare in places, the plastic leather was dull and lacked lustre. The curtains were a garish red and blue and the flower bowls were full of plastic flowers which had been salvaged from the local Tescos. Bob's first impressions were not good but Marianita, the current girl friend, was suitably impressed. Since Bob was driving around in a Sunbeam Alpine and since he was quite lavish in his style of expenditure, she didn't care much anyhow. Bob went to the bar to order tequila for Marianita and vodka and lemonade for himself. The barman seemed to be lacking in *joie de vivre* and came over to serve him with as much enthusiasm as a rabbi for pork scratchings.

'Can I help you, boyo?' said the part-time barman.

It was Taffy Owens from the Fanshawe Secondary School. Taffy supplemented his teaching income by working part-time on Mondays, Tuesdays and Saturdays, thus enabling the full-time barman to have Mondays and Tuesdays off.

'A double tequila with Canada Dry and a double vodka and lemonade,' said Bob.

Taffy wondered if he had heard things properly and interjected 'Pardon' somewhat incredulously.

Bob repeated the order. Taffy was used to beer, brandy, whisky and sherry. Indeed, there were Worthingtons', Newcastle Browns', Tennants', Tetleys', even draught Guinness. There were twelve varieties of whisky, seven of brandy and there was Harvey's Bristol Cream and amontillado and fino in the sherries. Taffy had never been asked for tequila before.

'Never heard of teq, whatever it is,' said Taffy.

Bob had so far been unable to satisfy Marianita's demands for tequila but he had ordered some from the local off-licence. Marianita had promised him a night of unbridled passion if he should ever manage to acquire some of her beloved tequila.

'Whisky with Canada Dry,' said Bob resignedly.

'What kind of whisky?' asked Taffy.

'What have you got?' said Bob without thinking.

Taffy pointed to the shelf and began reeling off the names.

'The cheapest,' said Bob. Marianita would probably go through a bottle anyhow but although she never succumbed to drunkenness she did allow him to take more liberties as the night drew on. After half a bottle, she would let his hands move higher and higher underneath the cover of the table until he reached the hot smoothness of her thighs just past the suspendered stocking tops. He had known Marianita for almost three weeks now and he knew, or at least he thought he knew, that he was very near to achieving the objective of seduction.

'We don't do cheap whisky, boyo,' said Taffy in a voice that implied that the service of cheap liquor cast aspersions on the integrity of the Southern Constellation Bar.

'The strongest then,' said Bob.

'How do I know what the strongest is?' asked Taffy who wanted to get things over and done with so that he could try to pick out the winner for the next day's three thirty.

'Well, anything, Teachers, Black Horse, anything.'

Taffy poured out a double of Teachers and asked if Bob wanted ice. Then he poured out the double vodka, at least that was limited to the single Cossack brand. Bob gathered the glasses together and almost knocked over a stout red-faced man who had just appeared in the bar behind him.

'Watch where you're going,' grunted the little fat man imperiously.

Bob glared at him but said nothing.

Marianita rapidly despatched the double whisky, leaving the Canada Dry untouched. She pushed the empty glass pointedly in Bob's direction and affectionately squeezed Bob's knee as she requested another. Bob felt an urge within his loins. Perhaps tonight would be the night. He downed his own glass and returned to the bar. The little fat man had been joined by his wife and was returning to the bar for a drink for her. Taffy looked up from his racing schedule and pointedly made for the little fat man first. Bob informed him that he had been first but Taffy ignored him. Taffy treated the little fat man with some deference, took the little fat man's order and served him before turning to look after Bob who was feeling somewhat irritated.

'Same as last time,' said Bob.

'I'm sorry, boyo, I can't remember all the orders people have,' said Taffy.

'But there's no one else here,' said Bob in disbelief. Bob requested a double whisky again, and another double vodka and lemonade.

'What kind of whisky, sir?' said Taffy. Bob couldn't remember.

'If you can't remember what you had, how can I be expected to remember?' said Taffy.

Bob felt very tempted to go elsewhere but the Southern Constellation was within walking distance of Bob's bedsit and Arthur, his co-tenant, was away for a few days. Bob swallowed his indignation and asked for another Teachers. Bob returned to Marianita and sidled closer to her. He put his hand around her waist and drew her to him as he kissed her gently on the cheek. The little fat man glared at him in disgust from across the room. The little fat man's wife looked round to see the reason for her husband's irritation.

'Do you remember how we were once in love?' she said wistfully.

The little fat man's Worthington seemed to go down the wrong way. His face puffed up and reddened. He almost choked. His wife deftly went inside his pocket to withdraw some pills. He swallowed a couple of these and seemed to recover. He withdrew a large white handkerchief from another pocket and mopped his brow. Marianita had been watching this in sympathy until the man had seemed to start recovering. The little fat man wiped his brow once more but this time was to catch the hair falling over the forehead. The hairpiece, for this is what it was, became dislodged and a large red bald patch came into view. The little fat man's disarranged toupee looked quite ludicrous. The effects of the doubles took hold of Bob who began to chuckle. Bob did try to control the chuckles, but to no avail. The little fat man struggled to his feet to demand an apology. His wife edged him back into the chair.

'Let's go back to the flat,' said Bob.

His hopes soared as Marianita agreed.

'Good ridddance,' said the little fat man in a stage whisper as Bob escorted Marianita to the door. Bob didn't care. The thoughts of the seduction of Marianita was much more important than a verbal barrage with the little fat man. He could hardly hit the little fat man and he was to be employed at the Southern Constellation on the morrow.

Marianita had not been to the flat owned by Mr Solomons, a descendant of Scrooge. Mr Solomons' god was 'Money'. He was more concerned with the wear and tear of carpets than the wear and tear of bedsprings. Officially he disapproved of mixed couples cohabiting in the bedsit rooms but as long as there were no babies or children, Mr Solomons cared not. Some of the rooms had young ladies, some had young men. There were no official couples, although Joe from Flat C would always move in with Jane of Flat J when Jane's flatmate Sarah went home for the weekends. Mr Solomons had caught them at it once and promised expulsion in the event of Jane"s pregnancy. 'No girls in the rooms,' he said to Bob and Arthur. They had rigged up a little screen between the two beds but Bob had been unable to develop the thick skin of Arthur with regards to performing sexual acts whilst the partner was in the room. Arthur was from Australia and had very few inhibitions. On one occasion they brought two girls back for a drink. Bob's girl had made it quite plain that a kiss and a cuddle was all right in private but Arthur's wandering hands in public was not for her. Bob had taken his girl home and had returned to the shared flat to hear loud snores from behind Arthur's side of the screen. About an hour later, having retired to bed himself, he heard squeals of joy, grunts and bed creaks, loud moans of obvious gratification. He lay in bed enviously and thought of looking behind the screen. Intervals of grunts and snores had been alternated with obvious sounds of sexual gratification. The next morning it was difficult to know who was more embarrassed, the girl or Bob. Whoever it was, it certainly was not the obviously run-down Arthur. Even after such a night of rut Arthur was ready for more but the girl could not get away fast enough.

Bob opened the front door and hoped that Mr Solomons was not around. There were thankfully no signs of disturbance from Mr Solomons' downstairs flat. Bob put the light switch down and beckoned Marianita forward. She entered somewhat reluctantly and they climbed together up the stairs.

'Quickly,' he said.

'Why we go quickly?' asked Marianita reluctantly. He didn't have to answer as the light went out suddenly and she let out a fortunately stifled exclamation.

'Stay put,' he said as he edged forward into the gloom to reach out for the position where the light switch should be. Thankfully he located the switch and the lighting was restored.

'Quickly,' he said, 'because the lights go out on a time switch.'

He urged her upwards whilst he remained on the landing below to give the switch another jolt before rushing up to join her. In the waiting period he noted that she was wearing black panties and he felt a further instalment of mounting lust. Every cloud has a silver lining. As he joined her on the second landing he used the third flush of darkness caused by Mr Solomons' economy light switch to advantage. She deftly moved his hand from her pert bottom whilst he claimed to be feeling for the light switch. Mr Solomons' economy light switch appeared to give a thirty second maximum of lighting before cut out.

Once within the flat Bob fed the meter for lighting. Bob had to buy, or should I say exchange, five pounds' worth of shillings per time. The meter yielded about 50 per cent profit to Mr Solomons even though this was illegal. Bob pulled her to him and managed to get a hand beneath her right breast at the same time. Marianita did not resist until he headed for her lower anatomy. Marianita wanted a drink and some music. Bob fetched out the bottle of whisky. The smell on her breath was a bit off-putting but the surge in his trousers was more than overwhelming in compensation.

They lay on the settee together and he kissed her gently as he undid her bra. His hands were rough and impatient and she had to help him. Out poured her beautiful soft abundant breasts and Bob squeezed and kissed them excitedly. He reached beneath her dress and headed for his ultimate goal but her hand blocked the way. He tried reaching for the waistband of her panties but her hand withheld him. Bob was getting desperate as his trousers swelled up obscenely. It was not to be. It was the wrong time of the month. Even the bottle of tequila would not have helped. Bob would need an alternative method of relieving his feelings.

Bob reported in at the Southern Constellation on the Tuesday lunchtime. The Australian lady in charge requested his presence in the bar. She was flanked by two poodles who growled at Bob in mistrust. They obviously did not like Bob at all but the Australian lady could see no reason for chiding their anti-social behaviour.

'Do you drink?' she asked, pouring herself a large scotch in the process.

'A little,' said Bob, in slight misinterpretation of the truth.

She poured him a half pint of bitter. He expected a pint but Mrs Kelly kept an eye on excess expenditure. When the Australian lady had established Bob's credentials she escorted him to the dilapidated kitchen which boasted a double stove and oven, a portable chip fryer and a salamander. There were only two small work tables and a small hotplate. She showed Bob the menu which was five sides of small print. Bob read the soup list incredulously. 'Clear turtle; mock turtle; sharks fin; clam chowder; lobster bisque; shrimp bisque; bisque of crab.'

'How do you cope with this wide range?' asked Bob.

He need not have worried. She showed him the stores. In it was a shelf stacked end to end with different canned soups. Below it were stacked rows and rows of canned sauces and below that was a shelf with rows and rows of canned fruit. There was, however, surprisingly little else. Bob decided to try it out: he was out of work otherwise and the courtship of Marianita was a definite drain on the pocket. He wouldn't be seeing her again until the weekend but he wasn't due for wages before then because of the week in hand. Bob would soon find that the dilapidated kitchen was but one problem in the Southern Constellation scheme of things. That night he was to meet Nola, the Irish waitress. Nola was new to the waitress job and was inclined to take the orders and forget to bring them through to the kitchen. It is traditional that the chef cooks the main course whilst the customer eats the soup or hors-d'oeuvres. Nola would take the melon boats or Florida cocktail from the *mise en place* but Bob would not know about the fried scampi or grilled *entrecôte* steak.

On Bob's first evening there was a dinner party for thirty, with melon boats, roast beef and yorkshire and Black Forest gâteau. Bob looked at the vintage oven incredulously. There was no bottom to it and he could make out the well-ingrained continuation of the originally red floor tiles. Bob put the oven on regulo 9 for the beef and soon turned it up to regulo 13 when he realized the puny amount of heat generation. The beef could roast effectively but the Yorkshire puddings were like leaden *chapattis*. The Australian lady was not impressed. She had come into the kitchen to inspect his progress, flanked by the horrible poodles. One of them started yapping loudly, having been startled by Bob's tall chef's hat. The other carried out a flanking movement and attached itself to Bob's chef's trousers. Bob normally liked animals but not in the kitchen. He aimed a gentle nudging movement backwards to dislodge the rear antagonist. In the process he lost balance and the whipped cream ready for decoration fell onto the dog's head. It fled, covered in cream, yelping miserably. The original yapping poodle fled too, tripping up Nola in the process. Nola had been dishing up horseradish sauce and the sauceboats flew into the air, to descend in a splattered heap. It was unfortunately the last of the horseradish.

The Australian lady departed to retrieve the delinquent poodles, having decided to leave Bob alone for the time being. Nola instructed two newly arrived casual waitresses to clear up the horseradish. Bob was left to clear up the cream. The two portly matronlike figures grumbled vociferously as they cleared up the horseradish but made no attempt to offer assistance to Bob. They sympathized, of course, and Bob learned that he was the twelfth chef in ten months.

'She keeps getting one of the lecturers from the college,' said number one, whose name was Enid.

'He's horrible,' said number two, whose name was Ethel.

'He swears a lot,' said Enid.

'He shouts a lot,' said Ethel.

Their duologue was interrupted by Nola who brought an order in for *sole bonne femme* and *sole mornay*.

'I thought service on the à *la carte* didn't start until 7 p.m.,' said Bob whose watch said 6.40 p.m.

'It doesn't,' said Nola, 'but it's Mr and Mrs Parable from Fanshawe Secondary School and they are very good customers.'

'They'll have to bloody wait,' said Bob who was not finding his *début* to be a happy occasion.

'They've got their starters,' said Nola, 'and I thought the fish would be easy.'

'They don't want any vegetables.'

Bob grumpily inspected the refrigerator and found a few unhappy soles. He also located the sauce *mise en place* which he had been told about. There weren't any labels but a greyish white paste was probably meant to be either fish *velouté* or *béchamel*. He tasted it gingerly. It was sweet. He put the soles in the oven to cook in white wine, then realized that the *mornay* should have been cooked in milk. 'Sod it,' he muttered under his breath. He left it unaltered though. He struggled to make up an instant *roux* diluted with milk. He diluted it in semi-thickened state in two pans.

One had extra cream. The second had the wine from cooking the fish, plus some sliced mushrooms and some grated onion. (Bob could not locate any shallots.) Nola came hovering in the background enquiring as to whether the sole was ready. It wasn't, she was informed testily.

'Mrs Parable is getting impatient,' said Nola, 'they have eaten their starters, and that was ten minutes ago, at least.' It was barely seven o'clock.

'You came with the order twenty minutes early,' said Bob patiently, 'but I started cooking nevertheless.'

'There's no *mise en place* and I'm more interested in the big party.'

'I gave them their starters at half past six,' said Nola. Nola had of course given out 'the starters' and then come through to the kitchen.

At this moment the Australian lady arrived, just as Bob was on the point of calling Nola a 'silly cow' or worse. The delinquent poodles were not in attendance. Bob was just about ready to walk out and the thirty guests for the special party could possibly be facing starvation. Nola was despatched to the dining room with a flea in her ear.

'She's always cocking the orders up,' said Enid.

'Ooh, do you remember when Mr Hector swore at her over the cod?'

'Ooh, yes,' said Ethel.

'Ere chef,' said Ethel. 'We had the principal from the college and he wanted some fried cod.' Enid broke into a cackling sort of laugh. 'She took the order, chef, just like now, and didn't bring it through.' 'Ere chef,' said Enid, 'Mr Hector said there weren't no cod, but she wouldn't believe him,' said Ethel. Enid broke out into another uncontrollable hysterical cackle. Ethel joined in the chorus.

Stifling the cackle for a moment Ethel continued with the anecdote. 'Mr Hector asked her to spell cod.' They both broke into fits of hysterical laughter once more.

'Mr Hector gave her the ticket and said, "write Cod",' spluttered Enid. 'What are the letters?' asked Mr Hector. Nola had eventually brought forth C O D. 'Is there an F

31

in it?' Mr Hector had asked.

'Of course there is no f in "cod",' Nola had said in innocent desperation.

'That's what I'm bloody well trying to tell you, you silly cow,' Mr Hector had yelled. 'There's no effing cod.'

The two matrons almost collapsed from the effects of their reminiscences but rapidly recovered their composure at the re-arrival of Nola who was looking distinctly flushed.

'You've no time to stand here yattering,' she stormed.

By now Bob had botched together the two fish dishes and Mr and Mrs Parable were eliminated from the current list of problems. By now the dynamic matronly duo were setting out the melon.

'There's two short, chef,' said Ethel.

'They're due in in a minute,' added Enid.

'There's thirty done,' said Bob categorically.

There weren't. There were only twenty-eight.

Bob knew he had got six out of each of the five honeydew melons and there were no more.

'Them two you just served had melon boat,' said Enid helpfully. Nola had struck again. Two of the guests would have to have an alternative.

The Australian lady arrived once more.

'We get eight out of a melon,' she said.

'Not these you don't,' said Bob, pointing at the diminutive-sized melon portions. Although not demonstrative in agreeing with Bob, the Australian lady privately conceded that Bob had a point. A choice of prawn cocktail was offered, at the same price. Enid and Ethel were given the job of making the thirteen prawn cocktails, leaving a balance of eleven melon boats for the casual customers. Although the diners were somewhat unhappy with the *chapatti*-style Yorkshires, the meal was a relative success in other attributes.

Nola was not seen in the kitchen for the rest of the evening. Enid and Ethel were to act as intermediaries. There were, in fact, only another seven casual customers after Mr and Mrs Parable and Mrs Parable had commented on the lovely *sole mornay*. As Bob had used Red Leicester instead of Cheddar and white wine instead of milk, Bob was unsure about its success. Mr Parable had even sent in a glass of wine for Bob and Bob had found a bottle of calvados for use with the Southern Constellation-style duckling. Bob needed reinforcement and felt much better after the liquid stimulation.

4

THE INTERVIEW

Mr Elliot Ness was the principal of Dronsley College of Further Education. He was aged sixty-one and certainly looked every single year of his age, plus a few extra years as well. He was rather rotund from over-eating in the college restaurant and he had a red face which would puff up like a blowfish when there was something which had upset him. Mr Ness was growing quite thin on top and so he had brought himself a toupee. Unfortunately, he found it uncomfortable and so he only wore it on special occasions such as governors' meetings or when entertaining important county dignitaries. Mr Ness managed to terrify everybody almost without exception. Sycophants would gain promotion, dissidents would end up with promotion prospects blocked off, and they would also often find themselves with bad timetables. The dissidents would have classes early on Monday morning and late on Friday afternoons. Severe defections would be rewarded with early morning classes and the twilight classes from 6.30 p.m. to 9.30 p.m. The unpopular groups were reserved for dissidents. Heads of department who disagreed with Mr Ness found their budgets cut back. Over the years Mr Elliot Ness successfully culled rebellious heads and appointed 'yes' men in their place. Dissident students would be expelled. Lecturers who had bad examination results would be carpeted and encouraged to find pastures new.

Every day without fail Mr Ness would do the rounds to ensure that litter was eliminated. Every day he would check to ensure lecturers did not finish classes early. He had a penchant for snooping around the laurel bushes looking to catch students smoking or worse. A first offence would be awarded voluntary clean-up duties. A second offence could be awarded expulsion. Sometimes Mr Elliot Ness would arrive unannounced and he would sit in the back of some unfortunate lecturer's class. This could be most disconcerting. Mr Elliot Ness was still under the weather from the effects of meeting Bob and Marianita at The Southern Constellation. Mr Elliot Ness was distinctly red-faced and irritable. He would have gone home but there was an academic board meeting that afternoon at 4.45 p.m. The academic board was supposed to be a meeting of minds to determine college strategy. In reality it was a rubber stamping body for Principal Elliot Ness. He presided like a Mafia godfather.

Principal Ness decided to do an impromptu tour of the college to see what was happening. As he exited tetchily from his office he crossed the path of Sam Brown, the caretaker. Sam hastily drew out a duster from within one of his pockets and began dusting the top of the glass showcase outside the principal's office. He managed to convey an apparent lack of observation as regards to the principal's presence.

'Everything all right, Sam?' asked the principal. Sam leapt to attention as though on parade. Principal Elliot Ness proceeded via the refectory towards the hairdressing department. There was a marked deference from students and staff alike whoever he encountered.

Meanwhile Jimmy Graham was actually dressed smartly in a suit ready for an interview with Mr Charles Potterton, head of the Food and Beauty department of Dronsley College of Further Education. Mr Graham had taken the afternoon off work and Mrs Graham was dressed in her best blue two-piece costume. The interview was scheduled for 3.30 p.m. and it was 3.10 p.m. already. The Austin Farina Forty had refused to start and Mr Graham's hands were black from mechanical activity under the bonnet. The car had eventually spluttered into life and was now ticking over spasmodically with Jimmy sat tensely in the back and Mrs Graham in the front. Mr Graham was despatched to the house to change his shirt, whose cuffs were black. He was also to wash his hands.

'Hurry up. We'll be late,' said Jimmy.

'Bloody car,' Mrs Graham reprimanded him vigorously.

Eventually Mr Graham appeared and set off at speed towards the Dronsley College.

'You should have had it serviced last week, like I told you,' she nagged. Mr Graham was not happy about Jimmy's pipedreams anyhow. Mr Graham had added up the cost of uniforms for chef work and waiting classes, plus the cost of chefs' knives and text books. It came to nearly £95, and Mr Graham received less than £24 per week.

'I don't know why he can't get a job at the garage,' he said. 'They are offering £4 5s 6d.'

'Yes, and look at the hours,' said Mrs Graham, 'Our Jimmy might end up as chef to the Queen,' she said. She also thought that perhaps Jimmy would cook a meal once in a while to give her a break from her kitchen duties. By now it was 3.35 p.m. as they approached the college gates. Mr Graham took the corner somewhat sharply and proceeded up the laurel-flanked driveway at 25 mph. A huge clearly marked notice demanded 'DRIVE SLOWLY 5 miles per hour'.

'You're going too fast,' nagged Mrs Graham.

At that moment the round red-faced apparition of Principal Elliot Ness lunged out of the bushes. Mr Graham screeched to a halt and Principal Ness jumped out of the way with remarkable agility for his age as the Austin Farina went into a skid. Mr Ness had donned the migratory toupee ready for the academic board later in the afternoon. The toupee and Mr Ness went flying into the bushes. Mr Graham jumped out of the car not knowing whether or not he had actually done damage to the red-faced figure. Mrs Graham got out too to render help.

'I'll go ahead,' said Jimmy, not wishing to be delayed

further. The red-faced figure was scrambling to its feet and was more in a state of shock from lack of dignity rather than source of injury. Jimmy left the three elders in the driveway, soon to be lost in a sea of bystanders. Some had come to render assistance to the esteemed principal, some had come with malice aforethought with regard to Mr Ness' state of health. Jimmy soon located a college entrance and was soon able to find the location of Mr Charles Potterton, head of Food and Beauty. Jimmy proceeded through an entrance indicating the department with yet another prominent demanding notice. 'FOOD AND BEAUTY DEPARTMENT : OUT OF BOUNDS TO EVERYONE UNLESS ON BUSINESS. VISITORS MUST EXERCISE DUE CARE.' Jimmy peered through a classroom door to behold several students dressed in pristine chefs' whites and overalls. Jimmy nearly jumped out of his skin as a voice bellowed in his ear.

'What do you want, lad?'

Jimmy looked round to see a tall ramrod-straight figure clad in chefs' whites with a red neckerchief. The embroidery on the front of the chef's jacket proclaimed H Britain, FAB. Jimmy deferentially asked to where he could find Mr Charles Potterton. Hector Britain informed Jimmy that the head of department would only see potential students when the said students were accompanied by their parents. Jimmy apologetically explained that his father's car had broken down and so Jimmy had run ahead with his parents following. Hector Britain decided to march Jimmy along to the head of department's office. It was by now 3.50 p.m. and Mr Charles Potterton was somewhat niggled because the interviewee for 3.30 p.m. had not turned up. His secretary, Joyce, informed Mr Potterton of the late arrival of a solitary boy. Mr Potterton knew that next year's student recruitment was down and was dreading explaining this at the impending academic board.

'You're too late, boy,' he informed Jimmy. 'Punctuality is most important in the catering industry.'

Jimmy breathlessly and deferentially and pleadingly

tried to explain the car breakdown.

'There's all the forms to fill in for a start,' said Mr Potterton.

'I'll fill in the forms,' said Jimmy.

'Parental permission is required,' said Mr Potterton, 'to begin the interview.' Jimmy had at least got a good reference from Miss Todd. Eventually Mr and Mrs Graham arrived, looking quite flushed. Mrs Graham was worried. Mr Graham was peeved. At least Jimmy was another firm recruit making twenty-seven out of the thirty-two required for the Dronsley chefs' and waiters' diploma. The baker's course, however, had only ten students and this looked potentially disastrous.

'Would you like to be a baker?' asked Mr Potterton suddenly. 'Bakers have good prospects and good wages. Cake decoration is really exciting.'

'What sort of wages?' said Mr Graham.

'I want to be a chef,' said Jimmy.

'He wants to be a chef,' said Mrs Graham.

The interview over at last, Mr Charles Potterton looked at his watch and realized in horror that it was almost 4.30 p.m. He picked up his papers and scurried off to the academic board. At 4.31 p.m. precisely he entered the committee room chamber. The other members were already assembled around the table but the esteemed principal was not present.

'You're late,' said Percy Brain, head of academic studies. 'You're pushing your luck.'

'If Hitler had been here you'd be shot.'

Percy Brain laughed at the discomfort of Mr Potterton. Percy Brain was the one irreverent head who had resisted all attempts of coercion by the megalomaniac principal. Percy Brain had once caught the principal with his trousers down in the secretaries' office. Percy Brain had resisted the inclination to publicize the liaison and was very pleased with the enigma of his obvious immunity from the principal's influence and coercion.

'Hitler's nearly been run over by some idiot bringing

their offspring here on interview. I wouldn't want to be in the shoes of whoever it is when he finds out who it is.'

'You don't know anything about it, do you? Yes you do. You're looking guilty. Dear oh dear. My word you do look pale.' Mr Potterton had indeed gone pale. He pleaded with Mr Brain to drop the subject before the dreaded principal came in.

At that moment the dreaded principal did come in looking redder and more puffed in the face than usual. He was helped in by Georgia Browne, his personal, very personal some might say, secretary. He staggered into a chair looking distinctly unwell. The infamous toupee was absent.

'Perhaps still in the bushes,' whispered Mr Brain but no one laughed. The Principal looked distinctly malevolent. He might not be well, but he was still omnipotent. The fire was gone from Mr Ness but the malevolent ashes were obviously still smouldering ready for re-ignition.

The meeting was thankfully brief and it turned out that Principal Ness had not discovered who the parents had been. Mrs Graham had managed to subdue her husband and kept him in the background whilst using her feminine wiles to calm the irate principal. No one admitted to carrying out the interviews and Mr Potterton resolved to change his records as soon as possible after the meeting to throw any investigation off the scent. Principal Ness left for home leaving a very lively bunch of departmental heads debating the mystery student. Mr Brain remained discreet and gave a knowing wink at Mr Potterton as they bade each other farewell.

Mr Potterton went home a worried man, especially so when he found out that Mr Hector Britain's class had left a chip frier turned on and it had caught fire. Sam Brown had arrived there just in time to save further damage. Sam Brown, the caretaker, was of course responsible for locking up. Sam Brown could also be guaranteed to ensure that Principal Ness would hear of the heroics. Mr Potterton was a very worried man. Mr Hector Britain was in line for deputy head of department and Mr Potterton had spent the last few weeks building up a case to support the promotion.

Surprisingly, Bob was still in gainful employment at the end of the week. Perhaps it helped that the Australian lady had been away for a couple of days. Saturday night was the night of the dinner dance with only a limited menu. The unsold melon had joined other fruits for the fruit salad. It seemed a well-booked occasion and Bob had eighty-three booked and he was on his own. Nola had tried very hard all week and had only once forgotten to deliver the main course requisition to the kitchen. Since it had been for omelette and chips it had not mattered. By 8.30 p.m. Bob had eleven requisitions lined up on the board as he deftly dished up the orders. Enid and Ethel seemed to spend most of the evening in the kitchen rather than in the dining-room.

'Ooh, isn't he quick?' said Enid.

'And doesn't he dress it up nice,' said Ethel.

Although flattered Bob wished they would go away and leave him in peace. The bottle of calvados had almost bit the dust and he didn't want them to see him drinking it anyway. Nola pushed past and requested a steak cooked medium.

'What table?' asked Bob suspiciously.

'There's no ticket, it's for Pierre,' said Nola.

'Write a ticket and stick it on the board at the bottom,' said Bob as he continued throwing orders together.

'It's urgent. I want it now,' said Nola desperately.

'You'll get it when I get round to it,' asserted Bob with menace. 'There's plenty more to do without anyone jumping the queue.' He stopped and turned as a thought hit him.

'You haven't cocked up the orders again, have you?'

The matronly duo turned away to hide their amusement and then they scurried around the corner out of sight. Not out of earshot, of course.

'No, it's for Pierre,' pleaded Nola desperately.

'I don't know who Pierre is but he can take his turn,' asserted Bob in firm resolution.

'It's for Pierre,' said Nola almost in tears.

'Who is bloody Pierre?' asked Bob who was getting annoyed by now.

'It's Mrs Kelly's dog. He barks a lot when he gets hungry.'

'If you think I am leaving off serving customers for a bloody dog, you can think again,' said Bob with belligerent incredibility.

'Please, chef,' pleaded Nola, 'Please.'

Nola, almost in tears, was despatched to report the chef's mutinous behaviour and Mrs Kelly came through herself followed by the yapping poodles. Enid and Ethel were collecting food for table seven and Enid tried to squeeze out of the way to let the Australian lady past. A sauceboat of tartare sauce tilted off the tray onto one of the poor dog's heads. The dog, Pierre himself, fled yelping loudly, hastily pursued by his partner in crime. Mrs Kelly chased after them. Bob continued with table three. He was a professional. Enid and Ethel tittered loudly. The tittering subsided as Nola returned looking flushed yet again. Enid was instructed to chop up some roast beef for Pierre instead. Although Bob had continued production it should be said that he was behind in orders and the incident had not exactly helped.

Nola sneaked in and put another order on the board whilst Bob's back was turned. The distraction of Pierre had given her a lapse of concentration but she dare not admit this to the belligerent Bob. She also made sure that the matronly duo didn't see her either. She returned innocently two minutes later.

'Is table five ready yet, chef,' she asked.

'What table five?' asked Bob, looking round to see what was ordered. 'Where's that come from?' It was an order for two well done fillet steaks.

'I'll tell them it will be a couple of minutes, chef,' said Nola, hastily retreating before Bob could interrogate her further. At that moment a short man popped his head around the door.

'Lovely meal, chef,' said the short man. He winked and thrust a five pound note into Bob's hand and disappeared quickly. Bob was taken aback. Chefs don't see many tips. Bob turned and collected the steaks and put them in the pan. Three minutes later Nola returned.

'Is table five ready yet, chef?'

'No they are not,' said Bob heatedly, knowing instinctively that there was something suspicious about this order.

The matronly duo followed Nola and joined in the chorus.

'Mr Ness is asking for his steak,' said Enid.

'Ee don't half get impatient,' added Ethel.

'And he's so rude and bad tempered,' said Enid.

'Can you speed it up?' asked Nola desperately.

'No, I can't speed it up,' shouted Bob.

Nola returned to the dining room to try to pacify Mr Ness. She was quite unsuccessful.

'Tell the chef we have been waiting twenty-five minutes, and we want serving now,' demanded Mr Ness.

'Cool down, Elliot,' said his long-suffering wife.

'I don't want excuses I want it *now*,' demanded the belligerent Mr Ness. Nola returned almost tearfully to the kitchen.

'It's not ready,' said Bob brusquely.

'Ee gets ever so impatient when kept waiting,' said Ethel unhelpfully.

'He'll have to have it, chef,' said Nola pleadingly.

Bob splattered the two steaks onto the ready garnished silver platter without comment. Bob knew that they were far from cooked. Nola scurried away optimistically. Enid and Ethel looked at one another and fell about giggling again.

'About time,' stated Principal Ness. 'About bloody time.'

Mr Ness' wife looked relieved but not for long. The demonstrative slash of the principal's knife revealed the raw meat inside the juicy-looking steak.

'It's bloody raw,' yelled Mr Ness.

Nola fled as Principal Ness demanded attention. Enid and Ethel scurried off to the far end of the dining-room to attend to table clearing. Mr Ness decided to go and see the chef himself. Mr Ness banged open the kitchen.

'Can't you bloody cook?' he yelled at the chef whose back was turned away from him. Bob turned to meet the eyes of the dreaded principal of Dronsley College of Further Education.

'Yes, I can bloody cook, you pompous prat,' yelled Bob. 'I said that it wasn't ready but the bloody silly cow of a waitress said you had to have it.'

Principal Ness was not used to being spoken to in such a manner. He reddened and spluttered in indignation and then clutched at his heart. He then collapsed. Fortunately, Bob had some basic first-aid training. He loosened the bald man's collar and summoned assistance.

'Get an ambulance,' he yelled.

5

DOCENDO DISCIMUS

Principal Elliot Ness had not discovered the name of the mystery interviewee and had now almost forgotten the incident. He had gone home after the academic board and had had a relapse. After the incident at the Southern Constellation hotel he had been confined to bed for a week and he had been put on a diet and a new course of pills. He had lost a stone and a half and was, if anything, even meaner than ever. Sam Brown had been bribed to keep quiet about the chip frier incident by supplies of tea, sugar and milk for his caretaker brew-ups. Mr Brain was not one for making trouble and the other heads were too dim to put two and two together. Mr Potterton had changed the records of the Graham interview just in case.

Today was the day of the college staff meeting, alias the party political decrees of Chairman Ness. A new stage was in the process of completion but it was behind schedule. John Lane wondered if he dare tell Principal Ness that the central struts were below specification. He walked up and down on the stage and decided that it should be safe as Principal Ness never allowed anyone else on the stage, since it detracted from Principal Ness's stature. Perhaps Principal Ness had studied Adolph Hitler's technique whereby Hitler was high and aloof from the massed ranks below as he, Adolph Hitler, presided from a raised rostrum, high above the clouds.

Principal Ness was not happy about the results of the examinations, especially those of the academic studies department. Although Principal Ness was unable to subjugate Mr Brain, it was also true that Mr P Brain was also unable to subjugate the academic departmental lecturers. Amongst their midst were a number of potential Red revolutionaries with beards, tatty jeans and red check shirts. The lecturer responsible for economics was an alcoholic who frequently slept under the stage after one of the departmental binges. The economics' results for this year were especially bad. Principal Ness was not happy. Mr Potterton was somewhat relieved at the good fortune of the food studies results.

The staff gathering was almost like a ceremonial parade. Only the death bed was an excuse for absence. Even the hirsute dissidents of the academic studies department turned out for this occasion. They stood out scruffily, or bizarrely according to sex, from the suited males in ties or two-piece suits and dresses of the females of the other departments. The academic studies staff scorned conservatism of dress. Ms Blenkinsop was dressed in a long black hippie ankle dress and sported pendulum earrings. Her face was coated in a white mask. Mrs Jones wore a sort of purple leotard top and tight sort of matching purple track suit bottoms. Lucy Juniper sported a miniskirt and eyes down look-in Bingo blouse. She had a voluptuous figure and displayed it proudly. She was flanked by the more rampant males of the academic studies department. Miss Mapleton wore a 'thirties' creation.

Mr Hector Britain was dressed in flannels with a large brown check sports jacket. He sported a regimental tie as he sat arms crossed in a sort of sedentary state of attention. Mr Saltpot, the head waiter, was dressed impeccably in pinstripes with white shirt and dicky bow. The Italian account's lecturer wore a cravat, a navy blue blazer with green corduroys. Most of the food studies lecturers, however, wore two-piece suits, and their female counterparts wore female two-piece suits.

The one thing that was noticeable about college staff meetings was the obvious departmental segregation. The food studies lecturers were conventional but they were accustomed to punctuality. As such they were the first in and had collared the rear seats. The unconventional academic lecturers had arrived late and had ended up at the front of the hall. Sam Brown had been told that there were 197 lecturers and 197 seats had been laid out. Six departmental heads seats were arranged in a cental bloc beneath the stage, with the vice principal and chief administration officer amongst them. Secretly the heads always arranged for checks on attendance in any case but if there was one empty seat Principal Ness would be guaranteed to order a post mortem. It was by now 9.28 a.m. and there were three vacancies. It would appear that there was one vacancy in the food studies department and two in the academic studies. In actual fact the food studies vacant chair was not so apparent because there was one somewhat large lady who overspilled somewhat to almost filling two seats. This large lady was dressed impeccably in a black dress, with pearls and brooch. She was a new member of the staff. A tall unshaven figure hobbled in to fill one of the vacant seats just as Principal Ness mounted the steps up to the stage. The hobbling figure was supported by crutches. He had the sort of bright checked shirt often sported by academic lecturers. He also had the customary worn jeans and unpolished shoes. Mr Ness was, of course, an out and out Fascist. He detested any leanings to the Left. He even regarded Enoch Powell as being too liberal in his political views.

'You're late, Mr Swinston,' said Principal Ness with obvious petulance.

Mr Swinston apologised and explained it was due to a broken leg injury.

'May we ask how you broke the leg?' asked Principal Ness unsympathetically.

'I was attacked by the RAF at a Ban the Bomb Rally,' explained Mr Swinston.

'You are supposed to be above that sort of thing,' ranted the principal. 'Lecturers marching up and down, protesting!

They shoot people in Russia for less. I suppose you'll be needing time off now.'

Mr Swinston was going to protest but thought better of it. Principal Ness was obviously working himself up to a frenzy. He began to stalk up and down on the stage, pausing at intervals to thump his fist on the table which John Lane had thoughtfully sited above the weaker area of the central stage. Principal Ness was becoming somewhat annoyed at the obstruction to the Principal Ness flight path. He also seemed to ignore the occasional creaks from the central stage area.

'Why is this damned table here?' Principal Ness suddenly interjected. He thrust it backwards and the central stage groaned ominously. Mr Lane put his hands over his face, prayed inwardly, but was too frightened to say anything. The academic lecturers nearer the stage looked more interested than usual. At this moment the door behind the stage opened gingerly and squeakily to admit another red-faced figure looking somewhat under the weather. It was the missing economics' lecturer. He was about to warn Principal Ness about the stage but first of all he had to apologize. He had been woken up by the principal's tirade and realized that he was not where he should be.

Principal Ness turned from berating the unfortunate Mr Swinton to start on the new source of irritation. Lateness was inexcusable; lateness was the height of bad manners; lateness set a bad example to students; lateness was one of the reasons for the adverse state of affairs in the once Great Britain. Principal Elliot Ness puffed in the face and became redder. The stage creaked more and more but withstood Principal Ness's stamping up and down.

Eventually Chairman Ness ceased from the party political broadcast long enough for the administrative officer to give a general update on the latest county requirements. After the brief interlude of the talk from the administrative officer, below the stage Principal Ness resumed command to go through the examination results.

'We have a record number of passes, record number of

credits. We have won the George Carter Award for retail, the Jack Teskow Award for hairdressing, the Jules Pilchard Award for the best college chef.' The list of successes was truly inspiring and Principal Ness missed out nothing. But the other side of the coin was not ignored either. There had been 19 failures in the GCE results and 13 of these were in economics.

'Who was responsible for GCE Economics?' yelled Principal Ness. No one answered. 'Who has spoilt the proud achievements of the Dronsley College of Further Education with such appalling results?' demanded the increasingly belligerent Principal. 'Mr Brain,' demanded the principal, 'who is responsible for these bloody awful results?'

The red-faced latecomer at last staggered to his feet and admitted guilt. Principal Ness grew redder and angrier. He forgot his dignity as he stamped up and down centre stage. The stage creaked and creaked. The red-faced lecturer cringed. The staff nearer to the stage hoped eagerly. Mr Lane prayed.

The mischievous prayers won the day. Suddenly there was a louder groan and creak and Principal Ness appeared to lose balance. The inevitable occurred as Principal Ness disappeared from view into a large hole in mid-stage. The scene was too funny for even the most obvious sycophants to deny. Stifled spluttered chuckles were hurriedly subdued further as the red-faced principal, toupee askew, struggled up through the hole in the stage.

'I want Mr Lane in my office immediately,' said the discomposed principal. 'This meeting is over. I have not done with you either,' said Principal Ness to the cringing red-faced economics lecturer.

Bob Malone was having great difficulty packing his many possessions into his Sunbeam Alpine sports car. The vehicle was a definite prestige symbol but it was not very functional. It was meant for driving at speed on motorways, not as a vehicle for goods' transportation. The boot was crammed full. The well of the front passenger footspace was full. Pullovers, shirts and ties were piled in an untidy heap on the passenger seat. His room-mate was not around to see him off but they had promised to keep in touch.

The car seemed to have a jinx on it, and would have cost a fortune to repair without the room-mate's assistance. It had had a new clutch, a new exhaust, a new gearbox, a new windscreen, a new union joint, new brake cylinders and new carburettor. Hardly a week went by without something breaking down. It did not seem to want to do anything this time. Phew; whirr; whirr; phew; whirr; whirr. Phew; whirr; whirr. Bob kicked the nearside wheel and cursed it bad temperedly. The excess choke flooded the engine. Bob decided to leave it awhile whilst he went round the corner to buy a newspaper. Ten minutes later he returned to try again. Phew; whirr; whirr, phew, whirr, whirr. Suddenly there was a bang, bang and the engine spluttered into life. Bob set out on the journey.

Twenty minutes later with only ten miles covered Bob hit a dense queue of traffic. The local gymkhana was creating traffic bottlenecks. The weather was quite warmish and the roadster reacted to the weather and the slow progress by starting to overheat. Bob turned off the engine to relieve the overheating problem. Bob was at this time in the middle of an apparent disused country lane access point and since the access road was partially concealed as well as being somewhat abandoned, Bob had not left any clearway. The traffic in front started to move but the Sunbeam Alpine was playing up again. The car behind tooted impatiently. The Sunbeam Alpine spluttered impotently. Bob was less than happy. The impatient driver could not pass because of oncoming traffic. Bob got out to look under the bonnet. It was, of course, an optimistic gesture. If there was oil and water and the plugs were clean there was little more that Bob could do. The car in front was by now vanishing in the distance. More motorists to the rear of Bob's car joined in the impatient hooter chorus. The plugs were OK, the car had oil and water.

'Push it out of the way,' demanded the impatient motorist

behind. 'Where would you suggest?' asked Bob with irritation.

'Anywhere. Just get the bloody road clear,' said the irritated antagonist.

Bob had noticed that the kerb was high and he knew that he was not capable of mounting the car on it, unless of course assistance was rendered. The causeway was narrow in any case. Bob pointed out these observations.

'I don't care where you put the bloody thing,' said the antagonist with obvious lack of compassion. The tooting chorus resumed.

A young scruffy looking boy had appeared and looked at the Sunbeam Alpine with a puzzled expression.

'What's up with your car, mister,' asked the boy.

'It's broken down,' said Bob with some impatience.

'It's in the way,' said the boy.

'Are you going to do something about the obstruction?' snapped the bad-tempered man.

'Why don't you have a look at the engine?' asked the small boy.

Bob snapped at last and selected the small boy as an easier target.

'Why don't you mind your own business and go home?' he snapped at the boy.

'Are you going to do something?' yelled the angry man.

'I cannot shift the car on my own,' said Bob with impatience.

By now two motorists from further behind had arrived on the scene. They either did not know much about mechanics or they did not want to demonstrate any mechanical proficiency. They did, however, supply musclepower and the Sunbeam Alpine was manoeuvred into the small side lane, where it was to become an obstruction there. The traffic procession was mobilized once more, without Bob to instruct it. It was obviously a job for the AA. Fortunately Bob remembered passing a telephone box and so he set off to retrace the source of potential assistance. It was only ten minutes walk. The small boy had disappeared in this time but Bob returned to find that the small boy had returned with an equally dishevelled little girl whose face was caked in some sort of red sticky confection.

'You can't park here,' said the scruffy little girl primly.

"Is car's broken down,' said the little boy knowingly. "E caused a big traffic jam. I don't think he knows much about cars,' the small boy added.

'Haven't you got a home to go to?' asked Bob hopefully.

'We live on this road, mister,' said the little girl. 'You'll have to move your car because it's blocking the road.'

'There's no other cars around,' said Bob. 'Even if there were, I couldn't do much about it. I'm waiting for the AA.' He paused and wondered why he need to explain the situation to these two scruffy urchins.

'My dad wanted a sports car,' said the small boy. 'My mum says they are for show-offs and ...'

'... for overgrown schoolboys,' chimed in the little girl.

'Can't you push it out of the way?' asked the little girl whose face was plastered in the red sticky confection. She leaned against the car leaving a red sticky handprint smeared on the white enamelwork.

'Get your sticky hands off,' yelled Bob, worried about the welfare of his pride and joy. The little girl jumped back in alarm.

'You're not threatening that little girl, are you?' interjected a passer-by.

The little girl was distinctly reassured.

'Sorry, mister,' she said. 'It soon comes off though.' With this she produced a grubby equally tacky handkerchief and began to rub at the red smearmark. She succeeded in wiping off some red but she replaced some of the red with black. This could have been liquorice.

'Just leave it alone, and go back home to mum,' asked Bob pleadingly. 'I'm sure it must be time for dinner.'

'We've had dinner,' said the small boy. 'Can I sit in the driver's seat.'

'No you can't,' said Bob shirtily. 'Go home.'

'This is *our* road,' said the small boy, 'and it is my home.'
'You're blocking our road, mister,' said the small girl.

Bob wished that the AA would turn up to rescue him from these *enfants terribles*. Another glance at the slow moving traffic made him realize that the fifth cavalry in the form of the AA could be a long time coming.

'Have you had dinner, mister,' asked the small girl.

'No, I'm not hungry,' snapped Bob.

It was then that he had a brainwave. He remembered that he had some small bars of Aero under the passenger seat.

'Do you like chocolate?' he asked the little girl.

'Why are you offering 'er chocolate?' asked the small boy. 'Our mum and dad says not to take sweets from strangers in case they are vampires.'

'*Ooh*, do you think he's a vampire?' screamed the little girl, backing well out of Bob's reach. 'Vampires have funny teeth, don't they?' she asked.

'I am not a vampire,' stressed Bob.

'Why are you offering 'er chocolate and not me?' asked the small boy.

'You can have some chocolate as well,' said Bob, 'provided you go away and leave me alone.'

At this thought the pair showed interest.

'How much chocolate, mister?' asked the small boy.

Eventually the bribe worked and the two tormentors left each clutching an Aero. Bob set about replacing the untidy pile of dislodged clothing back on the passenger seat. He had, of course, had to move it to gain access to the Aero bars secreted underneath. In the process he found a copy of *Penthouse* which his flatmate had thrown at him earlier that morning. He was busy flicking through the rude photographs when he heard a chomping in close proximity to the car. He looked up to see that the two scruffy urchins had brought along yet another family instalment who was even smaller and younger.

'Martin wants a bar of Aero as well please, mister,' said the little girl.

'I haven't any more, and you said you would go home and leave me in peace,' said Bob.

'Martin keeps crying 'cause he 'asn't got any chocolate,' said the little girl. "Ee said he was going to tell mum.'

"E's a dirty old man,' said a small boy's voice from the other side of the car. "E's looking at ladies with no clothes on.'

'Come away from him,' he yelled at the little girl.

'I want some chocolate,' screamed the smallest monster.

'There is no more chocolate. Give him some of yours,' said Bob.

The little girl hastily swallowed the rest of her bar.

'Mine's all gone,' she said with a mouth full of chocolate. The small boy was more considerate. He broke off a half inch square before swallowing the rest of his bar. The smallest boy eagerly accepted the morsel, swallowed it and then started crying once more.

'Are you sure you 'aven't any more chocolate for Martin?' asked the little girl.

'Keep away from him, he's a dirty old man,' repeated the elder boy.

Another passer-by stopped in mid-step and turned on Bob.

'What are you up to with those young children?'

Bob reddened. 'I'm not doing anything. I've broken down.'

'Serves you right for having a flash car,' said the passer-by.

'But you leave them kids alone.'

Bob thought to remonstrate then thought better of it. By now nearly an hour had elapsed and so Bob set off to retrace his steps to the phone booth. Halfway back, on looking over his shoulder, he saw an AA van approaching in the opposite direction. He broke into a run to return to the broken-down Sunbeam Alpine. The AA man pulled across the road to block the traffic once more. A couple more volunteers helped push Bob's car further up the access road so that the AA vehicle's rear-end no longer caused obstruction.

'You are supposed to stay with the vehicle,' stated the AA man. 'You should have pushed it in further as well.'

After a couple of further interchanges the AA man set about checking the ignition. There was little response, so the bonnet was lifted. The AA man began to poke around looking at the connections.

'There's a loose wire,' said a young voice.

'Go home,' demanded Bob.

'So there is, son,' said the AA man. 'You're a bright young man.'

'*He*'s a pain in the bum,' muttered Bob under his breath.

'He's a dirty old man,' said the young girl who had also returned. '*He*'s got rude pictures of ladies with no clothes on.'

'He did give you some chocolate,' said Martin, the youngest monster.

'He wouldn't give me any chocolate.' At this Martin started sobbing.

'What's this?' asked the AA man suspiciously, visually bridling.

Bob reddened and hastily tried to explain the situation. Thankfully, the AA man believed the story and soon repaired the minor breakdown. It was merely a case of broken high-tension lead. In the process Bob was coerced into disturbing the passenger seat clothing heap once more to gain access to the Aero bars' supply. Martin stopped crying and the three urchins disappeared once more. The AA man disappeared too, leaving Bob to replace the dislodged ballast of clothing. By now the traffic was clearing a little too.

Just as Bob was backing out into the main road once more he heard a scream from a middle-aged lady in spectacles who was attempting to run to catch him up. The floral-dressed lady was waving an umbrella threateningly.

'Wait,' she screamed.

'That's the dirty old man,' shrieked a little girl's voice excitedly.

Bob did not want to wait. He took off as quickly as he could leaving the floral-dressed female chasing his disappearing car.

The jinxed car had not finished its jinx effect for that day. Bob also managed to acquire a puncture *en route*. This entailed a further delay, including a total repacking of the car boot. The spare wheel was buried underneath the luggage. In the process Bob acquired black hands, black face and black shirt cuffs. He arrived at Garnstone College reception just as registration had been finalized. Bob managed to locate the college and managed to find a car park space well behind the scheduled 16.30 to 17.30 p.m. arrival time. It was in fact 18.23 p.m. and only two staff remained. They were Maisie Welling and Agatha Todd, bursar and deputy bursar respectively. Maisie Welling was one of the old school, member of the Institutional Management Association, daughter of a major who had served in the Indian Army. Her father had been brutal and totally dedicated to military matters. Her mother had regretted the marriage and mostly slept in rooms separate from the Major. The one thing her father had taught her was that appearances were most important. Maisie Welling insisted on everything being in its place cleaned and polished. Males should always have ties, be clean in appearance and clean-shaven. They should have shiny shoes and along with females too for that matter, should be punctual. Bob was dishevelled. The shoes lacked polish. Black cuffs, black grubby hands and a black-smeared forehead.

'Can I help you, young man?' she asked in a voice which conveyed the impression that Miss Welling did not really want to help at all. In fact, Maisie Welling conveyed the impression that Bob was an insect which should return from whence it came. She looked him up and down with a hint of contempt.

'I'm sorry I'm late,' said Bob apologetically.

'Late, late?' said Miss Welling with questioning tone.

'My car broke down.'

Miss Welling was not one to offer sympathy, in fact she

implied that an early start might have eliminated the problem.

'Are you a student teacher?' she asked in apparent disbelief that Bob could ever be held responsible for training young minds.

'Go and wash your hands and I will arrange for your documentation to be completed,' she said. She delegated this job to her prim assistant.

'Where's the boys' room?' asked Bob, instantly regretting such a phrase.

'Boys' room?' questioned Miss Welling.

'Don't worry, I'll find it,' he almost stuttered.

The mirror in the 'boys' room' revealed the reason for her scepticism that Bob might be a potential teacher. The wash completed, Bob was left hauling in extra lengths of roller towel to hide the black smear marks. He used half a toilet roll in an endeavour to remove all traces of grease from the sink. It was by now 6.45 p.m. and the deputy bursar was waiting impatiently to complete registration. Bob had left the acceptance letter in the car. There was further delay as he returned to the car to fetch the papers. By the time his room key had been issued it was turned 7 p.m. Bob located the dining-room only to find it almost empty. He approached the service counter.

'Evening meal terminates at 1900 hours,' said Miss Welling imperiously.

The shutters came crashing down. Bob was starving.

6

JIMMY SETTLES IN

It was a full week after the Principal's beginning of term staff address, with the culmination of the vanishing act by Principal Ness. The new course of heart treatment was obviously effective because he had not been driven home by the faithful secretary. John Lane, resident clerk of works, had been summoned. John Lane emerged from his meeting with the principal in an advanced state of shock. The rest of the week had seen much activity and the stage was completed in record time. The heaviest volunteers available from Hector Britain's territorials had conducted a PT display on the stage. John Lane had been compelled to act as compere as a means of getting him on the stage in case anything went wrong. Hector Britain looked well on his way to becoming senior lecturer. There was one little cloud on the horizon though. The case of the burning chip frier had come to light as the principal went through fire safety reports. Principal Ness was paranoic about fires. He had been in charge of a smaller college which had burned down. Although Principal Ness was not guilty in any way he had lost his place of work and had been very lucky to obtain a post as deputy at Dronsley College of Further Education. Hector Britain's prospects were further handicapped by the business studies lecturer who was handling Principal Ness's sister's divorce proceedings. Sam Patel was also angling for promotion. The food studies department student intake was assembling in the main hall for the opening address by Principal Ness. The staff were below the stage with seating facing the new horde of students. Hector Britain and Sean O'Riley were acting as ushers, demanding that the students fill the front rows first. The letter of acceptance to parents had emphasized the importance of punctuality and dress and had put down the assembly time as 8.45 a.m. instead of 9 a.m. as the time for the opening address to take place. At 8.58 a.m. the caretaker took up position at the bottom of the stage steps. At 8.59 a.m. Hector Britain and Sean O'Riley marched to the two vacant staff seats, having established that there were no more late arrivals. At 9 a.m. sharp Principal Ness entered and the caretaker Sam Brown jumped to attention and threw up a salute. There was almost an expectant hush. Principal Ness took the centre of the stage and banged down a gavel sited on a small table there. There was now an expectant hush.

'Good morning. Welcome to Dronsley College of Further Education. I am Principal Elliot Ness. . . . The food studies department has a long proud tradition. . . . Our students in all departments have a reputation for winning awards and trophies. . . . We have a record number of passes, a record number of credits. We have won the George Carter Award for Retail, the Jack Tescow Award for Hairdressing, the Jules Pilchard Award for the Best College Chef. . . . Dronsley College of Further Education has. . . .'

At this point Principal Ness was disturbed from the party political broadcast by a latecomer.

He was only temporarily nonplussed. He thought he knew the boy, but couldn't place him.

'You are late, boy. Don't you know that it is the height of bad manners to be late. Who are you, boy? What course are you following?'

A lecture on the unfortunate boy's criminal lateness followed with the 'boy' being unable to answer any questions at all. Eventually the unfortunate boy was allowed to answer to name the course.

'Have you noted those, Mr Potterton?' Mr Potterton did

not need to note things down. He remembered who the boy was quite clearly for once. Jimmy Graham's father's car had broken down again, more than likely.

After the principal's address Mr Potterton took centre stage. Principal Ness returned to his office puzzling as to where he had seen the late-coming youth. At last the opening induction session drew to a close. Mr Britain and Mr Saltpot were told to keep an eye on the delinquent Jimmy Graham. The stout lady, a new member of staff, intervened on Jimmy's behalf. Miss Todd had had enough of Mr Parable and the Fanshawe Secondary School. The post at the Dronsley College of Further Education offered more money and at least a code of discipline. Mr Millipede had referred her to the college principal, as Mr Millipede was on the college board of governors. Miss Todd had been promised a timetable with full-time students as these were more easily disciplined than the part-time day-release students. She had also been promised her own pastry department.

Miss Todd had noted one other student from the Fanshawe Secondary School, and she was somewhat surprised. Beverley Smythe Browne was an unlikely candidate for the food studies diploma course and was not there with the blessing of her father. He would have preferred that she had gone in for something more academic but she had had more than enough of her father's influence at school. Beverley wore spectacles like her twin brother and she dressed somewhat plainly. She wore a baggy blouse and knee-length skirt. Her appearance certainly gave the other feminine members of the group little cause for worry in the competitive stakes. The male students were more readily attracted to Stella Pavrotti, a voluptuous and equally temperamental Italian girl. There was Nancy Wee Wee, a diminutive but shapely Chinese girl. There was Rosalinda, a pretty but shy girl from Hemel Hempstead. Linda Carter had a father in the building trade. Her dress-sense indicated no shortage of money. Susan Miller was an attractive West Indian girl, with dark sultry ebony profile. Eileen Hunter was tall and lovely and mature in outlook for her tender years. Sheila Hancock was older than the others. At twenty-five she was a divorcée, something relatively rare in the sixties. Whereas the student males would be interested in Stella, Rosalinda and Linda, the male staff would become enthused with Sheila. Sheila was, moreover, a real blonde and there is a little truth in the adage that gentlemen prefer blondes. Non-gentlemen prefer them even more. The final member of the female contingent in Jimmy's group was Debbie Harris. Debbie's father was a group captain and as such had given his daughter everything she might ever have wanted. The one thing he had not given her was brains. Debbie was totally dizzy. She was bubbly, to put it mildly, but she was plain. She was clever with her hands but totally unbelievable in thought. Debbie was probably the most innocent girl in the group. She had believed in Father Christmas until nearly twelve years of age and she still was not certain about how babies were brought into being. She had been at private boarding schools all her life and as she had no brothers, Debbie found the new proximity of boys a little unnerving. Her plain looks would save her from their attentions for a while, though, whilst the sirens in the form of Stella, Rosalinda, Eileen, and Susan were around.

The male members of the group lacked the female members' overall sparkle, with only David Fretwork having an animal magnetism which attracted females. David was good-looking, talented and charming. He rapidly latched on to Stella, rapidly forestalling Jimmy's ambitions in that direction. After a group meeting with their tutor, Hector Britain, they had been given timetables and told to report back for the afternoon for his lecture demonstration. He had set up everything ready for his induction to knife drill, stocks code of practice. He returned to the staffroom for a cup of tea and a snort of brandy to get the adrenaline going. Fortified and refreshed, Hector returned to the lecture theatre to find the students gathering and collecting generally towards the rear of the room. Beverley Smythe

Browne was conspicuous by her solitude on the front row. She had a foolscap pad ready for taking notes and she was writing down recipes from the chalkboard. Jimmy was trying his luck with Eileen but she was totally unimpressed. Arthur Shaba was one of two black students but whereas Arthur sported an Omega watch the other lad a very commonplace Westclox version. Arthur was also older, at twenty-three he was a mature student. He tried his luck with Sheila but she informed him that she had had enough of men to last a lifetime. Actually there was relatively little interplay between the two sexes other than that between David and Stella. Arthur and Jimmy had soon been rebuffed and the other lads were chatting with each other at one side whilst the girls chattered with each other in other areas.

Hector Britain arrived relatively unnoticed. He immediately noted Beverley's apparent diligence, plus the location of Jimmy Graham who had been noted as a potential troublemaker. The students were chattering away almost oblivious to Hector's presence. 'Ahem, ahem,' he coughed to draw notice. Notice was not immediately forthcoming as Debbie was deep in conversation with Rosalind. Rosalind was not actively involved in the conversation. She was the recipient of Debbie's one-sided dialogue and was far too polite to want to interrupt. As a southerner she felt out of things and was grateful to find someone to team up with. The two had an unease of boys and Debbie had nothing in common with the northern girls' social background either.

Hector picked up a large cleaver and brought it down sideways with a loud bang. Rosalinda nearly jumped out of her skin. Debbie was speechless for once.

'Four on a row, front four rows, *move*,' bellowed Hector.

'There's only sixteen of us,' said someone.

'Who said that?' demanded Hector.

'I did,' said Arthur Shaba in a tone denoting Oxbridge diction.

'Well, there'll be thirty-two in a minute, cleverdick. So

shut up until you are spoken to,' said Hector condescendingly.

In truth, Hector was not quite prejudiced. As he often boasted, Hector Britain treated all students equally badly. Arthur Shaba did not quite appreciate this however.

'I am not a dog to be spoken to like this,' said the petulant Arthur.

He was still smarting from his rejection by Stella. Arthur was not enthusiastic about associating with the other coloured lad. Tommy Nunn, the other coloured lad, spoke with a broad Yorkshire accent and got on well with the other males in the group.

'Shut up, and don't argue,' yelled Hector.

By now one or two students had edged forward but Beverley was still on her own on one side. Five girls were squashed together on one row and David Fretwork was still at the back with Stella. Hector Britain turned from Arthur Shaba to Jimmy.

'You, down here next to this young lady.'

He referred to Beverley who edged further up the seat. She conveyed the impression that she did not fancy Jimmy's proximity.

'Lover boy,' said Hector to David, 'you can sit on the front as well. Not you, my dear,' he said to Stella. 'You may stay where you are.'

The seat movements had generated more noise as conversations resumed.

'*Quiet,*' yelled Hector.

'Can I say something?' asked Arthur.

'*No you can't, shut up,*' yelled Hector.

'I thought this was an adult college of education,' said Beverley quietly.

'I think we should see the principal,' said Arthur haughtily.

'Quite right too,' said Sheila, who had teamed up with Eileen. 'I'm not going to be treated like a ten-year-old.'

Hector had never had a start like this before. Normally Hector would have had the new group in a state of trepidation by this time. Why had he suddenly received older students, the potentially delinquent Jimmy Graham and moreoever, more than one barrack-room lawyer?

'*Shut up,*' he roared. '*We'll deal with any questions one at a time.*'

At this time there was the sound of more students approaching. There was a timid knock at the door.

'Are you ready for the other group. Mr Britain, sor?' asked a very Irish voice. Hector allowed entry with a repeated demand that there should be only four students on a row and only the front four rows were to be occupied. There was a marked disinclination to make up a foursome with Beverley, Jimmy and the reluctant David Fretwork. The group of five girls remained squashed together.

'Would you please come and join the front row?' said Hector to Linda, who happened to be on the end of the row. Linda declined to argue and moved, albeit unwillingly. Arthur once again tried to speak up.

'Can I say something?' he asked.

Hector swung round and glared at him malevolently.

'You can say what you want at 5 p.m. but I would like to get on with the afternoon's work, if you don't mind, and we are already quarter of an hour behind schedule. Perhaps you too would like to have a word at 5 p.m.,' he added in a more friendly tone to Sheila.

At forty-two Mr Hector Britain still had a great susceptibility for attractive young ladies. Dark mutterings had been heard about some of Hector's TA weekends being alibis for other more carnal activities. He was, moreover, quite fit-looking and attractive to quite a few women. Sheila knew that he was not her type but she was sensible enough to realize that she had had enough confrontation with her divorce for the time being. Arthur seemed to be on his own and decided to eat humble pie until later. The demonstration was allowed to continue.

Hector set about explaining the system of recipe annotation.

'Looseleaf files are to be used, with sections for soups,

stocks and sauces, eggs and farinaceous recipes, fish dishes, meat dishes and vegetable dishes.

'What about pastry dishes?' asked a quiet voice on the front row.

'Miss Todd will be teaching pastry,' said Hector paternally. 'Could you please save questions until the end? Could you also please stick your hand in the air if you wish to ask a question?'

He said this patronizingly but he did not really want another confrontation with Arthur or Sheila. He was also a bit unsure of Beverley. Mr Potterton had mentioned that her father was a deputy headmaster and as such he might have friends in the education department at county hall. He had heard about the appointment of Mr Parable and hoped that they would not do something similar at the Dronsley College of Further Education when Mr Ness retired next year. Hector did not like Mr Ness but he knew that Mr Ness did have a beneficial presence where discipline was concerned. Hector was a firm believer in the 'jankers' system set up by a former national serviceman from the RAF. Delinquent students would practise practical hygiene via copper polishing or silver polishing. The new pastry teacher had thought this an excellent extension of her own systems. The studious looking Beverley had her hand up in the air.

'Yes, Beverley,' he said patiently. Hector had a penchant for remembering dissident names and he had never known so many students' names so quickly before. He noted that the second groups seemed very quiet in comparison. He had soon crushed the small mumblings of dissent immediately after their arrival.

'There is only one N in farinaceous, I believe,' said Beverley demurely.

Hector rapidly flicked open the index page of the repertoire. She was right. Grudgingly he accepted the criticism.

'What are you grinning at?' he demanded of Jimmy, who was perfectly innocent.

''Nothing, chef,' said Jimmy politely.

Arthur thought to ask a question but thought better of it.

7

POLITICS AT GARNSTONE

Bob was to find that Garnstone wasn't so bad after all. The accommodation was comfy and clean. The meals were appetising too, provided you arrived on time. There was a well-used bar at very reasonable prices. The grounds were set in a sylvan setting but there were some open spaces for the more athletic to play sports. Two large tower blocks built nearby, however, tended to dwarf the block in which Bob had been accommodated. It was a pity that they flanked the college so closely as it did spoil the sylvan effect somewhat.

The students were a mixed bag. There were a large batch of younger students who seemed not long out of university. These dressed somewhat casually compared with the teachers destined for food studies, engineering and managerial subjects. The younger batch seemed to be predominantly disposed towards social studies and the arts. The males were largely unshaven and long-haired. The females were often dressed like hippies from a San Franciscan commune. It soon became apparent that left wing politics was quite important to the social studies and arts students and they were well organized for the election of the student union which was to take place within the second week. Bob soon made friends with neighbours in his block, including Sandy McPherson who had worked for seven years in South Africa. Sandy was quite concerned about the influence of the left wing, especially when he found out that the union officers had a large say in the allocation of funds from the central grant elected to the student union. 'We ought to take a stand against those hairy red chancers,' said Sandy. He made this announcement to the associates including Bob who sat quietly reminiscing in the bar two nights before the mandatory student union meeting in which the union executive would be elected. All the students had received a brief outline of the function of the union in the opening induction assembley. Only forty-eight hours' notice was required from nominees. Election was done by show of hands. It seems that it was usual for volunteers to be elected just by volunteering. Very few students wanted extra responsibilities. The sociologists had drafted out a team and there was apparently no one interested in standing against them.

'It's sewn up,' said Gavin, adding that nominations had to be in at lunch-time the following day. 'They even have a well-drafted out manifesto.'

'I've noticed,' said Sandy dryly. 'Look what they are going to do with the money.'

'Guest speakers from the unions,' said Gavin to no one in particular. 'Support for Che Guevara – Peace demonstrations and Ban the Bomb.'

'Someone should put up a stand though,' said Myra Williams who had joined them within the last few moments. 'I'll stand if someone will second me.'

Myra turned to Bob and suggested that there were several in the food section who were totally averse to the sentiments preached by the sociologists and arts student teachers. Each agreed to canvass his fellow theme group early in the morning and if they could they would put forward as many nominations as possible by the 1 p.m. deadline due the following day. There were president, vice-president, treasurer, secretary and four others to subscribe to. Each position required a proposer and seconder and these could be the same for all eight posts under the terms of the constitution. The only other thing required was a three minutes' maximum election manifesto speech from each candidate and then the show of hands.

That night after the nominations was a very hectic one as they met to draft a rival manifesto. The meeting was expected to be brief but Sandy pointed out the importance of presenting a good case. In the event, the election was to present five candidates for president but the vice-president evidently went to the runner-up on the presidential head count. This was probably a good thing because it potentally ensured fairness as it resulted in Myra as president and the very hirsute John McTavish as left wing vice-president. Bob ended up as secretary and wondered what he had let himself in for. Sandy became treasurer and Myra had two 'blue' supporters whilst John McTavish had two 'red' supporters. The meetings looked like being heated as proposals were drafted by the executive union cabinet for submission to the student union electorate at open meetings.

One of the first problems of union was to be the use of the student union office. They were given one key and that was all. Bob said he would go down to the local locksmith to get another seven keys cut. The local locksmith could not or would not oblige. He met with similar responses at other locksmiths and in one was put off by having to wait whilst the locksmith went to make a telephone call. The locksmith's apprentice looked at the key and said casually, 'You won't get one of those in a hurry.' And so Bob left.

Bob was soon off down the road and was nearly run down by an erratically driven police car, but he thought nothing of it. It was obvious that there could not be someone in the office all the time but chairs, tables and other furniture would go wandering to other locations. Papers would go missing or would be used for messages. Some people would use the office as a picnic centre or the others would moan if Bob had locked up. There were also implied allegations of incompetence until Bob thought of trying a locksmith he knew in Sheffield. Bob was very pleased to achieve success there but the bill was not small.

In the meantime Bob had settled into the Garnstone

routine and had become very friendly with Ben who was an ardent socialist in the old terms of the word. Ben was on the student union and had taken over as entertainments secretary. Ben had also landed a part-time job in the bar on the weekends which provided revenue and a source of free beer. Bob was looking for a source of part-time work himself so Ben invited him to become involved with the Nine Elms Restaurant working on Saturday nights with free beer, a steak supper and £5 for the night. Bob could not believe his luck. He had only been working a couple of weeks when he was asked if he would help out on a late October barbecue to be held at Blackberry Farm. Bob had never had much involvement in barbecues but agreed to go along as there would be a couple of bonus bottles as well as the normal lucrative fee.

Bob arrived at Rudi's house. Rudi was the Nine Elms German chef who had taken a night off to organize the barbecue. He could not very well take another member of the Nine Elms team and Bob was a first-class substitute because the Nine Elms clientele were potential Blackberry Farm party-goers on this particular occasion. The day was a golden October one, even quite warm. The trees had not started to brown yet and the Indian Summer had postponed the cold unwelcome winter approaches.

They set out at 2.30 p.m. in a large white van loaded with gateaux, salads, beautiful 10 oz entrecôte steaks, crockery and cutlery. Rudi's wife, who was very attractively dressed in a short mini-skirt sat provocatively in the middle with Rudi driving and Bob flanking her on the other side. Rudi's daughter aged eleven and son aged twelve were squashed in the back. Bob tried to control his thoughts and tried to avert his eyes from Erika's warm sensuous body. Erika seemed to know the effect on him and deliberately provoked him as Rudi drove on apparently oblivious to the effects that his wife was having upon Bob. Rudi was a thick heavy-set muscular man not to be tangled with. He was typically Teutonic. He was methodical, efficient and hardworking. He also lacked a sense of humour.

He was quite good-looking which no doubt had enabled him to succeed in finding such a lovely wife. Erika would not have wanted to change him but she did not get much romance out of him and she had a very lively disposition in marked contrast to Rudi. Bob did not know that she was teasing and did not want to give offence by open rebuttal. He was also very appreciative of the need not to upset Rudi.

It was only twelve miles to Blackberry Farm but the last three miles were over a very bumpy country lane. As they bounced over the holes in the road Erika's skirt rode up higher and higher. She made little attempt to push it down. It did not help when she 'accidentally' steadied herself using Bob's leg for support. She soon realized that Bob might have control over his mental reactions, but some parts of the body have a mind of their own.

'I like driving in the country, Bob,' she said. 'Don't you? Rudi used to take me in the country and we would find places to kiss and cuddle. You never take me out now, Rudi,' she said, kissing him gently whilst her hand again slipped onto Bob's lower anatomy ostensibly to steady herself. 'I'm sorry,' she said unconvincingly. 'Do you take your girlfriend in the country for naughty naughties?' she asked demurely.

Rudi drove on stolidly. Bob hoped that Rudi would concentrate on looking ahead.

Finally they arrived at the back of a huge cowshed with a very small door through which the provisions and crockery would be unloaded for the evening's work ahead. Bob climbed out uncomfortably and held the door open for Erika to climb down. Her ungraceful exit displayed more than just her shapely thighs and her scanty semi-transparent underwear hardly offered Bob the opportunity for his emotions to die down. The door would only offer temporary respite to cover Bob's embarrassment.

'I'll be back in a minute,' said Bob as he rushed off to the well-marked toilet.

A quick spent penny allowed him to recover his composure

and then the preparation work began. He returned to find Erika unloading with the two children but he was called by Rudi to lend a hand in moving the twelve-foot-long solid built barbecue. There were two farmhands present as well but even though the barbecue was in two parts it was still heavy movement action. Rudi wanted the barbecue between the two wide open barn doors and he wanted an emergency cover in case of rain. Having got the barbecue positioned, kindling began. Paper and sticks to begin, then coal was added. Ultimately coke would be used. Rudi had had this contract before. When the cooking began the steaks would drag out the heat considerably and an ordinary charcoal fire would be quickly spent.

In the distance a few clouds appeared. Rudi asked again for the tarpaulin for over the scaffold flanking the doors. The farm labourers rigged it up grumpily, keeping it unfurled so that it would be less inclined to scorch or catch fire even though it was poised at least six foot above the rapidly heating barbecue. A lonely wasp had arrived to disturb Erika within but it escaped the attempted swatting procedure. It arrived seeking reinforcements in the meantime with obvious success.

'Leave the gateaux in the boxes,' demanded Rudi. 'Clingfilm the salads. Clingfilm the strawberries.'

By now the solitary wasp had roused two squadrons. They zoomed around in fury and Erika and the children cowered, Bob swatted and Rudi cursed in German. The skies had begun to cloud over more and a few splashes of rain fell now and again. The distant sky was blacker.

The intention had been for the guests to approach the barbecue from outside and then they could choose to dine outside next to the lake or they could dine within. It would now appear that Rudi's Teutonic thoroughness in requiring cover would be badly needed. The raindrops began to fall more quickly and the tarpaulin was unfurled. It seemed likely to scorch underneath whilst it steamed above. The Porsches, Rovers, Rolls Royces, Daimlers etc. began to arrive and the well-dressed passengers scurried across the make-shift carpark to the sanctuary of the steam-cleaned cow shed. The band quartet played Beatles' numbers and the guests were happy.

The consolation prize was that the wasps were not enthusiastic about the wet either. Twenty-three casualties to the wasps one casualty Bob with sting. Erika dabbed some cream on it from within the confines of her handbag and Bob was aroused again by her sensuous closeness. Rudi was outside prodding the bulging tarpaulin which had begun to droop with its water content. The water came down in cascades at each prod. It also loomed threateningly as though it might subside onto Rudi's head. Underneath it was somewhat blackened and scorched.

The dining time was almost ready and Rudi and Bob had coached the coke into glowing red fierce heat. It was so hot that they could feel the heat transmission through the dampened aprons. Bob wished that he were back at the Nine Elms restaurant. Erika and the children were to oversee service of the salads and gateaux which were now uncovered. Bob and Rudi had to reverse positions of service so that the well-heeled guests did not need to venture out into the torrential rain. The steaks were soon sizzling away on top of the red hot barbecues and Bob and Rudi had a choice of fierce heat to the front or cold wet rain to the rear. As they performed the barbecue two-step the guests were suitably amused. Rudi's face was grim and Bob's wasn't exactly happy either.

The rain continued in torrents, and the tarpaulin began to bulge ominously now that the chefs were busily engaged in culinary duties. At last the service was over and the guests resumed their dancing, alternating between square dancing, rock, the Charleston, waltz, twist etc. Although black and singed on front and grey and sodden behind, Bob and Rudi joined the others in a steak supper before loading the van. The process was a wet one and Erika's clothes clung to her like the fur of a drowned rat. Even she was not up to teasing Bob on the way back. They had just about completed loading before leaving when the inevitable happened. The embers were still fierce when the tarpaulin finally gave way and it sploshed down into the embers sending up big black sooty waves. Some nearby trendies had been watching in drunken stupor. They rapidly sobered as they were cascaded in water, soot, cinders and mud. Bob and Rudi had, of course, forgotten to pull back the tarpaulin to render it safe.

Rudi cursed in his heavily German accent. 'It is *gut* that we have the money *yah*,' he said. 'I will I think not be here next year.'

Bob sympathized. Bob had inwardly decided that he was not in a hurry to feature on any further barbecues anyhow.

Bob was given six bottles of red wine on top of his £5 fee and so he soon cheered up. He arrived back at Garnstone to run into Ben, along with Roger Buckstone who was also in the student union. There were three girls there and Ben and Roger were very pleased to invite Bob to join them in a party in Ben's room. Bob was still in chef's whites, black at the back and damp grey at the back and was obviously not the sort of sight to sweep the unattached girl off her feet. It seemed that Ben had invited the two girls from the nearby Jodie Foskett Teacher Training College so that she could keep Roger company. Unfortunately, Roger's fiancée had turned up and the girl was an embarrassment. It was still wet, however, and so Sylvia was loath to leave immediately until the rain abated.

Bob changed in five minutes flat and dowsed himself in aftershave. He threw off the dirty chef's whites into a corner and rushed to join the party in Ben's room. Ben had a huge candle burning away and had changed the normal light bulbs for red ones. Ben introduced Bob to Sylvia and poured liberal sherries out for the girls. The males drank Newcastle Brown but these were rapidly exhausted. Ben had soft music playing and Ben, Roger and partners were smooching together in the darkened reddish glow. Roger soon decamped with his fiancée but not before Bob had persuaded Sylvia to 'waltz' with him. She did so with serious misgivings but the sherry had loosened her inhibitions. She had to leave the room for personal reasons and Ben pointedly told Bob 'to get on with it'. Bob did not expect to get so far on a first date but suggested she joined him for a glass of wine before he walked her home. It was not until he had lured her into his room that he remembered the state he had left it in. She laughed at his discomfort and got to talking about her brothers. Bob was able to relieve all that tension sustained by Erika after all. He woke up to find her gone and thought it all a dream until he found her stockings and suspender belt. Unfortunately, the only thing he knew was that her name was Sylvia. 'Who is Sylvia? What is she?' he sung to himself. He went to seek out Ben who was obviously not at his best. Ben had locked himself out of his room.

'Try my key,' said Bob.

The door opened before Bob realized that he had used the union office door key. It was strange as it was shaped differently. Ben's key also fitted the accommodation door, it was found.

8

SERVICE WITH A SMILE

The term was soon developing into a patterned routine with the course dovetailed in kitchen production and food service. Sheila found her charms had many of the male lecturers eating out of her hand but only one over-amorous food service lecturer made her slightly apprehensive. Sheila and Hector had a sort of truce. She had realized that his disciplinary manner was a means of survival and discipline was essential in the realm of the dangerous kitchen environment. Behind his back she sometimes supported his role; he in turn treated her with respect and avoided confrontation. Sheila and Beverley had become close friends, with Sheila playing an older sister role. Needless to say, Beverley was also treated with extra respect by Hector but there again Mr Hector Britain rarely had problems with the female students. Most female students had a more mature attitude to work than the male adolescents. Female students mainly caused problems because of male distractions or female physiology. There was, of course, rivalry between girls, and jealousy, but at least there was less likelihood of horseplay and lack of diligence.

Jimmy had not been keen on food service at first but he realized that it had compensations. The girls wore black skirts and stockings and white semi-transparent blouses. Even the prim Beverley took on a new guise in her waitress uniform. She was a brunette of slim build but the skimpy blouse demonstrated that she was certainly not flat-chested. Her long shapely legs were well displayed in the dark stockings. She had apparently discarded the spectacles for contact lenses. Jimmy looked twice before he realized who the changeling was. How could she be a twin to that dreadful Giles? he thought to himself.

Stella Pavrotti 'wore' a skimpy black bra which was a credit to material structural design in the way that its wispy structure contained the fulsome cleavage so provocatively. The first year students had alternating weeks practising on the staff. If there were spillages it would not matter so much if only staff were involved. On the second week the first years would act as runners for the second years and they would help and supposedly learn from the observation of the second year students. Stella was in the midst of half a dozen rampant, ogling second year students, basking in their lustful admiration.

The restaurant door swung open and in strolled the food service lecturer, Mr Simon Naunder. He was the lecherous food service lecturer disliked by Sheila. His eyes fell upon Stella's ample bust supported by the skimpy black bra displayed through the semi-transparent waitress blouse. The semi-transparency was accentuated by the tightness of the blouse which was probably two sizes too small.

'Only white bras are allowed in the restaurant,' he said, having mentally undressed Stella and each of the other female students in a way that only Mr Simon Naunder could achieve. 'I do not want to see coloured bras when we return from break. Nor do I want to see technicoloured socks,' he said to Jimmy who was wearing luminous green creations somewhat harsh on the eyes.

'Please, Mr Naunder, I haven't got any black socks here,' said Jimmy.

'I have not got a white bra,' said Stella provocatively as she thrust out her bust like a Dolly Parton look-alike.

'I am not interested,' said Mr Naunder. 'No black bras allowed in the restaurant and no luminous green socks.'

Susan Miller, the sultry West Indian girl, turned to Linda and stated her preference for black underwear. Mr Naunder knew the county obsession with regards to racial discrimination. His eyes rested on her ample bust as he stressed that the rules applied to everyone and preferences did not come into it.

'He's disgusting,' said Sheila to Beverley but if Mr Naunder heard he did nothing.

Mr Naunder continued with the day's routine, hoovering, plate sorting, table laying, accompaniment preparations, glass polishing etc. There is a lot of planned preparation before the customer arrives into the restaurant to dine. All too soon it was break time and the students set about their own catering needs, with the additional dress requirements necessary in the case of Jimmy and Stella. The old geriatrics had begun to gather in the foyer. These were the usual customers who were part of the college diners' club. The senior citizens were the main source of customer to the college because most people of younger age would be at work in the weekdays nine until five. Jimmy was conspicuous by his absence. Stella was wearing a cardigan over her waitress uniform. Mr Naunder's attention was temporarily distracted by Mr Ness, the principal, who was peering through the glass doors of the restaurant. Mr Ness was sporting a toupee which meant that the two people with him must be dignitaries or HM inspectors.

'Cardigans not allowed,' he said to Stella loudly. 'Take it off immediately.'

'You told me my bra showed,' said Stella.

'No, I did not,' said Mr Naunder.

Mr Ness outside was obviously going red in the face as he must have been able to hear what was being said.

'I said black bras not allowed, so stop being stupid and take off your cardigan.'

At this moment Jimmy arrived breathless.

'Where have you been?' asked Mr Naunder irritably.

'I'm sorry I'm late, Sir,' said Jimmy in his most apologetic manner. 'I had to go down the High Street to buy some black socks.'

It seemed obvious that Jimmy was telling the truth. Mr

Naunder swung round on Stella.

'Take off the cardigan,' he yelled at Stella.

Stella took off the cardigan to reveal the fact that she had also removed the offending black bra as well. Unlike Jimmy, though, Stella had not obtained a substitute garment. Her firm nipples stood out proudly thrusting into the tight semi-transparent blouse. Mr Naunder's eyes nearly popped out of their sockets and the reverie was only broken by the indignant half-throttled yell from Mr Ness, the principal.

'Cover yourself up, girl,' he spluttered.

Stella reddened in shock. She realized she had gone too far. The male students' grunts of approval such as 'Cor', 'Oooh' and more explicit vocabulary were instantly silenced. Mr Naunder was given an afternoon appointment with the principal but a later inevitable heart attack would defer this to a later date.

It was not the amateur striptease, however, which had aroused Jimmy's interest. Food service had enabled Jimmy to move from a job of kitchen chores at the Southern Constellation into the dining-room as occasional waiter. Jimmy's chat and new-found waiter skills had produced a small source of pocket money to subsidize Jimmy's amorous leanings. The students were supposed to put their tips at college into the *tronc* used for an end of term party but Jimmy managed to keep some of this back. It also was not unknown that students occasionally intercepted some of the bar stocks for afternoon consumption. Food service was conveniently followed by non-compulsory liberal studies. Jimmy's afternoon was involved in liberal studies in the loosest term of the word. Jimmy had found himself a nice little second year redhead.

Mr Ness had his guests brought in whilst he excused himself to return to his office. Mr Ness needed some special calming pills very badly. Mr Naunder had allocated his best second year student, Sally Surtees, to look after the principal's table. He did not take any chances with the first year *commis* either. Sheila was designated for this position.

Stella was dismissed to don the black bra once more and she was sent to work on the still in the kitchen. Mr Hector Britain was in the kitchen so the second year and first year males were unlikely to be distracted. Stella was also allocated 'jankers' in the form of silver polishing as a punishment for her display. John Greenwood, a second year Arthur Daley type, was enquiring as to whether she would do a strip show for the local rugby club and Stella appeared to be unwilling until she heard what the rate of pay would be.

Jimmy was allocated as *commis* to Michael Jackson. Michael was a willing lad but Michael was also a disaster area. Michael had been sent to the furthermost reaches of the dining-room at the opposite end to the table allocated to the principal. The curtains and low ceiling tended to make this dining zone less conspicuous. Michael had received an order for *crêpes Suzettes* and had the gueridon lamp lit ready for action. The wick was high, though, and there were scorch marks, well, soot marks anyhow appearing on the low ceiling. Beverley, who was working nearby, spotted this and suggested that the lamp was moved out or turned down. Jimmy pulled the trolley out from under the low ceiling and returned to the kitchen with some cleared plates whilst Michael crumbed down. Michael pushed the trolley out of his way and it rolled near to the curtains and low ceiling again. The two ladies on the adjoining table were into deep conversation.

Principal Ness had just about recovered his composure as he reassured the two visitors, who turned out to be inspectors, about the high standards of Dronsley College of Further Education. Good food and good wine are remarkable for brushing aside feelings of doubt and apprehension. Mr Simon Naunder gushed and wheedled and generally made an extreme effort to regain the confidence of Principal Ness.

There was a roar from the kitchen as Mr Hector Britain was obviously demonstrating his lack of approval for student misbehaviour. Mr Naunder excused himself as he went to intercede on behalf of Principal Ness. The engrossed nattering ladies continued in deep consultation. Michael was busy reading the *flambé* notes. The curtains smouldered.

Jimmy, on his eventual return from the kitchen, spotted the potential fire hazard from the far end of the dining-room and waved. Michael continued reading the *flambé* notes and was not conscious of Jimmy's waves. Meanwhile, Mr Ness had observed the wave and he looked round to see who the wave was for.

The ladies nattered on. Michael read on. Someone pointed out that Jimmy was waving and Michael looked up and waved back. At this point two things happened. Mr Naunder returned and took in the scene at a glance and the curtains finally caught fire. Principal Ness clutched his heart. The ladies continued nattering. Beverly snatched the water syphon from a second year student's hand and sprayed it upon the burning curtains. The nattering ladies were caught up in the spray too and ceased their engrossed conversation. Mr Naunder raced across the room, tripped over one of the nattering ladies' handbags and went reeling onwards to fall into the soggy smouldering curtains. He inadvertently clutched at them desperately as he tried to retain his balance. The curtains came hurtling down onto a table next to the principal who was still clutching at his heart. The screams of panic soon changed into peals of laughter at the unexpected cabaret. The two drenched nattering ladies resumed nattering and Mr Naunder clambered back on his feet as he attempted to regain his composure. The students behind the bar hastily secreted a bottle of brandy underneath the empty bottles due for the dustbin. The two visitors were attempting to relieve the principal's symptoms of heart distress. The geriatric customers seemed to have been given the elixir of life as they chattered excitedly.

The efforts to compose Mr Ness meant that Mr Naunder's appointment with fear would be at a later date. The ever-faithful secretary was to take Mr Ness home whilst the inspectors put forward a recommendation for his early retirement.

9

WHO IS SYLVIA?

The left-wing elements at college were very unhappy about the threats to student grants. The TUC and trade unions were very unhappy about the legislation planned to curtail union activities. The left wing proposed support for the day of action and the student union meeting for once had a sea of faces in support of proposed activities. John McTavish proposed an excursion to the House of Commons to lobby the MPs. There should be a coach or coaches paid for by student dues because there was a promised strike by public service bus and train employees. Bob was appalled. He stood up angrily and refused to organize anti-government activities. A red-bearded check-shirted heckler whom Bob had never ever seen before jumped up and demanded Bob's resignation.

'Sit down, you fool,' said Myra, 'and do it.'

Bob would not sit down and agree to organize demonstrations. He offered to soldier on with the other duties until a new election could be organized.

The following Tuesday began with dire threats of suspended transport systems and mass demonstrations at the House of Commons. At midday a charabanc arrived as the student executive carried out the left wing resolution to: 'Lead the student body into a lobby against the trade union proposed legislation'. As the charabanc set out for Westminster, a taxi discreetly pulled out to follow behind *en route* to Westminster.

Bob set to work on the mandatory thesis so that he could

get out early for the bar. He wanted another reunion with Sylvia but he had not found out who she was. Unfortunately for him, the female Jodie Foskett Teacher Training College was off-limits to all males. (This had not stopped the more willing Jodie Foskett maidens from staying at Garnstone overnight.) Even Ben had not been able to help as he had met the girls only once that particular evening and he had been in an even worse alcoholic stupor than Bob.

The demonstration coach did not get all the way to Westminster as police barricades blocked the way.

'This is as far as we can ride,' said Myra to the left wing activists.

'We can walk the rest of the way via the backstreets,' said John McTavish. 'We'll meet you here at 6 p.m.,' he said turning to the coach driver.

'You won't, you know,' said the driver. 'I've another arrangement booked for this afternoon.'

'Didn't you book a return trip?' John asked Myra. 'We might be stranded here.'

'The resolution called to lead the student union to Westminster,' said Myra.

'You didn't ask to be led back again and the bus did not come cheap,' said the driver.

The Marxists at the back had, of course, not heard the discussions and they were eagerly pushing forward to proceed with their demonstration. The executive were the last to disembark. Myra, Sandy and the 'blue' supporters gathered their composure whilst Myra looked back for the mysterious taxi.

'We'll see you back at Garnstone,' said Myra coquettishly as the four scurried across the road into the mysterious taxi. There were howls of discontent as the activists realized what had happened.

'We'll have a vote of censure on this,' yelled John.

Back at Garnstone, Bob was having difficulty with his thesis and so he decided to go out for a walk. He was just in time to catch a pint of beer at the Wellington. The college bar was closed because Ben and the other barman were out demonstrating. Bob was just looking up from his pint when he saw Sylvia sneaking out via a side door. He yelled after her but she either did not hear him or she was ignoring him. He dashed after her but she rapidly got into an Austin A40 which zoomed away before he got a chance to accost her. He hastily scribbled down the registration number, SYL 699F. He returned to the pub to find his remaining unconsumed half pint rapidly disappearing down the gullet of a well-built well-tanned roadworker. He declined to have an argument, and was unable to buy a further pint as the barman yelled, 'Time, Gentlemen Please'. Bob felt that there was not a lot to be gained by staying at The Wellington and so he returned to Garnstone. He decided to call in the union office to see if Myra and Sandy had returned from leading the lobby at Westminster.

The 'blue' party were indeed in the student union office and they had a case of Newcastle Brown which Myra was drinking as liberally as the male companions.

'Did you get this in advance then?' said Bob innocently.

'Not exactly,' said Sandy, 'but it has been paid for! Did you know that the student union office key is the same as the key to the bar?'

Bob began to have some misgivings about the keys which had been cut. For the moment, though, he forgot the misgivings as he contributed towards the kitty for the Newcastle Brown.

It was much much later that the lobbyists returned. There was a limited public transport service of sorts but it was somewhat infrequent. The activists were not averse to travelling on 'blackleg' transport and Ben was even quite good humoured about the state of affairs. Ben could not, however, throw any light on the ownership of the red A40 registration SYL 699F. Nor could he gain any information from the Jodie Foskett Teacher Training College. The hall porter, Bouncer, did not know and did not want to know. His responsibilities were to discourage rampant males of all persuasions from pursuing the Jodie Foskett teacher training maidens.

Bob returned to the accommodation block and then he remembered that he needed a clean ironed shirt for studies on the morrow. The following day was to be the day when they would find out where their placements would be. Then they would have a week of induction to get to know what their teacher training placement would be like. Following this they would leave for 'battlefront' teacher training practice in a fortnight's time. Bob climbed the stairs to the communal utilities room. He opened the drying cupboard to find his shirt and someone else's socks sharing the space with an array of very skimpy provocative female underwear. There were also a couple of blouses but these did not have the same psychological effect as the array of wispy underwear. As if to answer the mental query as to where the underwear came from, the door swung open and a beautiful young lady dressed in a very short housecoat entered.

'Oh, hello, I'm sorry if I've filled the cupboard up,' she said in a well-educated and seductive tone.

Bob could have fallen in love with her voice without the vision as well. Her housecoat fell open revealing a short pink nightie underneath. The vision was wearing nothing else underneath but she made no rapid atempt to cover her semi-nakedness. The vision seemed quite innocent of the havoc she was playing with Bob who even felt a little embarrassed as well as lustful. The vision introduced herself as June, gathered her clothing and disappeared into Charlie Brown's room so quickly that Bob had to pinch himself in case he was dreaming. The sounds from Charlie's room obviously quelled any thoughts of Bob's imagination running riot. 'Oooh. Charlie. You mustn't. Hmmm HM.' The two made no attempt to disguise the creaks of the mattress springs.

Bob woke up next morning wishing for the luck of Charlie Brown. The suspender belt and stockings hung over the tie rack as trophies from the previous memorable night. Bob wanted to return them but most of all he wanted contact with Sylvia again. For the time being he had other diversions, though, as there was a persistent knocking on the door. Since his shouts of 'Who is it?' were unheard or ignored, Bob angrily went over to open the door.

'Miss Welling would like to see you at 8.30 a.m. in her office,' said the burly middle-aged cleaning lady who appeared to be trying to peer within the portals of Bob's room.

Bob hastily remembered to fasten his flies and started buttoning up his shirt. The middle-aged *hausfrau* looked at him disgustedly. He had not expected a female at the door as normally the cleaning staff waited for the students to go to their lectures.

'What for?' asked Bob.

'You'll find out,' said the cleaner gloatingly. Bob looked at his watch. 8 a.m. already. He had obviously missed breakfast and the appointment with Miss Welling gave little opportunity to visit the newsagents for confectionery.

Miss Welling recognized Bob as soon as he entered her office. She inspected him as though he was some nasty little insect that she would like to sweep up and deposit outside in the trash bin. 'It's you again,' she said coldly in words that conveyed sinister overtones. 'Have you read the Garnstone Residential Guidelines?' Bob answered in the affirmative. 'What does it say about entertaining members of the opposite sex?'

The word 'sex' appeared to have offensive implications when uttered by Miss Welling. Before Bob could make any contribution to the virtual monologue, Miss Welling launched into a tirade about student morals, the reputation of Garnstone, the assaults on the innocence of the female sex and the embarrassment of residents of the adjacent tower block. Initially Bob had thought that the seduction of Sylvia was the cause for the summons and the potential cause for Bob's removal from the Garnstone halls of residence.

'It is absolutely intolerable that you should carry out such depraved behaviour for all the world to see and Mrs

Jones was speechless with embarrassment and disgust.'

'I'm sorry but I don't know what this is about,' said Bob almost innocently.

'Do you deny having female visitors in your room and having sex there?' said Miss Welling coldly. Before Bob could answer with an incriminating response, Miss Welling continued. 'And to tie the girl to the top of the bed whilst you . . . err . . . whilst you . . . err. . . .'

Miss Welling could not bring herself to say what Bob had supposedly done in this bondage sequence. Bob could at least state quite categorically that he had not tied any girl to the bed.

'Fetch Barbara,' said Miss Welling to her assistant. 'Do you deny having female underwear in your room?' asked Miss Welling. 'The same, ahem, the same item of female underwear used to tie a young lady to the, ahem, bed.'

'It's not me,' said Bob woefully. 'I've never tied a girl to a bed, not ever.'

'Mr and Mrs Jones saw you,' said Miss Welling distastefully.

'How could anyone see me do something I have not done?' asked Bob hopelessly.

'You left the curtains open.' At this point there was a knock at the door.

'Come in,' said Miss Welling. It was Barbara.

'Is this the student who has ladies' underwear in his room?' she demanded of Barbara.

'It is, Miss Welling,' said Barbara firmly.

'What is the reason for female underwear in your room?' demanded Miss Welling.

'I would rather not answer that,' said Bob evasively. 'But I am innocent of these allegations. I do not tie young ladies to beds.'

The interrogation continued with Miss Welling convinced of Bob's guilt and Bob sure that he had been set up by the mysterious Mr and Mrs Jones. Miss Welling informed Bob that the case would be referred to the principal with a recommendation that Bob was expelled from the campus and even from the course as a potential corrupter of morals.

'Am I allowed to meet Mr and Mrs Jones?' asked Bob, 'or am I sentenced without even meeting my accusers?'

Miss Welling informed him that it was bad enough that outsiders should have been subjected to such corruptible behaviour, without being dragged in for a confrontation with Bob.

'It wasn't me,' said Bob desperately. 'I'm innocent.'

The looks on the matronly trio, Miss Welling, her deputy and the burly chambermaid, seemed to indicate that all three considered Bob to be a pervert, rapist and woman molester. If they had absolute power, a big set of scissors would be used to bring Bob to book.

Bob was ten minutes late for the departmental meeting, and he had not had time to purchase a bar of chocolate as an interim snack.

'You're late, Mr Malone,' said Miss Pringle imperiously.

Miss Pringle was another matronly figure like Miss Welling. Miss Pringle was however only 5ft $2^{1}/_{2}$ ins tall, and she was slim and wiry. She could, in spite of her diminutive size, make anyone look small in spite of their physical height superiority. She did this by means of an icy tongue and piercing eyes. 'The bigger they are, the harder they fall' was her apparent family motto. Before Bob could explain the reason for his lateness, she continued.

'The principal wanted to see you first thing.' Miss Pringle looked at her watch. 'You are already twelve and a half minutes late and he is in a stinking temper. You can explain your lateness when you return.'

'Blimey, Miss Welling did not waste any time,' said Bob. 'It was about nine o'clock when I left her office.'

'What were you doing in Miss Welling's office?' asked Miss Pringle curiously. 'No, don't tell me now. Go down and see Mr Jamestown immediately.'

Hell hath no fury like Mr Jamestown scorned. Bob rushed off to the principal's office. Mr Jamestown had been an officer in the Black Watch. He was due for retirement at the end of this academic year and dreaded the inevitable final drift into anarchy which was certain to transpire when he retired. Bob knocked gingerly on the outer portal door of Mr Jamestown's office. He was summoned in by Mr Jamestown's secretary and he found another guest waiting inside. It was Sylvia. She blushed deep red when she saw him and, though he was pleased to see her, he knew that his days at Garnstone were obviously numbered. He did not have chance to talk to her, though, because the dulcet tones of Mr Edward Jamestown demanded that Mr Malone came into the inner lair immediately.

'Mr Malone, isn't it?' stated Principal Jamestown firmly.

'Yes, sir,' said Bob, standing to attention as though back in front of an officer in the RAF.

'Are you an ex-serviceman?' asked ex-Major Jamestown (Black Watch) in a somewhat more friendly tone. Bob gathered a few twinges of optimism.

'Yes, sir, RAF, sir. I didn't do it, sir.'

'Shut up, man,' said Principal Jamestown. The RAF were soft Brylcream boys to ex-Major Jamestown. Still, at least Mr Malone wore a collar and tie, had a short haircut, had clean shiny shoes and did not look like a Che Guevara revolutionary.

'I haven't accused you of anything yet, and you did do it,' said Mr Jamestown emphatically.

'I don't know who Mr and Mrs Jones are but I'm sure they have mixed me up with someone else, sir,' said Bob pathetically.

'I don't know what you are going on about, man,' stated Mr Jamestown. 'I am concerned as to how you got hold of the master-key for the whole college. I want it back and you will be held in suspicion of anything untoward that might have happened as a result of your having access to such a key. I know you paid for the Newcastle Brown but I cannot have students helping themselves from the bar or whatever.'

Further discussion elicited the information that Bob had been seen opening the bar, a fellow student's room, and the student union office. It then dawned upon Bob that Principal Jamestown was referring to the student union office key.

'Is this the key?' asked Bob, profferring the key-ring with the offending key. Bob realized that he ought to set the record straight.

'All the student union officers have a key like this,' he said to the principal who was clearly shaken as Bob explained the circumstances of taking office with only one key between eight of them.

Principal Jamestown called in the secretary to make immediate contact with all the others immediately. In the meantime Bob was asked to explain the previous outburst.

'I have not had any girls tied up in my bed, sir,' said Bob.

'I should bloody hope you haven't,' said the principal brusquely. 'What's this got to do with Mr and Mrs Jones? Who are Mr and Mrs Jones anyhow? I'll ring up Miss Welling whilst I'm waiting for the other union people. I am not keen on the student union you know, but I did hear that some of you stood up to those Communist blighters.'

Principal Jamestown picked up the telephone and dialled.

'Hello Maisie, Teddie here. Got a chap called Malone here. What's he been doing?'

Bob could hear Miss Welling recounting the shameful and incriminating evidence at the other end of the telephone.

'I'm surprised that Malone person had the nerve to approach you, Teddie,' said Maisie on the other end of the telephone. 'I suppose he's claiming he has not done anything.'

After the telephone call to Miss Welling, some of which Bob heard and some of which Bob had not heard, Mr Jamestown turned to Bob.

'Helping yourself to drink from the bar, even though

you left the money behind to pay for it is serious.'

Bob realized where the Newcastle Brown had come from for the office party now. He'd also begun to realize why it had been so difficult to get the keys cut. He could not very well say that it was not him who had obtained drink out of hours. He had, in actual fact, been an accessory after the fact in the consumption of the aforesaid Newcastle Brown.

'It is not half as serious as gratuitous bondage-type sex in the halls of residence.'

'I have not been involved in tying up women to my bed, sir,' said Bob. As an afterthought he added, 'How could Mr and Mrs Jones have seen me anyhow, even if it was true?'

'Surely you cannot be so stupid as to forget that the halls of residence are overlooked by the tower block?' stated Mr Jamestown. At last the picture was becoming more complete. 'And you have women's underwear in your room?' added Principal Jamestown.

'The fact that there is women's underwear in my room is not evidence that I tied a girl to the bed. Anyhow, any normal girl would have probably screamed.'

'I think the girl was enjoying it as well,' said Principal Jamestown, but he left this thought very quickly. 'Do you deny that there is women's underwear in your room?'

Bob admitted to the underwear and then thought of Sylvia in the outer office. 'Why was Sylvia in the outer office?' he asked himself. There was a tap on the door.

'Come in,' yelled the principal.

'They are all here,' said the secretary.

'I'll see them in a couple of minutes,' grated the principal.

'Do you deny that there is ladies' underwear in your room?' demanded the principal. 'You're not queer, man, are you?' he asked suddenly.

Bob could, of course, not reveal the reason for the underwear being in his room, but he was put out at the thought of being linked with homosexual behaviour.

'It does belong to a young lady, sir, but not one who had

been tied to the bed. If I had a girl in my room, IF,' he said slowly, 'I would close the curtains.'

'You have had a girl in there? Haven't you?' Ex-Major Jamestown, ex-Black Watch, could not condemn Bob for that. He had been a bit of a lad himself. For a moment he thought back nearly half a century to his time in India. Maisie Welling had not always had an aversion for the male sex. He remembered one occasion very well when Maisie had been under the influence of a hot sultry evening at an Officers' Mess party. They had both been aged fifteen.

'I think we'll sort out the matter of the keys first, Mr Malone, and I shall be making more enquiries. In the meantime, do not even think about breaking any rules. Send them all in,' he said, having opened the door slightly.

The puzzled union officials entered. The assembly had to surrender the keys and they were interrogated one by one about the existence of further keys. In the process Sandy admitted to taking the Newcastle Brown and leaving payment. The previous day's events were uncovered by shrewd interrogation. Bob gained a few lost Brownie points as the principal uncovered the story of Bob's resignation. The union members were dismissed and the registrar was sent for.

'Why was it that Bob had been given a master-key to the whole college?'

Bob was left to sweat it out about his Garnstone future. As he was released whilst enquiries were pending, he looked to see if Sylvia was in the outer office. She was not. She had disappeared. The secretary either could not or would not enlighten Bob as to who she was. He returned to the department to join in a lecture on student teachers' code of behaviour whilst on teacher training practice. He also learned that he was to be on practice with Veronica Lake. Veronica was nicknamed 'Hothouse Veronica' behind her back. She was forty-three and came from Nigeria. She was jet-black, slim and was reputed to have two grown-up married daughters. Veronica hated England. She really felt the cold and was always swaddled in a thick brown coat. She generally wore a scarf around her neck and she wore high leather boots that had thick socks oozing from the tops. Veronica always sat next to any radiators that might be close by. She insisted that windows were closed and she clearly longed for the day when she could return to hot sunny Africa again. Bob and Veronica were to go to the Dronsley College of Further Education.

'The principal is to let you stay with him,' stated Miss Pringle.

Miss Pringle obviously did not know about Principal Jamestown's present enquiries.

10

OUT OF THE FRYING PAN

It was now week six in Hector Britain's scheme of work. Week six was deep-fat frying. There was a strong rumour that Hector Britain might get the new upgrading if Principal Ness were fit enough or willing enough to sign it. Hector had all the big potatoes sized up for demonstration of deep-fried potatoes, *Pommes pailles, pommes alumettes, pommes mignonettes, pommes frites, pommes Ponts Neufs, pommes batailles, pommes crisps, pommes gaufrettes*, straw potatoes, matchstick potatoes, mini chips, french fried, jumbo chips, cubed potatoes, Smiths crisps potatoes and latticework fried potatoes.

The fish too were lined up, *filets de plie A 'l' Orly, filets de plie frites à la Française, filets de plie frites a L'Anglaise, goujons de Plie*, plaice in batter, plaice in milk and flour, plaice in breadcrumbs, plaice in breadcrumbs like fish fingers. Hector was also cooking whitebait and he had a small *friture* on the stove for this because the fat is useless after cooking whitebait in it.

The students were assembling and jockeying for positions, preferably on one of the back rows. Some like Beverley would make sure they were on the front but these keen ones were predominantly female. In the first few weeks one or two paired-off couples had attempted to sit on the back row for a place of secretive fumblings but Hector Britain had soon put a stop to that. Jimmy had been very humiliated when told to wash his hands after one such interlude. Jane from Sean's group had never spoken to him since but the embarrassment had been long since forgotten.

Jimmy nowadays was the conspicuous male exception to the rule as he was now permanently assigned to the front row so that Hector could keep an eye on him. David Fretwork and Stella were the last to arrive, beating Hector's deadline by one and a half minutes exactly.

'What's on today?' David asked Jimmy casually as he sat on one vacant place on the front, whilst Stella took a seat behind him. 'Fish and chips,' said Jimmy. 'I never realized that anybody could make fish and chips into a thesis, but he can.' Jimmy was not exactly quiet of speech. Mr Hector Britain looked up.

'Something to say, Graham?' he asked.

Hector did not pursue the subject further as he had noted that for once there was a full class. This was one of the benefits of having four on a row. If there was any row incomplete it meant an absence. Find the absentee and fill in a 0 and then a neat line of ticks could be drawn in for those present.

'Well now that Romeo and Juliet are here we can commence,' said Hector.

'With fish and chips,' muttered Jimmy under his breath.

'Who said that?' asked Hector disagreeably.

There was silence as the group tried to look interested. Hector began with the safety rules.

'Do not fill small fritures more than two thirds full. Do not leave heat turned on whilst friture is unattended. Do not lean over friture. Do not add wet food to friture.'

Then he continued with the use of asbestos blankets for suppressing combustion. He reminded the students of the fire drill. Then Mr Britain reminded them of the fires of hell visiting upon any would-be arsonist like Michael Jackson who had not so long ago set the dining-room curtains on fire with the ill-fated *flambé* dish. Michael cringed at Hector's forbidding stare.

Hector had completed the fire precautions, the fire drill and the potato dishes and was half way through the fried fish demonstration when it was time for the morning tea break. He was about to send the students for break when the alarm bells clanged incessantly. Principal Ness had struck again. The weather was fine, a fire drill was imminent. Principal Ness did not like to waste time on tea breaks. Principal Ness always arranged fire drills in the morning or afternoon tea break period.

'Follow the exit signs and we meet in the carpark,' said Hector. He cursed the principal under his breath, turned off the power, closed the windows and followed the group outside to the carpark. He had his register at the ready for roll-call.

Outside was like Blackpool at a bank holiday. Students sprawled around or milled around aimlessly. The academic lecturers could scarcely be differentiated with ease as their standard of dress was generally casual to say the least. Two figures stood out from the massed shambles. These were ex-RSM Hector Britain and Miss Todd and the reception girls. Miss Todd was reading out her register primly and had one girl, Rebecca, missing.

'Rebecca,' she yelled out shrilly, 'Rebecca Naismith.'

Hector Britain was roaring out the names on his list as though on the parade ground at Catterick.

'Where's that bloody Jimmy Graham?' he yelled.

Miss Todd looked at him in disgust and hastened her girls to the other end of the carpark away from Hector's corrupting influence. The academics looked on in disbelief. Principal Ness seemed impressed until Hector suddenly spoiled the image with a load roar.

'You randy little man, get yourself over here at the double,' he yelled.

Jimmy Graham hastily removed the wandering hand from Rebecca's shapely bottom. He had been ushering her towards the proximity of the bushes.

'Disgusting boy, I'll see you later, Jimmy Graham, when Mr Britain has dealt with you. Come here, girl,' she demanded of Rebecca.

The interlude was soon over and the all-clear was sounded. Jimmy was awarded two hours' copper polishing. Rebecca was sentenced to three days' hoovering the catering department staff room. Hector allowed his group twelve and a half minutes tea break and he set off himself to put the stove on again, plus re-igniting the *friture* for the demonstration. He then set off for the staff room for a quick pot of tea. The tea had not been delivered. He cursed as he set out to collect it.

'He won't be back in ten minutes,' said David Fretwork to Jimmy. 'Let's all go back late and say that we were held up in the queue.'

Hector Britain was indeed late. He thought at the last minute about the *friture* on the stove set up for the whitebait. Cursing under his breath, he dashed down the corridor. He made it half way when he heard the crash of glass and the alarm bells started out all over again. He dashed into the lecture theatre to find Beverley struggling to unwrap the blanket to put over the raging inferno. It was she who had broken the fire glass alarm.

'Bloody hell, what did you do that for?' he asked.

He hastily turned off the gas and ushered her out into the corridor almost into the arms of Principal Ness. The promotion would appear to be deferred. Principal Ness had gone red in the face. He left for home. He thought to himself that perhaps early retirement was a good idea.

It was on the same morning that Bob and Veronica were due to travel to Dronsley for the teaching practice. The morning had begun with a distinct chill. Veronica was not apparently visible to Bob as he arrived for an early breakfast. There was a sort of bundle of clothes tucked up against the radiator. It was indeed Veronica. She had knee-deep boots which disappeared under a thick long ankle-length skirt. A chunky cardigan oozed through a tiny gap underneath the collar. A four-foot-long scarf was draped around her neck and she sported a 'Noddy' cap with red bobbin on top. Two whites of eyes could be seen peering out from the clothes bundle. She was clutching a cup of tea for dear life as though it were a heat talisman of protection from the cold. Bob did not cast her as a ray of sunlight at all but he felt some sympathy for her. He tucked into his bacon and eggs and hoped that the living quarters in Dronsley would not be too bad.

The journey to Dronsley was quite uneventful as the car behaved for once. The plan was to stay at Mr Ness's house but they were to visit the college first. They arrived to find a milling throng outside the college, the throng being in a state of alarm as a fire-engine came careering down the drive in answer to the call-out. It was a false alarm. They reported in to see Mr Potterton, who was not happy. Mr Britain had been summoned and informed that disciplinary action might be called for. Mr Ness had left early for home and Mr Potterton suggested that the Garnstone guests have lunch in the restaurant and they could return for a briefing later at 2.39 p.m.

Veronica was assigned to Miss Todd as mentor and Bob was assigned to Mr Britain. Since Hector had to report in to Mr Potterton, so as to try to think up some creditworthy excuse prior to the return of Mr Ness, Bob was given the task of giving the A group a theory exercise to pass away the time. Bob arrived to find the students in uproar.

'*Quiet*,' he yelled in best parade ground manner.

He too had been an NCO in the RAF. If you are an NCO in Her Majesty's Forces and wish to establish command, you yell. David Fretwork, who seemed engrossed with Stella's voluptuous cleavage, nearly jumped out of his skin.

'Who are you, mister?' asked the inquisitive Jimmy Graham.

'He's a nice man,' said Stella. David Fretwork decided he was not going to like Bob at all.

'Oh, he's only the student teacher,' said Susan.

'How do you know that?' asked Jimmy.

'Shut up,' said Bob.

'I saw . . . ' said Susan, cut off in mid-stream by another louder '*Shut up*,' voice from Bob.

Somebody whispered, 'Set the race relations board on him, Sue', but when Bob swung around to locate the new source of interruption, yelling out an even louder '*Shut up,*' the group realized that Bob meant business. He set out to introduce himself and the group had some degree of control for a few minutes as they sought out some background. It always helps to have some measure of the opponent even if he was only a student teacher. After a potted biography which obviously omitted some details the questions began. Bob had mentioned Hector's test and the group knew that if they stalled for time the test might get overlooked. Bob might have been a student teacher but as an ex-serviceman he was aware of military philosophy of pursuing a preset objective. Two more questions then the test, he decreed. There was more stalling but Bob would have none of it. He demanded a clean sheet of paper and pen in front of each student and he demanded 'No copying.' The latter is usually only achieved in examination conditions but an attempt has to be made. Bob began writing on the board.

'Isn't his writing terrible?' said Susan.

'Your head's in the way, mister,' said Jimmy. Bob had so far achieved, 'Write down five derivative sauces from Bechamél, Espagnol and Mayonnaise.'

'*Sauce anchois, fromage, aux ouefs, oignons, soubise, persilles, mornay,*' said some know-all at the back.

Bob swung round from his writing in time to see David kissing and fondling Stella. She blushed provocatively and thrust David away quickly. The talking stopped as Susan pushed her written paper answers forward.

'Is that right, chef?' she asked.

Bob declined to comment, asked for cooperation and started to write out the next sentence.

'*Demi glacé, Oporto Xeres, Marsal, Maderé, Picquante . . .*' began the know-all. Bob swung round too slow to trace the information leak.

'Do you carry on like this with Mr Britain?' he asked.

'They wouldn't dare,' said Beverley. 'Why don't you give Mr Malone a chance?' she asked the group.

'We donna creep like you,' said Stella.

'Mr Britain writes the questions on the board before we get here, chef,' volunteered Beverley.

'Mr Britain writes the questions on the board, chef,' echoed David.

'We could go to teabreak early so that you could write them on the board, chef,' said Jimmy helpfully.

This time the echoes were different. 'That's a good idea,' the group chorused. 'Isn't that a good idea, chef?'

Bob did not think it a good idea.

'I'll look after that repertoire,' he said to Jimmy who had casually flicked open the sauce section in what he thought was not a line of vision within Bob's grasp.

'I've got a better idea,' said Bob. 'I will dictate the questions from question 2.'

The group did not think this a good idea at all. Bob, however, like Hector, did not believe in student democracy.

'Will Mr Britain get the sack?' asked Jimmy, desperately seeking a new source of diversion.

'Question two,' began Bob. 'We haven't had enough time for question one yet,' said Debbie.

'Question two. List *five* safeguards applied to deep frying.'

'Do not leave fryer unattended,' said David, laughing at his own joke.

The group burst into fits of laughter.

'What's your name?' asked Bob menacingly.

'Robin,' answered David respectfully.

'Robin Basket, I suppose,' said Bob, forgetting that such responses are not appropriate for chef lecturers. 'Or is it Robin Day?'

David stopped and thought for a moment, 'Robin Smythe Browne,' he answered.

Beverley was about to erupt at the thought of her family name being brought into dishonour but Bob had approached David by now and seized the answer sheet.

'Right, David, I'd just like a few words outside if you don't mind.'

'You lot be quiet for two minutes,' he said, perhaps optimistically.

Outside the classroom Bob reverted to RAF procedures learned at square-bashing at West Kirby.

'Right, you little bastard,' he said, 'We can play this two ways. We work together and Mr Britain need not know about this. Or you can try and stitch me up as a potential teacher and I can stitch you up as a student. You can come back into the classroom in the present seating plan and cooperate or you can piss off.'

'You don't frighten me,' said David who in actual fact had a broader build than Bob.

Bob grasped David's tie and pulled David towards him.

'What's it to be?' he asked menacingly.

For the time being at least David decided to cooperate. Although the incident had barely taken a couple of minutes, there was a rapid scurrying away from Bob's desk as he opened the door.

'He's coming,' said the watchperson.

David tried unconvincingly to swagger back to his desk next to Stella.

'You could have him for that,' said Susan.

'Shut up,' said David. 'Nothing happened.'

'Question three,' began Bob.

'We haven't...' said Debbie, interrupted in mid-sentence.

'*Shut up*. Question three,' continued Bob.

'Mr Britain did say something about copper polishing classes.'

'God, he's worse than bloody Hector,' said Jimmy.

The few murmurings rapidly subsided. The dictation style of test made it much easier to control the proceedings. Bob had learned a cardinal rule in teaching: *Never turn your back on a student unless you have to.* He already knew the other guideline to class control from his RAF days. Firm control is necessary when attempting to attain set objectives. The target was achieved early and so Bob applied a bit of Garnstone philosophy as well. The students were dismissed as reward for their belated cooperation.

'Can I see you, David,' asked Bob.

Grudgingly David stayed behind.

'Thank you, David,' said Bob. 'I hope we can be mates and forget about today.'

Bob stayed in the classroom and spent the last ten minutes glancing through the answers. It was obvious that the first two question responses were fairly consistent, with just about a hundred per cent listing 'Do not leave fryer unattended' as first response to question two.

Hector arrived just as Bob was about to return to the staffroom.

'Where are they?' he asked. Bob said he had let them go early. 'Too much for you, were they?' asked Hector sarcastically.

Bob bridled. He did not reveal the full tale of the afternoon's proceedings and Hector did not pursue the matter further. Hector had enough problems of his own. A student teacher was yet another straw on the overloaded camel's back.

11

AT HOME WITH PRINCIPAL NESS

Principal Ness sat at home in the front lounge supping at a cup of tea. The heart attacks were not so bad as they had been and since his new treatment and diet he recovered much more quickly. He still remembered that dark day when the previous college had burned down. He was paranoiac about fire. He then remembered that the student teachers were due and he should have been at college to welcome them.

'Don't worry, Elliot, they'll understand,' said his wife soothingly. His wife, in fact, had been the responsible agent for the arrangements. Their daughter was receiving help in her master degree with support from Miss Pringle and had offered hospitality to Miss Pringle in response to her requests for information about potential short-stay accommodation. Since their son had left home there was only the daughter left. The house was large and rambling and seemed deserted nowadays, apart from the times when Principal Ness was having meetings or parties. Principal Ness was hardly a talkative partner, and there were times when she welcomed external contacts. It was true the son came to stay over the holidays but term-time left barren patches of hermit-style living broken only by the meetings of the Dronsley Townswomen's guild. Miss Pringle and Barbara Ness had been at residential school together and had kept in touch. Sometimes Barbara stayed with Miss Pringle for a few days as she went up to 'the Smoke' for the occasional shopping spree. Principal Ness had not been overhappy about his wife's *fait accompli* but had been reassured by his wife Barbara that Miss Pringle would not send up just anybody.

'You ought to go and see the doctor again for a check up,' said Barbara gently.

Meanwhile, Bob and Veronica had completed their first day at Dronsley College of Further Education. The principal's secretary had offered to drive them to Principal Ness's home but when Bob explained that he had his own transport she drew them a map instead. Soon they were underway with Veronica navigating and Bob driving.

'It's somewhere near here,' she said, as they drove along a narrow road signposted 'Gymkhana'.

Bob felt misgivings.

'It's here,' said Veronica.

It was the drive with the approach from which the dreadful children had emerged when he had been suspected of being a child molester.

'It can't be here,' said Bob, pulling in to look at the map.

It was the right place though. Bob pondered and decided that he would have to bluff it out. He drove down the lane hoping not to meet the small boy and the little sister. Bob and Veronica went to the door and pushed the bell. A middle-aged lady i.e. Barbara, came in response. Barbara was younger than Principal Ness but was still, in fact, older than she appeared. Barbara was fifty-four and looked ten years younger, especially when not wearing her glasses. She was short-sighted without her glasses and could not see overwell without them but she did not wear them for most of the time.

'Are you the student teachers?' she asked. 'Have we met before,' she asked Bob suspiciously.

'No, Ma'am,' said Bob truthfully.

Bob wondered if she could be the previous pursuer. Barbara, however, was more concerned about how Principal Ness would react to a black person in the house. Principal Ness was not exactly racist, it was just that Principal Ness still thought of the African and Indian parts of the world as part of the British Empire. Her husband had had a bad turn once when their daughter had brought a West Indian graduate home for the night. The fact that they were merely classmates had not been realized at the time. In fact, their daughter had never formed any long lasting romantic links at all, but if she had felt inclined towards an inter-ethnic liaison the daughter would have probably gone ahead anyhow. Genetically she was as headstrong as her father but she had the more homely and compassionate side of her mother.

Mrs Ness ushered them in offering to help with Veronica's baggage. Bob declined feminine assistance and said he would bring the things in. Mrs Ness apologised for her husband's absence and set about making tea for the duo. Bob brought in the bags and Barbara showed them the rooms and told them that tea would be at 6.30 a.m. and breakfast at 7.30 a.m. She enquired about any specific dietary likes and dislikes and chattered about things in general. Barbara even managed to get Veronica to talk about herself a little, though Veronica was most loath to shed the swaddle of clothing wrapping even in the warm front room environment.

After the *tête-à-tête* the two went to their rooms to unpack. They heard the principal's car approach but Principal Ness did not appear for the evening meal. Barbara had prepared a buffet tea for this first occasion with homemade apple pie and an extensive cheeseboard. She had already prepared them for this in explaining that she did not know anything about them at the time of shopping and the buffet tea with cheeseboard should supply the needs of most people. Bob had already gently suggested that they hadn't expected meals and delicately he posed the question of payment. He had been told that the accommodation was free and the food would cost the same as that at Garnstone and she already knew that level of charge which she would expect at the end of each week. Both Bob and Veronica knew that the food cost would nowhere near meet this type of menu but Barbara would hear of no objections.

College principals are overpaid she said. Bob knew this was true but he was too polite to say so and he hardly expected charity. Bob did insist on helping with the pots and the two of them did the washing up whilst Mrs Ness refrigerated the left-over buffet items. Just as clearing up was almost complete another car was heard to draw up outside. Mrs Ness reached out for her spectacles to see who it was and it was then that she noticed the white sports car outside. She started to think back but was puzzled for the time being.

'It's my daughter,' she said in surprise. 'What is she doing here?'

The daughter by now had alighted from her car and she was coming into the house.

'Come and meet my daughter,' said Barbara to Bob and Veronica.

Barbara embraced her daughter as Bob and Veronica followed her into the lounge. The daughter looked up and Bob's eyes and hers met in recognition. It was Sylvia. Barbara sensed the recognition instantly and Sylvia had coloured slightly.

'You two have met, haven't you?' she stated unequivocally. 'Is there something I should know?' Yes there is and I know why I recognize that car outside.'

'Oh God,' exclaimed Bob miserably. 'I'll go.'

'You are not going anywhere, Mr Malone,' said Barbara. 'Not until I have had some explanations, beginning with last summer and my grandson and granddaughter. I might be calling in the police.'

Sylvia was puzzled but Mrs Ness transferred the interrogation to her daughter. First of all, though, she apologised but requested that the investigations were carried out in private as she did not think that Veronica would want to know about what was about to be said. Needless to say that whatever might develop Veronica was not to be affected by the outcome. Sylvia by now had recovered her composure and she confronted Bob, almost ignoring her mother's proposed interrogation.

'What do you mean following me here?' she demanded.

'I did not follow you here. How did I know that you lived here?' asked Bob hopelessly.

'What do you know about him?' asked Mrs Ness.

'I looked for you everywhere around Garnstone but how could I even dream that you live in Dronsley?' asked Bob.

'What do you know about him?' repeated Mrs Ness.

'Shut up for a minute, mother, please,' said Sylvia.

'What are you doing here then?' asked Sylvia.

'What do you know about him?' repeated Mrs Ness yet again.

'Shut up, mother,' said Sylvia, less politely.

'I am attached, probably *was* attached, to Dronsley Further Education College. The principal offered accommodation here whilst I am attached to the college,' said Bob pitifully. 'I looked all over for you at Garnstone but no one would tell me who you were.'

'What do you know about him?' asked Mrs Ness yet once more.

'Oh do shut up for a minute, please,' said Sylvia.

'I wanted to see you again, you must have known that. Then there was the time I met you in Jamestown's office but you'd gone and his secretary would not tell me anything. Nothing at all,' he added.

'That night was a mistake, it's over,' said Sylvia determinedly.

'Ah, some sense at last,' said Mrs Ness. '*Now, can you please tell me what you know about him,*' she almost screamed.

'We met in the Garnstone Bar,' said Sylvia desperately.

'And he tried it on didn't he? To think that I thought him such a nice young man.'

'No woman or female is safe with him, he even tried it on with Susan and Bobby, too. He offered them chocolate.'

'Mrs Ness, I am not a pervert,' said Bob.

'He is not queer,' Sylvia screamed almost simultaneously.

'He tried it on with you, didn't he?' shrieked Mrs Ness.

'As a matter of fact he didn't. I seduced him,' said Sylvia, instantly regretting her lack of discretion. 'It was a mistake,' she flung back at Bob in a swift afterthought.

'Please give me another chance,' said Bob desperately.

'If your father was here he'd go mad,' said Mrs Ness equally desperately. 'Mind you, it's perhaps as well he isn't here after the day he's had. You Mr Malone, pack your bags and go. I have no evidence on you and I cannot believe that you could be a pervert really but I want you out of this house. To think that I thought him such a nice young man,' Mrs Ness said to no one in particular. She stopped in her tracks. 'No, it won't do. I want to know what happened last summer. Why did you give my grandchildren sweets?'

'Yes, I want to know why as well,' said Sylvia.

At this point there was a knock at the door. Sylvia opened it.

'I'm going as well as Bob,' said the swaddled figure. 'I don't think Bob would attack little children. He-man, but he not pervert. I sorry I listen but you shout so. I go pack too.'

'He is not a pervert, mother, that I do know,' stated Sylvia categorically.' He shouldn't be made to leave as I'm only here for a couple of days anyhow. We may be sleeping under the same roof but it's over, OK?' she said to Bob.

'He's leaving after I've had my questions answered. You're staying,' she said to Veronica firmly. 'And since you've heard what has gone on so far you might as well stay in here too whilst I get some explanations.'

Bob was made to explain the events of the previous summer.

'It does ring true,' said Barbara. Charles' children are spoiled rotten and run amok. They should not have even gone down the driveway unattended. Any pervert could have got at them. Now, young lady,' she said, turning to Sylvia, 'what's this about you seducing a man? Not as I believe it,' she said abruptly to Bob. 'You are still going.'

'We met in the Garnstone bar and had a couple of drinks together and I kissed her afterwards. That's all,' said Bob unconvincingly.

'We went to his room and slept together,' said Sylvia brazenly. 'We'd both had too much to drink. He snored and did not even know when I left him. It was a one-off and it won't happen again.'

'This man took your virginity as casually as that?' said Mrs Ness in horror.

'It's not quite like that and you know it,' said Sylvia hurt by these developments.

'All men are after one thing alone aren't they, Veronica?' she said to Bob's classmate as a person with mature experience like herself. Even your father was, in better times, she thought to herself desperately.

'It was my fault,' said Bob, trying to defend Sylvia's lost honour.

'Shut up,' said Mrs Ness and her daughter in unison.

After further discussion it was decided that Bob would be allowed to stay but there were dire threats about what would happen should he try to press his suit with Sylvia. A telephone call was received stating that Mr Ness was going into Sheffield for more tests, especially bearing in mind that Mr Ness was due to fly to Munich for a week's international principals' conference. The group settled down for the evening to watch *Die Fledermaus* on television. At least Bob and Sylvia were talking together, though she was obviously trying very hard to remain distant. Surprisingly, Veronica gave him sudden quiet support.

'You play your cards right, man, and you be OK. But don't you go rush things. Slowly, slowly, man. Slowly, slowly.'

As they retired for the night Bob wished that he could once more feel Sylvia's warm body beneath the sheets beside him. He did not deserve the second chance but he relished it. There was a little misgiving in the back of his mind though. He had met Mrs Ness in another location. Where was it? It was then that he realized who Principal Ness was. How long could Bob's luck hold out. Time was the enemy.

12

PARTNERS IN ARMS

The next morning saw Bob and Veronica off to college. Hector was very friendly towards Bob, thinking that he might be a key to persuading Principal Ness that Hector Britain was indeed worthy of promotion.

'I'm away next week, you know,' said Hector confidentially, 'so if you like I'll let you do the demonstration. We can keep it simple and I'll work in a test to fill in the time. You know those questions yesterday. . . .' He continued as Bob acknowledged by a tense look. 'They were obviously cheating on the first two questions, just as you suggested. Then there is a marked difference in style.' He paused.

'It's sorted out,' said Bob. 'Can we leave it at that?'

Hector did leave it at that. He had not got much time for the Brylcream RAF, but at least he recogized some of the military philosophy in Bob. He had learned also that Bob had starred at the Southern Constellation.

'How did you get on with Mrs Kelly?' he asked. 'My, she takes some beating.' They got to relating stories about the Southern Constellation. 'Do you know she's had thirteen chefs this year? She sends for me when they walk out. The last chef has been there for three months now. Probably because the old cow moved up to London to see more of her daughter. The previous chef was a card.' It suddenly clicked.

'It was you, wasn't it? No it can't be, Hitler would not let you in his house after giving him a heart attack. Anyhow, he's very jealous about his daughter and I heard that that particular chef was having it off in the dining-room with Marianita. She was a one as well.'

Bob had reddened. 'What else did you hear?' he asked. 'How did you get round the old man yesterday?' The questions flew thick and fast and then Hector realized that Bob was in a similar state of apprehension about the future meeting with Principal Ness.

'The daughter's away, come to think of it,' said Hector. 'She's a cracker. Bloody cold as ice, though; going for a doctorate or something. Wouldn't talk to a bloody chef.'

'She's very nice, actually,' said Bob bridling.

Naturally Bob would not reveal how well he had got on with Sylvia but he did say how attractive he found her. He also confided as to how he'd like to take her out. Hector sagely advised him to forget it.

'If you are going to get through your teaching practice here you'd better keep out of Hitler's way. I should ask for a different college if I were you, as you can't avoid him next term.'

The established rapport had given Bob food for thought but he had fallen for Sylvia badly. The last time he had been in love he had ended up in the divorce courts. His previous wife had now gone to South Africa, taking their son with her. Bob had vowed never ever to find himself in the same predicament again. Somehow, though, the forbidden fruit is always more tempting than the ones within reach. Murphy's law in blackberry picking is 'That the luscious and most succulent fruit is always just out of reach'.

Back in the Ness household Mrs Ness had finally cornered her daughter for a coffee in the kitchen. Mrs Ness was worried. Her daughter was evasive. Both were sufficiently empathetic to recognize the other's symptoms. Both wanted to get some answers first.

'What's worrying you, Mum?'

'You love him, don't you?' said Sylvia and her mother simultaneously.

'I'm not worrying.'

'Don't talk rubbish,' came back the simultaneous untruths.

'You do, and you know it,' said mum.

'You are, I can tell,' said daughter.

'This is ridiculous,' they chorused in unison and in this they agreed.

'You first, Mum,' insisted Sylvia.

Her mother needed to get her feelings off her chest. 'You know that young man is so polite and, well, he can't be completely bad but I think he's bad news. I'm worried about you giving yourself to his charms.'

Sylvia blushed at this and bridled. 'I thought we were discussing your worries first,' she interrupted.

'We are,' said her mother. 'Don't interrupt.' Her mother then went on to explain how she suspected that Bob had been the chef at the Southern Constellation. 'You know how short-sighted I am without my glasses,' she explained. 'Actually the chef saved your father's life but I think he was the one who was canoodling some flashy Spanish girl. Your father was once romantic you know,' she added wistfully although this seemed completely beside the point. 'I'm wondering how we can get him transferred, Bob I mean, so that your father doesn't get another turn and so that you are spared from his attentions. He seemed such a nice young man but there was the incident with Susan and Bobby. Then there was this ahem . . . well, ahem. . . . You know. *How could you Sylvia*' she burst out. 'A one-night stand. How could you? One minute I think you'll grow up to be a spinster or end up in a convent and then a *one-night stand*. Oh Sylvia, I'm worried about you. You will forget him, won't you?'

Sylvia embraced her mum. 'Don't worry. It's over, Mum. I'll see Bob and ask him to ask for a transfer before Dad gets back. You can see Miss Pringle as well and explain the situation and ask her to move him. That will be that. I doubt if Father wanted lodgers anyhow. As for you, Mum, it's time you had another holiday.'

It seemed that the heart-to-heart was over and they got

to talking about other things.

Suddenly Barbara asked quite out of the blue, 'Did you really go to bed with him after just one meeting?'

Sylvia was taken completely unawares. 'Yes, I did,' she blurted out. 'I don't do things like that all the time you know,' she spluttered indignantly. 'I only did it once and you would think I was a prostitute.'

'You were a virgin,' said her mother triumphantly. 'I didn't think you could let us down like that. He'll have to go, oh, he'll have to go. Oh, why can't you find a nice boy like Wilfred Parable?'

'Forget it mother, forget it,' Sylvia almost screamed.

Sylvia was not impressed by Wilfred Parable and Sylvia found the Parable family all pretentious. At least Bob was a man, perhaps not as innocent as she had thought, but there again the male animal is expected to sow a few wild oats before settling down. Privately she agreed that Bob was a bit of a jinx but he was the only male who had made her at ease since her ill-fated romance with Willy O'Dare. Willy O'Dare had made Sylvia feel like a woman and they had made wild passionate love on numerous occasions. She had discovered that he was courting her and possibly half the available females in Dronsley and Willy had fled back to Ireland at the first warning signs of a potential paternity case against him.

Hector had completed the day's work and had briefed his stand-ins as to what he expected covered during the week's absence. His car was loaded with his uniform and six crates of beer. Hector considered the NAAFI prices somewhat high and so he had some back-up. Hector was to be attached to Never Wallop for the week with a permanent unit on manoeuvres with an Indian Regiment. He picked up Taffy Owens, the woodwork teacher, from the Fanshawe Secondary School. Taffy had decided to give the TA a go, on Hector's inspiration. It was Taffy's first weekly camp and Taffy was looking forward to a week away from school on legitimate grounds. He was even getting paid twice, if you count the TA bounty, that is. The two exchanged chat about how Miss Todd was settling down, and Jimmy Graham and Beverley.

'Bloody girls at woodwork, it is?' said Taffy. 'They are all over the place, whinging and whining, it is. They are young minxes as well. They are so sexy with it as well. Not as I want to know,' he added quickly.

'You don't have to tell me,' said Hector. 'I've got one not old enough to be my daughter. I-tal-ian. Tits like Gina Lollobrigida and she hangs them out like prize melons. Jimmy Graham positively drools over her, and gets nowhere. I don't think he could handle her anyhow. This one, though, has all the lot eating out of her hands, and I reckon one of 'em is screwing her rotten. Me, though, I like them older. I've got a lovely divorcée but I leave well alone. Don't shit on yer own doorstep eh, Taff.'

The conversation ranged from women, to football, to work problems. Taffy moaned about Mr Parables and Hector moaned about Principal Ness. All too soon they reached their destination. Hector, Taffy and the NCOs unpacked and settled in for a heavy drinking session before settling into military routine at 5 a.m. the following day.

In spite of consuming nine and a half pints and three treble brandies, Hector was up sharp at 4.30 a.m. Hector swigged down a can of beer and donned his chef's whites. He reported into the mess to find one solitary soldier cook frantically trying to prepare breakfast.

'You must be the sergeant cook,' said the solitary figure jumping to attention.

'You're in charge, Sergeant. All the rest have gone sick.'

'Gone sick, man? What do you mean gone sick? Who's gone sick?'

It turned out that the permanent staff had been out celebrating getting rid of the catering officer who had been promoted to captain.

Good riddance to that bastard,' said the overworked cook.

'Who is in charge now then?' asked Hector apprehensively. 'And Captain Britain is not a bastard. *He is my brother,*'

Hector shouted at the poor bemused figure.

'Sorry, Sergeant,' said the pathetic figure. 'You're in charge though, Sergeant, until Monday, Sergeant. The new officer doesn't come until Monday, Sergeant.'

It was obvious that the pathetic figure was frightened of Hector since Hector was related to the formidable 'illegitimate' catering officer. Privately Hector would have conceded that his brother was a bastard. He had achieved officer status through the ranks, hadn't he? Further interrogation revealed that the pathetic figure had not gone to the celebration dinner of roast turkey and things because the pathetic figure was a vegetarian and did not eat meat. He also didn't drink, didn't normally swear and did not like the army at all. He was, indeed, a very unhappy National Serviceman, one of the last who had been coerced into signing on. He wasn't even keen on cooking, but they had told him that cooks did less drill and fighting and he could be a cook if he signed on.

'What's your name, soldier?' asked Hector.

'Walter Wimple,' said the sad figure.

'I shall call you *Wimp*,' said Hector.

Hector set to work preparing breakfast, deciding that lunch was another battle that could be fought later. A quick reconnaissance revealed that there weren't so many to feed until the Indians arrived. The medical officer duly arrived and declared that the whole Catering Corps on permanent staff were not to handle food. He would see the commanding officer to see if Hector could get acting promotion with pay, but in the meantime Hector and the TA were in control.

'Fancy all the bloody cooks going sick, what? Could have been a bloody war on? Good job we've got you TA chaps, what? Never thought we'd ever need to rely on you *wallahs*.' The MO suddenly burst into fits of laughter. 'Just fancy the whole camp without a single Army Catering Corps.' The MO burst into fits of laughter again.

'What about the officers' and sergeants' mess?' asked Hector. Hector had reported directly to the other ranks' mess as a matter of course. Hector didn't usually eat anything until about ten o'clock. 'And Wimp here is ACC, sir.'

The sergeants' mess and officers' mess were run by civilian cooks it turned out, as Never Wallop was a skeleton transit camp.

'I'm afraid I'll have to stand that man down as well, Sergeant,' said the MO, referring to Private Wimple.

'Wimp did not go to the party, sir,' said Hector desperately.

'Didn't go to the party, man?' said the MO in disbelief.

''E's a vegetarian wot don't drink, sir,' explained Hector.

The MO, a jolly man, thought this funny too. He peered over his monocle at the unfortunate Wimp in disbelief. He left muttering, 'Strange chap,' under his breath. Stifled splutters of laughter erupted spasmodically from the MO from time to time as he progressed towards the CO's office.

Hector soon had a team of four as he was joined by two TA cooks. It looked like being a working TA week. He gained access to the stores and found it full of compo rations. For the uninitiated, and at a risk of breaching the Official Secrets Act I will explain what compo rations are. They are long-life rations designed for use in the event of nuclear war. They are usually made up in ten man boxes with just about everything you can imagine. Tins of cigarettes, tins of cakes, tins of chocolate and sweets were usually cooks' perks. There would be tins of custards, tins of sponge pudding, stews, bacon and eggs, pies, sausages, fruit, potatoes etc. Compo rations also came with packs of hard tack biscuits, dried shredded cabbage, dried plastic like strips of runner beans, swede, carrots and cabbage. There was the potato powder ancestor of 'Smash'. There were yellow coloured sugar powders designed to make 'lemonade'. All manner of strange things were to be found in compo rations. In this case, though, the compo rations had been opened up and the contents were disseminated in neat piles with names on: potatoes canned, pilchards canned, bacon and egg canned, sausages canned, stewing steak canned, baked beans canned, processed peas canned. The cigarettes, sweets, chocolates, and cakes were conspicuous by their absence.

'Captain Britain had those,' said Private Wimple gently.

'My brother *is* a bastard,' said Hector.

Hector remembered how his brother had often stitched him up as a child. Hector had dug up the garden to plant seed potatoes. They never came up. His brother dug them up when Hector went to the Scout camp, and they had been sold long before Hector returned home. His brother had offered him sixpence for eating this little green pod. Hector had to chew it, of course. It had been a red hot chilli. His brother had woken him early two days before Christmas Eve gently saying that Hector should creep downstairs to see what he had got for Christmas. Hector had believed him and had ended up disturbing his father who was trying to sneak in without waking up their mother. The ensuing disturbance had woken the mother who thought there were burglars. Hector had been soundly thrashed. Hector conceded that his brother was a 'bastard'.

Hector located the menu book and discovered that curried beef and rice was planned for the arrival of the Indian troops. There was eighty pounds of chuck steak ordered for this. Wimp had protests thrust to one side. He would dice the meat, Hector would make the curry. Hector liked curry. Hot curry was what Hector liked, with lots of fruit in it. Hector substituted bread and jam fritters for the pineapples planned for tea. He soon had the aroma of the East drifting through the camp, lots of tomato puree, apples, chillies, pineapple, coconut milk, curry powder.

'What about the vegetarians?' asked Wimp delicately.

'Sod the vegetarians,' said Hector. 'Tinned Pilchards,' he said.

'Vegetarians don't eat fish, sergeant,' said Wimp daringly.

Hector settled for cheese omelette, by request, ten minutes waiting. The beef curry did smell good. Those that liked curry even complimented Hector on the authenticity. The Indians were late and Hector served up the

British servicemen, but refused to serve seconds.

'Must have plenty of curry for the Indians,' said Britain's cultural ambassador.

At last the buses arrived and the smart turbanned figures disembarked. They were soon lined up at the servery savouring the rich curry smell emulating from the beef curry. A smartly dressed red-faced British expatriate officer pushed past to ask if Hector was ready.

'Damned good curry by the look of it, Sergeant,' said the officer.

'Thank you, sir,' said Hector proudly.

'I like a good curried lamb,' said the officer.

'Is this curried goat, Sahib?' asked one of the Indian figures, addressing the question to Private Wimple.

'It's curried beef,' said Wimp.

'I say, old chap, it's not beef is it?' the red-faced officer asked.

There was a muttering and jabbering from the soldiers lined up on the servery. Some were rubbing their kukri scabbards menacingly.

'I say, old chap,' said the red-faced officer quietly, 'don't you know about Indian Sikhs?'

'No, Sah. What's that got to do with it?' asked Hector, who was getting qualms in the bottom of his stomach.

'The cow is a sacred animal,' explained the red-faced officer quietly. 'You'll have to give them something else. It looks bloody good curry too. You should not have said it's beef. I'm going to have an awful job soothing the blighters down.'

The Indians were jabbering menacingly and Hector pondered how to escape if they came after him.

'They don't look very happy, Sergeant,' said Wimp timorously. 'I don't think they eat beef.'

'I know, I *know*,' yelled Hector. 'My brother is a *bastard*.'

'Hey, steady on Sergeant, old chap,' said the red-faced officer.

'Ahem, I'll try to stall them for a few minutes. What are you going to substitute?'

Hector hadn't a clue, and then he thought of the compo rations.

13

BACK TO GARNSTONE

Hector had been very relieved to return to the Dronsley College of Further Education after the TA camp. The experience with the Indians had upset him somewhat. It had indeed been fortunate that he had remembered the case upon case of compo ration pilchards. The Indians had tucked into the rice intended for the curry together with the canned pilchards. The skeleton staff and Hector had had rather a lot of curried beef that week and Hector was heartily fed up with curried beef and all things Indian.

Bob had spent the week apprehensively worrying about the sudden return of Principal Ness. Sylvia had disappeared back to London and Mrs Ness had taken to asking probing questions about Bob's background. These would appear, an odd one at a time, out of the blue when Bob was least expecting them.

It was the Thursday before Bob's last day that Bob invited Mrs Ness for a thank you meal at the Southern Cross. He invited Veronica, Mrs Ness and Sylvia but there was no sign of Sylvia. Just half an hour before they were due to set out a car drew up the drive. No car was expected and Bob feared the worst – that Principal Ness had returned early. Bob had intended to request a transfer as soon as Principal Ness returned to Garnstone. He looked through the window but did not instantly recognize the car. The boot was open and Bob could not make out the occupant.

'Who is it, Bob?' asked Mrs Ness.

'I don't know, I can't see,' answered Bob. Mrs Ness did not recognize the car either, the boot was still up, but there was the loud clamour of the doorbell. She went to open the door and was almost knocked over by the mad scramble of two children whom Bob had met before.

'It's the dirty old man,' said the young girl loudly.

'Have you got any sweets, mister?' asked the horrible boy.

'Oh God,' thought Bob.

'Children, children,' appealed Mrs Ness.

The two horrible children were rapidly followed in by their mother.

'Where's Martin?' asked Mrs Ness.

'He's having a couple of days with Maud,' answered the horrible children's mother. 'How do you children know this gentleman?' she asked.

'He's a dirty old man who gives us chocolate,' said the horrible little girl.

Bob reddened in embarrassment. The children's mother recoiled in horror and pulled the children protectively to her.

'He's a teacher . . . er . . . student teacher,' said Mrs Ness. 'He leaves for Garnstone tomorrow.'

'Can I have a ride in your car, mister?' said the horrible boy. 'It is mended, isn't it? I like sports cars.'

'Children, children, it's rude to keep asking for things, especially when you don't know the person. Now, how about some lemon tarts,' said Mrs Ness.

'Ooh yeah,' said the small boy.

'Have you got any jam ones?' said the dreadful little girl.

'Who is the black lady?' asked the small boy suddenly. 'Are you from Africa?' he added. 'We've been to Africa, on safari. It's full of flies in Africa,' he added to no one in particular.

'Them elephants make big whoopsies wot the flies buzz round,' added the dreadful little girl.

Eventually the children settled down to cake the pastries all over their faces.

'How did you meet my children?' asked their mother

suspiciously. 'And why were you giving them sweets?'

Bob explained about the embarrassing breakdown. Mrs Ness listened for any breach in the original version of the story.

'Why does Susan, the little girl, call you a dirty old man is what I want to know? And you never told me about this incident, Barbara,' she added.

Bob reddened and explained that he had been reading *Playboy* which his flatmate had given him. The children's mother still seemed suspicious and thankfully kept the children away from Bob who was quite pleased about this as it meant that they kept their sticky fingers away from his suit. Veronica, however, loved children, even overpowering ones like these two. She was soon telling them stories of Africa and exchanging memories of their holiday in Kenya. Veronica volunteered to stay behind to look after the children and the children's mother, Deidre, took her place for the Southern Constellation night out. They were just about to leave when another car arrived. It was Sylvia, escorted by Wilfred Parable, and Sylvia was obviously anxious to get away from him.

'I'm sorry I'm late, Bob,' she said as she quickly came over to Bob to wrap her arm around him.

Bob could not believe his luck. Deidre's face posed a hundred and one questions and Mrs Ness was wondering what her daughter was up to.

'Pleased to meet you,' said Wilfred Parable very unconvincingly. 'Congratulations on your engagement.'

'What?' asked Mrs Ness, Deidre and Bob simultaneously.

'We must rush now as we have an appointment at 7.45 p.m. haven't we, darling?' she said to Bob.

Wilfred was ushered away and Deidre and Mrs Ness's questions were deferred for the time being. Bob's Sunbeam Alpine was, of course, unsuitable and he had planned a taxi but Mrs Ness had insisted on being the chauffeuse. If Bob had expected to get Sylvia in the back, however, he was sadly disappointed. She insisted on going in the back with Deidre. Only when the party was underway did the motive for the phantom engagement come to life. Sylvia was desperate to get rid of Wilfred's attentions. She could not stand him.

'It's not on Sylvia,' said Deidre. 'You hardly know Mr Malone. Fancy taking advantage of him.'

'Oh, she does know Bob quite well, don't you dear?' said Mrs Ness.

'We met,' said Sylvia tersely. 'But that's in the past.'

'Perhaps you'll tell us something about things, Mr Malone,' probed Deidre.

Neither Bob nor Sylvia would say much at all. When they got to the Southern Constellation Sylvia was going to sit apart from Bob but her mother spotted Mr Parable dining at the other end of the dining-room. Sylvia was made aware of the situation. 'Damn,' she spluttered.

'Perhaps you should throw a ring at him and walk out,' said Deidre helpfully. The situation was forced into climax as Mr Parable came across and offered his congratulations for the engagement. 'When are you going to buy this lovely girl her engagement ring?' he asked.

'We're going to choose it on Saturday,' said Bob, holding on to Sylvia's hand lingeringly.

'Wilfred is so disappointed,' said Mr Parable. 'You're a lucky man.'

'Yes, you don't know how lucky,' said Bob.

'Don't get any ideas,' said Sylvia to Bob when Mr Parable was out of earshot and on the return to his table. 'This is a one-night act in which I expect you to play the part of a gentleman.'

'I know and I shall remember it like another occasion, not so long ago,' said Bob. 'I wish things could have worked out differently.'

'There is something more to this than meets the eye, isn't there?' said Deidre but her suspicions remained unanswered.

Sylvia and Bob remained distant in spite of Bob's attempts to rekindle their previous empathy. One barrier was brought down though. 'At least you're not the pervert that I thought you were according to Susan. I should watch him though, Sylvia. I've seen that sort of lust in Charles's eyes. That's why we've got three children,' she added.

'Sylvia knows all about Mr Malone,' said her mother sternly. 'The relationship terminates after tonight and Sylvia will need to find another excuse to keep Wilfred at bay. Won't you, dear?' she asked menacingly.

The meal proceeded well and Bob offered congratulations to the chef and asked the waitress to invite him for a drink.

'Who is the chef now?' asked Bob. The chef was Hector called in at very short notice. Since Bob had left him at college in fact. Once again the permanent vacancy was available.

There was a guest trio playing and the small dancefloor attracted a few dancers. Bob pushed his luck and managed to coerce Sylvia onto the floor, after first setting the scene with Mrs Ness and Deidre. Deidre, of course, used the opportunity to ply Bob with questions but they remained unanswered. Sylvia mellowed with the wine when her turn came and the band played *Moon River* very slowly. Bob put his arms around her and felt quite stirred with the softness of her perfume.

'I would give anything in the world to marry you,' he said suddenly.

She stiffened and the mood was gone. She demanded that they return to the table, where Deidre had by now obtained one or two answers from Mrs Ness about the relationship between Bob and Sylvia. Obviously the onenight stand had not been discussed but Deidre had sufficient intuition to realize that Bob and Sylvia did not have a previous platonic friendship. Mrs Ness too had realized that Sylvia was showing the same symptoms as she had with Willy O'Dare. Mrs Ness felt that Bob was a better bet than Willy O'Dare. She had found Willy O'Dare charming but she had known that he had been an altogether unreliable proposition with regards to forming any lasting, faithful relationship with any one single female. Bob's history did not look good on the surface but she somehow felt that he was not altogether untrustworthy. Bob had one last chance when another waltz came up and Deidre declined his offer and more or less pushed Sylvia into his offer.

'It is your last time together, and you might as well part friends.'

As they danced Bob promised that he would not be returning after the morrow. She looked into his eyes and saw the poignant sorrow in his expression. Impulsively she kissed him and was shocked at the passion with which he returned her kiss. She forgot to pull away as well. Her mother saw it all.

'I don't think this will be an easy parting,' she said to Deidre.

'This is quite something,' said Deidre. 'Does Elliott know?'

'Elliot doesn't and mustn't ever know,' said Mrs Ness quietly. 'This affair must end.'

Mr Elliot Ness, however, was to be made aware of the situation much sooner than anyone of them would realize. Shortly afterwards they set out for home and Deidre nipped sharply into the front seat. Bob climbed into the back of the car with Sylvia who promptly reminded him that he should not get so close. Deidre mischievously asked Bob what he was doing. Bob reddened with more embarrassment but fortunately no one could see this in the dimness of the back of the car. Bob tried to move his hand onto hers and was rewarded with a quick light smack. However, Mrs Ness rounded the next corner forcing Sylvia off balance and she rolled over almost on top of him. He gently held her to check her balance and she was not exactly swift in moving away from him. He knew that, given the right circumstances, he could well be in with a chance. He had felt this way about his first wife, but he knew that the feelings weren't quite so well reciprocated from her as he knew Sylvia was ready to reciprocate his feelings this time.

They soon drew into the driveway to the Ness household

and as they drew up to the house a different car was in addition to the Sunbeam Alpine and Deidre's car. It was a large grey Rover.

'Good God, Elliot's here,' exclaimed Mrs Ness.

'Perhaps I'd better not come in,' said Bob.

'I wouldn't miss this for the world,' said Deidre.

'Oh I wonder what he'll say about Veronica, he's a bit racist you know,' said Mrs Ness.

'He isn't over enthusiastic about children either,' said Deidre. 'He might not even notice you, Bob. Mind you, he might be surprised to hear of your impending engagement.'

'There is no engagement,' stated Sylvia very, very firmly.

'Please, Deidre, don't get him more excited than we have to,' said Mrs Ness wearily. 'Mr Malone, please wait outside for a few minutes,' she added.

'I'll stay with him,' said Sylvia 'I want a few words in private. Come on, Mr Malone, we'll sit in your car and talk,' said Sylvia in a tone which brooked no argument.

Bob escorted Sylvia to the car whilst Mrs Ness apprehensively went indoors with Deidre. She was met by a red-faced Mr Ness who tersely greeted his daughter-in-law by informing her that Charles was in the lounge wondering where she had been.

'Who is the person inside playing the African Queen with your grandchildren?' he asked. 'And what's this about Sylvia being engaged to the student teacher? I knew there would be no good come of your bloody stupid lodging house ideas,' he added. 'What the hell is going on? Where is this fiancée person. She can't have known him for more than five minutes.'

'Please, Elliot, sit down and I will explain,' said Mrs Ness hopelessly and wearily.

'I want them out of here,' spluttered Principal Ness. 'Tomorrow morning first thing.'

'Yes, dear,' said Mrs Ness, knowing, unlike her husband, that tomorrow was the last day anyhow.

Principal Ness was reassured. He was on a winning

streak. 'And how long are Charles and Deidre with us?'

'It's only for tonight. They are going up to Scotland and stopped off here to meet up and break the journey,' said Mrs Ness wearily.

Principal Ness was on a second winner. 'And where will we all sleep tonight?' asked Principal Ness.

'I don't know and I don't care,' said Mrs Ness.

'Haven't you spoken to Charles.'

'Not had time. He was in the front room playing cowboys and Indians with the black woman and the place is a bloody madhouse. Where is Sylvia, anyhow? I thought she was out with you and the bloody fiancée. I *want to meet him. Who the bloody hell does he think he is getting engaged to Sylvia without asking me. And he's only a scruffy chef.*'

'Please sit down, Elliot,' pleaded Mrs Ness. 'Prepare yourself for a couple of surprises, one of them being that Sylvia isn't getting engaged anyhow. She made it up because she wants to avoid Wilfred. Oh dear, if only she went out with the right people.'

'I think Wilfred's a mummy's boy. No wonder she's not keen,' muttered Principal Ness under his breath.

Eventually Principal Ness sat down and circuitously and evasively Mrs Ness explained about the student teachers, without explaining that Bob was the chef at the Southern Constellation.

'Now you know this Bob,' she said, 'and that is why Sylvia knows that the relationship must not go any further.'

'*What relationship?*' demanded Mr Ness suspiciously. 'It's not like that O'Dare person, is it?'

'Er . . . no,' said Mrs Ness unconvincingly. 'Not quite.'

'*Barbara, you are hiding something,*' indicted Principal Ness. 'Who is he? Where have we met? *Where are they?*'

'I thought you went out together on a celebration dinner. Is this man too cowardly to come in? *Where are they, Barbara?*'

'Oh, they are outside in the car waiting for me to prepare you. Mr Malone is the . . . was the . . . chef at the Southern Constellation. He did save your life.'

'*I knew it, It's him. and my daughter is outside alone with that lecherous bastard.*'

'*Elliot,*' remonstrated Mrs Ness. '*How dare you use such* foul *language in the house,*' she almost screamed at him.

Principal Ness, however, was halfway across the room heading for the hall way. He stormed through the door and out into the grounds. Mrs Ness looked round for his spare pills.

'Charles, I might need your help with father,' she said as she thoughtfully went through into the lounge. 'I think your father is due for another heart attack.'

'Oh, dear, no,' said Deidre. 'I'm sorry about what I said earlier. He's a pompous old sod but he's not a bad old stick.'

In the car park Bob and Sylvia had got past the talking stage and Bob had actually got so far as to holding Sylvia's hand. He was preparing to reach forward and kiss her when the housedoor burst open with the grim menace of Principal Ness.

'Take your hands off her,' he yelled. Bob rapidly moved out of the intended clinch.

'Well, here goes,' said Sylvia as she flung open the Sunbeam Alpine door and she struggled out to meet her father half-way. Bob struggled out of the other door.

Sylvia rushed forward and flung her arms around her father. 'Oh, Daddy, it's so nice to see you,' she said.

Principal Ness was halted in mid-stride. He loved his daughter dearly.

'You can't marry him,' he spluttered. 'Young man, I want you out of my house, out of my college and out of my daughter's life. I forbid you to have anything further to do with him,' he said to his daughter. 'How could you possibly get engaged to a . . . a Lothario like this? Anyhow, I won't give you permission. No. No daughter of mine will marry *him.*'

At this final remonstration Principal Ness stiffened and clutched at his heart. Bob rushed forward to steady him but he rallied.

By this time Charles and Deidre and Mrs Ness were

emerging from the house. Veronica and the children followed in their wake.

'Is grandad having a heart attack?' asked the dreadful little girl.

'*Keep away* from me and from my daughter,' valiantly spluttered Principal Ness.

'Shall I ring for the ambulance?' asked Deidre.

'No you won't. I'm all right,' shouted Principal Ness weakly and unconvincingly.

Principal Ness was helped into the house and onto the settee. Mrs Ness had located his pills. He took two and demanded a brandy to wash them down. Mrs Ness refused and gave him a splash of lemonade instead. She offered a cup of tea and, having assured herself that this attack was nowhere near as critical as previous ones, offered a cup of tea for them all.

'I think the children should be in bed,' said Charles tactfully. Naturally they were not enthusiastic.

'Are you going to be our uncle, mister?' asked the dreadful little girl.

'You can buy me a motor car for Christmas,' said her horrible brother. 'When will you get married?'

'*They are not getting married. I forbid it,*' yelled Principal Ness who appeared about to have a further heart attack.

'Deidre, please take the children to bed,' said Charles. 'I'll help you. Where shall I put them.'

'I hadn't planned it yet,' said Mrs Ness.

'Give them my room,' said Bob. 'I'd better be leaving. I'll just possibly get in at the Southern Constellation.'

'First bit of sense all night,' rallied Principal Ness. 'And the engagement is off. O F F,' he spelled out. '*Off.*'

'I'll decide whether it's off or not,' interrupted Sylvia.

'Are you going to kill him, grandad?' asked the morbid little girl.

'Get them off to bed, please,' said Charles.

'We can sleep in the attic in the camp beds,' said the horrible little boy.

'We want the man as our uncle 'cos you'll give us

chocolates, won't you, mister?'

'Ooh, yes,' said the dreadful little girl. 'Have you always got chocolates in your car, mister?' she added hopefully. 'Er ... please don't kill him, grandad.'

Bob was rising to go but Sylvia walked across to him and pushed him back into the easy chair. She promptly sat on top of him across his knee and Bob had little option but to either put up with her or throw her unceremoniously onto the floor.

'Don't I get a say in anything?' he pleaded to the world in general.

Principal Ness was about to get up and cross the room when Mrs Ness thrust the first cup of tea on his lap. She had just returned with teas and lemonades for the children. Deidre decided she had best get the children out of the way and she suggested that the camp beds in the attic was a good idea. Veronica excused herself as she was finding the scene embarrassing and Charles said he would go and help Deidre with the children. Bob and Sylvia and Principal Ness and his wife were left to sort out the situation.

'I will marry whoever I want, Daddy,' said Sylvia firmly.

'He'll never ever get a job in teaching after I've done with him,' said Principal Ness.

'Are you sure this is really what you want?' asked Mrs Ness.

'Don't I get to say anything?' asked Bob.

'*Shut up*,' said the Ness family in unison.

'We are never having student teachers here again,' vowed Principal Ness.

By the time the discussion was over there was no time for Bob to find accommodation anywhere. The sleeping arrangements left the children in the attic, Mr and Mrs Ness together in their matrimonial bedroom, Charles and Deidre in Charles' old single bed, Veronica in her room, Sylvia in Bob's room and Bob downstairs.

'You had *better* stay downstairs as well,' demanded Principal Ness.

It was now 2 a.m. in the morning. Deidre and Charles

were obviously not asleep.

'I can see them having a fourth,' muttered Principal Ness who was listening out to see if Bob betrayed his trust.

'I remember when we were like that,' said his wife wistfully.

Downstairs Bob was lying half-awake, half-asleep. He thought he heard the door go. He was about to say, 'Who's that?' when he was urged to 'Shhh'. The cover lifted and he felt the warm sensuous body of Sylvia nestling up to him underneath the covers. He felt a stiffening in his nether regions.

'You can forget that. We've got to talk,' said Sylvia whispering softly.

'He'll go mad if he knows you're here,' said Bob, stating the patently obvious.

Nevertheless Bob put his arms around her and felt for the softness of her right breast.

'Stop it. Anyhow, you can't. It's the wrong time,' she said with sudden inspiration.

Wrong time or not does not necessarily make much difference in the initial male responses. He could still hold, caress and cuddle, even if the ultimate fulfilment was not at hand.

'I'm only here to talk,' she said moving the seeking hands away from the intimate areas of her breast. Delicately he had restrained himself from the other areas because of her remonstration that it was the wrong time. As they whispered together his hands wandered back to her breasts. He gently undid the top buttons to expose them further and he gently kissed and suckled her firm nipples.

'Oh I give up,' she said pliantly. He felt her hand reach down. 'I don't suppose you'll listen to anything whilst you're in this state, will you? Anyhow, you're not doing it.'

Bob then had the suspicion that she had not been telling the truth. He gently placed his hand on her knee and slowly caressed upwards, kissing her ardently as he did so. Her restraining hand grew weaker and he gradually got higher and higher. After a nominal resistance he was soon able to fulfil his goal and the two were oblivious to a small figure which had come into the room. Suddenly the light crystallised the scene into the harshness of reality just as Bob and Sylvia were, to coin a phrase, making the earth move.

'I want a drink of lemonade. What are you doing, Auntie Sylvia?' demanded the horrible little girl.

Auntie Sylvia hurriedly fastened the top buttons to hide away her ample cleavage.

'*Shh,*' she whispered. 'It's our secret and if you keep quiet I'll buy you some sweets tomorrow.'

'What's going on?' said a voice upstairs.

'I'm just getting Susan a drink of water,' said Sylvia, ushering her into the kitchen.

'Wot were you doing with the dirty old man?' demanded the horrible little girl. 'Why was he kissing your naughty bits? He's rude. I'm going to tell Grandad. My Daddy does that to Mummy. I seen them once. Bobby didn't believe me.'

'Susan, I thought you liked me,' said Sylvia desperately. 'Wouldn't you like Bob as an uncle?'

'I want a new dolly as well,' said the dreadful blackmailing little girl.

'Is everything all right?' called Deidre.

Yes, it's OK,' said Sylvia desperately. 'A new dolly and three Mars bars,' she said desperately. The deal was clinched.

Next morning Sylvia had left early. She had thrust a note under the door for Bob asking him to meet her at the Southern Constellation at 2.30 p.m. before he left for Garnstone.

Principal Ness, Mrs Ness, Deidre and Bob were all in a state of uncertainty about what was going on. The only person who knew whether the engagement was on or not was Sylvia, but the little girl had attached herself to Bob as her new uncle. Her dreadful brother knew something was the matter but he had slept all through the midnight activities. Mrs Ness was most suspicious but had not told her husband that Sylvia's bed was apparently relatively undisturbed. Sylvia had indeed given the little girl a drink of lemonade and had taken her back to the attic. She had been blackmailed into getting in bed to cuddle the little girl to sleep and had fallen asleep herself. By the time she had crept downstairs after waking at daybreak she had decided to set off early to sort out her local business arrangements. She was due in London but she knew she had to sort things out with Bob first. He had found a pair of Sylvia's panties to add to his collection. He thrust them into his inside jacket pocket to hide the evidence.

'Goodbye and thank you for everything, Mrs Ness,' said Bob and Veronica.

14

THE CHRISTMAS PARTY

Principal Ness had willingly accepted his wife's logic that it would be unwise to set about pillorying Bob in revenge for the seduction of his beloved daughter. First of all she had tactfully pointed out that it was Sylvia who had claimed that she had seduced Bob. This seemed a very incredible proposition but he did have his suspicions that Sylvia had joined Bob downstairs and not *vice versa* on the night of his untimely homecoming. Secondly was the fact that only a few insiders knew the story of the alleged engagement. It had emerged that Sylvia had not really recovered from the effects of Willie O'Dare and did not want a repeated broken heart. She had decided that she wanted to complete her doctorate in educational studies before she thought of settling down. Her meeting with Bob had brought to his attention that he too was midst studies. The two were to have a six months cooling-off period. They would meet at Easter next year, if Bob still felt the same way, but there were no ties either way and she would not write to him. If he still felt the same way, and if she felt the same way, the relationship could resume. There was, of course, no official engagement, even though Bob wanted to buy a ring. In the meantime her mother was effectively barred from matchmaking, especially to Wilfred Parable.

Meanwhile Principal Ness faced a further shattering blow. The inspectors had decided that he should face an early retirement, and he was to complete his thirty-seven years at Dronsley, coincidentally at Easter too. He was devastated. In vain he pleaded that his health was much better and that the college couldn't run without him. The secret, of course, quickly leaked out and this coupled with rumours surrounding the possible engagement of his daughter to a student teacher in the Food and Beauty department, served to make Principal Ness less awe-inspiring. He cancelled several of his hatchet appearances and he even ratified Hector Britain's promotion. Hector thought Bob had helped and wrote to thank Bob who, of course, disclaimed credit but did offer congratulations. Bob, incidentally, had had his request for transfer turned down in spite of strong pleas.

'Mr Malone, you have a good report from your Dronsley mentor, Mr Britain. You have some inside knowledge and rapport with the students there. You are staying,' said Miss Pringle.

During the interview Bob tried to explain about the problem with Principal Ness and Bob's relationship with Sylvia. Miss Pringle claimed that she would sort it out and requested that Mr Malone concentrated on his present studies prior to the return to eight weeks teacher training practice in January. Miss Pringle, of course, rang Barbara Ness to hear the other side of the story and the two exchanged what little private knowledge was known about Bob, including his previous divorce. This was a further shock to Mrs Ness, but Miss Pringle could or would not venture further information about Bob's social life at Garnstone. At least Bob had been cleared with regards to the public sexual acrobatic displays. The real culprit had almost been expelled, but an appeal had resulted in a move to quarters adjacent to the private staff quarters where Miss Welling resided. It had resulted in more discreet behaviour with any sexual Olympics restricted to playing away. The female underwear found in Bob's room left some questions unanswered but it was hardly an indictable crime. Meanwhile, at Dronsley it was the end of term. The students had traditionally always featured two weeks of Christmas lunches but this year it had been extended to three weeks because of the revenue raised. The traditional menu of tomato soup, roast turkey and accompaniments, and Christmas pudding and mince pies was a good profit-maker. The second years could almost bone out turkey legs blindfolded. The legs were then filled with a chestnut stuffing made with white breadcrumbs, chopped sweated onions, sausagemeat, lemon zest, juice and parsley and thyme and chopped chestnuts.

In order to keep students busy Hector insisted on *pommes château*, which meant that each potato had to be turned. The trimmings were made into mashed potatoes. Hector used button Brussels sprouts which meant four or five times as much work. The carrots were hand-peeled and sliced for Vichy carrots. Hector, of course, insisted on smaller carrots. Then there were the dozens of mince-pies.

'I hate Christmas,' said Hector to his students prior to the first Christmas dinners. As the days passed with the boning of the turkey legs, the shelling of the chestnuts, the peeling of the small carrots, the topping and tailing of the button sprouts, the turning of the *château* potatoes, the sieving of the potato parings for the mashed potatoes, the chopping of the parsley and the making of the dozens of mince pies, it was noticeable that some of the anti-Christmas Scrooge behaviour began to rub off on some of his *protéges*. Even the waiters began to tire of the same Christmas menu to eat every day.

Hector stopped eating lunches in the restaurant. He took to having rolls filled with turkey on some days, and he fried some of the turkey livers for paté for his rolls instead of using the liver in the stuffing on other days. A pint of beer would wash down the repast. Hector would frequently be heard to mutter 'Bloody Christmas'. It was reputed that Hector had almost ended up divorced because he refused to serve turkey at Christmas, even when the dreaded mother-in-law came to stay.

Only second year students were permitted to sit down for their own Christmas dinners. Afterwards there was a disco and free drinks for all the students, first year ones as well. This year there were some murmurings of discontent. The students too were all heartily sick of turkey dinners, the second years had previous memories of the endless turkey dinners only twelve months before.

'We want something different,' they demanded.

'Tell them to get stuffed,' said the newly promoted senior lecturer.

'The turkeys are all ordered anyhow,' said the larder chef, 'and we have to put up with bloody Christmas dinners every year, so they can as well.'

Two days before the meal the second years delivered their ultimatum. If it were to be Christmas dinner, they wouldn't come.

'Sod them,' said Hector.

'I'll freeze the turkeys. Well, I will if I can find room,' said the larder chef whose fridges were bulging with whole turkey birds and partly boned turkey birds.

Mr Potterton was aghast with horror when he heard of the threatened boycott.

'Oh dear,' he said, 'whatever are things coming to?'

Then he added that the chairman of the board of governors always liked to come and serve the wine. He did too. He also managed to drink rather a lot as well. His wife would help out and she too could tuck it away.

'They are wonderful students,' he would say every year. 'They are our future. They all work so hard. Dronsley is lucky to have such conscientious and hard working staff and such wonderful well-behaved students.'

Principal Ness always managed to have prior engagements and sent the deputy principal in his place. The deputy principal always ended up in the departmental office supping sherry. Meanwhile, the chairman and his wife really enjoyed helping to serve the wine, helping to drink the wine and helping to put the official sanction on the proceedings. The chairman and his wife were totally oblivious, of course, to the hysterical behaviour of the students. Meanwhile, the FAB staff would usually have a glass of Dutch courage themselves in the face of serving the wild hordes of students.

After various threats the number of boycott students had been reduced to twenty-five stalwarts. Threats of failures, expulsion, etc. were shrugged off. A further fifteen had already made known their intentions to be earning money by trade experience and so numbers were indeed down. The waiters promised returns of all the £2.50 deposits to all who turned up, plus extra wine. The forty absentee nominates decided to stand fast. A desperate cover-up was needed. Hector rose to the occasion.

'We'll invite some first years,' he said.

It was decided by the staff to invite first years but it would not be possible to take them all. Finally, it was decided that it should be Hector's group. Hector duly announced the honour to his group.

'Is it turkey bird, chef?' asked Jimmy Graham.

'Yes, it *is*. What of it?' asked Hector threateningly.

'Er . . . nothing, chef. I like turkey,' said Jimmy unconvincingly.

'I'm a vegetarian,' said Debbie, 'otherwise I'd simply love to go.'

'*This is the first time any first year group has ever had the bloody honour of attending,*' screamed Hector. '*You will all bloody be there in your best bib and tucker or else,*' he threatened menacingly.

'Or else what, chef?' asked Sheila.

'Or else I won't be wanting to see you next year,' said Hector quietly, menacingly and desperately. 'I stuck my neck out to get you this chance,' he added. 'It's only this group that's been invited because of your good reputation.'

'You said we were bloody useless,' said Jimmy.

'Shut up Jimmy,' said Beverley. 'He only spoke to you at the time.'

'*We'll* be glad to go, won't we, Sheila?' she added.

'We should all go,' said Sheila, realizing how much it obviously meant to Hector.

'And Debbie can have an omelette, can't she, chef?' she added.

'Yes, yes. She can have an omelette,' agreed Hector desperately.

'I don't eat omelettes,' said Debbie.

Hector bore down on her. 'We'll get you something you do like, all right?' he said softly but very menacingly.

It was agreed that the group would go unanimously. Jimmy would even miss out his Thursday part-time job. The second year volunteers were not keen on the first year group joining them and it leaked out that omelettes were an option. There were forty-five requests for cheese omelette. It could not be allowed. Finally it was agreed that there would be a change from the straightforward turkey dinner but it was to be a secret menu. The vegetarian lobby was reduced to five students. There was a last minute request that Christmas pudding was still served. Mr Potterton was desperate. It was the last year for Principal Ness. He did not want any unhappy occurrences reporting by the chairman of the governors to Mr Ness. Mr Ness might be on his way out but the next year's financial arrangements were still not resolved and Principal Ness was the main driving force as to what would happen. The new incumbent would arrive too late to help out the FAB department's next year's budget and financial allowances.

'Mr Britain,' he said, 'I'm relying on you to ensure that the party runs smoothly. Incidentally, your promotion has a six months' probationary period. I might have forgotten to mention it at the time.'

Mr Potterton could react well in a crisis.

Thursday came and all the students, even the dissidents, were sent home. The menu was still secret except for the potatoes. The students had been coerced into turning lots of *château* potatoes. The art of turning was mastered by all Dronsley students. There was, however, no sign of sprouts, nor carrots, nor even turkey cooking. Turkeys were always cooked in advance but not this time. There were known to be some uncooked raw prepared turkeys in the larder refrigerator. The refectory curried chicken seemed to have a high proportion of turkey into the big refectory bratt pan. Even the cottage pie tasted of turkey. Two dissidents sneaked back to ask if they could come, they had after all paid their £2.50.

'No you can't. Piss off,' said Hector.

'Yes you can, but no one else,' said Mr Potterton who had come out from hibernation in his office to see what was going on.

'What is on please, chef,' asked one repentant dissident. 'I don't mind if it's turkey, chef.'

'Piss off,' said Hector. 'It's a secret.'

It was two hours to go and the volunteer staff, which was all of them, had split into chefs and waiters. The accountants, science teachers, domestic science, technicians etc. were naturally waiters. Hector and close associates manned the kitchen under Hector. The newer chef lecturers would also end up as waiters and the bakery lecturers would also have the dubious pleasure of food service. Hector locked the outside corridor doors so that the only way through from the outside was via the laid-up restaurant. It was now time for the staff tea. Although a new member of staff, Miss Todd had declined the honour of food service. She was in charge of the Christmas pudding and fruit salad for the four vegetarians. She had also hidden away several mince pies.

The tables had been laid and the waiting staff were resting in the staff room or dining-room prior to the ordeal. Hector sent Sean to round the staff up for their tea.

'It's not bloody turkey, is it?' said one of the new chefs who had seen enough turkey recently to put him off for life.

'No, it's bloody pork,' said Hector.

Hector was lying, and not convincingly, but they gathered round anyhow. The meat did look remarkably like turkey, but there was a lovely rich brown sauce with sliced mushrooms to mask the turkey effect.

'Can I have an omelette, please?' asked Mr Cohen, one of the science teachers.

'You're not bloody *kosher*,' said Hector irreverently. 'I

saw you eating rare roast beef in the Southern Constellation.'

'Oh I eat beef, but not pork,' said Mr Cohen apologetically.

'It's bloody turkey,' said the novice chef lecturer, 'but it's a lovely sauce,' he added quickly before Hector could take offence.

'This *pilaff* is OK,' said one of the waiters.

There was not a sprout in sight, not a carrot, no chipolatas and bacon rolls. The staff were not going to get any potatoes either. Miss Todd arrived late and tucked in heartily. She offered Christmas pudding or scones. Some declined Christmas pudding but some had double rations. Some had scones and some had double rations. Some had Christmas pudding and scones. By the time the chairman of the board of governors and his wife arrived there wasn't much left. The waiters supplied three or four jugs of beer which had also disappeared. George Farrant had got hold of the rum for the sauce for the Christmas pudding. Sean was helping him. Hector had got hold of the brandy for the brandy butter.

'Is there any red wine for my good lady?' asked the chairman of the board of governors.

Mr Simon Naunder grumpily left his place to fetch some wine for the chairman and wife. Mr Potterton popped in and said he was catching up on paperwork and fled.

At 6 p.m. sharp Hector called his brigade together.

'Naunder,' he said, 'Keep those bloody students out of my kitchen,'

'Hector, you should't speak ill of those wonderful students,' began the chairman. 'These FAB students are wonderful, aren't they dear?' he said to his wife and anyone who would listen. 'I feel so proud when I bring guests into the college restaurant.'

The rhetoric continued. The lecturers hastily set out to do whatever they had to do to get away from the chairman's party political broadcast.

'Where's the melon?' asked Mr Cohen.

'How do you know it's melon?' asked Mr Britain suspiciously.

'It always goes with roast pork, my boy,' said Mr Cohen with a wink.

'I hope you haven't told the students,' said Hector.

By now the earlier students were gathering. They soon discovered they were locked out. Two blackboards obscured the vision lines for three-quarters of the kitchen.

'We want to see the chefs,' went up the cry.

'Piss off,' was Hector's response.

It was obvious that many of the students had already been for a drink. David Fretwork had his bottle of vodka, which was half empty, confiscated. The male students were dressed in suits and ties which was a considerable metamorphosis from their usual casual and scruffy attire. The girls were dressed formally, too, with a considerable proportion of tight dresses and low bodices displaying pert posteriors and ample cleavage. Stella Pavrotti appeared at one of the two uncovered windows asking to see Hector.

'Piss off, tell her,' he said to Sean.

'Oi think you should see her to be sure,' said Sean.

'Cor look at the tits on her,' muttered one of the others.

Hector permitted himself a quick look. He had to concede that Stella looked very adult, very seductive, very provocative and also somewhat indecent. He could almost see her nipples.

'Looks good, don't she?' said David Fretwork, placing a hand underneath her lovely bottom.

'Ooh, stop it,' she giggled half-heartedly.

'I think our students are really wonderful and so adult in turn out, don't you?' said the chairman over Hector's shoulders. 'I wish I had been to a college like this,' he added, looking quite lecherously for the moment down Stella's cleavage. 'Mind you, we wouldn't have been allowed to wear things like they do now,' he added quickly as he perceived his wife coming to see what he was looking at.

'Can I take your photograph, chef?' asked Beverley who had also approached the window.

She too looked ravishing but in a much more modest way than Stella. Hector's group of girls had obviously done him proud in their turnout, even though Stella and Nancy Wee Wee had gone over the top. Nancy had a very tight *cheongsam* with a split up to her waist. When she walked she displayed ample thigh meshed in lightish brown flesh-coloured tights. It was doubtful as to whether she had anything on underneath. Hector declined the photographic poses until later. He had a meal, a secret meal, to prepare.

The students were finally sat down for their first course of the melon boat.

'I'm glad it's not tomato soup,' said Jimmy Graham.

Jimmy had been unlucky, or so he thought, in his choice of dining partner. He had ended up at the end of the table sat next to Beverley, although he had to admit that she was beginning to look very attractive. Jimmy was somewhat dissatisfied with life. He was nearly seventeen and still a virgin. He would, of course, never admit to this. He had had his hands in girls' blouses, he had had his hands underneath girls' skirts, he had had his hands in girls' knickers. He had even managed to have Mavis Riley's knickers down to her ankles before some loud roar made him realize that her father had suspected that they weren't exactly playing leapfrog in the porch outside her house. It was true he wasn't caught but it was also true that Mavis was not going to take chances with him again in case she was caught. He couldn't admit that he was a virgin, of course, not when people like David Fretwork were always hard at it. Jimmy looked at Beverley in her long white dress. She did not display much cleavage but the contours of the dress curved provocatively around the young maiden's figure. He looked across the table at Stella Pavrotti and felt pure lust. She was obviously not on his menu though and Beverley was unattached except that she was with Sheila. There was no one who would be likely to interest Sheila here, though there were several of the male staff who found her most attractive.

'Dining-room looks nice, doesn't it?' he said to Beverley.

However, her responses were not exactly encouraging.

'Ah well,' thought Jimmy, 'the night is yet young and there are plenty of girls who will be available at the disco.' He resolved to make the most of the meal for the time being. There was plenty of entertainment too. Several of the lecturers were obviously not at home serving, and there was the chance to make a few snide remarks. John Bamber, one of the second years, had produced a water-pistol and was squirting Mr Naunder. The novice chef lecturer let him half-empty the barrel before confiscating the water-pistol using a pressure on the neck resemblant of that seen by Mr Spock of *Star Trek*.

'Aren't the students wonderful?' said the chairman as he scurried round filling their glasses.

And now came the surprise main course. There were dishes with thick slices of white meat surrounding a heaped mound of rice with peppers in it. The meat was coated in a brown Madeira sauce with mushrooms in it. Each portion had a tartlet full of sweetcorn.

'I think it's turkey,' said Jimmy shrewdly.

'What we got?' asked David Fretwork.

Actually this question was framed in several different way by several different students.

'It is *dindonneau Louisiane*,' answered Mr Simon Naunder.

'What?' asked several students at once.

'Bloody turkey,' said David and Jimmy simultaneously.

It was indeed turkey. It was served with the inevitable *château* potatoes but Hector had substituted peas and braised celery. Frozen peas and tinned celery hearts are much easier to prepare than button Brussels and Vichy carrots. They were, moreover, better appreciated by the students who were so heartily sick of preparing sprouts and carrots. The main course gamble was a complete success. The four vegetarians had the vegetables and sweetcorn tartlets, they got two each. Actually, Hector had even dodged making tartlets. They had been prepared by Miss Todd, and they were delicious. When it came to the service of the Christmas pudding the first major problem came to light. Mr Naunder received demands for rum for the sauce and brandy to set the puddings on fire.

'You've had it,' he spluttered.

'No, we haven't,' said George Farrant with a few choice expletives.

If someone had ignited George's breath, George could have been a dragon. George enjoyed a glass of rum. He was an ex-navy man. Mr Naunder had to fetch some more rum and brandy and he added the rum to the sauce himself and he put the quota of brandy on the pre-heated sugared Christmas puddings himself. The students had begun a chorus of 'Why are we waiting?' until the puddings began to go into the dining-room. One of the vegetarians demanded Christmas pudding and was served some by Mr Cohen who should have known about the suet content. Not as Mr Cohen bothered much one way or another. He had indeed enjoyed his *dindonneau Louisiane,* alias roast pork.

There was only the mince pies and coffee to go and the students were knocking back the wine like there was no tomorrow. The chairman and his wife had withdrawn to join Mr Potterton and the vice principal in the departmental office.

'If he says "Aren't the students wonderful"? once more, I'll bloody kill him,' said Hector.

Stella was by now sprawled across half a dozen male admirers' knees. Someone decided to pass her round. As she did so enjoy the furtive hands that went under her dress, felt at her bust and almost all parts of her shapely anatomy, it was a wonder that she was not undressed. As it was, her bra did become unfastened and her large fulsome breasts with their darkening mouth-watering nipples were displayed for all to see. At this moment Miss Todd arrived with the last of the mince pies and she hastily and haughtily decreed that Stella cover herself up. Stella did so much to the distress of the male population, blushing fetchingly as she did so. Mr Naunder rapidly did a U-turn about the promised liqueurs as some of the students began a mince-pie fight in one corner of the dining-room.

Someone managed to obtain a cessation from hostilities and the call went out for the chefs. Hector and the chefs reluctantly came out to take the curtain-call as it seemed that the students would stage a sit-in unless they did so. The students let out a tremendous cheer. Hector and the chefs rapidly withdrew, carrying George Farrant with them. Then the mince-pie fights began again. By now the first years were arriving for the disco. The night was yet young. Gradually the dining-room emptied, leaving one or two waifs and strays behind. One of them was Stella.

'I feel sick,' she said to David who had his arm around her. With that she threw up all over his trousers.

'You'd better get a taxi, and take her home,' demanded Miss Todd, brooking no argument.

David sat looking sodden and forlorn in the college foyer as he waited for the taxi. He dreaded the thought of meeting Mr Pavrotti, Stella's father. It was reputed that he came from Sicily. In spite of all the appearances to the contrary, Stella was, as far as he knew, a virgin. He had fondled her and indulged in heavy petting but Stella was, she said, saving her virginity for the wedding night. He had come very close to the real thing, and the nearer he got to her, the more he became incensed into wanting intercourse with her. If only Jimmy had known this. However, David Fretwork had lost his own virginity about four years earlier. He had since tried out several of the local wenches but not Stella. She was the ultimate challenge. Sheila suddenly felt sorry for him as he sat there in his smelly soggy trousers. The stains and smells of sick were quite disgusting. Stella was remarkably clear of her own sick, but she didn't look well.

David had tried to swab down most of the sick in the male toilets but sick is remarkably difficult to remove. To coin a phrase, sick sticks like shit to a blanket. Sheila offered to come with David and she indeed took Stella home, which was very fortunate for David. David was despatched home after he gallantly paid for the taxi. Sheila returned to the orgy, sorry, party, to enjoy herself dancing with all the male lecturers she could, even Hector. The only one she did avoid was Mr Simon Naunder. As it happened, Mr Potterton was holding him responsible for letting the students drink too much. The chairman and his wife had been ushered off the premises still saying, 'How wonderful the students are.'

Hector, Miss Todd and a few others were postponing the disco until as late as possible. They set about sweeping up the mince-pies, Christmas crackers and other general Christmas-fare debris in the dining-room. In response, Mr Naunder allowed them to finish off the last three bottles of red wine. Meanwhile, the Martinis and sherries had been withdrawn from the free disco bar. Plastic half-pint glasses were issued and if the student lost their glass, there were apparently no replacements to be found. Anyone generally looking incapable was reduced to lemonade or Coke. Then at only 10.45 p.m. it seemed that even the beer had run out. There were no pass-outs and any sources of imported drink were confiscated.

The disco was lively and noisy. The frenetic rock and roll sobered up people who danced very quickly. Miss Todd placed a ban on slow waltzes after seeing the effect of one or two close clinches by over-amorous males. Three-quarters of the way through the evening it was realized that there were quite a few visits to the temporary cloak-room. In a corner behind the coats sat a piano. Two people were apparently underneath it completely devoid of concern for the world about them. George Farrant was feeling much better and he tiptoed across and quietly perched on the piano stool. There was the grunting and groaning and writhing of passion beneath him. George quietly pulled back the cover and struck up a rousing rendition of the *1812 Overture*.

'Ah,' screamed out a female voice.

The tones were remarkably quiet and well spoken. Debbie Harris was finding out about the facts of life. Jimmy too, but the act was not fully consummated.

Only George and Hector witnessed this act.

'You horrible little man,' raged Hector. Debbie fled in embarrassment but Jimmy was not allowed to follow her.

'You can help clean up the mess,' said Hector threateningly.

Meanwhile, Hector located the light switch, to uncover lots of closing of buttons, fastening flies, tucking away pieces of anatomy which should be covered up. Some students had sneaked out as the tone of the *1812 Overture* struck up. Miss Todd had finally relented for the last waltz to be played. Someone lowered the lights in the hall. The last waltz extended to two then three waltzes.

'It's time they bloody went home,' said Hector. He went to put on the lights and hands quickly left female bottoms, kissing subsided and the students set out for home.

'I hate bloody Christmas,' said Hector.

The staff, with the assistance of Jimmy Graham, set about cleaning up the mess in the main hall.

'Isn't Jimmy a good lad, helping out like this?' said Miss Todd.

'Isn't he just?' said Hector.

George Farrant fell into a helpless fit of laughter. Hector sat him on a stool which unfortunately had only three legs. George fell hard on his backside on the floor and the laughter from him subsided. It was now the turn for Hector and Sean and also the embarrassed Jimmy Graham.

'You won't be laughing if she gets pregnant,' muttered Hector. '*And for your sake let's hope she does not get pregnant.*'

The mess was cleared up, the staff drank black coffee and went home. The 1960s were golden years. 'Drink driving' wasn't such a heinous crime. For a start there were fewer cars on the road and it was the hardened adult drinkers doing most of the driving. The worst that Hector did was to back into the neighbour's wall and knock it over.

'I hate bloody Christmas,' said Hector as he clambered out of his car.

He crept upstairs to bed, undressed in the dark and felt for his wife's warm body.

'Get away from me, you've been drinking,' she snapped.

'I hate bloody Christmas,' said Hector.

15

I'M DREAMING OF A WHITE CHRISTMAS

Whilst Hector is not exactly alone amongst chefs for having somewhat uncharitable thoughts of Christmas, Bob himself was optimistic about it. The lovely sports car, his pride and joy, was going to have to go. Not only did things keep going wrong with it, it also seemed to carry a jinx with regards to minor accidents. Some unmentionable person had cut off his aerial, he kept getting rear lights or headlamps smashed, and he had a couple of minor prangs. As it was, the insurance was high anyhow, but there was now a £25 excess. Twenty-five years ago, a £25 excess was quite a sum. Bob had decided to keep it for a final fling over Christmas as his meeting with Sylvia had eventually culminated in an emergency contact system. Sylvia had been dreading Christmas, too, because her father's social life would have inevitably brought her into contact with Wilfred Parable. This is where Bob had, in spite of the trial separation, pulled off a major *coup*. Both Bob and Sylvia faced evacuation from halls of residence over Christmas and although Bob would like Sylvia to stay with his parents, Bob really needed a cash-flow input. Bob had, therefore, answered an advertisement for Christmas work at Dotheboys Holiday Camp near Bournemouth. The job had also specified that chalet maids' posts were available. Sylvia, of course, knew little about such work but she had readily acquiesced to Bob's suggestion that there would be nothing to it. It would give her a little extra cash and she was looking forward to seeing Bob again, in spite of some misgivings. Best of all it would allow her to escape the endless Christmas parties where she met Wilfred Parable and her mother's matchmaking charades. She had made it plain that there would be no hanky-panky but Bob remained quite optimistic that he might enjoy more pre-marital cohabitation or, at least, just being with her would be very very welcome. They arranged to drive to Dotheboys separately.

Bob set out for the long drive from his parents loaded with plenty of clean shirts, clean underwear, but certainly no vests, and plenty of aftershave and deodorants. Bob was feeling very very happy with life. He was so happy that he was blissfully unaware of the heavy gatherings of cumulo nimbus clouds. Bob's estimated time of arrival was for 3.30 p.m. With a further eighty miles to go, it was only 1.30 p.m. However, the skies were darkening already and the odd snowflake smattered ominously on the windscreen. Gradually there was a build-up. Bob had twenty-five miles to go and it was nearly 3 p.m. By now there were flurries of snow and it was beginning to settle. Bob was on a B road, which means that it wasn't used very much and therefore Bob was not driving on compact ice yet. The snow began to fall in big flakes and the wipers thudded heavily as the snow was crushed onto the lower half of the windscreen. He was down to twenty-five miles per hour, twenty, fifteen and then finally about ten miles per hour. Some of the hedges were low and the ditches found adjacent to some fields were becoming blurred as the snow drifted to fill them up. It was now 3.30 p.m. with about twenty miles to go. Bob was so concerned in holding the car on the road that he passed the turning for Bognor Coldfield which is where he should have turned off for Dotheboys Holiday Camp. He did not realize this until he arrived at the next signpost five miles and a further half an hour's drive down the road. There was a secondary road from here which was virtually a one-way track. Rashly Bob took this road, only to find it to be very obscured by drifting snow. He decided to turn the vehicle round at the earliest opportunity, which came up a few minutes later when he found himself arrived at the open gate of a farmhouse courtyard. He backed into the courtyard to turn round, only to hear a loud crunch from the back regions of the car. He got out into the flurries of snow to hear the hissing of air exuding from a punctured rear-wheel tyre. He had to delve under the clothes and cases to locate a topcoat needed for protection while delving further for the spare tyre needed as replacement for the punctured one. At this juncture Bob could hear the noisy whirr which indicated the approach of a farmer's tractor. Bob's vehicle blocked the way into the snow-covered courtyard. The tractor ground to a halt about eight inches from impact.

'Bloody silly place to park,' said the irate farmer. 'Who are you, and what do you want?'

The irate farmer clambered down from the tractor and was then able to see what Bob was doing. He tried to explain his predicament.

'You're bloody trespassing and blocking my access,' said the impatient and apparently unsympathetic farmer.

It was obvious though that Bob couldn't go anywhere on three wheels. It was also obvious that the crunch was caused by Bob's reversal over a snow-covered piece of farm equipment.

'Just look at it,' yelled the irate farmer. 'It's ruined,'

The farmer had yanked the piece of equipment away from its white snow-covering to reveal in the dim light available a piece of rusty distorted ploughing attachment. Bob thought that it looked decidedly obsolescent and tactfully suggested this.

'That cost me £430 last year,' claimed the farmer.

'It shouldn't be left lying around like that,' said Bob desperately.

You shouldn't bloody trespass and drive round my property smashing my farm equipment either,' said the irate farmer menacingly.

'I don't have that sort of money,' said Bob.

'Well now you've got a big flash sports car and you're

going round vandalizing poor farmer's equipment,' retorted the farmer. 'You are not leaving here, matey, until it's paid for.'

The poor farmer looked at his Omega watch and declared that he had to go to milk the cows.

'I need to get my tractor off the road,' he declared as well.

Bob was made to remove the jack and the farmer watched Bob struggle to push the three-wheeled car back a few paces. The farmer just cleared the track outside but left the tractor obstructing Bob's evacuation route. The farmer went to milk the cows whilst Bob set about completing the wheel change. By now Bob's top coat was white and sodden and the luggage was coated in snow too. Eventually the wheel change was complete, which was just as well as it was getting quite dark. It was 4.30 p.m. The snow was still falling heavily. The farmer had not returned and the tractor still blocked the way. Bob decided to walk over to the farmhouse to see where the farmer was. He could not see any sign of life at the front of the house and so he decided to walk round.

'Who is it?' screamed a frightened female voice.

Bob looked in through the window to see a well-fed, scantily dressed female figure in the process of washing her hair. The woman, in spite of the cold, was almost naked down to the waist. A heavy-duty but scanty bra struggled to contain a bust that would be comparable to Dolly Parton, if the proportions had been better. As it was, the timorous female must have weighed going on for twenty stone.

'I'll set the dog on you,' she said, and at that a huge black snarling Alsatian leapt at the window. The fierce-looking, frightening demon dog almost came through the glass. The window pane shook at the fierce assault and saliva from the dog's mouth dribbled down the window.

'What is it, Mum?' asked a younger voice.

A small boy of about twelve appeared. The woman had turned round and was making attempts to cover the rolls of exposed fat.

'It's a peeping Tom. Set the dog on him.'

The boy rushed to her bidding with pleasurable anticipation.

'I'll go and open the door,' said the small boy with relish.

Bob tried to explain but the small boy was persuading the dog to leave the window so that the small boy could release the dog by the side door. It was obvious that the large farmer's wife and the small boy were not going to listen to any of Bob's pleas. Bob broke into a trot, skidding a few times as he did so. He was three-quarters of the way there before the side door opened to relese the dog. It bounded across the courtyard at him, slavering and barking excitedly.

'Get him, Duke, get him,' yelled the small boy.

At this time Bob slipped. He wasn't going to make it. He remembered his friend's advice when threatened by the unhappy student. Bob swung round.

'Sit,' he said loudly. The black Alsatian ignored the order and leaped through the air.

'Sit,' yelled a louder firmer more confident voice. The dog somehow fell to miss his throat by inches and, remarkably, it sat. It sat, however, on Bob's chest.

'Duke don't like ee,' said the newly-returned farmer. 'I've a good mind to let him have you.'

After negotiations culminating in Bob's written promise to claim on the car insurance for a skid in the snow which damaged the plough attachment, Bob was allowed to go. The tractor was backed out only to leave tracks which Bob's car got stuck in. The farmer had to tow Bob's vehicle out onto the track and Bob set out to retrace the journey back towards Dotheboys Holiday Camp.

The journey up to the B road was horrendous as Bob struggled to keep within the tractor tracks. The B road had had some traffic and the compacted snow made it somewhat treacherous. It was half-past seven before Bob eventually located Dotheboys Holiday Camp. A welcome sign was partially obscured by drifting snow and the white-flecked barbed wire surrounds had something in common with square-bashing and prisoner of war camps. It seemed that Dotheboys had once been an RAF camp as the catering block stood like a huge, ominous ex-aircraft hangar. A second hangar was the entertainment block. There were chalets made from converted Nissen huts. All visitors had to report in to what had probably once been the RAF camp guardroom.

'You're late and you've missed tea,' Bob was told.

He was given an arrival form for collection of blankets, sheets and pillowslips.

'You'll be sharing B16 and you are responsible for returning all bedding before you get paid. Losses or damage will be stopped out of your pay.'

Bob set about trudging through the snow to find the billet.

'You start at 6.30 a.m. in the cookhouse,' he had been told.

It was an old Nissen hut of probable pre-war vintage. Bob struggled to locate the key in the lock and once within struggled to find the light switch. There was a heavy smell of whisky. The light served to disturb the denizen within, a scowling face relatively lacking in vitality peered blinkingly at the new arrival.

'Whoo are yooo?' asked a distinct Scottish voice.

The voice did not serve to inspire Bob with a feeling of camaraderie. It turned out that the other inmate was Tom McClaughlin, who worked in one of the bars. To Bob he did not seem an appropriate custodian for alcohol.

'Yooo can call me Jock,' said Tom magnanimously. 'Doo yooo have a cigarette?' Bob was unable to help. 'Yooou're not much guid,' muttered Jock.

With that Jock turned over and went back to sleep. The new position soon resulted in loud snores. Bob decided to see if he could return to reception to get a transfer but was unlucky.

Bob went to collect his sheets and blankets. Someone in front had returned torn sheets.

'You'll have to pay for them,' said the grumpy storeman. Further argument resulted in referral to the stores manager on the morrow. In the meantime a reference to the sheet's damage was annotated on the arrival card. Wisely Bob checked his sheets. The first had a large grey patch in the middle, the second was torn.

'You should have been here earlier,' said the grumpy storeman.

Bob had had enough trouble with the farm incident. 'I want a decent pair of sheets,' he demanded, 'or I'll come round the back of that counter.'

It was time to close the stores and Bob was persistent and so the storeman conceded the exchange. Bob was issued three blankets and requested more. This, however, was not authorized. Bob returned to the billet and made up the bed to the strains of the snoring Scotsman. It didn't look as if he'd be able to bring Sylvia back here, especially not with the smell of the whisky.

Bob had discovered that Sylvia had arrived and that Sylvia was billeted in W12. Evidently the holiday camp authorities didn't mind what the holiday makers got up to, but workers were not encouraged in licentious behaviour. Sylvia had fared better in her companion, as she was sharing with a youngish-looking grandmother who had a daughter of Sylvia's age. Sylvia's disclosure that her boyfriend was working at Dotheboys as well had resulted in some timely advice.

'Be careful,' she had been told. The grandmother's grandson was illegitimate. 'A lot of men are only after one thing,' she had warned Sylvia.

At reception they had learned that the guests would arrive on the morrow and that it was an old time dancing Christmas. Bob had noticed that most of the Dotheboys inhabitants were well-advanced in years anyhow. Sylvia trudged over to the entertainment block where the strains of musicians practising could be heard. One bar was open for the staff. There was virtually no heating and the mainly vintage users sat well-wrapped up but there was still some shivering. Bob's pint was flat and Sylvia's sherry was certainly not the Harvey's Bristol Cream which appeared on the outside of the bottle. The only food available was crisps, dubious looking pork pie and some tired-looking sandwiches. Even the nearness of Sylvia made only a slight improvement to such bleak surroundings. In spite of the bleak weather, although the snow had stopped, it was decided to try the public house Bob had passed two miles down the road.

Bob and Sylvia set out down the road in the Sunbeam Alpine. He courteously held the door open. The advantage of low-slung sports cars is that girls in short skirts are inclined to display more leg than they normally intend. Bob felt familiar urges as she swung into the seat displaying those provocative panties and stocking tops which turned him on.

'I've got something for you,' he said, thinking of the bra from Garnstone and the panties from the Ness household. He then realized that it was not good form to let her know of where he had been looking.

'What's that?' she asked, but did not press further when he said nothing.

The car was reluctant to start but did go eventually. He hoped he would not get a puncture since there was no spare wheel. It seemed a long two miles on the deserted road but eventually they arrived and went into the room marked *snug*. They had had so much to talk about that he had not got round to telling her about the farmhouse incident. However, after he had collected their drinks and sat down with his arm around Sylvia he heard laughter in the next room and a very familiar voice.

'Oi got 'ome to find this poser in my backyard, wet as a drowned rat and covered in snow. Oi asked ee what ee were doing blocking my backyard so oi couldn't get in. When oi got down oi see'd ee were changing 'is tyre 'aving punctured it on that rotor plough thing that oi tried to part-exchange last year.'

'Well, they gave you the allowance, Bert, even though they didn't take it, so I don't know what what you are grumbling at,' interrupted one of the audience.

'Ar, but they didn't take the bugger away.'

'Well, it was about thirteen years old, anyhow. A few more years and you can flog it to the museum,' said another.

'Not now oi can't. This bloke in the flash sports car backed all over ee. It's squashed now and ee got a puncture,' said Bert.

'That was me,' said Bob quietly. 'I'm going round there, big as he is.'

'You'll come off worst. Leave it, Bob,' said Sylvia, clinging onto his arm.

The story continued as Bert told about his wife screaming 'Rape!' and setting the dog on the sports car stranger.

'Christ, it would be a brave man who'd want to rape your missus,' said the first listener, who, realizing that he should not have said so much, hastily regretted it. 'She even frightens you, Bert,' he said hopefully in jest. 'She's some woman, she is.'

Bert did not quite know whether to take this as an insult or a compliment. The group's laughter decided him to accept it as the better option of the two.

'Oi told him it would cost £430 to replace,' said Bert. '£430, and he wrote me a letter for the insurance.'

Bob had finally extricated himself from Sylvia and was heading round into the public bar.

'He must have been mad, no one would pay that,' said the first listener incredulously.

'Eee were blocked in and didn't have a lot of option,' said Bert. 'Oi got the letter 'ere,' he said, waving it in the air.

By this time Bob came through the door behind him and snatched it out of Bert's waving hand. Bob hastily tore it up as Bert swung round to see who had taken away the valuable piece of paper.

'Oi'll kill ee,' said Bert, falling over a chair as he said this.

'I'm the poser,' said Bob in explanation to Bert's cronies.

This new development was even funnier than Bert's stories as Bert struggled to his feet by clutching at the nearby table of drinks. The table fell over on top of Bert, cascading him in beer from the half-empty glasses spread around the table. Bert lost his balance again and his cronies fell about in healthy helpless laughter.

'I think we'd best get out of here,' Bob said to Sylvia who had apprehensively followed him into the public bar.

Bert was staggering to his feet once more when a voice from behind the bar said, 'Leave it, Bert. That was not a nice thing to do and if any harm comes to this young man, I shall be the first witness for the prosecution. *Especially if any of my bar gets smashed up. Get it? Peace and love.*'

The barman turned to Bob and suggested that he returned to the snug.

'The car had best not be touched either,' added the barman as an afterthought.

'Oi'm goin' 'ome,' said Bert disgustedly.

Bert left and there was a squeal of brakes and engine. Bert had obviously not delayed to interfere with Bob's car. They stayed a further hour and then Sylvia said that it was time to return to Dotheboys and leave the warmth of the cosy pub. Outside in the cold the car was once more reluctant to start. Bob pulled out and there was a loud crash on Sylvia's side. A car had come from apparently nowhere and was oozing steam and water everywhere.

'Are you all right?' asked Bob to Sylvia anxiously.

She was shaken but entirely unharmed, in spite of some broken glass.

'Your car isn't,' she said bravely.

Bob went to the other driver's assistance. It was Bert and his gargantuan wife.

'I told you not to speed down here,' she said as she steadily beat him around the head with her large handbag. 'Ooh, it's him,' she said as she realized that Bob was the erstwhile peeping Tom.

She interrupted her assault on Bert's head.

'Oi've got you now,' said Bert menacingly.

'I don't think so, Bert,' said a uniformed figure who had just arrived on the scene. 'I was just coming out of The Unicorn and I saw everything. Your driving is bad enough without a drink. The young man hasn't drunk much. He's been too busy with the young lady.'

'Are you all right, Miss?' asked the kindly policeman.

'Can I have your name as a witness, please, constable?' asked Bob.

'No, lad, you can't, because I would have to say that both you and Bert had been drinking. You two can sort it out peaceably without me.'

Details were exchanged and Sylvia was driven back to Dotheboys. Only then did Bob discover that the passenger door was jammed. Sylvia displayed even more underwear clambering out than she had done clambering in.

'Forget it,' she said to Bob whose lecherous look was making him temporarily forgetful of the original concern over the accident.

Sylvia allowed him to escort her back to her quarters and he kissed her goodnight.

'It's too cold to stay out here all night,' she interrupted as he attempted a long passionate embrace.

Bob returned to the chalet. It was cold as the electric fire boasted one single worn-out bar. The three blankets offered little warmth and so he donned pyjamas and put an overcoat on the bed. Bob normally slept in the raw but the pyjamas had been intended in case of oportunities for getting Sylvia in bed. He had forgotten that such charades were superfluous in view of previous developments. The one thing he had noticed was the absence of Jock. The whisky smell lingered but not the snores. Thoughtfully, Bob doused the room in deodorant to disguise the brewery smell.

Jock staggered in in the small hours singing the *Northern Lights of Aberdeen* very loudly. He clambered into the top bed, narrowly missing Bob's head in the process. Bob had to get out of bed to put the lights out.

Sylvia returned to her warmer billet than Bob, although the furnishing was almost equally bare. The grandmother was a Dotheboys veteran and had brought a couple of rugs and a kettle. She made some cocoa and she and Sylvia had a cosy chat before turning in. The grandmother, Doris Becksworth, had sadly lost her husband five years ago and her daughter had emigrated to Canada with her husband. Doris was a supervisor and reassured Sylvia about the job.

'I'll look after you, love, don't you worry. I need somebody fit for the issues and a lot of the staff are a bit worn out, like me.'

It should be said that Doris was far from worn out.

The female Nissen huts actually had hot water radiators as they were sited near the boiler house which generated steam for the cookhouse. This was, of course, in marked contrast to Bob's frozen billet. Bob slept fitfully as the overcoat kept falling off. Above him there was a background of drunken snores. Bob felt a couple of drops of something wet fall from above and thought it must be condensation or something. He had just managed to drop off when he was awakened by a hefty upheaval as the man mountain above erupted to meet nature's call. A size eleven foot narrowly missed Bob's head as the figure clambered down in the partially lit gloom of the billet. There was a street light outside which permeated the thin curtains which did not close anyhow. Bob was determined that he was definitely not having another night with this roommate and since he was unaware of Sylvia's circumstances he was feeling guilty that she might be faring like himself. Perhaps she could be coerced into coming home with him to his parents. It would be a surprise but he knew they would like her. He could do with the money but he would rather have long unpaid sessions of bliss being next to Sylvia, even though the prospects of naughty nights was even more unlikely at his parents' house than here. Bob heard the grunts and groans as the Scottish barman completed discharging the surplus alcohol. At the back of Bob's mind there was a horrible thought that there was no sound of tinkling water, as is common when males go to the toilet for a Jimmy Riddle.

Jock staggered back into the upper bunk and seemed better as his foot fell away from Bob's head for once. Soon afterwards the snores resumed and Bob returned to a fitful sleep.

Clang, clang, clang, clang, clang, clang, clang.

Bob reached out blindly for the alarm clock under the bed.

What's that? fire, fire. The drunken barman had sobered somewhat and awoken in shock. Perhaps he had had a previous experience of fire and this trauma was still there in the recesses of the mind.

Bob located the source of the disruption and clambered out of bed. He staggered across the room to put the light on.

'What time is it?' enquired the drunken barman.

'Half-past five,' answered Bob tersely.

'Put the light out, I want to go to sleep,' demanded the barman.

'*Tough*, get knotted,' answered Bob who was heading towards the toilet cubicle to have his early ablutions.

Normally Bob had been trained to dress in the gloom very quietly so as not to disturb colleagues who were not on early shift. In the RAF there are cooks on duty for twenty-four hours a day. Some sleep in the day, some at night. Do unto others as they do unto you is the motto i.e., if the early man wakens the day man, this will be reciprocated when shifts change. If the day man disturbs the night man, justice is more swift. The night man will leave his duties to collect something from the billet in the middle of the night. The source of discomfort will be singled out. 'Psst, want to buy a battleship?' was a favourite byline. At RAF Halton it had been the prerogative of the fire picket to ring a large bell at the end of the twenty-man room for reveille. There is something sadistic in many men's outlook after a night of boring but spasmodic rest whilst on fire picket. There was four hours on, four hours off, but you slept with boots on so as to be in a state of instant readiness. The other four hours were spent walking to and fro around the cold windswept base carrying a large club-like thing. This was not to put out fires but to deal with any suspicious interlopers who might presumably be potential arsonists, terrorists or burglars. The sight of all those lucky people sleeping away peacefully in comfort and warmth was too much. If there was someone you didn't like there was the perfect revenge. You could creep up on the sleeping victim and then *clang, clang, clang, clang, clang, clang* in the victim's ear. This was the culmination of the perfect revenge. It could, though, possibly have potential disaster if the victim overreacted. The tormentor, of course, did have the advantage of being awake and alert allowing escape. In this case Bob did not feel very charitable towards the Scotsman but he didn't care about the consequences anyhow. He was not a hero but when in the right mood cared nothing for potential adverse consequences.

'Splosh.' Bob had stood in something wet. There was a huge puddle of urine adjacent to the toilet bowl. 'You dirty bastard,' he shouted.

'Whoo are yooo callin' a dirty bastard?' asked the Scotsman threateningly.

'You, you dirty bastard,' explained Bob. 'You've pissed all over the floor.'

There was an angry roar as the Scotsman clambered and then fell out of the bunk. He lay sprawled and groaning on the floor.

'*Shit*,' said the Scotsman.

Bob looked out to see what was happening. It didn't look as if the Scotsman was capable of inflicting much harm. Bob completed his ablutions and transferred his effects to the car before starting work. It was too early to go and awaken Sylvia but he would have a long talk tonight. He might as well go to work for now. Perhaps he might find someone who would give him a transfer billet when the management came on duty. Bob left his bedding behind and he left the drunken Scotsman lying on the floor. He had fallen asleep again, having pulled Bob's bedding over him. Bob had extricated the overcoat. It was then that he found out what the condensation had been. It was not condensation. The drunken Scotsman had wet the bed.

'You dirty bastard,' said Bob.

16

HI DE HI

If Bob had thought that his trials and tribulations were only to be in the Dotheboys' billets, he was sadly mistaken. The converted aircraft hangar could have been likened to a Victorian workhouse. Bob's shift was 6 a.m. until 6 p.m. The cooks prepared and cooked all three meals: breakfast, lunch and dinner. There would be the first guest arrivals later in the morning and so the meal for lunch would be served at 1 p.m. until 3 p.m. on this first day.

Bob went through the campers' entrance. A huge picture of Charles Dotheboy hung above the portals, beaming down benignly on all and sundry. The publicity said that Charles Dotheboys had made his money in a chain of London Victory V restaurants set up for servicemen passing through London during the war. Rumour had it that Charles had really made his money selling black market meat, including the pigeons in Trafalgar Square and the squirrels in Regents Park. It was said that the odd camel or hippopotamus from London had featured in the Victory V steak and kidney pie, but this was probably malicious rumour. Suffice it to say that Charles Dotheboy had, perhaps rashly, sunk most of his capital in setting up this holiday camp on an ex-RAF airfield bought on the cheap from the hard up post-war government. Charles Dotheboy had figured that what was good enough for Billy Butlin was good enough for him. Unfortunately, he lacked the Butlin charisma, flair and style.

Although the huge converted hangar was draped and

festooned with Christmas decorations, it still looked like what it had once been, an aircraft hangar. The roof made of corrugated iron was painted on the underside but was too high to give a congenial family environment. The long lines of tables and chairs looked like the pictures of bygone warehouses. The service counters at the end adjacent to the kitchen were like those which Bob grimly remembered from RAF West Kirby in the long past days of square-bashing. Behind the counter were large glass cupboards which Bob would learn later were for reheating by steam the plated dinners. A large yet dwarfed Christmas tree reached up towards the painted corrugated iron roof high above. The few workers present, laying up for staff breakfasts, echoed and resounded around the huge converted hangar. 'Who on earth would want to spend Christmas here?' thought Bob to himself. The few geriatric workers laying up should perhaps have given a potential answer.

Bob found the dining-room lacked warmth but the kitchen behind was even colder. The steam rising from the boilers below had risen and condensed in the cold above beneath the unpainted kitchen corrugated iron roof. It poised above in a formation of embryonic stalactites. Bob was shown the staff changing room and was advised to keep a shirt on under the chef whites. and he was also advised not to leave anything valuable lying around. Bob heeded this advice and got changed. He returned to be introduced to the kitchen superintendent.

Henry Higgins, the kitchen superintendent, was a bluff Yorkshireman, another ex-wartime, ex-black marketeer. Obviously this was not made apparent to Bob at this stage. Henry Higgins was the most unlikely kitchen superintendent you could ever hope to meet. He sported a bowler and a thick tweed overcoat. He wore brown boots and complimented Bob on his choice of footwear. Bob was wearing his ex-RAF boots, having decided that such footwear might be appropriate for large scale cookery.

'You can be veg cook,' said Henry Higgins. 'Nice and young and fit, got to be veg cook, hasn't he, Joe?'

Joe was a toothless veteran of about sixty-seven.

It was readily apparent that Bob was the youngest person dressed in chef's whites.

'I'm down as second chef,' said Bob who wasn't keen on this sudden demotion.

'You might be paid as second chef, but you are going to be veg cook,' said Henry Higgins.

Bob got the impression that Henry Higgins might have been in the forces. He had, Bob learned later, been an ex-Sergeant cook, which was how he had gained access to rations to sell on the black market. This was how he had got to know Charles Dotheboy.

'We need a nice fit fellow like you for the veg,' said the toothless old veteran.

Terry Finch, the veteran, was the head cook who ran the kitchen. Henry Higgins organized the supplies. Charles Dotheboy did not trust him but gave Henry 4s 11d per day, together with a pre-set menu. Henry got whatever he made from judicious planning, buying and scheming. Charles Dotheboy planted various people at various times to check up on standards. Henry still managed a sizeable cut. In actual fact, Henry Higgins could often spot potential spies. He looked at Bob suspiciously. It was far too early to tell.

'It's a special job, the veg,' said the veteran soothingly. 'The second chef usually cooks the veg, doesn't he, Henry?'

'You cook the veg or you can piss off,' said Henry. If Bob was a spy he wouldn't be inclined to go.

'I might just do that,' said Bob. 'After a night with a drunken Scottish moron who's peed the bed, pissed on the floor and kept me up half the night I'm thinking of leaving anyhow.'

'You won't get any travel expenses and you'll get charged for overnight accommodation if you go,' said Terry. 'The veg is not that bad. You can have Alfred here to help you with the lifting.'

Alfred was the only other young-looking person present. He was a thirty-year-old Jamaican who had just come out of the army and was working his holiday to get enough money to buy his own house.

'Give it a whirl, mate,' said Alfred, who seemed quite a friendly chap.

'Please yourself,' said Henry Higgins.

Bob decided to work the day, but for now he wanted a change of accommodation.

'I'll stay on condition I get a move from sharing with the moronic Scotsman,' he said.

'Wha's a marrer with the Scots?' said another bespectacled geriatric threateningly.

'Do you wet the bed?' asked Bob in answer to the question. 'I was underneath as well.' There were unsympathetic chuckles at this.

'Henry will help, won't you?' asked Terry, wheedling on Bob's behalf. Terry wanted a fit veg cook to lift the bins of potatoes boiled up in the huge boilers for mashed potatoes.

'Write down the details of your billet and I'll see what I can do,' he said in a somewhat non-committal manner. 'But you're veg cook if you're staying.'

Thus it came to be that Bob was veg cook for the day. He set to work with the lunch menu. Roast pork, roast and creamed potatoes, vichy carrots, garden peas, blackberry pie. The roast were boiled, four bins full, standard dustbin size, and then coloured in the chip fryer. They were replaced in the boiler with more potatoes for creamed potatoes. Dozens of tins of carrots were opened both ends so that the tins could be flattened under boot power. The compactor had not been invented in those days. The flattened tins, of course, took much less space in the dustbins and the Dotheboys' camp dustbins were charged for and taken away by number not according to load. All the bins' contents were squashed down and crammed as full as possible.

The cooks were given a breakfast break at 10 a.m. The congealed beans, shrivelled up bacon, the plastic style India rubber eggs and the mushy tomatoes looked foul. Bob ate lots of toast with margarine.

By now huge coaches were appearing and this included two from Newcastle, over three hundred miles away. They gave up their loads of vintage crones from the frozen North who greedily tucked into the breakfast that Bob had so ungratefully declined. Times were hard in Geordieland and wages up there were poor. Charles Dotheboy knew well where to recruit the cheapest staff. It was a wonder he had not brought in immigrants from South-East Asia but shipping would have been expensive. It was during this break that Bob was fortunate enough to run into Sylvia who was also having breakfast. In the brief interchange he learned that she was enjoying the experience. She was having cereal and milk. Bob was not a cornflake person. He decided that he would chase up the kitchen superintendent about the accommodation. If Sylvia was staying, Bob was staying. Sylvia said she was definitely staying.

'That Scots bastard has done a case of whisky,' said someone talking to Henry Higgins.

'What do you want?' said Henry Higgins to Bob, having seen Bob out of the corner of his eye. Bob explained once more about the accommodation.

'Oh, go and see Mrs Becksworth in D3,' he said. 'Tell her I sent you and let Terry know where you are, and don't be long.'

Bob set out in chef's whites to locate Mrs Becksworth. He found her with Sylvia in her issues department.

'It's one of those Herberts who ruin the food,' said Mrs Becksworth. 'What do you want, young man?'

'This is Bob, whom I told you about,' said Sylvia.

'Oh you're Bob are you?' said Mrs Becksworth.

Bob explained his problems and about the soiled bedding.

'Bloody animals, some of them,' said Mrs Becksworth in a surprisingly unladylike way. 'I'll put you in with Joe but if you upset him you'll have to go back.'

Joe was permanent boilerman and Mrs Becksworth had a soft spot for him and normally it was ensured that he was on his own.

'Can I change my bedding, please,' asked Bob.

'Yes, of course you can, but don't worry, I'll arrange for some bedding to be put in with Joe's room and I'll collect the old stuff. I'll see he gets charged for the extra laundering too,' said Mrs Becksworth grimly.

Bob learned that he would be in the Y lines, which were also served with waste steam from the cookhouse block.

'But if you upset Joe, you're out,' he was reminded. Bob resolved that he would be very polite and friendly with Joe.

Bob returned to the workhouse kitchen. The geriatric females from Geordieland were setting up piles of plates along lines of tables opposite the mysterious glass cupboards.

'Hurry up with the mash,' demanded Terry. 'Alfred has started frying the roast.'

'I thought lunch was not until one,' said Bob.

'We start plating up at 11.30 a.m. today and 10.30 a.m. from then on,' cut in Henry Higgins.

'Hurry up and get those bloody ducks in, you Scots git,' yelled Henry Higgins at the ancient Scotsman.

Bob looked over to see the vintage Scotsman busily unwrapping frozen ducks and tossing them into trays half-full of water. Another ancient porter was carrying these over to the huge rotary oven where they were being loaded three trays at a time by another porter.

'Balls,' muttered the vintage Scotsman.

'What's that?' asked Henry Higgins.

'Yes, Mr Higgins,' said the Scotsman politely and with deference.

'He's getting past it,' said Henry to the not so young head cook.

'He's a good worker, Henry,' said the ancient head cook.

'Things I do for money,' thought Bob, wondering what the rest of the day would bring.

It wasn't long before the women were lined up along the tables ready for plating up the dinners. It was nowhere near as sophisticated as the Ganymede system but it worked. The women, like Henry Higgins, retained their topcoats. It was somewhat incongruous to see the women in topcoats and scarves, some with headscarves on, sat along the table lobbing on a spoonful of peas, a blob of mashed, a spoonful of carrots, two fried roast potatoes and a blob of stuffing.

Terry was in control of the pork issue which went on first. The joints had been steam roasted by the look of it and they came from the biggest pigs Bob had ever seen. There was certainly no crisp crackling and the joints had been cooked the day before. Bob decided he would not be eating this for dinner.

The plated dinners were loaded into the cupboards, and Bob learned that these cupboards would have jets of steam blown in to bring the meals up to temperature. In another corner of the kitchen another porter was opening boxes of blackberry pie which came from the local bakery. This would fare for a quick filler for lunch until some other substitute could be found. Perhaps Bob would lose some of the spare weight he carried around.

At 12.45 p.m. the camp Tannoy started up with loud echoes of tinny Christmas carols and regular bulletins of camp entertainments. The geriatrics staggered into the dining-room and the vintage Geordies discarded their top coats and donned white overalls and Christmas aprons to serve the guests. There was no changing-room as such but most retained their cardigans underneath anyhow. Sweet white wine was lobbed out under the close supervision of Henry Higgins and the person who had been talking to Henry earlier. The old folks loved it, Christmas carols, lots of wine and plenty of similar geriatrics to talk to. They were grateful for the disgusting meals which Bob disdained. Meanwhile, the Bluecoats had appeared and they were here, there and everywhere in the dining-room jollying along the old folks. After lunch was over the cooks had a half-hour break. Everyone except Bob, Terry and Henry Higgins tucked in. Bob ate his blackberry pies whilst Terry and Henry disappeared somewhere.

'Are you a vegetarian?' asked the vintage Scotsman.

It was soon time to resume work and the vintage Scotsman went to see how the frozen ducks were going on. They had shrunk somewhat and the trays of water were nearly brimming over with a fatty oil extrusion. The ducks were spread out on trays to cool, which was relatively rapid in the cold kitchen. When they had cooled a little the vintage Scotsman set about removing the paper packets of entrails still left inside the ducks.

Terry was pouring orange cordial and water into a large boiler. He added some of the greasy duck extrusion, some Bisto and some cornflour. Bob was appalled.

'Do people eat that,' he asked.

'It's Duck *à l'orange*,' said Terry indignantly.

Bob spent the afternoon boiling and frying more 'roast' potatoes. He reconstituted some potato powder for *duchesse*. He opened up dozens of tins of celery pieces for braised celery and he cooked some frozen broad beans. In a separate corner one of the geriatrics was cutting up sultana slab cake to be used as steamed sultana pudding. Bob had a huge chunk of this for tea. He would be eating out tonight.

The workday was done and Bob set about removing the sodden soiled chef's whites. It was not so much sweat, but the condensation which fell like drizzle throughout the day which had caused the trouble. He would be very tight for chef's whites at this rate unless there were some laundry system on the camp.

'Whoo were yoo sharing with?' asked the vintage bespectacled veteran Scotsman.

'I don't know his name,' answered Bob truthfully.

'Yoou're no Dotheboys spy, are ya?' enquired the old Scotsman.

'We did over the last one,' said another vintage chef who whistled through his false teeth. 'Ya shopped him, didn't ya?'

Bob did not know what the old chefs were on about.

'If you're not telling the truth, you're a bloody good actor,' whistled the old-timer.

'Forget him,' said Terry, who had just entered. 'The

cleaning staff went to collect me laddo's sheets here and found Jock with a case of whisky that had gone missing last night. That's why the police took him away. It's not me laddo here, he knows nothing. He's been here all day, hasn't he?'

Bob was exonorated. He went wearily over to find the new billet. The new billet mate, Joe, was also Scottish but he renewed Bob's faith in the tartan. Joe had installed carpets and, as permanent staff, he had a cooker. He was frying up some steak. Bob looked at it longingly.

'I don't eat the rubbish you lot serve up,' said Joe.

Joe was not exactly surprised that Bob didn't eat it either.

'There's no cafe round here,' Bob was informed, 'but there was a good fish and chip shop.'

Bob got changed and set out to find the fish and chip shop. He had two fish and two lots of chips and felt normal again. He then set out to find Sylvia. He found she too was unimpressed with the food but Doris had let her share some cold provisions for lunch. They too had had fish and chips for tea. They decided to go down the road for a drink as neither of them could do old-time dancing. They had both forgotten the jammed door. Sylvia clambered in ungracefully, displaying all her lower underwear again.

'You could be a gentleman and not look,' she said, staring at the bulge which was most apparent in Bob's trousers.

There was no one around and so she left her skirt hitched high.

'Seen enough?' she asked shamelessly. Bob grabbed hold of her and kissed her, moving one hand up her skirt.

'Behave,' she said. She allowed kisses and hugs but she was not letting Bob anywhere near her knickers. She explained that she had thought he had got her pregnant the last time and she was not taking chances again.

The next day Bob left quietly in the morning so as not to disturb Joe. Joe had come in later than Bob and so they had not spoken. Bob had fared better today because he had cooked his own bacon rolls for breakfast. He ate some of the bought-in cooked turkey, a new product from the

USA, in rolls for lunch, and he planned to have fish and chips with Sylvia for tea.

'Didna see you dancing last night,' said Joe.

Bob explained that he did not know any old-time dancing.

'Make it up as you go along,' said Joe sagely.

Bob was invited to go halves on the self-catering and willingly offered to cook.

'Can I invite my girlfriend round and we'll wash up?' asked Bob hopefully.

'Aye ye can, if ya bring Doris as well,' said the cunning Joe.

And so it was. The foursome later went to the dancing together and this became a regular set-up for the remaining days. Bob and Sylvia would go for a kiss and cuddle in her car before they went separate ways. Sylvia had decided that the sight of her underwear coupled with the no escape route because of the jammed door was tempting fate. She was not going to be intimate again unless they did actually decide to make a go of it and marry at some future date.

On the last night it was obvious that Doris and Joe were becoming more than good friends.

'Since it's the last night, Joe is coming back with me for a nightcap. He'll be back sharp at 12.30 a.m., won't you Joe?' said Doris.

'Don't do anything we wouldn't do,' she winked at Sylvia.

Bob was ecstatic.

'Down boy,' said Sylvia. 'You're not getting it.'

'I can get something,' said Bob who had, in fact, never tried contraceptives before.

'If you are thinking what I think you're thinking, I'm disgusted,' said Sylvia. 'We will leave them to get on with whatever they are going to get on with but we'll go to the Blue Lagoon Cocktail Bar where I'll be safe. Doris can't get pregnant anyhow,' added Sylvia malevolently.

Bob did manage to persuade her to return to Joe's billet where he did almost everything he could to seduce her, but she was resolute. At 12.35 a.m. there was a whistling man approaching and there was a subtle tap on the door. Joe seemingly took a long time to unlock the door which wasn't locked anyhow, but it gave Sylvia time to fasten her top buttons and push down her skirt which Bob had kept disrupting in his assaults on her womanhood.

'A hope this man was a gentleman,' said Joe mischievously.

'Don't worry, he wasn't, but I behaved,' said Sylvia confidently.

Bob hoped that the bulge in his trousers wasn't too apparent but Joe would not have said anything anyhow. Bob took her back to chalet. As they had the last kiss she felt down and gently massaged his maleness. He was obviously aroused as she thrust him away and bid him good night.

'Serves you right,' she said.

Bob remembered a friend in RAF Muharraq hospital who was always free with his hands with the nurses. He was in for a circumcision. After the operation his vital organ was very tender. The nurses seemed to bend over or titivate in other ways quite a lot. He was in agony. Only when he left did they reveal the intended revenge.

The next day Bob went to draw his pay but was told that the card must be signed by the various departments before the pay would be awarded. Bedding had to be handed in, he had to gain clearance from the cookhouse, clearance from the stores. Eventually he collected his pay and set out to say farewell to Sylvia. She still wouldn't come home to his parents but they agreed to meet at Dotheboys for Easter again, if they could be accepted, that was.

17

BACK TO DRONSLEY

Bob and Veronica were back at Dronsley for the most useful part of their teacher training course. They were also back at the house of Principal Ness. Mrs Ness knew about the Christmas holiday camp and the unofficial *ad hoc* engagement, or probationary engagement. Mr Parable had been very inquisitive as to where Sylvia had been over Christmas and as Mrs Ness had tactfully pointed out, it would be odd that Bob should stay somewhere else if he was engaged to Sylvia. Principal Ness was not overhappy, but his own imminent early retirement was placing some stress on him. 'What would he find to do with himself?' Mrs Ness was having second thoughts too. 'Could she stand him around the house all day? Principal Ness privately abhorred the thoughts of losing the power and influence which principals are able to exhort over staff and students. 'I hope he doesn't start throwing his weight about at home,' thought Mrs Ness. She could put up with small doses of Principal Ness-style authoritarianism but days or weeks of it would be too much. She had already lost some friends because of the Principal Ness attitude.

Principal Ness grudgingly welcomed Veronica and Bob to the Ness homestead. Both Bob and Veronica were very much ill at ease but Mrs Ness did her best to make them at home. Sylvia was away on her course and so there were only the four of them present for the buffet tea supplied on Bob and Veronica's arrival. Principal Ness was going to give Bob a lecture but Mrs Ness dissuaded him. He retired very quickly from the table after the meal and the remaining trio were soon chattering away happily. Mrs Ness used the opportunity to try and find out how Bob and Sylvia got on together at Dotheboys Holiday Camp.

The next morning Bob and Veronica set off early for Dronsley, and so they missed Principal Ness. This was to happen most mornings. Bob and Veronica usually missed the principal in the evenings too, as they worked late or the principal was late due to various committee meetings or social engagements. Bob and Veronica often asked to be excused as the workload of producing acceptable teacher training lesson plans is quite considerable. Although lecturers only taught for twenty-two hours per week, with ten hours' preparation time, the figures were reversed for teacher training. Some one hour-spells took six or seven hours for Bob and then a further hour as he typed out the plans in duplicate. The truth was that Bob's handwriting was somewhat illegible and the typing partially covered up this shortcoming. Bob tried to use Letraset and stencils on the overhead projector acetate sheets as well but Principal Ness had not encouraged the purchase of such modern technology and so there was a bit of a problem in getting hold of an overhead projector. Hector was not helpful either, he was a chalk and talk man. The chalk would chatter rat tat tat tat like a volley from a machine gun as Hector conveyed his ideas onto the chalkboard. Sometimes the chalk would snap from the stressful impacts and then Hector would swear and blaspheme. He had acquired some new chef's whites emblazoned with Smiths Catering Supplies in luminous purple and green in a semi-circular swathe on both shoulders. The whites were supplied free and Hector got 2s 6d commission on every jacket sold to Dronsley students. Hector was temporarily nice to each student buyer, and non-buyers received a little pep talk if the chef's whites showed the slightest tear or showed the slightest stain or fading. 'Why can't you get some smart chef's whites like these. . . ? he would say.

The news of Bob's engagement had somehow got round

before Bob's renewal of Dronsley activities.

'Congratulations, sir,' said Jimmy with the oily charm sometimes found with certain head waiters.

David Fretwork, always a born opportunist, offered help in selection of an engagement ring. 'I can get you 25 per cent discount,' he said. 'You're all right then, sir,' he said knowingly. 'The ladies are very affectionate with a ring on their finger,' he added.

'Is that why you are going to get engaged to Stella?' said Jimmy. 'Mind you, you seem to do all right without engagement rings.'

If only Jimmy knew. David was not allowed near the Pavrotti household, even though David and Stella were almost inseparable at college. Stella was too frightened of her father to allow David to have his way with her too. Bob was not to know this, but he was embarrassed and concerned that the innuendoes were getting out of hand. David was advised to peddle his wares somewhere else. David did, in fact, use the lesson breaks to try and sell some cheap brooches at £2 7s 6d to the girls. Half way through the morning Hector almost caught him and David secreted the samples underneath the box of spinach which was ready for preparation for fillets of plaice Florentine. When the lunchbreak arrived one brooch was missing.

The box of spinach was gone too and the remnants were in the bin together with a lot of discarded spinach which was either yellow or, more likely, had been buried because the students had become bored with the tedium of removing the green fleshy part of the leaves to separate them from the stalks. David bent over the bin rummaging through the leaves looking for the brooch. Hector was busy involved in assembling the lines of plaice fillets Florentine, each fillet being stuffed with cooked spinach. Some of the smaller fillets were enhanced in size in this process, making the portion of fish much larger.

'Where's Fretwork?' asked Hector, looking round the kitchen. His eyes caught sight of a male bottom covered in chef's checks looming over the bin.

'He's over there, chef,' said Beverley respectfully. 'I think he's lost his vegetable peeler.'

'Stupid boy,' said Hector. 'Fretwork, come here. Why are you scavenging in the bin, you horrible shitehawk?'

'I've lost something chef,' said David.

'What have you lost, other than your brains, which you probably never had in the first place?' said Hector unsympathetically.

'It's a brooch, chef,' said David quietly.

Hector looked round at Beverley.

'Did you say, brooch?' asked Hector, looking at David.

Beverly picked up a vegetable peeler and waved it frantically behind Hector's back. 'It's here, David,' she said.

David knew the brooch wasn't in the bin and he did not want further hassle from Hector and so he gratefully accepted Beverley's lifeline. Hector was still suspicious but continued with his instructions about final cooking and service.

Bob was helping in the background of Hector's class and Bob, of course, knew about David's sideline. Later on he found the opportunity to talk to David to find out what the problem was.

'Nobody here would take it, chef,' said David. 'I would trust any of our group with my life. They might pinch the odd packet of crisps from the refectory, or eat buns which are being delivered there, but none of us would steal from one another.'

'Wait a minute,' said Bob. 'I think there was another bin went out earlier. I'll go and check for you so that Hector doesn't miss you again.'

Bob excused himself to Hector and set off to see if he could help David out. Hector was feeling magnanimous and had sent the girls for an extended break. Stella Pavrotti urged David to hurry up but he said he'd got problems. Meanwhile, Bob had located the second bin with spinach near the top and he was bent over sifting through the discarded spinach when he saw a glint and sparkle which was possibly the missing jewellery. He bent over further.

Meanwhile, Stella had also had a brainstorm and she too had remembered the second bin. She would go and see if she could find the brooch, she thought to herself. As Stella approached the dustbin compound she spotted the familiar bottom in chef's whites which she thought was David. She crept up on him and gently cupped her hand between the legs and gently squeezed the testicles.

'What the . . . ?' yelled the startled voice of Mr Malone.

Stella blushed up in embarrassment. Bob felt an embarrassing growing bulge underneath his apron.

'What do you think you're doing?' asked Bob who was very conscious of the dangers of too close an association with female students, especially those below the age of sixteen.

'I thought you were David, chef,' said Stella. 'I'm ever so sorry, chef. Please donna tella my father,' she added plaintively.

Bob had no intention of telling anyone but unknown to him there were witnesses. The other girls had come to help out Stella but they had held back to witness the prank. Now they broke out into fits of helpless giggling.

'I want this forgotten about and nothing said,' said Bob optimistically as well as firmly. 'Stella, I am not bending over there again. The brooch is at the bottom of the bin. You get it out.'

Bob instantly regretted this decision as the girls accused him of being a dirty old man who would do the same to Stella. He turned round to talk to them whilst Stella looked in the bin. Stella bending over the bin was a much better vision than Bob. He could obviously not look at her himself and so he chivalrously kept his back to her. Stella bent over further and her skirt, which was always ridiculously short, rode up to reveal a pert bottom with thin, wispy laced panties through which all was displayed down to the last pubic hair.

'You can turn round now, chef,' said Susan Miller mischievously and Bob did so.

Stella had located the brooch but it fell from her clutches

and she reached forward further and over-balanced. Bob had the erotic sight frozen in front of him and was temporarily frozen with lust.

'Pull her out,' he screamed desperately turning away from the provocative sight.

Unfortunately, the bulge in his trousers grew if he looked at Stella and it showed if he stood facing the girls.

'I'm going to the staff room,' he said hurriedly evacuating and leaving the girls to rescue Stella.

'Oo, isn't he horny?' said Debbie uncharacteristically.

Bob's request for secrecy was, of course, completely ignored. The girls started to play up in Bob's afternoon class and he was compelled to take reprisals by means of silver polishing. Susan Miller decided to take her own reprisals and she whispered to the other girls that they should all keep staring at Bob's flies. It should be mentioned that Bob was now changed into a suit for the cookery theory. Bob turned round from the writing on the board to see what the whispering was about.

'Nothing, chef,' said Susan staring at Bob's flies. Embarrassed, Bob turned away. He then noticed that Stella was staring at his flies. Debbie started giggling.

'What's the matter, Debbie?' asked Bob.

'Nothing,' said Debbie who gazed briefly at Bob's flies and then fell into helpless laughter.

'What's going on?' asked Jimmy who had not been let in on the secret.

Bob rounded on the new interruption. In fact, none of the boys had been let in on Susan's diversion, even though they all knew about the dustbin episode. In fact, the luckier ones had even caught the tail end of the diversion and David Fretwork had gained even more envious adulation from his male contemporaries.

'I think it's something to do with lunchtime,' whispered Clive.

Even Beverley had seen the funny side of this escapade as all the girls without exception were on silver cleaning duties. Beverley gazed at Bob's flies. The penny clicked.

Bob said to himself, 'My flies are undone.' He could hardly look down to check, nor could he adjust them in class. 'Excuse me a moment,' he said, blushing red.

Bob hastily sped outside the door. He looked around and saw the coast was clear. He looked down to see if his flies were undone. Behind him in the classroom there was uproar as the males were let in on the secret. The classroom door adjacent swung open to reveal the large silhouette of Miss Todd. Bob looked up hastily and guiltily.

'What on earth is going on, Mr Malone?' she boomed.

'It's nothing, nothing,' said Bob desperately.

Bob hastily and angrily swung back into the vacated classroom. He was livid with anger. The titters and giggles rapidly subsided. Bob had no more trouble that afternoon and the whole class was awarded homework as penance to cover the lost ground for the theory session. The girls were given a large consignment of silver to polish. Miss Todd looked in on them.

'I see you're learning something about class control, Mr Malone,' she said. 'I trust that this is not male chauvinism in so far as there are no male participants in practical hygiene.'

If Miss Todd had hoped for an explanation she was to be disappointed. However, Miss Todd being Miss Todd, she would find out later what had happened. Part of the story emerged very quickly. Hector was explaining the incident in loud stentorian tones to male colleagues in the staff room. There were only three female lecturers in the department and male conversation was often somewhat coarse unless the female presence was showing a high profile.

'You should have seen Malone's face, when Stella squeezed his balls,' said Hector. 'Seeing her bent over the bin was a bloody sight for sore eyes an' all,' he added, stopping from further outbursts as he noticed the large figure of Miss Todd out of the corner of his eyes.

Bob was in his third week of teacher training when the series of minor thefts began. It was small things generally, things which did not take much carrying. Miss Todd's small cash box for pastry sales disappeared from her locker. Hector lost a large bottle of expensive aftershave. Odd bottles or half bottles of brandy disappeared from lecturer's cupboards. Many of the demonstrations of French cuisine required brandy, Grand Marnier, red wine, white wine etc. and the bottles would be left in the lecturer's cupboard overnight for safety as the stores closed at four o'clock and some classes finished later. Some lecturers, of course, kept the brandy for future classes or medicinal purposes after the stress of teaching particularly difficult groups of students.

Expensive pens or watches would go missing. It usually seemed to happen at night time after people had gone home and the night cleaners were especially suspect. It appeared to be someone with keys and access to the staffroom and teaching rooms. As a student teacher, Bob had been given the status of receiving on loan a set of keys. Although nothing was said, he did not feel happy that the thefts began after he had joined the department. Although the missing items seemed to disappear at night, it was, of course, possible that the thefts took place in the early morning. Bob, of course, often arrived very early to set up class, especially when due for an external assessment by the Garnstone regime. Principal Ness had been informed of the thefts and so had the night cleaning superintendent. In spite of extra vigilance, the thief remained undiscovered.

On the fourth Saturday Bob had agreed to represent Hector as host to some of the parents who were sending their sons or daughters to France. He was going to join Hector and the students in France for the spring bank holiday week. The meeting place was to be the main hall. It was a cold February weekend and the heating was only on half-power to stop pipes freezing up. Fifteen parents were expected but only six turned up. The six were lost in the huge, cold chilly hall. After ten minutes all were shivering and cold and it seemed improbable that any more would turn up. Bob decided to use some initiative.

'We'll go in the bar area,' he said, 'but I'm afraid I do not have access to the drinks.'

Bob wrote the new venue on the blackboard in case there were any latecomers and the small group set out for the bar area next to the restaurant dining-room. They were soon settled comfortably for proceedings to take place and they were rapt in their deliberations. It was certainly much cosier than the huge draughty hall. After about fifteen minutes of proceedings the group were much more at ease. Suddenly the door burst open and framed in the doorway was Clive Batman, the resident engineer, and Sam Brown, the veteran caretaker. Each held a large baseball bat.

'Stay where you are,' yelled Mr Batman. He paused with an astonished look on his face. The group were equally astonished. 'Who are you? And what are you doing here?' asked Sam Batman, then, belatedly recognizing Bob he added, 'You're the student teacher,' in answer to his own question.

Bob hastily explained his business as the chief engineer and caretaker relaxed from the threatening baseball stance.

'You've no business in here,' said the chief engineer officiously. 'You are now the chief suspect. This place is alive with booby traps.'

In spite of Bob's protests, the group had to return to the draughty hall. The meeting proceeded fairly quickly after that because of the hostile surroundings. The parents departed, except for one dark-haired Mediterranean type figure displaying a luxuriant dark moustache. Bob guessed quite correctly that this was Mr Pavrotti, alias Stella's father.

'I amma very concerned a over Stella on this trip,' confided the Italian representative. 'I donna like this Davida Fretwork,' he said. 'He is afta her honna and if he getta her ito da trouble I'll castrate him like I do da stallion,' said Mr Pavarotti very malevolently. 'My a Stella, she wear a da shortage skirts. Hay she showa all a of her legs. Have you seen her?'

Bob pleaded ignorance in the face of this potential Mafia hitman. He thrust the vision of Stella bent over the bin from the back of his mind. He thrust the thoughts of Stella's provocative brushes against him as she always seemed to need something in the silver cupboard at the same time as Bob away from the back of his mind. He thrust the thoughts of the cavernous cleavage yawning before him as she insisted that he see her new necklace. It was Stella who always seemed to hang around after class to ask innocuous questions bristling with innuendo. What had she been saying to her father about himself? Fortunately nothing dangerous emerged. Stella spoke well of Bob and Mr Pavrotti was depending on Bob to protect Stella's honour when the school party including David and Stella stayed for the week in France. Mr Pavrotti was concerned that the male and female students' dormitories were well separated.

'My little Stella, she issa innocenti,' said her father. 'I tell her to keepa covered up and be careful becausa the boys only wanta da one a thing.'

Bob reassured Mr Pavrotti that the girls would be most safe in Hector's hands. If anything did go wrong, Hector should share the blame, he thought. With Stella in France away from paternal influence a potential 'situation' existed.

18

HECTOR BRITAIN AND BOB MALONE INVESTIGATIONS

Hector was most unhappy. He had lost a half bottle of brandy and a bottle of red wine from his chef's whites' locker. This had been his new hiding place after thefts from his desk in the staff room. Unfortunately, there were few cupboards or lockers which did lock and in the past there had been no need for it. Hector had been to the bar and acquired a hock bottle. He had filled it with urine diluted with water to the right colour and carefully recorked it and placed it in ambush in the chef's whites' locker. Two days later there had been an anonymous letter made up of cutouts from newspaper cuttings.

'WATCH YOURSELF, SHITHOUSE.' Hector had been in great stitches of mirth when he found the bottle of urine gone from his locker.

'That's *really* taking the piss,' he said to Bob.

Bob was disgusted but did regard it as somewhat appropriate for the petty sneak thief as he had lost a pair of cufflinks which Sylvia had bought for him.

'When I was a kid there was this bastard who used to bully me and pinch my sweets,' said Hector.

Bob could not imagine anyone daring to bully Hector. Perhaps this childhood bullying had made Hector the way he was, thought Bob. 'I didn't get many sweets either,' continued Hector. 'It was the great depression with hardly any work and money was tight in the family. Sometimes

Granny Hawkes would buy me some sweets and they always came in a red striped bag with 'Wimples Sweetshop' printed on it. Anyhow Aloysius Inchy always seemed to know when I got some sweets and he nicked them off me three times before I had my master plan. I got some rabbit currants and rolled them in sugar and put them in the 'Wimples' bag. Aloysius Inchy nicked them and scoffed the lot. He was off sick with the 'shits' for two days. The doctor made him go through everything he'd eaten and eventually they made it out to be my rabbit turd sweets. He daren't beat me up because it also came to light that he'd been nicking from other kids as well. Serve the bastard right. I got tanned by my father for nearly poisoning Aloysius but my father was proud of me and didn't hit me that hard. I became a hero and never looked back. I think that's why I became a chef,' said Hector. Hector broke into laughter at his own joke.

'Now there's a thing,' thought Bob.

Hector had not had the last laugh, though, as Hector had arrived home to find a ton of horse manure blocking the drive. No one knew who had delivered it, and the mousetrap set for the phantom thief had another message made up from newspaper cuttings.

'THOSE THAT TAKE THE PISS END UP IN THE SHIT.'

Hector was inflamed. The students had a rough time from the sharp edge of his tongue, Bob kept out of his way and the brothers of the department were careful to keep their mirth to themselves. It was not often that anyone pulled anything over on Hector and this was the funniest thing since Hector's TA curry incident. As a matter of fact, someone else was very upset with the phantom thief, namely Principal Elliot Ness . The phantom thief had disappeared with the Harveys Bristol Cream and the gin kept by Principal Ness in the principal's office. Worse still was the fact that the large box of Havana cigars had also been stolen. Principal Ness had not lost anything before but it would appear that the Hector comeuppance had made the thief bolder. Hector had not told the principal about booze going from his locker, it would not have been wise to do so, but the principal did know about the aftershave theft.

Hector went round all the local stables before he found the source of the horse manure delivery. Euphoric, Hector asked for the name of the person who had placed the order. The bespectacled middle-aged woman peered into her diary. 'A Mr Hector Uriah Britain,' said the lady, and she followed up with the address. Not many knew Hector's middle name as Hector was not exactly proud of it. The thief had been through Hector's desk pretty thoroughly. However, Hector had put some wine away one afternoon when in a fit of amnesia. It had remained untouched. A one pound note with four half-crowns dusted in green powder had remained untouched until Bob turned up with green fingers. Bob had been putting some notes in Hector's desk and had intended to move the money for safekeeping. Hector had been somewhat suspicious but Bob did have an alibi for one set of thefts as Bob had had to return to Garnstone for a two-day debriefing in the middle of the teacher training.

'What did this Hector Britain look like?' asked Hector, livid that anyone should dare to impersonate him.

'I never saw him myself, I'll ask Jane,' said the bespectacled lady. She disappeared and returned with a skinny, spotted teenage girl who turned out to be Jane.

'I'm so sorry to keep you waiting. By the way, it cost £2. Will you be paying, Mr Er . . . I did not catch your name,' said the bespectacled lady.

'*No, I will not be paying and I am Mr Britain,*' shouted Hector.

'It was supposed to be cash on delivery. Mr Britain said he would pay then,' said the dopey, spotty girl helpfully.

'*I am Mr Britain and I did not order a load of horse shite,*' shouted Hector, as though addressing a bunch of army recruits or a bunch of students.

'There is no call for coarse language, Mr Britain,' said

the bespectacled lady primly. 'If you had the manure and you are Mr Britain, you owe me £2.'

'I *did not order the horse manure, madam,*' said Hector patiently.

'How did you know to come here then?' asked the bespectacled lady.

'I *have been round every stable around Dronsley, Madam,*' said Hector slowly, loudly and patiently in the tone of voice used by Britons abroad to talk to damned foreigners who do not speak the Queen's English.

'Has Mr Britain had his bill, Jane?' asked the bespectacled lady.

'I don't know, Miss Hunter,' said the dopey-looking girl. 'I'll go and check. The girl disappeared to look and see if the bills had gone out.

'You needn't bother billing me because I am not paying,' said Hector quietly. 'I want you to take it back.'

'Mr Britain, we do not want it back,' said Miss Hunter. 'The £2 is a delivery charge.'

'*Madam, you can just undeliver it,*' yelled Hector. '*How many more times must I tell you. I do not want your horse shite.*'

The girl returned with a bundle of stamped but unfranked envelopes. There was one addressed to Mr H Britain, Esquire on top of the pile.

'They . . . er . . . don't seem to have been sent, Miss Hunter,' said the dopey girl apologetically.

The dopey girl proffered the unopened, unsent letter to Hector timidly.

'Mr Britain,' said the prim Miss Hunter. 'We sent the . . . ahem . . . horse S H I T E,' she spelled out the latter word with repugnance, 'in good faith and we expect you to pay. I'm sure you will find your roses will really thrive on it.'

After a further verbal crossing of swords Hector ended up paying out £5 for the manure to be collected. It was pointed out that the manure was of no further use to Miss Hunter and although she was unhappy about the loss of £2 for transport fees, it would become very smelly before

Hector could get a county court injunction order for the manure to be collected. It was indeed quite smelly already and this was in mid-winter. Hector had already lost half the argument by spelling out that his garden was too small to use such a large amount.

'I can go to the county court anyhow for payment,' said Miss Hunter thoughtfully. 'How long do you think it would take?' she asked Jane thoughtfully.

'Ooh, I really don't know,' said the dopey girl.

'*This is blackmail,*' stormed Hector, '*you swindling old cow.*'

'Mr Britain, I can leave it there with some more besides, if you do not behave in a more gentlemanly manner. You sound like my niece's cookery teacher.'

Miss Hunter, furthermore, would only accept cash. Quite shrewdly she had deduced that Hector might well stop a cheque.

'*I am going to have that bloke's balls on toast,*' confided Hector to Bob.

Bob had thought of a way to get round the principal by catching the thief. Bob and Hector would secretly lay in wait in the middle of the night armed with trip-wires and other devices which Hector used in the TA. They would tell no one, not even the night superintendent cleaner. Hector still thought the night superintendent's staff were responsible. Hector loosened off the nuts from one of the panels in the boilerhouse.

The two crept in the building that night at 11.30 p.m. and they sneaked into the flat above the bar area. When all was quiet they set up a series of trip-wires linked to bells and buzzers and they settled down in the gloom of the flat for a quiet nap awaiting developments. Both had warned Mrs Britain and Mrs Ness respectfully of their whereabouts. Bob had made a particular point of informing Mrs Ness just in case anything went wrong and he needed a further alibi. He had sworn her to secrecy, much against her better judgement. He did not want a security leak via the principal's office.

Bob soon fell asleep and began to snore. Hector poked

him in the ribs to wake him up.

'If you're going to give the game away by bloody snoring, we might as well go home now,' said Hector.

Bob was very tired as he had been coaching Jimmy Graham and Beverley with pastillage work. Miss Todd had had major success with them in a cake decoration class where they had come up with a first prize for Beverley and a third for Jimmy. As a result, Beverley was not quite so distant. Jimmy's luck with Debbie was over and done with. She was horrified when she realized what she had done under the influence of alcohol. She had secretly enjoyed her sudden popularity with the boys but vowed that it would never happen again, especially not with Jimmy Graham. He was now kept at a safe distance. Debbie had been in deep stress for two months after that in case she had become pregnant. The monthly miseries were actually a welcome sign of relief for once. Meanwhile, Beverley had tired of being regarded as a prig and a swot. Jimmy Graham's company offered her a chance to soil the chaste image without actually giving much away. Since the other girls were giving him a wide berth, Jimmy was glad of Beverley's apparent friendliness. She even let him take her out for a glass of Babycham after the late night practising of cake decoration. Tonight Jimmy was taking her out a second time after the late night practice session. Beverley had put the finishing touches to her pastillage church and Jimmy completed his pastillage Roman galley. Beverley's artefact was a work of art. Jimmy's boat was suffering structural stress. The competition was scheduled for the following afternoon and all they were needing was transport into Sheffield. Jimmy had been permitted the loan of his father's car for the evening and he was taking Beverley to a late night dance. Jimmy had told his father that Beverley's brother had passed the test and would sit in the seat adjacent to the wheel whilst Jimmy drove under 'L' plates. Jimmy did not like Giles but Giles had turned up and served his purpose. Giles was not quite so spotty looking and had grown some confidence since staying on in the sixth form. Giles disappeared from the dance with some horsey-looking girl who had her own car. Beverley was not amused. She and Jimmy had got on well and she had even allowed Jimmy to kiss her. She had enjoyed the kiss, but she had firmly pushed the wandering right hand away from her breast with the comment, 'You can pack that up,' to the rampant Jimmy. She had also firmly removed the steadily lowering right hand from her bottom when Jimmy had tried it on in the low lights of the last waltz. As for the hard bulge in Jimmy's trousers as he tried to pull her close to him in the waltz, she had cooled the ardour with a loud, '*Stop it, You're disgusting.*' Naturally everyone nearby looked round and Jimmy was somewhat deflated by the unwelcome attention. Beverley allowed him to continue dancing with her and when they were halfway round the floor again she gradually unstiffened and allowed the romantic mood to return.

'We'll have to get a taxi,' she said.

Jimmy had not got enough money for a taxi. He was not happy about the thought of going home to confess to his father that the car was not ready for Mr Graham to drive to work on the following day.

'I haven't any money left,' said Jimmy. He had kept the promise to his father about not drinking. Jimmy had, in fact, drunk shandies but Beverley had had Babychams and they weren't cheap.

'None of the police will see us in the dark,' said Jimmy. 'I'll take the L-plates off.'

Beverley was not overkeen on this idea but her father had only let her out because Giles was with her. She did not want to endanger this new-found freedom. Jimmy cursed Giles but thought it would give him a second chance at Beverley's honour on a back road somewhere. Should he have an electrical fault, a flat tyre or how could it look authentic? Jimmy had rampant thoughts.

Beverley without glasses, with her long hair down to her shoulders, with her firm well-formed bust and long legs was very attractive indeed now that he had seen her in her long, low-cut silken ballroom gown. It might have been embryonic love or pure lust but Jimmy was definitely stricken.

Beverley, meanwhile, was not drunk but the Babycham had mellowed her feelings towards reserve. Jimmy had a friendly personality and was good company. She had not been out with boys before and had not had kisses other than the messy squashy ones of childhood blind man's buff. Although she had rebuffed Jimmy, her latent female passions had been roused by Jimmy's tentative caresses. As they set out for home she hoped Jimmy would not be completely frightened off.

'It's been a wonderful evening, Jimmy,' she said, putting her hand on his knee gently. She instantly regretted this as Jimmy returned the compliment. 'When I marry I shall be a virgin,' she said firmly. 'Don't spoil things like you did with Debbie. I'm not drunk and won't be and so I know what I'm doing. If all you want is sex you'll have to find someone else.'

Jimmy did not at that moment want anyone else. He reassured her and kissed her gently before setting off for home.

BRRRR BRRRR BRRRR BRRRR CLANG CLANG CLANG BRRRR BRRRR CLANG BRRRR.

The booby-traps had gone off in resounding cacophony. Hector and Bob rapidly woke up with a start. Hector fell over Bob's holdall reaching out for the light switch. The two scuttled off downstairs, Hector gripping two blank thunderflashes exultantly. They were just in time to see the rear of a very alarmed retreating figure running down the corridor. The figure disappeared into the gloom of the pastry room.

'Keep away from me. Oi have a noif,' said somebody with an obviously Irish accent.

Hector had found out that the telephone request for horse manure had been Irish. This was the phantom burglar. Horace lit a thunderflash.

'Is that wise?' asked Bob.

'I owe that bastard,' said Hector exultantly.

After counting ten he tossed it into the gloom. Two seconds later the red sparks flared up into a loud boom. Hector lit up the second thunderflash.

'Oi surrender, Oi surrender. God, oi surrender, Have mercy,' screamed the desperate voice.

Hector could not stop the thunderflash in his hand and so he tossed it back in the corridor behind him where it went off in a second deafening boom. The phantom burglar did surrender. Mr Batman came out from his house dressed in pyjamas and dressing-gown to find out what the noise was about. The police were called and the phantom burglar was pleased to be taken away to be locked up safely in a police cell. The phantom burglar was a night cleaner sacked six weeks before. He had had skeleton keys made and the thefts were revenge for the sack.

Meanwhile Jimmy Graham was so elated at the possible seduction of Beverley that he did not notice the police car parked down the side lane.

'That car's going very slow, Sid,' said constable Nicholas Yule, nicknamed Nick U for short.

'The right rearlight isn't working either,' said Sydney Shorthairs, nicknamed the Short and Curlies by irreverent colleagues.

The Z car set out in pursuit with some suspicion.

'There's a car following and I think it's a police car,' said Beverley.

Rashly, the worried Jimmy decided to try and shake it off. Jimmy turned off down another side road and put his foot down to try to lose the following police car before it turned the corner. Nick U and Short and Curlies were used to this sort of evasive response.

'Put your foot down,' said Nick unnecesarily.

Sydney rapidly accelerated. Jimmy, meanwhile, turned off sharply down the nearest side-road on the left.

'That will shake them,' he said confidently.

Unfortunately, there was another car proceeding towards him and there was not a lot of room for manoeuvre. Jimmy pulled up with a screeching of brakes. The approaching car did likewise.

'You stupid berk,' shouted the alighting driver.

Meanwhile, Constables Yule and Shorthair had gone sailing past the one-way street and realized that the lead car could not have evaporated into thin air.

'He must have gone up the one-way, the crafty sod,' said Constable Yule. 'We could whip round and try to head him off.'

'Back up carefully. No, you go round and I'll stay here and see if he comes out this way,' said Constable Nicholas Yule.

They arranged to meet up when constable Sydney Shorthairs had gone round the block. Jimmy was reversing back into the main road as Constable Yule turned the corner.

Bang. Bang. Constable Yule banged on the rear window of Mr Graham's car to intimate his presence. Jimmy observed the police uniform in his driving mirror.

'You are a prat,' said Beverley.

'Hello, hello, hello. What have we here then?' said Constable Yule in best police-style diction.

'May I have your driving licence and insurance please, sir?' asked Constable Yule. 'Did you notice the one-way, sir? Do you know that your right-hand side rear light isn't working properly?'

By now Jimmy had searched and located and handed over the driving documents.

'Do you realize that this is a provisional licence?' added Constable Yule unnecessarily.

A further two cars had drawn up behind the car facing Mr Graham's wrong direction one. The second one began tooting loudly for clearway. A third car drew up behind it and the driver got out quietly and took in the situation skilfully. Tap, tap. The impatient car horn-tooting driver looked round to see the uniformed figure tapping on the window.

'Kindly refrain from creating a disturbance, sir, or you will be nicked as well,' said Constable Shorthairs quietly. The tooting ceased forthwith as Constable Shorthairs joined his colleague.

'Where are the L-plates?' enquired Constable Yule.

'They must have fallen off,' said Jimmy unconvincingly.

Beverley cringed. How could she live this down? She would never be allowed out ever again.

'You berk,' she screamed at Jimmy.

Bob and Hector, elated by success, decided to return home for the few hours sleep available to them. Bob drove into the Ness household drive and quietly entered and crept up to his room. As he had entered the drive he had observed an extra car parked there. 'I'm sure that is Sylvia's car,' he thought to himself. As he undressed the door opened and in crept Sylvia. She *Shh*'d him but the two were heard. 'What's that?' said a heavy male voice.

'It's only me, father,' said Sylvia who had to make a point of crossing the landing and flushing the toilet.

'Blast,' thought Bob. Reluctantly he rolled over and eventually dropped off to sleep.

Twenty or thirty minutes later and he was just nodding off when a gentle hand covered his mouth.

'*Shh, shh,*' she said gently.

A warm figure crept in beside him.

19

NEMESIS

Bob was sat at the breakfast table narrating about the excitement of the previous evening's events. Mr and Mrs Ness and Veronica were listening intently. Normally Principal Ness avoided early morning encounters at the breakfast table but his wife had mentioned that the thief had been caught and he had made an effort so that he could come and hear the news firsthand. Principal Ness was very very pleased that the criminal who had dared to steal the sherry and cigars had been caught. The previous thefts had been an irritant, but a theft from the office of the principal himself was unthinkable. Bob had just finished his tale when Sylvia arrived and kissed him lightly on the cheek as she sat down next to him. Principal Ness almost forgot the previous *bonhomie* at this brazen display and then he was quickly reminded of the tentative betrothal.

'I was just telling Principal Ness about how we caught the midnight thief,' said Bob, forgetful that he was not supposed to have seen Sylvia since then.

She kicked him under the table. Bob winced.

'What midnight thief was this, Bob?' asked Sylvia innocently.

If Principal Ness had noticed anything, he said nothing. Mrs Ness said nothing untoward but the look in her eyes said quite a lot.

'You must tell Sylvia what you have been up to, Bob. I'm sure you have a lot to tell her since you haven't seen one another for some time,' said Mrs Ness with no hint of the implied sarcasm in the tone of her voice.

'Well, I must go now,' said Principal Ness who did not want to hear the story all over again.

Bob began the story all over again but in a briefer vein.

'Don't go missing bits out,' said Mrs Ness. 'Tell her who the thief was. Sylvia is very interested and wouldn't want to miss any details, would you dear?' said Mrs Ness, turning round to her daughter.

'And when Bob has told you all his news we can have a little chat later, can't we, Sylvia?' she added with a small hint of menace.

Hector had arrived early at college anxious to remove any traces of the thunderflashes. The Irishman had complained about hand-grenades on the previous evening but the police hadn't taken much notice. Mr Batman had been anxious to lock up and go back to bed. Hector had managed to retrieve the cartridges and stuff them down his shirt but there were probably marks on the floor of the kitchen. The smell had been dispersed by opening the windows wide to blow in fresh air, with a few whiffs of gas from an unignited gas stove to blur the smells. Hector removed the scorchmarks skilfully with some paintwork off the bottom of the door as well. The pastry kitchen was easier to clean but Jimmy Graham's Roman galleon had not fared well in the blast. Beverley's church, however, was built more skilfully and was undamaged. Perhaps the galleon would have collapsed with or without the explosive repercussions.

Jimmy arrived looking worried, the galleon was only a minor type problem. He had only entered to be near Beverley anyhow.

'Put it in as "The wreck of the Hesperus", lad,' said Hector who had completely misinterpreted the cause of Jimmy's concern.

Jimmy had spent the night in the cell at Mr Graham's request. Mr Graham had been enjoying the joys of matrimony when his conjugal enjoyment had been disturbed by the ringing of the telephone.

'Ignore it,' Mr Graham had said with obvious displeasure at the *coitus interruptus*.

'It might be something serious,' Mrs Graham had said.

'Nothing is that serious,' Mr Graham had said.

Mr Graham Senior had been relieved that the car and Jimmy had been safe. Jimmy would not be let loose in the car again, though, and there was also the unwelcome publicity of the future court appearance. Would Jimmy go to jail? Would he ever drive again and would Beverley ever speak to him again?

Beverley was also in trouble with her parents. Mr Smythe Browne pointed out that Jimmy had always been a fool at school. Although Giles had also faced the music for absconding for potential pleasures of the flesh, there were such things as telephones for contacting the parental home. Apart from the dangers of driving with an unqualified driver, there were also the dangers of being out late at night with an unchaperoned male. He could have driven her anywhere to have his wicked way with her. Now Beverley was likely to be grounded and would have an early curfew. What would her friends think of her as well? She would be the laughing stock of the college when they discovered that Jimmy had taken her up a one-way road in the wrong direction.

In fact, Beverley had enjoyed the evening up to the last unfortunate episode. She had been looking forward to a kiss and a cuddle with Jimmy but she had had absolutely no intention of it going further than that. Now her father was implying that she could have been a road casualty or an unmarried mother in a typically parental Dooms day-type scenario.

Beverley met Susan Miller on the bus and was coaxed into disclosing an account of the previous evening's events. Beverley needed a confidante badly and also some reassurance and, perhaps, guidance. Beverley swore Susan to secrecy.

'It was bad enough anyhow and then he said that the L-plates must have fallen off in the chase,' said Beverley.

At this point Susan almost collapsed in hysterical laughter. She had tried to keep a straight face about Jimmy driving up the wrong way on a one-way street but this was too much. Beverley was hurt at first, but Susan's laughter was infectious. She joined in and felt much better. She then disclosed how Jimmy had been escorted to a cell in the police station.

Jimmy couldn't keep secrets very well at all. David Fretwork soon wheedled his way into Jimmy's confidence to ask how the previous night went.

'Did you get anything?' he asked Jimmy somewhat coarsely.

'I wouldn't tell you if I did,' said Jimmy with chivalry. 'As it was I was locked up for the night.'

As a result, the story of the night's events was public knowledge by the time Beverley arrived. Far from being regarded as a comic figure, Beverley had developed a sort of notoriety. She liked this new image but she still displayed a very cold aspect towards Jimmy. It was no use being regarded as notorious when her parents would be looking over her shoulder every five minutes in an attempt to maintain the threatened chastity.

Bob arrived at college in a very happy frame of mind. Jimmy's vandalized galleon was a minor setback but it never looked likely to achieve Gold Medal status. Bob heard of the previous night's events and felt sorry for Jimmy. He was encouraged to go along with Hector's 'Wreck of the Hesperus' idea and was allowed the morning to make repairs. Bob acted as matchmaker and persuaded Beverley to do a few additions to the church, as a potential means of giving Jimmy company and perhaps even inspiration. Beverley soon thawed. Jimmy had not disclosed all. Even when Jimmy had been caught under the piano with Debbie in a state of *in flagrante* Jimmy had sworn that the whole incident had been totally exaggerated. Eventually Beverley even gave help and guidance on Jimmy's competition entry. She agreed to travel with Jimmy in the back of Bob's car when they went to the exhibition on the following day. Sylvia was travelling in the front seat of Bob's Farina as she wanted to see her aunt for advice and Bob had agreed to drop her off at the aunt's house.

It was the day of the salon. The coach was due for 9 a.m., but Hector had told the students to be ready at 8.45 a.m. Hector and Miss Todd had the onerous chore of travelling with the first years. Miss Todd had entered some students in the puff pastry goods and the decorated tartlets class. Hector was inspecting the shoes and the attire of the students. He had banned short skirts on the girls and he had demanded that the boys wore suits. They looked quite smart for students, he thought to himself. Stella and David were missing when Hector carried out the register check. The students were allowed to mount the bus which had arrived early. The front seat was to be reserved for Miss Todd and himself, who might need to navigate the last stages of the journey to assist the driver. There was a mad rush for the back seats when the students heard this.

At 9 a.m. Hector was about to order the bus departure when Stella and David put in an appearance. Stella was not wearing a short skirt but she might as well have been. Her coat fell open as she reached the bus step to reveal that her shapely limbs were clad in very short hot-pants.

'You are not wearing those,' stated Hector.

'Get 'em off,' yelled some coarse male at the back of the coach.

'Don't be disgusting,' stormed Miss Todd in the general direction of the offender of public morals.

'You said we could wear suits, girl's trouser suits,' said Stella.

'You are not wearing those, miss,' said Hector.

'I paid fifteen shilling out, are you going to give me my money back?' asked Stella realizing that she might have gone too far this time.

'You are not going with us dressed like that and you are

not getting your money back,' said Hector.

'You said we could wear suits, chef,' said Stella in a wheedling manner. Perhaps she could soften him up. 'Don't you like me dressed like this?'

Hector did like her dressed like that and he tried not to show the admiration felt for that sensual body with the erotic thighs.

'What did you say to them about dress?' said Miss Todd to Hector.

'He said that we shouldn't show our bums, miss,' said Stella who then burst into tears. 'You can't see my bum, miss he said we could wear trouser suits.'

'Be quiet, child,' said Miss Todd imperiously. 'Pull yourself together.'

'I've got a pair of chef's trousers what would fit Stella,' said a male student sat near the front.

'They are only in my car boot.'

Stella departed with the male benefactor for a quick change and the coach set off ten minutes late. Stella, being Stella, still looked fetching in the chef's trousers underneath a tight jumper.

Miss Todd sat at the front of the coach perched with one cheek on the seat and one cheek protruding over the coach aisle. David was sat on the inside of the opposite front seat with Stella between David and Hector. David had not wanted to sit at the front but the late arrival had meant that that seat was the only seat left vacant. David had put one arm around Stella and one hand on Stella's knee.

'You behave yourself, lad,' said Hector jealously.

There was a scream from the back and a 'Stop it.'

'You lot at the back can behave yourselves as well,' yelled Hector.

The singing began shortly afterwards.

'Shut up!' yelled Hector.

'Shut up!' echoed several students.

Each time the coach rounded a right-hand corner Hector almost ended on Stella's lap. Round about the seventh or eighth time this happened Hector sprawled over and his hand fell between Stella's legs by accident.

'Keep your hands to yourself,' said Stella, forgetting her normal dread of the Britain presence.

Meanwhile, Miss Todd was not overkeen on Hector's proximity and inadvertent jabs in the ribs either.

'Perhaps you should change places with David,' said Miss Todd helpfully. She was not that keen on Mr Britain's proximity.

'An excellent idea, Miss Todd,' said Hector who had been wondering how to pull off such a stroke without upsetting her.

'And Stella can sit beside me,' said Miss Todd. 'And David can sit in the middle.'

'It's not fair,' said Stella.

'Shut up,' said Mr Britain.

'We never get to be together,' said David.

'What a shame, *never mind*,' said Hector.

The seating was rearranged and David found the situation quite bearable after all. Stella seemed to come off and rub up against him when the coach rounded the right-hand corners. Stella didn't complain when David's hands accidentally touched private female no-go zones. The singing began again and Hector once more demanded silence.

'I should ignore them, Mr Britain,' said Miss Todd. 'Let them sing if they want to.'

The singing was allowed to resume until 'It was on the Good Ship Venus'. Miss Todd stood up and identified the instigator immediately.

'We will not have those sort of songs sung,' she remonstrated.

'I'm surprised you have even heard of the "Good Ship Venus",' said Hector.

'My father was a rugby supporter,' said Miss Todd. 'I know all about the German officers crossing the Rhine and all about the four and twenty virgins coming down from Inverness. I might know some you don't know but I am not going to listen to them here.

The coach arrived at the *Salon Culinaire* with Hector issuing last-minute orders that the students should re-assemble at 16.15 p.m. or they would be left behind. Miss Todd was busy sorting out her competition entries and so Hector used the opportunity to sneak away to join Mr Simon Naunder who would be in the alcoholic beverage food symposium. Mr Simon Naunder purchased the college wines and therefore knew all the trade suppliers. He was thus able to enjoy the hospitality of would-be sellers of wine and he was allowing Hector to join him because Hector would reciprocate and keep Mr Simon Naunder amply fed back at college. On his way to the drinking assignation Hector bumped into Mr Niconinni, the lecturer responsible for the second years. Mr Niconinni was the opposite year leader to Hector and Mr Niconinni had been Hector's previous rival for the post of senior lecturer. Mr Niconinni had arrived earlier as he had several second-year competitor entries.

'How are we doing then?' asked Hector.

'Not bad, really,' answered Mr Niconinni noncommittally.

'How good is not bad?' asked Hector.

Eventually Mr Niconinni revealed that Dronsley had achieved three golds, one silver and five bronzes. Hector was impressed.

'How about my first years' pastillage?' asked Hector.

'Doing that now,' said Mr Niconinni tersely.

Surprisingly Jimmy's 'Wreck of the Hesperus' received a bronze, Beverley had been more than helpful in its renaissance. Beverley herself achieved a gold for her church. She had £15 which was a lot of money then. Jimmy had £5 which he could put towards his fine, she said.

Mr Simon Naunder could not be found in the drinks symposium and so Hector decided to have a look around the *Salon Culinaire* exhibits with Mr Niconinni. A small screen covered the entrance and the queue looked quite small. Hector joined the queue just in time to see the tail end of the first-year group disappearing ahead of him into the salon. There was, unknown to Hector, a large queue behind the screen and the small queue did not progress very quickly. By the time Hector got round to the other side a huge queue had formed behind so that Hector could not do a u-turn. The only way forward was left as an option. The commissionaire released access to about ten viewers at a time.

Miss Todd appeared at a side door reserved for salon organizers and was waved ahead, alongside the others in her party, by the commissionaire. Hector tried to attract her attention but if she saw him she certainly didn't show it. He was left fuming, to wait his turn.

The salon was magnificent. *Pastillage* (Dronsley gold and bronze in the juniors), pulled sugar, potato work, dressed salmon, boar's head, wedding cakes, gateaux, marzipan scenes, heraldic plaques, petits fours, shellfish and crustacea, terrines etc. This year was a vintage year and Hector was very impressed. Once he had entered the salon he was able to mingle and he ran into Mr Niconinni again.

'I thought you were imbibing,' said Mr Niconinni.

'Oh, that will do later,' said Hector sanctimoniously.

As they drew near the exit they noticed that there were several empty spaces on the platters which presumably had displayed puff pastry goods and small pastries.

'The students get worse,' said a prim lady in front. 'There was a girl in chef's trousers with some rampant male running his hand up and down her bottom.'

'Disgusting,' said her friend with distaste.

'Isn't that Stella and David?' asked Mr Niconinni.

Hector kicked him and pretended to trip up.

'Do you know those students?' asked the prim lady.

'Pardon,' said Hector. 'Were you talking to me?'

'*Do you know those students*, the girl in the chef's trousers?' asked the prim lady.

Hector pleaded ignorance but as they emerged from the salon he found the group waiting outside eating cakes.

'It's good isn't it, chef?' said Jimmy Graham, talking with

a mouthful of sausage rolls.

David had his hand perched on Stella's lovely tight bottom as usual.

'You do know them?' asked the prim lady.

'Disgusting,' said her matronly friend.

'Let's get the commissionaire,' said the prim lady.

'You bloody shower,' said Hector.

'Disgusting,' said the matron.

A commissionaire was approaching and the prim lady bustled off towards him.

'I'll deal with you lot later,' said Hector.

'What's a matter, chef?' asked Jimmy.

'They're the ones who nicked the sausage rolls,' said some other accuser.

'Get out of here,' said Hector, 'Come on, let's move it, Mr Niconinni,' he said.

Mr Niconinni and Hector disappeared into the crowd, not before Hector had told Stella to go and change out of the chef's trousers.

'Let's go to the wine symposium,' said Hector.

Mr Niconinni was only to glad to escape from any potential confrontation.

'We'll be disqualified and we'll lose all the prizes if they find out it's our lot,' said Mr Niconinni.

Fortunately, the duo were able to locate Mr Naunder and were able to hide in the back of Flintlock's Wholesale Spirits Company. Mr Naunder had hid there before but Hector had run into Mr Naunder on the way to the toilet and so the assignation did take place after all. It was a very successful trip for Hector after that. Mr Naunder knew everyone who was everybody in the drinks' trade. Hector even got a half bottle of brandy on the strength of the visits and Hector would be able to drink this on the way back to Dronsley.

The group of First Years were all on the coach by 16.15 p.m. and Hector arrived two minutes later, somewhat puffed and red in the face.

'Let's go without him,' said several anonymous voices.

Miss Todd ushered Hector onto the back seat amid a chorus of 'Whoah hohs'. Hector demanded to see David Fretwork and Stella and Jimmy Graham. He was going to take reprisals.

'*Mr Britain*, you have had too much to drink,' said Miss Todd. 'Please sit down and do not make a fool of yourself.'

'They have been nicking the cakes,' said Hector.

'No, they haven't,' said Miss Todd.

'They pinched the sausage rolls and cakes that Stella Pavrotti, David Fretwork and Jimmy Graham had made,' said Hector.

'I gave them sausage rolls and cakes, Mr Britain,' said Miss Todd. '*And if you thought they had stolen them, you should not have run off to evade the issue*,' she added.

'I never ran off,' said Hector.

'We saw you,' said Miss Todd.

Hector produced his half bottle of brandy. Mis Todd took it away from him.

'I'll look after that,' she said.

She did too. She drank the lot on the way back to college.

Meanwhile, Bob had enjoyed his day at the salon. Jimmy and Beverley had rejoined him for the trip back to Garnstone and he was on the way to pick up Sylvia from her auntie's. Sylvia did not see her auntie very often these days but she wanted some advice about her romance with Bob. The trip to the salon had been a good way of introduction without it being an obvious inspection of the potential groom. Sylvia's aunt liked Bob as soon as she met him. He was full of charm and won her over completely.

'I wish I were younger,' said the aunt who had lost her husband three years previously.

'We'll see you at the wedding,' said Sylvia and Bob.

'Are you getting married, chef?' asked Beverley who had thought the proposed matrimony a put-up job. She and Jimmy had been invited indoors for a quick tea and cakes by the hospitable aunt.

'Are you thinking of getting married then?' asked the aunt.

'Certainly not,' said Beverley.
'Not for some time yet,' said Jimmy.

Back at Dronsley, Principal Ness had had visitors. Constables Yule and Shorthairs had had a busy night. After arresting Jimmy and Beverley they had gone on call out to pick up the midnight college burglar. They had been asked to call at the college before their late shift started, so as to interview the Principal about the allegations of use of explosives. The Irish interloper wanted to take out proceedings against Hector and Bob for the undue use of threats and firearms. Principal Ness dismissed the use of explosives as preposterous.

'I haven't heard of any use of firearms,' he said.

Paddy O'Toole had confessed to stealing the principal's sherry and cigars. He had confessed to other thefts. The only part of the story which did not fit was the explosives, or firearms or whatever it was that caused the bangs. Paddy confessed to ordering the delivery of horse manure to Hector's house. Hector had tried to poison him with tainted wine and Hector had tried to blow him up. This could have been a murder charge. Principal Ness went along to the scene of the crime with the two constables. PC Shorthairs found some evidence of carbonised deposits which Hector had overlooked. Principal Ness promised that he would look into it. The son-in-law and Hector would be interrogated separately, when they returned from the day out at the salon, vowed Principal Ness.

20

THINGS THAT GO BUMP IN THE NIGHT

Feeling safe in the back of the car which was, of course, dark, Beverley allowed Jimmy to nestle close to her. By the time they were half-way home they had even got as far as holding hands and he kissed her and thanked her for her help in the competition. It was a brief kiss but she didn't pull away and even kissed him back. By three-quarters of the way back they were cuddling as it seemed that Bob and Sylvia were almost oblivious as to anything that would happen in the back seats of the Farina. Jimmy had his left arm around Beverley by this time and he was trying to fondle the parts of the left breast that he could reach. She tingled at this caress and let his hand linger awhile but when Sylvia made as though to turn round she gave Jimmy a right elbow in the ribs. Jimmy grunted and winced quietly and desisted for a while. Beverley did not allow replacement of the encroaching hand but firmly pushed the trespassing hand away from her erogenous zone. In the meantime, Jimmy's right hand, which had been released for a few seconds whilst Beverley dealt with the wandering left hand, strayed down to her knee. Since it was unlikely that Bob could turn his eyes from the road ahead and the lower part of her anatomy was hidden from vision, Beverley ignored it. Slowly Jimmy manoeuvred his hand beneath Beverley's skirt. Slowly he moved upwards beneath her skirt up to the thicker stocking tops and then onto what was called the 'whoopee zone' in the days of stocking tops. Jimmy stiffened with rampant ardour as he felt the warm smooth flesh between Beverley's thighs. (The 'whoopee zone' was the penultimate point to female surrender in those days.) Beverley allowed him to touch her through the thin nylon panties for about thirty seconds. She liked the feeling a lot. She reached over to feel the back of her hand onto Jimmy's manhood. It was true what the girls had said. Wasn't it marvellous what a girl could do to a man, or boy. Beverley pressed down slowly but firmly, gradually increasing the pressure which made Jimmy wince. His right hand refrained from its trespass of Beverley's intimate area. Beverley slowly pulled the hand away by pressure at the wrist. She then took Jimmy's right hand and held it firmly to prevent further wanderings. Jimmy did not get past the 'whoopee zone' again that night. He contented himself with having discovered that Beverley did not wear tin knickers and was certainly not frigid either.

Sylvia had not wanted to be seen in public amongst Bob's student teacher novitiates but since Bob was to return to Garnstone on the following day she had condescended to accompanying Bob to the buffet supper laid on for the returning students at Dronsley. Mr Niconinni had telephoned ahead with the news of the accumulated six gold medals, three silver medals, and nine bronze medals and Mr Potterton was so ecstatic that he had telephoned Principal Ness.

Principal Ness in turn informed the press and arranged to drop in and see the returning students. He was very proud and had visions of appearing on the front page of *The Weekly Dronsley Review*. The duty officer said that they would send someone along to take photographs the next day. The buffet was, in fact, a buffet launched under Trades Description Act deficiencies. It was gala pie, sausage rolls and various cheeses. The part-time bakery class had made a vast amount of *baguettes* and there were cream gateaux made on the preceding afternoon. There was wine and coffee. Principal Ness, however, was impressed until he thought about who was paying. Mr Potterton hastily reassured Principal Ness that the 15s payment from students covered both the hire of the charabancs and provision of food.

Principal Ness appeared to be reassured that the departmental budget was not being mis-appropriated.

Hector had completely sobered on the journey back and Miss Todd returned a brandy miniature drawn from her handbag. His half-bottle sample was completely empty but Miss Todd promised that she would refill it provided Hector let her deal with Stella.

'You don't know what else they have been doing,' said Hector.

'*What else have these poor students done to you now, Mr Britain?*' she asked. 'The first years have achieved eight awards in the salon and you are going to punish them? What on earth have they done?'

'*They nearly lost us the lot by stealing the entries from the display,*' said Hector. '*I even caught Jimmy Graham still eating the evidence.*'

'And what did you do about it, Mr Britain?' asked Miss Todd sweetly.

'Er . . . I . . . er . . . left the situation to be sorted out at college when we get back,' said Hector. 'Anyhow, Jimmy Graham is in the car with Mr Malone.

'David Fretwork is also involved,' added Hector.

'Mr Britain, you slunk away to the beer festival having told the students to scatter. Jimmy Graham did not take any sausage rolls or currant buns either. He didn't have to. I gave the students sausage rolls and buns, and, *Mr Britain, I explained* as much to the commissionaire who you ran away from. Do they teach you to run away from trouble in the Territorial Army nowadays, Mr Britain? And do you enjoy bullying the students?'

Hector was stunned. Miss Todd had, in fact, given food supplies to the competitors of the first years. She had been able to prove this. What she hadn't said was that this had given some students the impression that the goods were stolen. Two wits had decided to go round themselves for free snacks. It had been pretty stupid leaving sausage rolls and bakery goods so exposed to viewers, sited near to the *Salon Culinaire* exit, thus allowing a quick getaway. Miss

Todd knew about some Dronsley criminals, including David and Stella, but she would deal with them in due time. Stella, incidentally, had been advised to take off the chef's trousers in the ladies' cloakroom. Another girl had taken charge of her coat. David had been advised to keep away from her until the time for the coach and Stella was now once more in hot-pants. Males found the sight of her shapely thighs far better to look at than looking for a girl in chef's trousers. There were suspicions but no proof that Dronsley was involved but Dronsley students had been joined by other college students seeking free food. Fortunately, no one attacked any other exhibits but the commissionaire had to be more vigilant in view of more potential anarchy. The commissionaire as a result lost out on the numerous smoke breaks. He hated students even more than usual as a result.

At Garnstone Miss Todd allowed all the students to alight except David and Stella. She invited the driver to park the charabanc and to come in for a snack whilst Stella and David cleaned up inside. She supplied a bucket and soapy water from inside the college. The driver was very pleased. He normally was responsible for the cleanliness of the vehicle himself.

'If there is any deviation from immaculate standards there will be trouble,' threatened Miss Todd. 'I shall inspect at 11.30 p.m.' This allowed forty-five minutes. The two completed the job in half an hour and David resolved to put the remaining time to good use. Stella had very sensibly removed her hot-pants and donned the chef's trousers to scrub the floor. David had stood guard whilst this took place but he had not turned away whilst the hot-pants were discarded.

'I'll stand guard whilst you get changed,' he said chivalrously.

'You'll look again,' said Stella provocatively.

'I won't do anything,' said David.

He was unlikely to promise this though. Stella undid the trousers and lowered them to reveal the dark stocking tops, the white thighs and lacy white panties in the gloom at the back of the coach. David reached forward. Stella couldn't back away far. He put his arm round her and kissed her whilst the wandering hands reached for her nether regions. There was a loud *bump* from behind. Stella dived for her hot-pants which David allowed her to don quickly.

'You haven't done the boot,' said a firm female voice. Miss Todd called them out to the rear of the vehicle. The *bump* had been the sound of the door hinge lifting. Miss Todd pretended that nothing untoward had been happening but she had returned early to forestall any such activity and also to invite the students in for a chance at the buffet remains.

By now the parents had collected their charges, except for the few wealthy students whose parents had purchased cars, motor bikes, mopeds and bicycles for them. Those within walking distance had walked home. In those days there were far fewer reports of rapes, muggings, assaults etc. A furtive hand on a female bottom and the occasional flasher was headline material, let alone rape. Jimmy had been introduced to Beverley's father as a runner-up to Beverley's *pastillage* church.

'I remember you well enough,' said Mr Smythe Browne.

How on earth could his daughter want to take up catering and how could she have a boyfriend like Jimmy Graham? Where had he gone wrong?

Bob had agreed to take Jimmy home. Bob also went to the door with Jimmy. The door opened to reveal Mrs Graham.

'You should be proud of Jimmy. He got a bronze medal,' said Bob.

'Oooh, fancy having a bronze medal. Father will be pleased,' said Mrs Graham.

Bob declined to come in as Sylvia was waiting outside. Mr Graham came to the door and appeared to be pleased by Jimmy's success. The previous night's escapade was temporarily forgotten. The ice had been broken with Jimmy's homecoming and his neck was still in one piece.

Bob took Sylvia home. Principal Ness and his wife were still downstairs and so there was no opportunity to get together on the sofa. Sylvia was due to return to her MA studies on the morrow as well, but it looked as if they would have to stay up a long time before the principal and his wife went to bed. The two went upstairs to their separate rooms but stayed for a cuddle in the corridor upstairs. They were even interrupted in this as Veronica crossed the corridor dressed in a thick long dressing-gown in order to visit the toilet. The embrace continued whilst Veronica paid a visit and the two disengaged at the sound of the toilet flushing. Then they heard the sounds of the radio downstairs being turned off. Principal Ness and his wife were about to come upstairs to bed.

'Goodnight, darling,' said Bob wth one long, last lingering kiss.

He was caressing her breasts as he kissed her but she pushed him gently away at the sounds of the creaks from the lower stairs as her parents came up to bed.

He took some time to go to sleep. He had lain awake hoping she would visit him again. The door softly opened and closed. A figure tiptoed across and quickly put her hand over his lips. The dressing-gown fell to the floor and he felt Sylvia's warm body snuggling up to him.

'We must talk,' she whispered. They had not had very much time alone together all day. Bob kissed her and caressed her and soon discovered that she had not put knickers on. She made no attempt to stop his premarital initiative. They were soon bound together in sexual conjugation, both enjoying the repeat of their first night together.

CREAK, CREAK CRRR . . . BANG. The bed collapsed.

'*What's that?*' shouted Principal Ness.

21

A PRESSING ENGAGEMENT

Bob was in disgrace. He would have been thrown out of the Ness household a second time but the return to Garnstone pre-empted this. Meanwhile, Bob was carrying out the last demonstration which was to be an illustration of the use of convenience foods. Bob had been informed that he was to have an external assessor as well as Harry Clarke from Garnstone. Bob had expected Mr Clarke, one of the social studies lecturers but not an external assessor from the University of London as well. He had enough worries about his love life without this added sword of Damocles. He brought out the battery of visual aids: the flannelboard, a magnetic wallboard, handouts in skeleton form. On one side of the room was a table with examples of dried foods, mainly pulse, canned foods and various sizes A10s A1s A2½s with leaflets on usage. For the frozen section Bob had to be content with empty packages and more leaflets. Bob was demonstrating the use of a packet tomato soup, all-in custard mix, the use of potato powder, the use of frozen puff pastry and frozen croquettes, chips and the frying of frozen cod fillets. Duplicate hand-outs and lesson plans were laid out on the back row for Harry Clarke, the assessor and Hector. Hector warned the group that he would be most upset if they dropped Mr Malone in the 'shite.'

Beverley and Jimmy sat on the front row together. Jimmy was as pleased as Punch. Beverley was obviously pleased with her new image. Hector had an appointment with Principal Ness re the 'explosives' thrown at the night interloper. Bob had quickly improvised a story about it only being 'jumping cracker fireworks' He had had but a few short words with Hector that morning and he had informed Hector that he had been caught in bed with Sylvia, by the principal.

'I have to see him this afternoon, before I finish here,' said Bob despondently. 'I haven't even seen Sylvia this morning.'

Hector had been told to see the principal at 10 a.m. but the visiting assessors would probably want him on the back row with them for his assessment of Bob's teaching abilities.

Hector set out to see the principal's secretary to seek a deferment. It was still only 8.30 a.m. but the principal's secretary normally started early. Hector knocked on the door and entered without knocking. Georgia Browne, the principal's secretary, had been with Principal Ness for twenty-two years. She had been his secretary as head of department in Elliot Ness's younger years. It was in those years that they had had a brief fling together and been intimate together. In latter years Principal Ness had lost his ardour and, apart from the one odd occasion when caught in the act by Mr Harebrain, nothing much had happened at all. Recently his secretary had been seeing the verger of her church and the two had become very friendly. She had told Principal Ness about this as the two were very close still, even though the friendship had burnt out into a platonic association.

This morning Georgia was very very upset. Her boyfriend had been seen kissing another woman by her best friend who had been to London shopping. The boyfriend had been away in London for two days on business. She had not seen him to demand an explanation but she feared the worst. She had broken down into tears and Elliot had tried to console her. She had ended up on his lap as Principal Ness embraced her and tried to soothe her. It was this scene that confronted Hector as he strode into the secretaries' office. Principal Ness stood up with a start and Georgia fell to the ground. Weeping louder than ever, she clambered to her feet with his assistance and then she hit the principal across the chops shouting '*Men*' as she did so.

'I'll come back later,' said Hector, turning round to leave.

The weeping secretary pushed past him whilst the reddening Principal insisted that Hector stay to complete the business which he had come about.

'I want nothing further to be said about this,' said the worried principal. 'Miss Browne is very very upset and I was trying to calm her down.'

'I don't know what you mean, sir,' said Hector. 'All I saw was your secretary in tears. It is nothing to do with me and it will go no further.'

'What did you want, anyway?' said Principal Ness, regaining his composure.

Hector informed the principal about the external assessors coming in for Mr Malone's teacher training.

'Ah, yes, I forgot about that. You two were the two who caught Paddy aren't you? What the bloody hell went on that night? That bloody thief alleges that you threw explosives at him. The police want to interview you. It's a serious offence. Did you not think of the dangers of burning the college down?' said the rapidly recovered principal.

Hector assured the principal that it had only been a small cracker to frighten the thief.

'It couldn't have hurt a fly,' said Hector. 'They wouldn't let people have dangerous explosives for children's fireworks, would they?' he continued.

'I hope you can convince the police, Mr Britain,' said Principal Ness. 'If that Irish sod gets off, you are in trouble.'

Hector refrained from reminding the principal about the earlier incident with the secretary. Mind you, he thought to himself, there was no evidence.

Hector got back in time to see Harry Clarke and the visiting assessor. It was a large woman with a very large hat. She had on a very strong perfume. She wore a bright red two-piece suit and dark red shoes. She had bright red lipstick and thick make-up. Hector was sat in the middle place between her and Harry Clarke, a large man who was the double of Fred Emney. Although Hector was not a small man, he felt dwarfed. Hector explained that he had to leave to meet the police at 11 a.m.

'Don't worry, Mr Britain, we shall only stay an hour,' boomed the large lady.

Beverley and Jimmy had been the first, David Fretwork and Stella Pavrotti were the last. The large lady was walking ahead and she deliberately went to the opposite end of the row so that there were two students in between. Since Hector had not been around the students had lapsed into an untidy array, leaving vacancies on the front row. Bob had let things slide whilst setting up the demonstration but he was now almost ready for action.

'Could you come down here with Jimmy and Beverley?' asked Bob.

Reluctantly the two came forward, David first. He sat down, expecting her to have to sit beside him. Instead, she walked round the front and sat with Jimmy and Beverley in between her and David.

'Move up,' she said to Jimmy. She added 'please' provocatively, as only she could.

'You don't mind if I sit beside you, Jimmy, do you?' she asked sensuously.

Beverley glowered. Jimmy might have been flattered in previous times but he sensed that Beverley did not like Jimmy's initial reaction. Stella was a threat to any female.

'Have you and David had a row?' he asked unnecessarily.

He moved closer to Beverley. Stella wasn't used to a brush-off.

'You want to watch yourself,' she said to Beverley. 'They are only after one thing.'

'I know,' said Beverley smugly. 'But I can handle it.'

'*Could we all please settle down,*' said Bob loudly.

'He's politer than Hector,' said Susan Miller on the back row, forgetting that Hector was just behind.

'*Shut it,*' said Hector tersely.

Susan was quiet. The class began and Bob set about reminding them of a previous theory lecture on preservation of food.

'I am going to begin with dried convenience foods,' said

Bob. He referred to the flannelboard and then the table stacked with pulse. He then made up a *duchesse* mix with potato powder and asked Beverley for some uses of *duchesse*. 'How do you make *duchesse*?' Bob asked another student.

'I love to see the 'foodies' at work,' said Harry Clarke. 'He's rather good, isn't he?'

Harry Clarke and the overpowering large lady obviously got on well together.

'I think we've seen enough,' said the large lady suddenly.

The two prepared to leave and excused themselves. Hector went with them to see them off before seeing the policemen.

As the three went through the door there was visible relief from the students. Two minutes later there was a loud cheer.

'*Don't spoil it,*' said Bob.

He went underneath the demonstration cupboard and produced some paper cups. He produced two large cans of beer and a sort of opener pourer device. This had been the unseen stimulus and tasted response as taught at teacher training. It was not normally interpreted in this way, though.

Veronica too was very nervous for her class on air circulation. She was swathed in thick, long woollen knee-length dress with a thick woollen cardigan over the top. The radiators were turned on full blast and the classroom was decidedly hot. Mr Clarke and the large heavily scented lady proceeded to the vacant places at the back of the class to join Miss Todd. This time Harry Clarke was flanked by two large ladies.

'There's a lot of meat there,' muttered some irreverent small girl.

Mind you all the students appeared small compared with this trio. The heat seemed to bring out the heavy scent even more. At the front of the class Veronica was setting up joss-sticks and she lit up two electric radiators. She placed a blanket underneath the door to cut off the intake of air coming from beneath the door. The pungent joss-sticks and the scent of the large lady were having a stifling effect.

'I can h h h ha hardly breathe,' puffed Mr Clarke.
'It's very hot, Miss,' pleaded a dark-haired girl.
'Please, give us some fresh air,' said a ginger-headed girl.
CRASH. The crashing sound came from the back.
'Open the door and windows, turn off the radiators,' said Miss Todd, pushing to the front of the classroom.

The large red-lipsticked lady was giving Harry the kiss of life. He woke up and asked if he was in heaven. His lips were bright red too.

'Well done, well done,' said the large lady, beaming.

She pulled Harry Clarke towards her and gave him another kiss.

'Oh, you're covered in lipstick. What would your wife say?' she asked.

'I'm not married,' said Harry Clarke in a bemused way.

'Oh, you darling man,' said the large lady. 'You should be.'

She kissed him again. By now the girls had been evacuated and were breathing in fresh air outside. They were sent for an early break.

'Oh, I'm so sorry, so sorry,' Veronica kept repeating.

Later on Veronica and Bob met up in the staff room. Hector had a note for each of them. Veronica read hers first, fearing the worst. At the end was the summary which was the most imortant piece of information: 'I have never ever seen such an excellent illustration of the importance of air circulation. Distinction. Marjorie Forsythe.'

Bob opened his and read it. He turned to the end first. 'Excellent use of materials, including flannelboard, leaflets, skeleton handouts, question and answer techniques. Credit pass. Marjorie Forsythe.' Scrawled as an addendum was: PS Excellent rapport and motivation of students using real visual aids. PPS Don't give students too much of potentially misleading motivation. Harry Clarke.

Harry Clarke had sneaked back to see through the

keyhole what the noise had been about.

'Oh, by the way, there's a letter from Sylvia. I should read it before you go and see the principal.'

Bob opened the letter. 'Ask my dad for permission to marry me, Easter. See you at 1.30 p.m. in the Southern Constellation.'

'Is it bad news?' asked Hector, seeing from Bob's expression that it did not appear to be.

'I think I'm getting married, if I can persuade the principal, that is.'

'You're both over twenty-one but if there's any trouble just say that Hector Britain and Miss Browne are on your side,' said Hector. Hector would not embroider on this though.

Bob had received a summons from the 'Great Man' anyhow, as Bob had left early that morning in order to set up the demonstration. The previous evening's post-mortem had been postponed as Sylvia had scuttled off to her own bed and the 'Great Man' Principal Ness had been subdued by his hard suffering wife.

'If I were a younger man I'd thrash him within an inch of his life,' he said.

'I know you would, dear,' said the patient wife.

'In Sicily they shoot despoilers of daughters,' raged Principal Ness.

'Yes, dear,' said Mrs Ness.

'We should throw him out now,' he raged on.

'He's leaving tomorrow anyhow,' wheedled Mrs Ness.

'You said that last time,' said Principal Ness. 'I told you something like this would happen.'

'Yes, dear,' said Mrs Ness patiently.

'If I were a younger man. If . . . Where are my pills?' said Principal Ness.

'Sort it out in the morning, dear. You'll get another of your turns. You know how I worry about you,' said the patient, long-suffering wife.

Principal Ness had been awake half the night thinking of what he would say to this blackguard student teacher and to his wayward daughter. When he had finally gone to sleep it was a heavy one. Mrs Ness had turned off the alarm and waited for the students to go to college before wakening her husband with a cup of tea and breakfast in bed. Sylvia and Bob had evaded him. Now he would be able to sort out this young whippersnapper. If only he were younger. As if this was not enough, his faithful secretary was weepy and snappy and not very co-operative this morning. He sent his secretary to do some Photostatting whilst he rang up the verger, whom he knew casually from their acquaintance at the local freemasons.

'Well, Hector, here we go. *Over the top*,' said Bob as he set out to see the 'Great man'.

'I'd say that was last night and this is a pressing engagement,' said Hector, not entirely unsympathetically.

Bob managed a weak smile at the pun and reported to the red-eyed secretary who buzzed the principal to say that 'A Mr Malone is here to see you, Mr Ness.'

Things were very formal this morning.

'Could you please see that we are not interrupted, Miss Browne,' said Principal Ness who was also very formal this morning.

'Come in, sit down, Mr Malone,' said Principal Ness in a very hostile manner.

'If I were a younger man . . .' began Principal Ness.

'I most sincerely apologise for . . .' began Bob.

'Shut up whilst I have . . .' continued Principal Ness.

'. . . last night and I should never have . . .'

'. . . finished. Shut up. *Shut up*,' demanded Principal Ness.

'May I ask one question first, please, Mr Ness, please?' asked Bob.

'*If I were a younger man I would* . . .' began Principal Ness.

'*I want to marry Sylvia*,' said Bob loudly and desperately.

The Great Man paused. 'What, man?'

'May I have permission to marry Sylvia, Sir?' asked Bob.

The Great Man, who had stood up to lecture Bob, height being a valuable psychological point when administering a rollocking, sat down sharply.

'Is my daughter pregnant?' gasped the Great Man. '*No, don't answer that.*'

'*She is not,*' said Bob in loud denial.

'I have a few things to say before I come round to this preposterous belated attempt to get round me after seducing my daughter. *Now shut up whilst I say what I have to.*' demanded the principal.

'Sylvia is not pregnant, sir, and I do want to marry her,' said Bob quietly.

'*Shut up,*' said Principal Ness. '*Shut up and listen.*'

Bob allowed Principal Ness to continue.

'If I were a younger man I would thrash you to within an inch of your life,' said Principal Ness. 'In many countries I would be expected to kill the despoiler of my daughter. You . . . you . . . you *repay my hospitality by going to bed in . . . in . . . in my own house. . . .*' The buzzer went. Principal Ness picked up the intercom.

'I thought I said no interruptions,' he snapped to the weepy secretary. He slammed the receiver down.

'*You repay my . . .*' be began, only to be interrupted by the buzzer again.

'It's the press about . . .' began the secretary.

'Oh, send them over to Mr Potterton,' stormed Principal Ness, banging down the receiver.

'*You repay . . .*' began the principal, only to be interrupted by the buzzer yet again.

'*What is it this time?*' he yelled.

'The Press are not here about the competition. They are here to see Mr Britain and Mr Malone about . . . er . . . explosives. Oh, and your daughter's here as well.'

The secretary did not wait for a response, but put down the receiver. The exasperated principal buzzed her back.

'Please could you ask them to wait for five minutes, Miss Browne?' asked the weary 'Great Man'.

'I've sent for Mr Britain. He's here. He says, "Could he join with me in congratulations with your daughter's forthcoming marriage to Mr Malone?" ' she said.

'*Five minutes, please,*' said Principal Ness grimly.

'*So now you come to me asking for my blessing and you've already told everyone else about it before asking. Can you support my daughter? Do you think she wants to marry a . . . a . . . a . . . bloody philanderer like you? Well, well. Just give me even one good reason as to why my daughter should want to marry you?*' shouted the principal. He sat down again and reached into the top drawer for his pills. 'If . . . if . . . if I were a younger man,' he gasped.

Bob rushed round the desk, thinking the principal was going to have a turn.

'Get off, get off,' spluttered the reviving principal. 'One reason, ONE REASON.'

'We love each other, sir,' said Bob weakly.

'LOVE? You don't know what love is. It's pure lust . . . *lust,*' spluttered the principal. 'Well, I can't stop you marrying but I won't give my blessing. How do you even propose to support a wife. You haven't got a job and if I put my oar in you'll never become a teacher,' threatened Principal Ness.

'WE. . . . We would like to marry with your blessing, sir, and I promise that I will take care of her, even if I have to take on two jobs. Your daughter does want to marry me. She would not have come to my room last night otherwise. That is *why* she came to my room,' said Bob sincerely.

'*I don't know what hold you've got over my daughter but you were not exactly playing at Chinese whispers last night were you, Mr Malone?*' stormed the irate principal, '*and you could have asked my opinion first before announcing the engagement.*'

'I have not asked Sylvia to marry me yet,' said Bob. 'I wanted to ask your permission first.'

'How come everybody knows about the engagement except Sylvia and me?' asked the exasperated principal.

'I only knew myself about twenty minutes ago,' said Bob.

'You've been with her again this morning haven't you?' stormed Mr Ness.

'I haven't seen Sylvia since last night, sir,' said Bob truthfully.

'She is pregnant, isn't she?' stormed the principal. 'I'll. . . .'

'Sylvia is not pregnant, sir,' said Bob firmly. 'We love each other.'

'How do you know she's not pregnant after Christmas?' said Principal Ness.

'Nothing happened at Christmas, Mr Ness, nothing happened.'

The door burst open and Sylvia came in.

'I told her she couldn't come in,' said a flustered secretary.

'Stop it, stop it, both of you, stop it,' interceded Sylvia. The press outside can hear everything when you shout. I leaked the information about the engagement because I knew you would do everything you could to break it up. He hasn't asked me yet either.'

'I should have known,' said Principal Ness wearily. 'And you want to be married to a woman who manipulates like this? How could you stoop so low, either of you? Both of you?'

'Will you marry me, Sylvia?' asked Bob. 'Not as if I am going to let this sort of thing go on if we do get married. And what's this about Easter? It's a bit early, isn't it?'

'You are pregnant, aren't you?' said Principal Ness quietly.

'*No I'm not*, well I don't think I am,' said Sylvia.

'*What do you mean, you don't think you are?*'

'Father, please, the press are outside. I don't think I'm pregnant but after last night. Well . . . well, I might be.'

'I was meaning to ask you, I mean talk to you, about last night. But what about the fortnight at Christmas?'

'Nothing happened at Christmas, father. As for the last night, well, it was something I once heard you say about trying a new car before you bought it.'

'*How dare you?*' stormed the principal.

'What's this about buying a new car?'

'Shut up,' said the principal.

'I'll explain later,' said his daughter.

'You deserve each other,' said the weary principal. 'I wouldn't want to marry a scheming bitch like my daughter.

As for her, I can't see why she wants to marry a wimpish sex maniac like you.'

'He's not a wimp,' said Sylvia. She did not say anything denying his sex maniac qualities though.

'I take it that you'll give me away then, Daddy?' said Sylvia. 'I'll go now and I'll see you at half past one in the Southern Constellation, Bob.'

'*Get out, both of you. I'll see you there too,*' said the 'Great Man'.

He had lost his touch. Was no one frightened of him anymore? Bob and Sylvia, however, had to run the gauntlet of the press first and *The Weekly Dronsley Review*, was to run the front page with: THINGS THAT GO BOOM IN THE NIGHT. PRINCIPAL'S DAUGHTER CAPTURES HER MAN and THERE'S GOLD IN THEM THERE SALONS. It was somewhat unfortunate that the photograph of the engaged couple appeared under the first headline. Hector and Bob were the reluctant heroes, or at least Bob was. There was no actual reference to the Irishman by name until the case came up in court but there was reference to a man helping the police with their enquiries. A somewhat quaint phrase that is. It always makes you think of some poor sod stuck in a draughty cell waiting for the early morning cup of tea from a tin mug, with a greasy plastic egg and congealed baked beans.

22

THOSE WEDDING BELLS

Bob had returned to Garnstone and Sylvia had returned to her studies. The wedding had been arranged for the Saturday a week before Easter, and this was only because the principal had valuable contacts through the freemasons. Unfortunately, Easter is a popular time for weddings and the venue for the reception was as yet undecided. Bob and Sylvia wanted a small quiet affair but this seemed to imply a cover-up to some people who were commenting on the speed of the arrangements.

'My daughter is not pregnant,' Principal Ness had informed several sceptics. The vicar had squeezed in a 4.30 p.m. wedding but the Southern Constallation was booked up, the Ness household was too small, a county directive forbade use of the college premises and time was running out. Principal Ness was in the bar of the Southern Constellation with Mr Millipede, the retired headmaster.

'Your daughter's wedding's a bit sudden, isn't it?' enquired Mr Millipede.

'Yes, but it's not what you are thinking,' said Mr Ness, on edge suddenly.

'I'm not thinking anything. What should I be thinking?' asked Mr Millipede genuinely.

Principal Elliot relaxed. 'I don't know why there's such a rush. He's not got a job, no money, and she's got him under her thumb. She could have had her pick. She went out with an Irish Lothario who broke her heart, and now, well. . . .' He didn't add more but continued in a new vein.

'I don't even know where to try next for the reception. I can see I shall have to see if I can put up a big tent in the deserted horse stables near me,' said the weary Principal Ness. 'Anyhow enough of that, what do you do with your time now you are retired?'

'I've got plenty to do with the freemasons. Outings, Dronsley Table meetings, charity. Actually, we are thinking of buying up those stables to form a golf club. We are waiting for permission from the planning committee but that should not be much trouble. We have set up a trust but we need about another £5,000. There should be a good return on it. I've got £5,000 in myself with a guaranteed return of £6,000 in five years' time, if I live that long. If not the wife or the kids get it back. Good investment really. I'm involved with quite a lot of things with the freemasons. They don't pay me but I get expenses. Anyhow it gives me plenty to do and I've got a good pension. You could do worse than come in on the committee yourself, you know,' said Mr Millipede.

Principal Ness thought this an excellent idea. He learned that the stables would be steam-cleaned. The deal was set to go through when the planning committee gave the approval. Principal Ness could sell some of his shares and easily raise £5,000. He was planning a secret wedding settlement on Sylvia but he had no intention of letting her know. Both Bob and Sylvia had made it plain that they did not look to charity. Bob was not marrying her for her money. He thought she had not got any money, she knew that he certainly hadn't got much. They were even planning to spend their honeymoon working at Butlins but in shared accommodation this time. Bob did not want drunken Scots barmen peeing on him in the middle of the night.

Principal Ness was very pleased with life. He was now a co-trustee of the new Dronsley Golf Club. He liked golf and now he could play for nothing without a long drive. Hector had agreed to do the catering with the first year students in the steam-cleaned stables. A tent had been hired, a great marquee, in fact, for the refreshments. Principal Ness had come round to accepting Bob. At least his daughter seemed much happier now than she had been after the break-up of her previous affair. Principal Ness's secretary was planning to get married as well, to the verger. The other woman was his sister who he had been kissing goodbye. She was back to waiting hand and foot on the 'Great Man' and was very grateful for bringing the verger back into her life.

Mr Parable had put in for the principal's post and Miss Todd was not so happy. She hoped that Mr Parable would not come to upset the discipline of the college of further education. She had been horrified when she had seen him marching round with the other interviewees for principal's post.

Meanwhile, there was a new chef at the Southern Constellation, the fifteenth in less than twelve months. Captain William Britain had been cashiered for misappropriation of cigarettes and chocolates from compo rations. There was no actual tangible proof that Captain William Britain had actually misappropriated the said rations but the cigarettes had gone at Captain Britain's new posting, just after Captain Britain arrived. The warrant officer who was the only other person with a key to the special stores was in sick quarters from before the delivery of the partially incomplete compo rations. The CO had always had the cigarettes for use as reward for various people who aided the army or himself in various ways. The CO was suspicious and had enquiries made at Captain Britain's previous posting. Private Wimple had blown the whistle in vengeance for much past ridicule and much army hassle as regards extra bull nights and kit inspections. Captain Britain had got off relatively lightly because no one knew what had happened to the cigarettes and chocolates. (In actual fact, Captain Britain's nine children had eaten all the chocolates and the cigarettes had been bartered for brandy. No money had changed hands and no incriminating packaging had been found.) A search of Captain

Britain's double-married quarter had proved fruitless. In view of the lack of evidence, Captain Britain had no criminal record entries on the pay book but it was difficult to get a reference because of the unanswered questions. Captain Britain had asked his brother for guidance. In spite of the curry incident, blood is thicker than water. Hector had put his brother in contact with Mrs Kelly and ex-captain Britain had moved in on a temporary basis whilst he could find accommodation for his wife and nine children. The large family were still temporarily housed in the double-married quarter at Aldershot, but the Roman Catholic padre was rapidly running out of stalling time. It should be mentioned that Captain Britain had married a staunch Roman Catholic girl who would not risk excommunication by practising birth control. Since Captain Britain was a once-per-night man, at the very least, the large family was inevitable. However, hope was yet eternal. Captain Britain had the Roman Catholic priest of Dronsley on his side and it seemed likely that council accommodation would be forthcoming.

There was also another part-time member of staff at the Southern Constellation. One, Jimmy Graham, was working as a part-time waiter. Jimmy was saving up for a motor bike. Mr Graham had promised that Jimmy should never ever borrow the family car again. Jimmy sometimes wanted a night out in far-off Sheffield but the bus service was not cheap and the last bus left Sheffield at 9.48 p.m. Since Mr Graham was unwilling to turn out after 9 p.m. which was even earlier, it appeared that Jimmy's social life would have to evolve around Dronsley and Dronsley was even less lively than far-off Sheffield. Beverley went to ballroom dancing classes in Sheffield but her uncle brought her home afterwards in his MG two-seater sports car. Jimmy was still regarded as *persona non grata* by Mr Smythe Browne. If only Jimmy could get transport back from Sheffield he could go down on the bus and stay until 10.45 p.m. when Beverley was picked up by her uncle. Mrs Graham had obtained a promise from Mr Graham that Mr Graham would equal whatever Jimmy could save up in a three-month period. Mr Graham thought that he was on a reasonably safe wicket. What Mr Graham didn't know was that Mrs Graham was in charge of the Yorkshire Penny Bank pass book and she was putting £1 per week in. Jimmy was doing quite well as a waiter and getting quite a few tips and was selling off his stamp collection to raise funds as well. He was also saving his dinner money, or most of it, because he received a big meal from ex-captain William Britain because Jimmy made sure any unused wine returned from customers went back to the kitchen. William Britain used this wine for cooking and kept the bottles of wine ordered from the bar unopened. In spite of this, William Britain maintained good food costs by astute buying and skilful use of cheaper ingredients. The bottles of unopened wine were used for the odd special party for such as the Dronsley Pigeon Fanciers of which Taffy the barman was an *ex officio* member, and the local branch of the TA. Such favours were returned in kind. Ex-Captain Britain was never short of a pint. Taffy dined well and often took home fillet steak for tea and Jimmy was doing very well in saving for a motor bike. Nola, the head waitress, suspected nothing as she kept out of the ktichen as much as possible. William Britain was even worse than Hector.

Beverley went dancing in Sheffield on Tuesdays and rarely went out at any other time. This dancing was a new venture because it seemed a useful way of introducing Beverley to boys other than those at college. It seemed that any boys at college could only be like that dreadful gormless Jimmy Graham. Her mother knew that Beverley was friendly with Jimmy because she had seen them together when she went to the college for lunch. The college had a diners' club and membership was a very valuable concession because the college meals were produced at cost and the food was generally top quality even though it was a teaching situation. Mrs Smythe Browne used her husband's card, as it was not often that he could use it himself, unless he could get away to entertain a county education official because Mr Parable was tied up. The chance to escape had been frequent under old Millipede's regime but Mr Parable had delegated nearly all the supervisory work to Mr Smythe Browne. Mr Parable was a part-time justice of the peace, he was a member of the newly-formed educational executive, he was in the masons and he was in the Rotary Club, Mr Parable regularly went to seminars at the education meetings at Whitehall. Most headmasters of schools would not circulate all that much but Mr Parable was going places. He had promised to recommend Mr Smythe Browne for headmaster should Mr Smythe Browne move on.

'I may be in with a chance for the principal's job at the Dronsley College,' he confided to Mr Smythe Browne.

Mr Smythe Browne wished him all the best. Taffy was stirring up trouble about the non-gender sex education and the new cookery teacher had had a nervous breakdown teaching the boys cookery. The incidence of staff sickness was very high, and there had been murmurings from the Parent Teacher Association with regards to concern about the lack of discipline. The school children knew there was no cane anymore and truancy was higher, the school certificate examinations would probably produce very poor results this year and some of the mud would splatter Mr Smythe Browne, he thought. Taffy had put this more succinctly.

'The shite is about to hit the fan, boyo, and you'll be buried in it,' he said.

Ex-Captain William Britain viewed his Southern Constellation appointment with mixed feelings. Mrs Kelly was constantly on patrol with her obnoxious poodles at first, but he had cured this problem.

'I think there are cockroaches here,' he said, but he had not put down insecticide. The dead cockroaches scattered around had been planted by William himself. 'I can get rid of them,' he said confidentially, 'and you don't want the health inspector round.'

William had used the money to purchase pepper dust

and another sort of animal repellent. The cockroach story was to cover up for the liberal quanties of repellent which William put down.

'The dogs don't like that insecticide,' she said as her obnoxious poodles took one sniff at the repellent and retreated, yelping in thwarted kitchen invasion mood.

'No, they don't, do they,' said William innocently.

Best pest control ever, he thought to himself, It was, in fact, a very, very good pest control system as ex-Captain William Britain found that by turning up the bottoms of the chef's trousers he could fill the turn-ups with more pepper dust and the pampered poodles refrained from nipping his ankle as reprisal. The other really big advantage was that Mrs Kelly rarely came in the kitchen now, which was why he was able to liaise with Taffy who was an almost full-time barman now. Taffy was planning to give up teaching. He had become somewhat disgruntled with his charges before Mr Parable but the girls were the last straw. Taffy virtually ran the bar now as the full-time barman was getting past it as regards the heavy cellar work. This was why the embryonic diversion of wines had started 'innocently' at an unofficial TA meeting.

William Britain's *début* had not been promising. On his first day there had been a wedding booked for one Arthur O'Dare, a brother of the Lothario who had seduced Sylvia and half the wenches of Dronsley. Arthur had begun to emulate his brother's example but when threatened with castration or worse by the girl's elder brothers, Arthur had proposed marriage. Taffy had ordered ten cases of Guinness for the wedding and normally the Southern Constellation used less than one case per month. Taffy was hoping to get hold of some real 'poteen' and was anxious that the drinks should not run out for the Irish wedding.

William Britain had loaned Jimmy to make piles of sandwiches. William had made fried bread hedgehogs which consisted of carved quartern loaves carved and shaped like hedgehogs. The spines were cocktail sticks filled with diced cheese, gherkins, olives, pineapples, small pickled onions, tomato wedges, diced cucumber etc. Gala pies had been cut up small and there were scotch eggs, cocktail sausages and cocktail sausage rolls. The party were due to arrive at 3 p.m., but 3.30 p.m. arrived and there was no sign of any of them. Hector Britain had introduced Taffy to his brother and so William at least had his pint lined up.

'Just the one, paid for, Mrs K,' said William.

It was the third actually and none had been paid for but it certainly did not show. Ex-Captain Britain had graduated in officers' mess bars and SNCO's bars, especially the latter, and had an infinite resistance to the effects of alcohol. Mrs Kelly was hovering and Nola seemed uncomfortable. Nola had taken the booking.

'Perhaps you should ring up the church,' said William Britain helpfully.

'I don't know which church it is,' said Nola.

'Try the booking's telephone number,' said William.

Nola went away to see if contact could be made but there was no reply.

'They are probably at the church. Try the Roman Catholic church,' said William.

Nola returned to say that there was no Arthur O'Dare booked there and that the priest had been very rude. Arthur O'Dare was well-known for trying to get Catholic girls into trouble. He was a 'filthy' Protestant. It was now half-past-four with still no arrivals.

'Try ringing round the other churches. It's a good job people pay deposits as there will be a lot of food wasted here.'

'I don't know what we'll do with the Guinness,' said Taffy.

Eventually, one of the churches disclosed the information that Arthur O'Dare had disappeared back to Ireland like his brother before him. The wedding had been cancelled two weeks ago. Further information from Nola revealed that she had not taken a deposit. Mrs Kelly went mad. William Britain called her a 'silly cow'. Taffy got a rollocking from the full-time barman.

'We'll have to have an Irish Night with half-price Guinness and free buffet,' said William with inspiration.

William had rung up his brother, Hector, who had contacted the nearest army camps. Mrs Kelly was most impressed at William's initiative which at least helped remove the stock of Guinness. The buffet was displayed in a fenced-off area 3s 6d per time but it did not bring in a lot of revenue as the hordes of off-duty soldiers demolished everything in sight. Nola escaped with a final warning, probably about the twentieth. In fact, it was really highly improbable that Mrs Kelly could obtain another employee so cheaply.

'If you pay peanuts, you get monkeys,' said ex-Captain Britain philosophically.

In fact, ex-Captain Britain wanted much more pay than that offered but first of all he had to gain a sound footing with Mrs Kelly.

Two nights later there was another cock up on the catering front. It was 5.30 p.m. when William arrived back on duty to find two legs of pork in the kitchen ready for cooking, together with a note saying that the meal would be for 8.30 p.m. for fifty people. This time the culprit was not Nola but the matriarch herself, Mrs Kelly. William had started off stating rather pointedly that he could not cook legs of pork in such a time, especially in a defunct oven with no bottom in.

'What about the vegetable preparation?' said William.

William considered walking out, but the Southern Constellation did have potential. He knew he could use the potatoes prepared for the following day and the menu was for peach melba, which was very easy anyhow. William was offered five hours' overtime if, *if*, the meal went all right. He would have to come in earlier in the morning to catch up, but he would cope.

Cream of tomato soup
Roast leg of pork with apple sauce
Roast and creamed potatoes
Garden peas
Buttered carrots
Peach Melba

William inspected the stores. There was only one gallon packet of tomato soup powder. There was no tinned apples. The fruit consisted of an A10 of pears, two A10s of peaches and an A10 of apricots. There were, however, three cases of potato powder tucked underneath six cases of Christmas pudding. There were lots of baked beans and tinned tomatoes and of course, the lines of various soups and the sponge puddings. Quick counter-measures were imperative.

William ended up slicing the pork and cooking it as escalopes. The potatoes were cut up and browned in the chip fryer whilst this happened and William put a few potato chunks on the stove to boil up for the mashed potatoes. Mrs Kelly wisely kept out of the way. She was a born leader. She was conspicuous by her painful presence in times of calm. In times of crisis she would keep a low profile. Nola was a good disciple. She had summed up William Britain very quickly. She knew about his relationship with Hector but she had not confided this to her aides, Enid and Ethel. They came through to inspect the new chef. They only worked on special occasions.

'Good evening, chef,' said Ethel pleasantly.

'Good evening, chef,' echoed Enid.

'How are you getting on here, chef?' asked Ethel.

'Bloody awful,' said William. 'I'm in the shit.'

'Oooh,' said Enid, 'he's another rude one, like Mr Hector.'

'What's on tonight, chef?' said Ethel. 'And how many?'

'Roast pork, and haven't you got something to do? I haven't got time to talk. I'm in the shit,' said William Britain.

'You need not be so unfriendly, chef,' said Enid. 'It's not our fault you're in the shit. Ooh, is that the pork, chef?'

'Yes it is. Piss off,' said William, rudely.

'He's worse than Hector,' said Ethel. 'If that's possible,' she added.

'I'm Hector's brother, so piss off,' said William.

'Oooooh,' exclaimed Ethel and Enid simultaneously.

'Aren't you going to put it in the oven, chef?' asked Enid timidly.

'No, I'm not. Mind your own business and *piss off*,' said William loudly, culminating in the shouted order to evacuate his kitchen.

'Ooh, we're going to see Mrs Kelly about you,' they said together.

'As long as you piss off you can go and see the Archbishop of Canterbury for all I care,' said William.

The two returned with Mrs Kelly and the yapping poodles.

'You've upset the waitresses,' said Mrs Kelly.

'They've upset me,' said William coldly. 'Am I going to try to get this meal out or am I leaving?'

'You must not get under chef's feet,' said Mrs Kelly, realizing that the kitchen without a chef was a real crisis situation.

'Aren't you going to put the pork in the oven?' she then asked.

'I'll have my cards, please,' said Hector. 'You know best. You take over and put those two in here.'

'Don't be hasty, chef,' said Mrs Kelly, in an attempt to placate him.

'He hasn't put enough potatoes on either,' said Ethel to her friend Enid, in a voice loud enough for Mrs Kelly to hear.

'*And* he minced up tinned pears instead of apples,' said Enid, in return.

Reason had won the day and William had been persuaded to stay. It was then that William's menu modifications had taken place. The final aberration was the need to substitute apricots to extend the peaches for the peach Melba. Mrs Kelly had discovered that all the shelves of fruits and sauces had been used up by the previous chef. The benefits to William from these initial set-backs had been considerable. Mrs Kelly recognized a professional cowboy chef when she saw one.

> Cream Malakoff
> Escalope of Pork with Cider Sauce
> Roast and Creamed Potatoes
> Garden Peas
> Buttered Carrots
> Peach Melba

William extended the tomato soup with potato powder and shredded some cauliflower leaves to impersonate spinach. He stirred some cider into the minced pears. He could hardly make apple sauce without apples, and pears were the same colour as apples. The few potatoes were boiled to make lumps in the powdered mash potato so that William did not need to use up all his *mise en place* potatoes for the following day.

23

THE GREAT OUTDOORS

Hector Britain had risen very early to organize the meal for Bob and Sylvia's wedding. College had broken up the day before and there had been a farewell reception for Principal Elliot Ness. The 'Great Man' had almost been reduced to tears as they gave him his farewell presentation of a beautiful oil painting of Victorian Dronsley. Mrs Ness had received a large bouquet of flowers and caretaker Sam Browne had plaintively played the last post on a bugle, in spite of a half-hearted attempt to shut him up.

The Elliot household had been deluged with mail, some with best wishes for the principal's retirement and much more for congratulations for the forthcoming bride. Principal Ness had been very pleased when Hector, at a fee, offered to organize the catering. Principal Ness had said that the stables were being steam-cleaned and Hector had inspected them and had approved their use. He had offered advice as to how a catering operation could work as he thought that this might be a useful sideline for his brother in case the Southern Constellation did not work out. William's wife had come over from Ireland with the youngest three children and they were staying with Hector. Hector wanted them out. He did not mind his brother's wife. He had had a close association with her in the past but although she was almost a nymphomaniac with her husband, Brigitte had never had sex outside marriage. She bore no malice towards Hector, in spite of a near seduction during William's detachment abroad, and he, in turn, still had fond thoughts. Surprisingly, Hector's wife and Brigitte got on really well together. In fact, nearly everyone got on well with Brigitte. She was a typical Irish rose, she was lovely, she was vivacious and she was very, very astute. The one really amazing thing was how such a lovely girl could have fallen for a barbarian like ex-Captain Britain or, indeed, nearly fell for a barbarian like Hector Britain.

Hector had planned a menu of appetisers for the immediate reception, to be followed by a sit-down meal in the evening. It was early April and therefore it was hoped for a reasonably mild temperature for the great outdoors.

Hector had borrowed some trestles for use as tables and he had also loaned some temporary cookers fuelled by Calor gas. There was an electric supply aleady set up but there were only two plugs for the electric friers, the mixer, and two electric hot plates. The sit down meal was;

>Melon boat or prawn cocktail
>Chicken Maryland
>New potatoes
>Cauliflower and peas
>Sherry trifle
>or fruit gateaux

The appetisers were:

>Open sandwiches
>Sausage rolls
>Scotch eggs
>Gala pie
>Quiche Lorraine
>*Goujons* of plaice
>*Beignets* with Parmesan

The major problem was the water supply, as stables only require cold water. There was a cold water supply at one end but this water supply was away from the zone most suitable for setting up the kitchen. Miss Todd had been subcontracted to carry out the baking and the sherry trifles and gateaux. She had sought and obtained permission to carry out the baking at college, using her students, and her commission had been donated to the Salvation Army. She had worked with Beverley, Susan and Debbie and the girls had been rewarded generously as well. Miss Todd had seen the primitive facilities and declined to work there. The gateaux and trifle completion was to take place at her house as the college was closed on Saturdays. She was not happy at the prospects of having Mr Parable as the new principal and there was no point in creating potential trouble before he assumed command.

Hector had had the equipment set up the previous day. The hot water was to come from a huge stockpot set up on a Calor Gas fired gas-burner stand. There was an extra large cylinder for this but the gas burners did not seem to show a lot of pressure when Hector lit up. There was plenty of time, though, so Hector was not unduly worried.

Hector connected the long, long winding hosepipe which was to feed into one of two large rain butts which had drain taps underneath. Jimmy had been solicited as one of the students working with Hector and he was to be put in charge of water supplies. If one butt became full, the water supply should be rerouted to the second and so on. It also turned out that the water supply was not strong either. Jimmy was on duty at the Southern Constellation that evening but he was not due on duty there until 6 p.m. He, therefore, started out at work with Hector first thing. The extra money would be another £6 towards the motor cycle collection. Jimmy had £61 already and the bike he wanted was only £160. He was looking forward to taking the bike out. What Jimmy had forgotten, though, was the court appearance. The wheels of justice grind very slowly. Mr Graham senior had not forgotten, though, and he was hoping that the wheels of justice would speed up. He had seen inside the Yorkshire Penny Bank pass book.

Sylvia had arrived home on the Friday and was ensconced in her bedroom which she shared for the night with Susan, her niece.

'Why do people get married?' asked the little girl.

'It's because they love each other,' said Sylvia.

'Is that why they sleep together?' asked the little girl. 'Mummy says you have to be married for ladies and gentlemen to sleep together. You and Uncle Bob were sleeping together so why do you have to get married again?'

Sylvia would have preferred to be in bed with Bob. The little girl kept rolling over and taking all the covers. She kept jabbing her in the ribs and she snored. This after all the earlier problems of the embarrassing questions which required very carefully thought-out answers. On top of this, Sylvia was concerned about whether she was doing the right thing. There was no second thoughts about how much she loved Bob. It was the time-scale that worried her. She was determined to complete her studies in June, but the qualification had limited use in the Dronsley location. She did not want to leave her father to live far away as she knew how badly the retirement might affect him. She had been very close to her father, even though it did not show. Sylvia and Bob could not move in together until he qualified in June, or should qualify in June, she added to herself as an afterthought. How would they get on together as well, she thought. The decision to get married so soon had been a desperate reaction because of the horror expressed by her father at knowing that they had been to bed together. The fact that her father had been as bad before he married her mother was not at issue. Many people have double standards and no father likes to think of the loss of his daughter's chastity any more than any mother thinks that there is a woman worthy of her son. Perhaps it might have seemed a better time in summer to be married but she had had to convince her father that she was serious. The sudden impact had convinced him and he had accepted the inevitable, namely that his daughter would marry the most unlikely candidate. She had also missed her last period and could be pregnant but she could not bring herself to tell Bob until after the wedding. That last night together had been quite a momentous one. She was not worried about the effect on Bob but she was worried about becoming a mother so soon before they had even chosen a home. Bob had to find a job as well.

Bob had an early rise that morning too as he was setting out from Garnstone. He had decided against staying overnight in Dronsley in case he ran into Sylvia. The honeymoon night was to be at the Southern Constellation and then they would drive down to the Dotheboys Holiday Camp, with two days to spare. Mrs Becksworth had arranged a chalet for them but apologised for the bunk beds.

'You'd better not pee on me when you have the top bunk,' Sylvia had said to him. They were in touch by telephone every Saturday and Sunday night since the engagement. They also wrote twice per week. These were the only concessions Sylvia had allowed from her studies.

'We both need to concentrate on our studies and qualify,' she said.

'When I said I would sleep on top, I had another arrangement in mind,' said the rampant Bob.

Bob did not have a stag night this time. He had decided to keep the event secret and had persuaded Miss Pringle to do the same. When Bob had married previously he had had to face a lot of baiting in the RAF camp. His mates had caught him and pulled his trousers and underpants down. Whilst spreadeagled helplessly his pride and joy and the family jewels had been daubed luminous green with food colouring. On top of this he got a rash from the allergy. His first wife had roared with laughter and it had been almost a week before he could consummate the marriage. Bob had no doubts about the marriage either but he wished that he had a job to go to. Now he was speeding up north with Veronica, the only one let in on the secret other than Miss Pringle. She would bring Veronica back so that Bob did not need a detour.

The day had remained dry with a watery sun keeping the

temperature quite cool. Hector and his students had prepared and covered the sandwiches to keep them from curling up. The Scotch eggs had been fried and the two hotplates had been heated one at a time before putting them on one adaptor. Hector put the two friers onto the second adaptor and the fuse blew.

'Bloody thing,' Hector blasphemed.

Hector went to his car to get some fuses. He got one frier hot before he plugged in the second. It remained operational.

The group, who claimed to be like the Beatles, were tuning up in the marquee. The washing-up water from the stock pot never seemed to get hot. There was problems with the potatoes, too, although Hector didn't realize it at the time as he had only just put them on to boil.

'Calor gas isn't very effective is it, chef?' observed Jimmy.

Hector told Jimmy to start frying the *goujons*. The first lot went in OK but when the second lot was added to the second friture the temperature went down and the fuse blew again. Hector sent Jimmy off down the road for more fuses but he coped temporarily by taking the fuses from the hotplates. He cursed loudly as he did so. David Fretwork took over on the *friture* when the fuses were replaced.

Stella and the remaining girls from the group were working with Mr Naunders who was also involved. Stella was wearing her hot-pants and a tight blouse on her upper body. She radiated sex as usual. She was waiting to see Bob Malone to give him a wedding kiss. She was also keen to inspect the bride.

'I wish it were me,' she confided to Susan Miller.

'You've never been the same since you squeezed his willy,' said Susan in somewhat poor taste.

Meanwhile, the zone around the water butts had become somewhat soggy. When Hector sent someone to turn the water off, the butts were rapidly emptied. When the water pressure returned the butts filled and overflowed. He couldn't put someone to work near the tap because it was so far away. David returned with the fuses. A packet of ten fuses had been requested. Hector tried to operate with a frier and a hotplate on each plug. The fuses blew. Hector decided to turn off the hotplates and work with a frier on each plug. This seemed to work but there was only residual heat in the hotplates to keep the *goujons* and cheese fritters hot. It was then that the advance party and the bride and groom arrived. Hector decided to compromise and made do with one frier. However, the fuses on the hotplates blew again. Hector used his previous ploy of pre-heating each hotplate once more on the separate plugs before putting the hot plates on one plug together. '*Shite!*' Hector kept exclaiming.

Meanwhile the Earwigs, a pun on the Beatles, had started playing. A loud throbbing beat echoed from the marquee. The remaining guests were arriving and Mr Naunders sent out the food service girls and boys to circulate with the appetisers. Hector had his frier going again to finish off the *goujons* and to start off on the cheese fritters. Since the hotplates were half-empty Hector decided to plug in the second frier again. Simultaneously the Earwigs started up their flashing lights display.

The DER DER DER : DER DER DER DER DER (If there is anything that you like) became DER . . . DER . . . DER . . . D . . . D. The flashing lights faded and died and Hector's fuses blew again.

'*Shite,*' exclaimed Hector.

Hector unplugged the friers to change the fuses. The lights lit up again and the DER . . . DER . . . DER . . . DER etc speeded up again. The puzzled Earwigs resumed their gyrations and off-key music making. Hector, being Hector, had not connected the two incidents, however, because he could not see inside the marquee.

Ex-Principal Elliot Ness came round to inspect the catering facilities as Hector was about to replace the plugs with their new fuses.

'Well done, Mr Britain,' congratulated Mr Ness.

He was enjoying being the centre of attention. His

toupee had been dusted and donned. He had congratulated Bob and Sylvia and he was feeling proud of this new venture with the masons. The Earwigs were in full throes and were producing considerable noise when Jimmy inserted another batch of *goujons* in each *friture*. The temperatures cut out and the *friture* elements cut in again. The distant noise slowed once more and cut out in succession to the pops of the *friture* blown fuses.

'*Shite,*' said Hector but not quite so loud as before. After all, ex-Principal Ness had only been an ex-Principal since yesterday and he was being paid as principal for another fortnight yet.

The cheese fritters were aborted and once it was realized that the *fritures* and band were dependent on the same circuit, Hector was forced to compromise with use of one *friture*. As a result the roast potatoes, which in actual fact were fried boiled potatoes, were to be late. The new potatoes were late in cooking because the gas pressure had delayed the boiling of the 'roast potatoes'. It was then that the major gas cylinder cut out completely. It was empty.

'*Bloody hell,*' said Hector.

Miss Todd arrived with the sherry trifles and fruit gateaux, fortunately assembled well away from the primitive steam-cleaned stables.

'I have to go now, chef,' said Jimmy, as he was due at the Southern Constellation.

'*Piss off,*' said Hector ungratefully.

'Have you paid him?' asked Miss Todd. 'And I do wish you would refrain from such coarse language. Come girls,' said Miss Todd to her girls.

Jimmy squeezed in the back with them and managed to squeeze Beverley's left nipple as though accidentally.

'Pervert,' said Debbie sat on the other side. They were speaking again but Jimmy would never be granted a repeat session, Debbie vowed resolutely.

David Fretwork took over on the friers whilst Hector set about frying chicken. The cauliflower was waiting to replace the potatoes on the other stove. Bob also came round to see Hector and he brought Sylvia with him. Stella and Susan did not see Sylvia who was trailing behind having stopped to look at the puddle which was slowly expanding due to an overspill from the rain-butts. Bob bent down to pick up something glinting on the ground.

'Now's your chance, Stella, grab him by the balls as you usually do,' Susan whispered to her.

Bob swung round, '*Don't you dare*,' he exclaimed.

Stella blushed and Susan would have done so but it would not have shown on her dark, smooth ebony skin.

'What's going on?' asked Sylvia. 'You surely can't have been fooling around with young girls. Oh, how could you?' Sylvia rushed off in tears.

'I hope you're satisfied,' said Bob, dashing after her to explain what had happened.

Sylvia would not talk to him but she went and hid in the ladies' toilet. Hector learned what had gone on and sent the two girls in to explain.

The peace declared and the function served up one and a quarter hours later, the wedding speeches over, there was nothing left but the festivities to continue into the night. Bob and Sylvia sneaked away in a taxi. There was an A40 in the carpark belonging to Giles Parable who had been invited along with all the Parable family for old times' sake. The students tied dozens of cans to the exhaust, daubed the windows with shaving foam and they had blown up contraceptives and fastened them to door handles and wing mirrors. Giles had brought the vicar's daughter with him but he would not find out about the mistaken identity until later.

Ten minutes after the departure of the bride and groom there was a final bang. The puddle had become a lake and the lake had found a gully which in turn had flooded and run downhill. At the bottom of the hill was the Earwigs disco cable together with the marquee lighting system.

Bob and Sylvia were oblivious to all this. The lovely white gown was removed and Bob had Sylvia laid out on the bed kissing her passionately.

24

RETRIBUTION

The Fanshawe Secondary School was returning to the former semblance of normality before Mr Parable had arrived. The cookery teacher had made a rapid recovery from her nervous breakdown since the boys were no longer allowed into the sanctum of femininity. Taffy had promised to soldier on until at least the end of the summer term. The staff were cooperative and helpful and wholeheartedly behind Mr Smythe Browne's bid for the headship. Better the devil you know than another liberal evangelist like Mr Parable. The cane was reinstated and used rather more than it had been in the old days before it had been banned with Mr Parable's cultural revolution. Prefects were selected by staff, not by democratic student elections. The numerous meetings had been replaced by a resumption of normal teaching schedules. It was quite imperative that the examination results, which had been jeopardized by the interrupted classes and lack of discipline, were not so bad that Mr Smythe Brown's position was jeopardized. The staff had seen the face of the future and did not like it.

The dinner ladies were jubilant too. They had not liked the insults received from students who did not want nut cutlets and salads and the like for lunch. The ladies did not like cleaning up the mess from bun fights. The caretaker was in high spirits because the piles of litter and graffiti had reduced overnight. The blackboards were no longer chalked with obscene messages and the seats were no longer stuck up with chewing gum.

There were even several students who were pleased with the return of law and order. The more mature had realized how far behind their studies had fallen. The bullied were not so bullied any more with the return of teachers' morale and vigilance. It was true that Mr Smythe Browne had tried to resist the tide but the ultimate arbiter, Mr Parable, had always supported the so-called underdog, which was the voice against authority. Like all so-called liberal modernist democrats, though, Mr Parable did not accept the democratic view unless it was Mr Parable's view. As an intellectual he knew best. The staff's misgivings were subdued by using sycophants to support the headmaster's ideas and these were rewarded by extra responsibilities and powers. Mr Foskett and Mr Johnson had been keen supporters of Mr Parable and had received extra responsibilities, allowances and grandiose titles of non-specific gender educational coordinator and student guidance mentor coordinator respectively. The first thing Mr Smythe Browne did was to abolish these posts and so that they did not lose out on money they became playground and luncheon liaison officer and buildings and maintenance liaison supervisory officer. In view of their lack of sympathy from other members of staff, this served to make their re-education acceptable. It also meant that the ancillary staff knew who to take their initial problems to. Perhaps not unsurprisingly, the two new officers were very quickly re-educated into the ways of authoritarianism. Dinner ladies can be very forceful in their ways. One or two undisciplined students had been complaining about short rations to Mr Parable. Some down-right creeps who had flattered the ladies about their new hairstyle, the lovely jam-roly poly etc, had seemed to receive larger portions. Justice was now served by the playground and luncheon liaison supervisory officer. Bun fights and references of comparison as regards the dinner ladies and bovinary mammals had ceased. Portion control was much more equitable as there was very little breach of etiquette. Furthermore, the buildings and maintenance liaison supervisory officer had reduced vandalism and graffiti down to negligible proportions. He had tracked down the person who had written on the staff tablecloth 'MR FOSKETT AND MR JOHNSON ARE POOFTERS' and in the process had also located the person suggesting that 'MR SMYTHE BROWNE SHOULD TAKE EARLY RETIREMENT'. This notice had appeared outside the meeting of the board of governors when the appointment for headship was being considered. It had been a substantial influence in the decision to promote Mr Smythe Browne. The chairman of the committee had observed the fall in standards during Mr Parable's term of office and he had noted the re-establishment of tidiness and discipline during Mr Smythe Brown's regency. The chairman was also on the Dronsley College of Educations board of governors and had been the one voice against the committee's decision to appoint Mr Parable principal.

Mr Johnson had a particular group of students as suspects. 5 X's homework had been checked.

'Look at the "Rs",' said Mr Foskett who had been called in by his friend as consultant.

The two were at the time studying the defaced tablecloth and comparing it with the defamatory notice. They might not have been so keen to solve crimes suggesting Mr Smythe Browne's early retirement but this new allegation was a personal attack.

'Look at the "Rs",' repeated Mr Foskett.

'Oh, yes,' said Mr Johson, the penny dropping belatedly.

'They are funny "Rs",' said Mr Foskett.

'Pardon,' said Mr Johnson looking out of the window into the playground.

'Oh, yes, I see what you mean.'

The culprit turned out to be a new boy, one Frederick Britain. Frederick was one of the new intake from the Britain family who was living in a caravan parked behind the Southern Constellation. He was a son of the ex-Captain William Britain. Frederick had welcomed the lack of discipline which had been the scene of his arrival. As the son of the officer class he had decided that the previous liberal *status quo* should be maintained so that he might possibly organize a Frederick Britain protection racket. Frederick Britain was the eldest and his Irish mother had brought him up in an admirable Irish tradition. When there is one child the mother will punish any wrongdoing. When there are two, and the eldest is old enough, she will delegate her authority. She punishes the eldest for the crimes of the younger. She then supervises so that the punishment is not excessive whilst the first punishes the second. She will similarly delegate her protection so that the eldest will try to protect the younger from any external bullying. This process of delegation is carried on down through to the third, the fourth etc *ad infinitum*. This is a primary reason for the closeness of Irish family life and it also maintains a semblance of order and relief from stress of maternity in large families. On the debit-side it might have ended up as very dangerous in the vacuum of law and order of the previous Mr Parable's regime. Frederick Britain had, therefore, already received three doses of the renewed caning system.

If the staff at the Fanshawe Secondary School were elated at the demise of the Parable regime, it should be said that this was not the case with the Food and Beauty staff of the Dronsley College of Further Education. The initial joy at losing the despot, Principal Elliot Ness, was being very rapidly tempered. Mr Parable had many contacts in the education ministry and he was well-known for his innovation in curriculum development: the negotiated curriculum, non-specific gender education, anti-corporal punishment campaigns, ethnic minority encouragement schemes, non-examination curricula etc were all part of the Parable doctrine. Miss Todd had had constant update from the Fanshawe Secondary School since she left and Mr Britain knew all to well what was happening as well from his TA friend Taffy.

Mr Potterton was not over-happy either. Mr Parable had introduced a NO SMOKING campaign. Mr Potterton inherited a regime whereby the principal's decrees were law. No one had argued with Principal Ness very much, not even in his last term. Mr Potterton had been puffing away at his pipe when notified by the principal's new secretary that Mr Parable was approaching. Mr Potterton hastily extinguished his pipe and put it in his pocket and opened the windows wide to dissipate the fumes from the pipe. There was a knock at the door and Mr Parable strolled in.

'I do hope I'm not disturbing you, Charles,' said Mr Parable.

'No, of course not, Mr Parable,' said Mr Potterton deferentially.

'What smells? *You are not smoking at work, Charles?*' enquired Mr Parable.

'Oh, no, Mr Parable, of course not,' spluttered Mr Potterton.

'Call me Horatio, Charles, Horatio, I do so hate formality.'

Mr Parable sniffed suspiciously.

'Perhaps the gardener is burning leaves,' said Mr Potterton helpfully.

'Do you mind if I close the window?' asked Mr Parable.

'Of course not, Mr Parable,' said Mr Potterton.

'Horatio, do call me Horatio,' said the new principal.

Mr Parable then set out outlining his proposed policies. The pipe in Mr Potterton's pocket began to smoulder.

Mr Horatio Parable went on about his negotiated curriculum and said that he would like to bring in a friend who taught plumbers at the Ecclestown College of Further Education.

'There's still a burning smell, Charles,' he said suddenly. 'I'm sure that that dreadful aroma of burning compost is coming from within this very room.'

However, Mr Parable continued and the smouldering increased. Mr Potterton could feel something hot penetrating through to his shirt. He reached down and let out a howl as he felt burning. Mr Potterton jumped to his feet and ripped off the offending jacket, much to Mr Parable's amazement. The pipe fell out of the jacket and splattered sparks everywhere and the jacket began to smoulder into flame. Mr Potterton jumped up and down on the zone of potential conflagration.

'*You were smoking, Charles, and moreoever, you tried to mislead me,*' said Principal Horatio Parable.

Mr Parable was also a firm believer in close contact with students and he had actually asked to be involved in teaching himself as well as also expecting heads of department to teach for three hours per week.

'Perhaps I shall take early retirement this year, Hector,' said Mr Potterton to Mr Britain. 'I did find Principal Ness somewhat overbearing but at least you knew where you stood. By the way, all classes are cancelled next Thursday afternoon as he is bringing in his plumber friend to instruct us in something called a competency learning.'

'I can't understand the bloody man,' said Hector, forgetting himself for a moment. 'I'm sorry, Mr Potterton, I should not have said that,' said Hector apologetically.

'It's quite all right, Hector,' said Mr Potterton. 'I can't understand him either. I've turned a blind eye to some of your rough army ways because it has meant that we can maintain standards but I'm afraid you will have to ease up a bit with this chap. Come back, Elliot, all is forgiven.'

The conversation continued about the increase in litter and graffiti. It then drifted back to the competency learning.

The catering department staff and the hairdressers were assembled to meet Archibald Parable who was an adviser from the Ministry of Education. Mr Archibald, called Archie by the new Principal, had been a plumber but had been unsuccessful. He had received top theory marks in the City and Guilds plumbing examinations but had failed the practical three times before passing. His employer found him invaluable as a sales person as he could make the most simple job sound like a major refurbishment and his employer had put in bills accordingly. When one of the fitters had been off sick Archie had been used as a temporary stand-in on the practical work. In drilling to lay new pipes Archie had hit a main water line and two blocks of flats had had to use standpipes for three days as a result. The water had blown the electric circuits of the blocks of flats as well and they had been without electricity, water and lifts for the same length of time. Archie had been advised to leave town and had ended up on a teacher training course. He had passed out with distinctions but his first teaching post had been disastrous. Archie had been showing his students how showers are connected. The showers were in the ladies' changing area for the second floor college gymnasium. It was bad enough that the practical work had disconnected the inlet valve causing the ceiling below to collapse. Two voyeur students had also installed inspection holes so as to peep in on the unsuspecting young ladies. The flooding had meant cleaning up after hours and the two voyeurs had been caught by the two formidable 'butch' cleaning ladies. The voyeurs were expelled and Archie left suddenly 'in breach of the probationary period'. Archie had soon found a job at the Ministry and was now closely involved in curriculum innovation and appraisal.

Archie was a little fat man with spectacles. He had thick bushy black hair, thick bushy eyebrows, a thick bushy handlebar moustache and piercing blue eyes. He sported grey flannels and had a very ostentatious chequered sports coat. His tie had vivid green and red stripes on it.

It was three o'clock in the committee room and a tea trolley had been supplied.

'It's my bloody early day,' said Hector. Hector was obviously not enjoying the prospects of two hours with anyone associated with the new principal.

'If he is as good at lecturing as he is at plumbing, things should be quite extraordinary,' said Miss Todd to Miss Hyacinth who was in the hairdressing section. Miss Todd knew a friend of a friend of one of the inmates of the tower block which had suffered from Mr Archibald Parable's handiwork. Miss Todd had not disclosed her knowledge to anyone other than Miss Hyacinth, however, and so they were unaware of the potential insinuations of Miss Todd's statement.

'I'd rather be here than teaching,' said Mr Naunder. 'If Parable had started sooner I might be senior lecturer now instead of him.' Mr Naunder was speaking to George Farrant who was unimpressed about Hector.

'I should be allowed to go home. In another three months I shall retire to my garden and Parable can take a running jump,' said George Farrant.

'Welcome to this innovation workshop,' said Principal Parable to the assembled minions. 'I'm sure you are all eagerly anticipating this educational initiative called the negotiated curriculum. It is essential that we must stimulate and nurture the students' quest for knowledge in order to maximize the potential benefits of college life. Archie, who is by the way my younger brother, has developed some exciting concepts and hypotheses. Our objectives should be to tailor the individualist demands by means of curriculum development which is appropriate to changing circumstances of student needs,' he said.

'What's he bloody on about?' whispered Hector to George Farrant.

'Sh hhh,' whispered the sycophantic Mr Naunder.

'I don't know and I don't care,' said George Farrant.

Mr Potterton was looking out of the window wistfully.

Mr Archibald Parable took centre stage and introduced his competency approach.

'Every student has a pre-set target of objectives,' said Mr Parable.

Mr Parable passed round a sheath of papers for every member of staff.

'It's all about bloody plumbing,' said Hector disgustedly.

By now Principal Parable had departed for greater things. He had heard it all before and many of the ideas were his ideas anyhow. There was a knock on the door and Mr Potterton's secretary apologized for the interruption.

'I suppose I'll have to pop out,' said Mr Potterton apologetically. 'I'll be back shortly.'

Mr Potterton had prearranged the interruption. The anti-climax of the reprimand on smoking from Principal Parable had removed any major terrors from Mr Potterton's mind. It was obvious that Principal Parable was a grey man without the autocratic personality of his predecessor, Principal Ness. Mr Potterton had no intention of going back if he could help it.

'Mr Britain, make sure you can explain how it works in case I am out for any length of time,' he said to Hector.

Hector Britain looked at the checklist.

BALLCOCK VALVE COMPETENCY

1. DOES THE STUDENT HAVE APPROPRIATE OVERALLS?
2. DOES THE STUDENT HAVE APPROPRIATE SHOES?
3. HAS THE STUDENT HAD A SHAVE?
4. DOES THE STUDENT HAVE HIS BAG OF TOOLS?
5. DOES THE STUDENT KNOW WHAT TASK IS TO BE UNDERTAKEN?
6. DID THE STUDENT SELECT THE OPTION AS A RESULT OF THE CORRECT NEGOTIATED PROCEDURE?
7. HAS THE STUDENT COLLECTED ALL REQUIREMENTS NEEDED TO FIT A BALLCOCK?

The list continued over three pages. There was a little box to place a tick after each stage. Archie was beginning to explain how the system worked but Hector had glanced through the first page in disbelief and anger.

'I don't wish to be rude, Mr Parable,' said Hector, 'but I don't see what relevance this has to catering.'

'Call me Archie,' said Archibald Parable disarmingly.

'Now Mr . . . er,' Hector continued.

'Call him Hector,' said Mr Naunder helpfully.

'It's not got much in common with hairdressing either,' said Mrs Jones.

'All educational philosophy is based in similar criteria,' continued Archie. 'There are two interrelating participants. On the one side is the novitiate seeking knowledge and on the other side there is the oracle disseminating knowledge.'

'He uses a lot of big words for a bloody plumber,' said Hector.

'What's it got to do with hairdressing or chefwork?' said Mrs Jones.

Mrs Jones and Hector got on very well together, though nothing tangible had been seen to happen at college. There had been rumours that Mrs Jones had been away to see her sister in Wales on occasions when the TA had been on detachment in Wales, but perhaps this was coincidental.

'It's a load of "ballcocks",' said George Farrant.

Meanwhile, the Graham household was settling down for Jimmy's court case with reference to 'driving without L-plates and insurance up a one-way street in the wrong direction'. The court case just happened to fall within the same week as the time set for the 'Double your money motor bike deal'.

'I'm not paying your fine either,' said Mr Graham. 'Mind you, you could end up in jail if you are not careful. You'd better plead guilty and say nothing,' advised Mr Graham.

Mr Graham had by now forgiven his son and was, in fact, worried about him. He need not have worried as Jimmy was to get off lightly with an overall £95 fine on all charges. Although permission was given to pay by instalments, Jimmy was advised to pay up and get it out of the way. Nevertheless, Jimmy lost out on the intended 500 c.c. motorbike. Jimmy was to end up with a 150 c.c motorcycle because the breach in the law made Jimmy a poorer insurance risk. Jimmy was very pleased to have the legal proceedings resolved and he now had a motor cycle so that he could stay out longer with Beverley. Jimmy determined to put in for a test so that he could take her on the pillion. Mr Graham had had motor cycles in younger days and so he was able to give free advice in motor cycle maintenance.

25

ON THE MOVE

Ex-Captain Britain was euphoric. He had been allowed two council houses to house the large brood of Britain offspring. The council had obligingly knocked a doorway through the wall where the two lounges backed onto one another. Mrs Kelly had gone off on a world cruise and ex-Captain Britain was operating on a sort of franchise. The council hadn't been told of this, though, when William Britain had submitted his application for advancement on the list. William Britain had brought all the children over from Ireland and stuck them in the caravan which had been moved over to Hector's back garden. Mrs Britain, Hector's wife, had stayed with Mrs Britain, William's wife, for a couple of nights and the others had been allocated into male and female squatters' dormitories. Even if the anonymous phone calls had not worked to put pressure on the council, the ploy would probably have worked because Nigel 'Nosey' Nosegay lived but two doors away from Hector. Nigel Nosegay was chairman of the housing committee and did not appreciate the boisterous cowboy and Indian games played by the Britain clan, especially when he arrived home to find his son Gerald tied to the clothes line post as a captive of the marauding Red Indians. His wife had gone out for the day, thinking that Gerald would be all right for a couple of hours or so as Grandma Nosegay had said she would look in.

Grandma Nosegay was a timid old lady who would not say boo to a ghost. She had very poor eyesight and was well-known for putting sugar in the stew or throwing away the current newspaper which had just arrived. She did not know about the arrival of the Britain clan. She pondered about the 'tents' in the garden as she arrived on foot having walked up from the bus-stop. As she put down her bag to go and investigate the 'tents' in the back garden, she was surrounded by whooping Red Indian braves with Irish accents. She was sufficiently composed to have noticed that it was Gerald tied up to the clothes post but she hadn't noticed that the rope used was the clothes line. She also had not noticed that the 'tents' were created from the sheets which had been put out earlier to dry by the absent Mrs Nosegay. Old Grandma Nosegay fled into the house and locked out the boisterous children. She dialled 999. The upshot was yet another supporting reason to house the Britain clan in an alternative neighbourhood.

Hector had been very relieved to see the departure of his brother's children. Hector had fathered one son, as known, and this son had joined the navy and had last been seen about twelve months ago. He was on a South Pacific posting, but Hector did not mind as the two did not get on all that well. Hector's wife had stayed for the social officer's visit but had departed soon after saying that she would return from mother's when the house was her own again. Hector had taken to working late at college, ex-Captain Britain was working late at the Southern Constellation and Captain Britain's wife had the house and children to herself. In reality, they were fairly well-behaved indoors, but they were boisterous, as young children frequently are. They preferred the great outdoors away from mother's supervision and Hector's normally well-kept garden was ravaged as they dug for buried treasure, played pirates with a plank across the ornamental goldfish pond and played cowboy and Indians with no respect for anyone's garden or flowered borders. Ex-Captain Britain came home every afternoon between the split shifts and he and his wife went upstairs for an afternoon 'nap'. The children were not to disturb their parents' 'siesta' but the elder ones were not so naive that they did not suspect what was going on. Since their mother had spent half her married life walking around like a female barrel due to pregnancy, they would have had to be pretty stupid not to know what was going on. Ex-Captain Britain was euphoric because he had just found a buyer for the caravan. Elliot Ness had been advised by Hector that it could be used as an office for the second access to the new golf course. It was sufficiently mobile to allow certain advantages and it offered overnight accommodation for the builders who were converting the old stables into the new recreation centre. William Britain had recovered the financial outlay with £100 profit for doing the caravan up. The six weeks' use of the caravan had therefore been rent-free. William had been given two complimentary tickets to see Tom Jones. He couldn't stand Tom Jones really but his wife raved over him and would no doubt be very responsive to ex-Captain William Britain afterwards. She probably would pretend that she was making love to Tom Jones instead of ex-Captain William Britain but who cared?

William Britain knew that his wife was in town getting the numerous sets of keys cut so that each one of the Britain clan could gain access in the unlikely event that no one was at home. It was true that there had not been any recent additions to the clan but there had been no obvious reason for this. William Britain had just been grateful. He arrived home to find the front door locked against him. He walked around the house to the backdoor, passing the kitchen window as he did so. He observed that there were several strange offspring in the kitchen but none of his own were present.

'Please let us out, mister,' said one urchin.

The backdoor was also locked. So were the windows so William could not get in. William was dependent on getting his key until his wife returned. William tried the right-hand neighbour.

'Have you seen where the boys and girls are?' he asked in his most charming manner.

'Ere you the father of all those bloody Irish kids,' said a broad Yorkshire voice. 'You don't sound Irish.'

'You never ought to 'ave all them kids running loose without supervision,' said the matriarch of the house. 'I brought my Arthur indoors.'

'Them bloody Irish kids tied him to the clothes post,' interrupted the male member of the household.

William Britain retired in the face of a further potential verbal onslaught. He tried the left-hand neighbour who turned out to be Irish as well. The mother of the household was a very, very attractive brunette wearing a mini-skirt and a tight white sweater. She had very shapely legs in dark stockings and William was instantly attracted.

'The children can't be far off, they are playing with my two girls, Jane and Karen,' said the vision.

William wished that he could be playing with the vision. He had wondered if his detachment to Christmas Island had made him sterile. If this was the case, he need not worry so much as he had about the paternal potential within him. He certainly felt more than a neighbourly feeling towards this young lady.

'Come in and have a cup of tea whilst you wait,' said the vision. 'Are you any good at handiwork, by the way? My husband is at sea and I sometimes don't see him for three months at a time,' she continued. 'My curtain rail has come down. It would probably be an easy job for a man but I am just a helpless woman.'

William decided to take up the offer of the cup of tea. The previous meeting with the other neighbour had not been very encouraging. A friendly neighbour is a very worthwhile asset, especially if she is as good-looking as this one, he thought to himself. William allowed her to persuade him to come inside and sat down on the sofa. It was a low-slung sofa which had the effect of giving comfort whilst making it difficult to get up once having sat in it.

The lady of the house was called Susan and soon insisted that he call her 'Sue'. She soon returned and sat opposite him. The mini-skirt rode up high, displaying frothy pink underwear. Sue kept stroking down the skirt in a ridiculous attempt to preserve her modesty.

'Ooh, this settee is terrible to sit in,' she said.

Susan kept crossing and uncrossing her legs. William tried hard not to look obvious at looking up her skirt but his eyes were unable to control themselves.

'My Freddy bought this skirt,' said Sue. 'Do you like it? My Freddy won't be home for another month, though. I do wish he would get another job. I get so lonely.'

William asked her what the job was as he might be able to do some handiwork.

'Follow me, William,' she said. She had soon wormed out his name.

She led the way upstairs and he was given a good view of the frothy pink panties once more. She led him into the bedroom where he surveyed the curtain rail and curtains laid across the floor. There was a chair next to the window which she mounted, displaying more thigh as she did so.

'It's this bracket here what has come out,' she said.

At this, the chair started rocking and William rushed forward to catch her. They fell on the bed together and she squealed in merriment.

'It's a good job Freddy can't see us,' she gushed.

The skirt had somehow risen higher and William could feel a mounting demand in his nether regions. He managed to move his hand onto her knee as though to steady himself. Susan put her hand over it so that he could not remove it, nor could he move the hand higher.

'You are so strong, like my Freddy,' she said.

Bang! Crash! A door crashed open somewhere below.

'*Mum, Mum,*' yelled two female voices. 'Can we borrow your lipstick?'

The mood was broken. William promised to return to fix the bracket when he could get in his house to get his tools. He descended the stairs, pulling his pullover down in an attempt to disguise the bulge in his trousers.

'Have you seen any of my lot?' he asked the girls in a paternal manner.

The girls looked at him suspiciously.

'I can't get in at home,' explained ex-Captain Britain, 'and I am looking for the boys to let me in.'

'Why were you upstairs with Mum?' asked Karen.

'She was showing me a broken curtain bracket,' explained William.

Why were kids so suspicious nowadays? It must be the things they learn at school, he thought to himself.

'We're playing with Jamie and Ryan,' said Jane and Karen.

Jamie was eleven and Ryan ten. The eldest son, Frederick, had been helping out as odd job boy at the Southern Constellation but this still left Theresa unaccounted for.

'Where are they? And where are the rest of them?' asked William.

'We're trying to get Billy Johnson down from the top of the apple tree,' said Jane.

'Why do you want my lipstick?' asked their mother.

'Oh, we are going to be saloon girls,' said Karen. 'Saloon girls always wear lots of lipstick.'

The girls showed William the way to the oak tree.

'Have you seen any children playing?' asked a bespectacled lady. 'They aren't down by the oak tree. They seem to be all Irish.'

The rest of the clan were there, including Jamie and Ryan and Billy Johnson.

Another worried mother came along.

'I can't find Joanna anywhere,' she said.

William saw Jamie brandishing a large bunch of keys.

'Hi, Dad,' he said cheerfully.

'Are those the housekeys?' asked William.

He then recalled the children locked in the kitchen.

'I think I know where Joanna is,' he said.

William returned home to find that Joanna was indeed where he had expected to find her. There were also another two mums demanding that their offspring be released from their incarceration. Jamie had informed his father that he Jamie was the sheriff, which is why he had all the housekeys. The Britain clan were his posse. The other unwitting children who had not joined the sheriff's posse were, of course, outlaws.

Ex-Captain Britain promised that reprisals would be taken, and the events would not happen again. The Britain posse were awarded seven days' 'jankers' each, with fourteen days for Jamie. The aggravated neighbours were appeased by free shoe cleaning or car cleaning or gardening, according to their whims.

Having solved the current crisis, William searched out for his tool kit and returned to offer assistance to his delectable neighbour. She was dressed in a housecoat this time and the top button was missing to display ample cleavage oozing out from a frothy pink bra which probably matched the underwear displayed earlier on.

'Ooh, you nearly caught me with nothing on,' she said provocatively. 'I was just going for a shower,' she added.

The two daughters hovered suspiciously in the background. They had been forbidden to don the lipstick and become saloon girls.

'Do you want to go out and play?' asked their mother, who contemplated that perhaps she had been hasty in her maternal role.

'No, it's nearly time for tea,' said Karen.

'Why is the man here again?' asked Jane.

'Shall I come back at a better time?' asked William.

'Oh no, I shan't be able to draw the curtains tonight and I might forget myself and walk around with nothing on. You wouldn't want me to be embarrassed like that, Mr Britain, would you?' she said provocatively.

Ex-Captain William Britain told a white lie. He liked what he had seen and in truth that was quite a lot.

'Come on, we'll get the little job finished as you must be a very busy man.'

Once more she led the way upstairs. He noted that the black stockings had been removed but she still sported the pink frothy panties. The girls were not going to leave them alone, though, and even when their mother pushed the door to, Karen made a point of coming in to ask if Mr Britain would like a cup of tea.

Jimmy Graham was very pleased with his new, well, nearly new, motorbike. He could get to college quickly and Beverley had been quite excited when she allowed him to take her round the recreation ground. She was not going to be a pillion passenger on the road, though, until she saw a legitimate driving licence, not a provisional one. She had enjoyed the notoriety of the court case but she was not being caught out again. She was only just beginning to obtain parental trust once more, although her parents were not happy about Jimmy Graham as her beau. She liked Jimmy but she was not going to get tied down with a steady boyfriend for a long time.

Jimmy was a bit unhappy today, though, because the bike was not performing as well as it might. Mr Graham came to the rescue of his son and remedied the lack of performance by cleaning the sparking plug and resetting the plug gap.

Bob Malone was up in Dronsley for an interview as lecturer in food production, to replace George Farrant who was retiring that summer. There were four other short-listed candidates and Bob knew that he was up against fierce competition. His examinations were a month away and Sylvia was due to take her examinations about the same time. Apart from the idyllic working honeymoon, the couple had not seen each other in spite of Bob's fierce attempts at persuasion. She had agreed to meet him at her parents' home, although Bob had suggested a room at the Southern Constellation.

'We're saving up to buy a house,' she told him. She also warned him that she had a surprise, a big surprise in fact.

Bob was to attend the interview first and so his first point of call was the college. He reported to the principal's office where he met Mr Parable and the other candidates. Mr Parable claimed to have a busy schedule and so Bob and the other candidates were handed over to Hector Britain for a tour of the department. Hector welcomed Bob warmly and asked him what married life was like. Hector was quite jolly now that his brother's family had gone and he was enjoying a sort of second honeymoon.

The other candidates included Anton Musseli who had recently appeared in a TV series.

'He is odds-on favourite with the principal,' warned Hector discreetly.

There were two chefs from restaurants in Sheffield and a lecturer from Brighton.

'There is quite an interviewing committee, I'm afraid,' said Hector. 'We now have student democracy.'

The lecturer from Brighton went in first. He did not stay long.

'I wouldn't want to work here with that prat and the students in charge,' said the Brighton lecturer as he donned his coat and left.

The two Sheffield chefs entered one at a time.

'You'll have to be clever to understand that principal chap,' they were warned.

Bob went in as the penultimate candidate. It looked as if the running order was based on reverse order of preference. Bob entered to find a long committee table in front of him. Arranged around the table were some he knew and some he did not know. Bob was introduced to each delegate and then the questions began led by Mr Parable.

'Ah, Mr Malone, I understand that you carried out your schedule of practical teacher training here at Dronsley, which no doubt served to motivate your application for employment here. Tell me, Mr Malone, how you feel about non-specific gender education.'

Bob responded in textbook manner as taught at Garnstone and as warned by Hector. Mr Parable was impressed. Bob was next referred to a second Mr Parable, an educational adviser from the ministry.

'Ah, Bob,' said the round figure informally, 'What are

your opinions on competency objectives?'

Bob knew about this as well but was unable to put up a convincing support for it. He reserved himself to saying that competency testing had its place in certain circumstances. Mr Parable broke into a lecture on competency theory and had to be restrained by Principal Parable. Bob was then passed onto the Student Union representative for ethnic and sexual minorities.

'Do you have any reservations about teaching black students?' asked Susan Miller, 'and do you treat all students the same?'

'I think you know the answer to that one, Susan,' said Bob.

Bob turned to the other delegates and informed them that he taught Susan during the teacher training practice.

'Does he have reservations, Susan?' asked a kindly-looking lady dressed in a huge feathery hat.

'Nah. He's OK,' s. . . .' Susan stopped.

'You should have seen him when Stella grabbed what?' asked the lady.

'Oh, nuthin'. He's OK,' said Susan.

'What did she grab?' asked Principal Parable.

'The girl grabbed the geezer's balls,' said the other student delegate, who was president of the Student Union. 'It was no big deal, she thought it was her boyfriend.'

'Nothing happened except that Mr Malone was very embarrassed,' said Mr Potterton. 'Students *do* lark around.'

'Oh, things have changed since my days,' said the lady.

Was it perhaps a little wistfully or did Bob misconstrue her tone of voice?

'What about your feelings on discipline?' asked the chairman of the board of governors when his turn came.

"E don't stand no muckin' about,' said Susan. "Ee is fair, though.'

'I'm asking Mr Malone, young lady,' said the chairman, 'but I think you've put me in the picture anyhow.'

It seemed that the last candidate would never emerge

but eventually he did. The candidates were kept waiting for a further twenty minutes before the appointments committee came up with their decision. The student delegates had swung the vote and Bob was to take up the post of lecturer in professional cookery next September, subject to passing the Garnstone examinations. Anton Musseli had been pipped at the post.

Bob set off to the Ness household to impart his news. He had promised to have a celebratory drink with Hector at a later date.

'Congratulations, my boy,' said ex-Principal Ness.

He had just walked in on Bob and Sylvia who were embracing in the hallway. He would have to get used to this mauling of his daughter. At least he was a man, not like the Parable's boy whom Elliot Ness looked down on in disdain.

'Can we be alone together for just a couple of minutes, please, Dad?' asked Sylvia coyly.

'You don't have to ask me. Go to bed for half an hour or turn in for the night now and I'll arrange room service meals,' said Mr Ness disgustedly.

'Dad,' said Sylvia slowly. 'We haven't seen each other since Easter.'

Dad left them alone.

'You're looking beautiful, let's go to bed,' said Bob lewdly.

'Don't you think you've done enough damage?' said Sylvia.

'You're in the club, aren't you?' said Bob intuitively. 'I'm going to be a daddy.'

'Shut up, you fool,' said Sylvia. 'How did you guess? It's serious, you know, as I won't be able to start work. I have to find a way of telling Dad.'

'Well, there's no time like the present,' said Bob. 'When is it due?'

'About Christmas I should think but it might be premature, in November,' said Sylvia.

'Not the night the bed collapsed,' said Bob. 'I think we'll

settle on Christmas, don't you? And why didn't you tell me?'

'I had to be certain and I wanted to see your face when I told you. Oh Bob, we're not ready but I don't regret a single thing.'

'Let's go and tell the old man,' said Bob.

26

TWILIGHT CLASSES

Hector Britain was not happy. Mrs Jenny Beeton, a part-time teacher, was off sick and there was not exactly a large amount of enthusiasm for looking after her class, even though the overtime rate was quite generous. Mrs Jenny Beeton was a small domestic science-type teacher who did all sorts of weird things, well they seemed weird to the hotel-trained chefs like Hector. Mrs Beeton claimed to be descended from the Great Mrs Beeton of Victorian fame but whereas the authoress was undoubtedly a good cook, Mrs Jenny Beeton was not. She walked around with the Mrs Beeton cookbook under her arm and it was not very compatible with City and Guilds styles. Most of the lecturers used *Practical Cookery* by Ceserani and Kinton and many of the City and Guilds examinations were couched in the same style of language. The other problem was the fact that the twilight class seemed to attract housewives and employees from the Post Office, the steel works, the sheep farms and any other form of employment other than catering. Perhaps the lure of the warm kitchens in winter, plus the surrounding supplies of food, was a lure offering havens of warmth and security to anyone successfully mastering the success of the final examination.

Hector had arrived to set up a demonstration. Mrs Beeton had planned to make cream scones, cream of parsnip soup, and poached darne of cod with dill sauce. Hector had intercepted the ingredients' order which included ready-prepared darnes of cod.

'Bloody typical,' he had commented. 'They probably haven't seen a real fish in her class.'

Hector had scrapped the scones. He had substituted fillet of plaice *bonne femme* using a *Duchesse* border, *Pommes fondants* and *petits pois à la Française*.

'If I'm teaching I'll give them real fish and knife drill,' he said. 'They'll enjoy peeling button onions as well,' he added.

If the twilight class had any false conceptions about catering being a clean healthy sincecure, Hector would put them right.

The students began to arrive for the theory session. Hector could not gain access to a training kitchen until 5.30 p.m. for a 6 p.m. start. It was nearly 3 p.m. and only five had arrived out of the dozen potentially accepted.

'Ooh, are we going to have a demonstration?' said a buxom lady aged about fifty-five, plastered in thick make-up and jewellery. 'How exciting. We never have demonstrations from Mrs Beeton.'

Hector was busy making last checks. He was also going to demonstrate fillet of lemon sole *Florentine*, fillet of Dover sole Suchet and *pommes Berrichonne, Hongroise, Bretonne* and au lard.

'Ee, we don't have owt like this with Mrs Beeton,' said a roundish Yorkshireman with a mid-forties middle-aged spread.

'Wot's all them different fish there, mate?'

Hector continued setting up the demonstration on separate trays so that the items were ready for individual assembly. This saved confusion where similar lists of ingredients were involved.

'He's totally oblivious, Mr James,' said mascara lady.

'Wot's them fish, mate?' asked Mr James more loudly.

Hector ignored him. He was just about ready. He was not anybody's 'mate' and treated such communications with the contempt of the head waiter dismissing the whistle from the ill-mannered poseur customer.

'I told you, Mr James, he's probably deaf,' said mascara lady.

'I am not deaf, madam, and I am not anybody's mate, either,' said Hector. 'I am Mr Britain or chef, if you don't mind.'

'Mrs Beeton let's us call her Jenny,' said a skinny youth, apparently the youngest present.

'My name is Mr Britain or chef,' repeated Hector. 'I'm sorry if I appear unresponsive when I'm setting up a demonstration but I like the demonstration to flow like a kitchen production line. If I have distractions, parts of the *mise en place* may get overlooked.'

The door swung open and in swept two burly lads with a quite attractive young lady.

'Is this Mrs Beeton's class?' asked the larger of the two.

'It is and you're late,' said Hector.

'Where have you been, Rosalind?' said mascara lady.

'Madam, may I continue with my lecture?' asked Hector.

'She's my daughter,' said mascara lady. 'Rosalind, I've told you about mixing with those two.'

Hector had managed to acquire the lecture theatre to demonstrate in and the eight students present were scattered around the large areas of empty rows of seats. The two late arrivals and the young Rosalind were heading towards the back of the class.

'I would like you all to sit on the front two rows, please,' said Hector.

'I am not going to wear out my voice shouting out for the back row.'

Another interruption brought the numbers up to nine. It was 3.12 p.m. already. Hector eventually had the students at the front of the lecture theatre. He carried out the register documentation, laid out his expectations and had almost caused mascara lady to storm out. Mr James had interceded on behalf of Hector.

"Ee's like the bloody corporal I had on National Service,' he said.

Hector was progressing through the potato dishes first of all when there was a timid tap on the door. Hector didn't notice it at first. The tapping resumed.

'I think there's someone outside, chef,' said Mr James.
'*COME IN*,' roared Hector.
A small but polite lad entered.
'Is this Mrs Beeton's class. I've been looking all over for it,' said the young lad.
'Yes, it is. Who are you?' asked Hector.
'I'm Dean Martin,' said the timid, polite youth.
'I suppose you've been making bloody pop records,' said Hector sarcastically.
The two burly lads fell into stiches of laughter at this.
'I don't think that's a nice thing to say,' said mascara lady.
'Madam, I am not a nice person,' said Hector truthfully.
Dean was number thirteen on the register of twenty. The twilight classes always had a high fall-out rate. If it had been earlier in the year the class would have folded.
Hector managed to finish on time and sent the students for a half-hour break. He told them to return promptly as they had a lot to do and told them that he expected them dressed in proper protective clothing. He was to be disappointed and they did warn him that most of them did not own proper chef's whites anyhow. Hector set about borrowing some aprons from the refectory staff. He also sold them some paper chef's hats. The two burly lads apologized but they had to go back to work. This reduced the potential group of nineteen down to eight but, there again, there were seven students who had not been seen for several weeks, so it could be assumed that they had left.
Mr James arrived in baker's trousers and a butcher's apron over a white shirt. He was a publican.
'Mrs Roberts sends her apologies, chef,' he said, referring to mascara lady.
'Rosalind won't be here either, as she has probably gone off with Mike and Luigi,' he added.
Mike and Luigi were the two burly latecomers claiming to be due back at work. Nice work if you can get it, thought Hector, because Rosalind was quite attractive. Hector did not, however, think the same about their mascared mother. He was quite grateful that she was not there. Dean was

the only one present other than Hector who sported real authentic chef's whites. The skinny youth had also disappeared but there was another lad in his place who was almost dressed like a chef but he had jeans on instead of chef's trousers.

'We didn't think we'd see you again, Charlie,' said Mr James.

Charlie was in the RAF and had been on a three month detachment with the RAF Regiment. Hector decided to double up on the fish to give the students 'extra practice'. This turned out to be a mistake as they only had three filleting knives between them, even after Hector broke the rule of a lifetime and let Mr James borrow his personal Hector Britain filleting knife. As an ex-serviceman, albeit a National Serviceman, Mr James was a singular kindred spirit. Moreover, he seemed to be a beneficial influence in this terrible undisciplined domestic science group. There were eight more weeks of term left and Mrs Beeton was unlikely to return for this term.

Charlie and Mr James worked together. Their work was first-class and they finished well before time. They cleaned their section and several others and asked if they could go. Whereas Hector had intended presentation at 8.30 p.m. as a complete meal and he had expected each student to draw up a time plan, he had received a large wave of protest.

'Wot's a time plan?' the skinny youth had asked.

Hector had, therefore, drawn up an impromptu plan, but only Mr James and Charlie had achieved par with it. In fact, they were the only two who started on time and they capped this by working faster than Hector's scheme. One girl had spread newspaper on the chopping board so that the board did not smell of fish.

'Wot's this? Are we going to read Egon Ronay's *Times*' food report or are we going to fillet the fish, madam?' said Hector in his friendly manner.

At 8.45 p.m. precisely Sam Browne had arrived jangling his keys ready for locking up.

'Where's Mrs Beeton?' asked Sam Browne. 'She's normally clear by now.'

Hector had already made three belated requests for immediate presentation.

'Present or destroy, but not the fish,' said Hector desperately.

'Classes terminate at 9 p.m., Mr Britain,' said Sam Browne, jangling his keys.

'You'd better get them moving, I don't get paid after 9 p.m.'

'PISS OFF,' said Hector.

'I shall have to report this to the principal,' said Sam Browne imperiously.

'You can report it to who you like,' said Hector. 'NOW PISS OFF.'

'I shall be back in ten minutes,' said Sam Browne.

Mrs Beeton normally gives him tea and cakes,' said Mr James. 'That's why he's peeved.'

'He'll get sod all from me,' said Hector.

He hurriedly cleared up and put things away in the refrigerator and broke the rules about putting hot food in the refrigerator in doing so. Sam Browne paced up and down closing windows, shutting doors before Hector had done, all the time jangling the gaoler's keys. He hovered in the changing-room whilst Hector changed. Hector's car was the last in the carpark. Sam Browne promised to claim for an extra half hour's pay.

Hector drove home to find that they had a returned lodger. His sister-in-law had moved in, having left his brother, ex-Captain William Britain, looking after the clan. Hector's wife was in full sympathy and Hector was being given the cold shoulder for committing the crime of being a member of the male species.

Next day there was not a lot to show for the twelve plaice supplied to the twilight class of the absent Mrs Beeton. A 1¾lb plaice should yield two portions. There were about fifteen recognizable portions out of the twenty-four expected. The *Pommes Fondants* were largely mis-shapen.

Mr James and Charlie were the only two who had served up the peas. Hector surveyed the previous evening's work. It was easy to get the full-time students to cook the unprepared peas. Hector put the mangled fish and mis-shapen potatoes through the mincer together with the *Duchesse* border. Golden fish cakes with tartare sauce were to appear on the staff restaurant menu. In the meantime, Hector had to report to the principal about being rude to Mr Sam Browne. Mr Parable had found Mr Sam Browne quite useful and so Hector was not on a very sound wicket. Hector ended up claiming for half an hour's less overtime and this was diverted to pay Mr Sam Browne for his being detained at work. Hector was furious. He was even more furious when he found that the principal's brother was going to join Hector to 'see how catering worked'.

'I'll put him in the part-time class, Hector,' said Mr Potterton. 'There's no point in letting him get near your full-time students, not the way you treat them. We'd both end up with the sack.'

If Hector thought that his troubles had reached ultimate crisis point he was to learn that there was even more trouble on the horizon. Ten members of staff were off sick and this meant more stand-in time. Normally staff had to be off for three consecutive sessions before they could claim for overtime, too, and so this was not popular with stand-in staff. All ten members of staff had eaten fishcakes in the staff restaurant. The local health officer and two assistants were brought in to investigate how the outbreak of food poisoning could have occurred. Hector had had fishcakes but was unaffected. He was sent to the hospital for a stool test but was confirmed clear. Nevertheless, Hector had not heard the last of it. The student handlers were also declared clear. It was the fish, it was decided, but there was no evidence remaining.

27

THE NEW TRIBULATIONS OF HECTOR BRITAIN

Jimmy's motor bike had broken down on his way back from Sheffield. It was late and so Jimmy decided not to ring his father. Mr Graham liked to be in bed by 10.30 p.m. and was asleep by 11 p.m. It was not a helpful promise towards assistance from Mr Graham should he be disturbed from his slumbers. It was not the sparking plugs this time. The lights were working and so it probably was not electronic. The sparking plugs, battery and electronics was all Jimmy knew about diagnostics. He pushed the bike for the remaining three and three quarter miles home, hoping that his father would be able to solve the problem of getting the motor cycle to operate effectively once more.

The health inspector, his two assistants and the trainee health inspector were not happy with the FAB department. The department had been using dreadful mahogany boards, whereas a new polystyrene board had been instituted in modern departments. Food handling operatives should be wearing disposable polythene gloves when handling foods. The FAB department did not have blast chillers to reduce food temperatures very rapidly. Fish should have been filleted on sterile surfaces. Something very new called a probe should have been used to ensure that internal food temperatures were in excess of 70°C. Tables and boards should be made of stainless steel and polystyrene respectively. There were appliances called chillers which should have been used to lower temperatures effectively for protein foods. Dronsley had none of these, however, and in fact, very few places did. Hector was interrogated as to what had actually happened as regards to the fish used for the fish-cakes. After the grilling Hector had felt like a criminal. After the visit of the health inspectors just about everybody in the food and beauty department felt like criminals, in fact. Hector resolved that the remaining classes taken for Mrs Beeton should be simplified. He had grieved on the loss of half an hour's overtime and now reconsidered that Jenny Beeton's class should be handled very, very carefully. It never even entered Hector's mind that the faults had been brought about by putting hot foods in the refrigerator, thereby raising temperatures within the refrigerator, so that the internal temperature of the refrigerator became hot, thus enabling the binary fission of pathogenic bacteria.

Hector was preparing to receive the dreaded part-time group of the absent Mrs Beeton. He had not been able to acquire the lecture theatre this week so had decided to do a demonstration instead of the practical session this week. It had seemed obvious that the dreadful twilight class had caused his problems. He would have theory in the afternoon and a lecture demonstration *in lieu* of the practical session. There were sixteen students present at the afternoon theory class.

Hector's theory class started late. The group had gone to the lecture theatre to disturb Mr Connell. At last they located him in their allocated classroom.

'We thought you would be demonstrating,' said Mr James. There were fifteen students present. The skinny youth was absent but four presumed departures had returned. The two burly youths were full of apologies for absconding with Rosalind. Rosalind was sat next to Luigi. Rosalind's mother was sat next to Mr James. Mike was sat sulking on his own. Dean had arrived half an hour early. Mr Parable's brother was sat in the front row taking notes.

Hector was obviously unhappy but he carried out a magnificent demonstration.

'Poulet sauté chasseur, poulet sauté Hongroise, balletines de volaille bonne femme, supremes de volaille Maryland and veloute Agnes Sorel and germiny and cock-a-leekie using stock from the bones of the chickens. The group clapped to drown out the clanking keys of Sam Browne who had arrived at 8.45 p.m. to seek the closure of activities.

'Piss off,' said Hector.

'Please leave us alone,' said the mascara lady.

Hector finished at 8.55 p.m. and was clearing up by 9 p.m.

'I get paid and I teach until 9 p.m.,' said Hector.

Mr Graham had spent some time on Jimmy's motor cycle. He even stripped the engine down. He had checked the electrics. He couldn't find anything wrong with it. He reassembled the bike and decided to interrogate his workmate, James Hunt. He couldn't really offer much advice without seeing the bike.

'I can pop round at the weekend,' he offered. 'I assume you did check the petrol.'

Mr Graham would not admit that he had overlooked the most blatantly obvious point.

'Of course I have,' he snapped.

Hector was home relatively early compared with the previous occasion. He was very pleased with himself. He knew he had given a good, a very good demonstration. What was so pleasing was the obvious appreciation of the group. This was the reason for the return of some presumed lost students. Hector never received appreciation from the full-time students. They were obviously more interested in each other than anything Hector was likely to show them. There were a few exceptions but generally the philosophy of appreciation of culinary expertise is a developed response which flowers with the passing of time.

His sister-in-law was pleased to see him. She was lonely.

Mrs Britain, Hector's wife, was not due back until nearly midnight. Hector invited her to have a drink with him. There was nothing to watch on TV and so he put on some Strauss and they sat and Hector supped at his brandy whilst his sister-in-law supped the Bristol Cream. As the alcohol took effect they decided to waltz together. She smelt warm and womanly with the exotic fragrance of her tinge of 'Evening in Paris' perfume. Hector's right hand gradually slipped down to her bottom. She did not stop him. They were soon on the settee cuddling and caressing. Her blouse was undone and her bra was soon to follow. Her breasts were soon exposed to Hector's lustful eyes as he kissed and fondled.

'Put the light out,' she said to him but he declined, saying that it would appear suspicious. They crept upstairs in the dark to her room instead. She let him undress her in the dark and she allowed access to the last barrier.

Hector was not fated to have his wicked way, though. Why, oh why, had he drunk so much brandy? He had an acute case of 'brewers droop'. No amount of stimulation would revive Hector's flagging manhood. His sister-in-law was gentle with him.

'It is God's way,' she said. 'We would both regret it. It was wrong in the first place.'

'I'll definitely regret it,' thought Hector.

She said she would turn in, anyhow, since she was already dressed, or should she say undressed, for bed. Hector slunk back downstairs. He stopped on the landing to check that he had left nothing undone. He was quick enough to find the discarded bra downstairs and he hastily returned it to his sister-in-law's bedroom.

'We could try again,' he said hopefully.

'Goodnight, Hector,' she said firmly.

It was as well that she had not let him try again as there was the sound of a car pulling up in the driveway outside. Hector's wife had arrived home early.

Hector was having breakfast which he had had to cook himself. His wife was sulking and suspicious. Hector's brewers droop' had not recovered for response to his wife's marital expectations either. Hector did smell of brandy but, there again, that was not exactly unusual for Hector. He was normally rampant and 'brewers droop' was not a common phenomenon as far as his wife was concerned. Hector was not always sympathetic with her occasional migraines, or at least he did not seem to be. Hector's wife suspected adultery had taken place. She was not especially sociable to the temporary lodger. She knew Hector had a soft spot for his sister-in-law but she did not expect her lodger to be so treacherous under her own roof.

'Nothing happened,' repeated Hector.

It was a futile act of conviction.

There was the sound of a car drawing up outside and the doorbell rang. It was ex-Captain William Britain seeking reconciliation with his wife.

'Nothing happened,' said ex-Captain William Britain to his outcast brother.

'Why the black eye, then,' asked Hector who was torn between self-pity and guilt at the unsuccessful attempt on his brother's wife's fidelity.

Ex-Captain Britain's wife felt guilty for what almost happened. She felt very uncomfortable at being the cause of the rift in family relations. She wanted to go home with her husband but she would not allow him to see that she would forgive him so lightly. She agreed to return home with him for the children's sake but she would be sleeping in separate rooms from her husband.

'Nothing did happen, you know,' she said to Hector's wife. 'Don't be silly, he was working late, he probably had a stressful night and drank too much. Have you ever seen Hector and I carrying on? I have more than enough to handle with one of the brothers let alone two,' she added.

Mr Hector Britain's troubles were not over. Sam Browne had expressed concern about Hector's attitude. Mr Parable's brother had expressed concern about Hector's attitude. The student union was expressing concern about Hector's attitude.

'It is deplorable that a lecturer can be insulting to the ancillary staff, to students and to my own brother. You cannot go around telling people to "piss off". I will not have it. I could have you sacked for this, Mr Britain,' said Principal Parable. 'My brother says you call the Competency approach "crap". He says you refuse to negotiate marks with students and you refer to this as "crap". What does "crap" imply, Mr Britain? It does not seem a nice word,' continued Principal Parable.

'A Mr Crapper invented a toilet-flushing device,' said Hector. 'Crap was always associated with his plumbing capabilities.'

Hector was really trying hard with his diplomatic skills. He decided that he might have to find somewhere else to work. He could not, would not, negotiate with anyone. He took orders, he gave orders. He did not, and would not, take orders from students or ancillary staff. Hector expected such categories to jump to it, when so ordered by ex-RSM Hector Britain.

Hector was not the only one who was unhappy with developments at Dronsley College of Further Education. Mr Potterton had decided to take early retirement. Miss Todd was wondering how to commit the perfect murder and other members of staff were privately thinking of the same solution to removing Principal Parable. It was fairly unanimous within the college that the principal must go. Even the hairy academics had discovered that student emancipation equalled student anarchy. Food studies' chef lecturers were either unable or unwilling to act as disciplinarians in the servicing of FAB classes. Mr Parable had been awarded a class of his own in teaching communications to the part-time bakers.

It was Principal Parable's second bakery communications class. He had decided to try Shakespeare, with a scene from *The Merchant of Venice*. Principal Parable was recounting the extract pertaining to the pound of flesh. Tom Jones was one of the better-educated bakers. He was trying to fill in *The Sun* crossword. Arthur Jason had his hand underneath Freda Aitken's skirt. William Burchill was almost throttling Graham Makepeace on the back row. Clementine and Ann were discussing their latest boyfriends. No one, not anyone, was listening to Principal Parable. Hector took in this scene as he waited outside for admission with his full-time group of students.

'He has got to go,' said Hector after a further traumatic session with the Principal's brother.

'I'm glad I'm retiring,' said George Farrant.

'He'll be here long after you,' said Mr Naunder.

'There's only one hope,' said Miss Todd. 'He has to be promoted.'

'You'll be even worse off when Potterton goes,' said George Farrant with the aplomb of Jeremiah the prophet of doom.

Jimmy was happy again. His motor cycle was working again. He even had a forthcoming driving test to look forward to. Beverley now occasionally let him put his hand up her knickers and he knew that he had passed the external practical of his City and Guilds 147.

All too soon it was the end of term and there were interviews for Mr Potterton's job. There was, however, no solution to the problem of ousting Mr Parable. The new candidates were short-listed for the food and beauty department. The candidates included William Britain, Hector's brother, someone from the great Westminster, Hector himself, Mr Harry Clarke of Garnstone, Mr Parable's brother and a clergyman lay preacher, the Reverend Doctor Gerbils who was a part-time TA padre. Mr Gerbils seemed to be a rank outsider. The odds were on Mr Parable's plumber brother or ex-Captain William Britain who had formed ties with some of the board of governors.

'I'm leaving if that bastard brother of mine is appointed,' said Hector, Hector and wife were now reconciled and Hector was enjoying a status similar to that enjoyed during his honeymoon days. The major problem was that it took him somewhat longer to recharge his batteries and rise to whatever was called for.

Jimmy had passed his motor cycle test and was taking Beverley for rides. Ex-Principal Elliot Ness was enjoying his retirement and spent much of his time at the newly-opened golf club. Bob Malone was standing in as temporary chef at the golf club and he and Sylvia were in an idyllic honeymoon residence in the redundant caravan of the ex-Captain Britain, even though Sylvia was obviously putting on weight. Stella Pavrotti and David Fretwork were engaged. David was frightened out of his wits about the dangers of the Mafiosi. Stella had still not surrendered her honour but he knew that he would do anything to achieve that ultimate submission even though it did mean the inevitable matrimony.

The FAB staff were left to spend their summer vacations finding a way to remove Principal Parable. They were also left to ponder the effect of the new lay preacher head of department, the Reverend Doctor Gerbils. Perhaps God would find a way of salvation for the FAB Department.

28

TIME FOR CHANGE

The Reverend Doctor Gerbils had arrived in Britain with his mother and father just after the war. The family name, Goebbels, was somewhat unpopular in their part of Germany because of the actions of the Third Reich propaganda minister. Heinrich Goebbels had a rough time at school too, even though he spoke excellent English, having an English mother. His father soon changed the name by deedpoll to Gerbils and his family conspired to place him in a different school with the name of Henry. By the time Heinrich, now Henry, had passed through grammar school and subsequent university the name had metamorphosized into Henry Gerbils, leaving no trace of the Teutonic heritage. Henry had read about the Nazi, Dr Goebbels, who was believed to be a distant relative. Henry had been indoctrinated into the effectiveness of propaganda and economy with the truth. It was not that the Reverend Doctor told lies. The Reverend Doctor would allude to and he would insinuate and his ambiguity would make many promises appear to come true. He was also ahead of the 1970s and ahead of Mr Parable in the use of the computer. Initially Mr Parable had put some files on computer but these had mysteriously been attacked by a computer virus. Some of the files had been an attempt by Mr Parable to document the activities of the new Food and Beauty head.

Principal Parable had brought in 'democracy' by introducing student governors to the staff selection board. All this had been indicated in the copious candidates' advisory programme sent to each short-listed candidate. The Reverend Doctor had stayed at the Southern Constellation on the night preceding the interview. Jimmy Graham had been very impressed by the friendly 'curate' who was so keen to talk to him about his college course.

The principal's secretary had been very impressed with the curate as well, when he had arrived and made friendly enquiries about the Food and Beauty department.

'I don't know if I'll be good enough,' he had said disarmingly. 'I'll bet there are a lot of people in for the job but it would be improper of me to ask such a question.'

'Could you check that I have put my new address on file as I seem to have been overlooked with regards to communications as to whether I have or not been shortlisted,' he said innocently.

In between this innocent query and the secretary checking her files there had been a temporary diversion. The fire alarm had gone off and they had had to abandon the building. In the process the Reverend Doctor managed to find out who the candidates were. Naturally, he was shortlisted. Reverend doctors in catering education are few and far between. Mr Parable had been very impressed.

It was probably coincidence that ex-Captain Britain's temporary separation from his wife had become well-publicised. Mr Harry Clarke of Garnstone had not turned up. Someone had told him that Mr Potterton had withdrawn his resignation. The Westminster candidate had received a similar letter. Mr Parable's brother had mysteriously fallen over in the refectory whilst being shown around the department with the reverend doctor and ex-Captain Britain. He had still attended the interview but the bulging red nose caused by the accident made the red dicky bow seem part of a jester's matching set of accoutrements. The chairman of the board of governors was not impressed anyhow. The student representatives regarded him as a pain and the 'curate' gave an air of philanthropy which suggested lots of potential day trips and parties. The upshot was the appointment of the reverend doctor as head of Food and Beauty. Moreover, the Reverend Doctor arrived before the end of term, working *gratis*, so that he could come in and take over the reins of office with at least some working knowledge gained before the official start. The reverend doctor had learned a lot that week about the state of staff morale. He had decided that Principal Parable and his brother were superfluous to Dronsley requirements. The Reverend Doctor had charmed Miss Todd most effectively and he had lured Hector into a state of false security.

The Food and Beauty Department had a very healthy list of enrolments in the September of the new term. The department had an excellent public image. The elections for student governors and the Student Union took place in early October. The elections for staff governors and academic board representatives took place at the same time. This should have happened in July for the staff but there had been allegations of false accounting when there had been 500 staff votes, which was over 200 votes above the number of staff entitled to vote. Only part-time staff teaching more than ten hours were awarded a vote, and many full-time staff said that even this was not fair. Principal Parable had drawn up a new constitution which an emergency board of governors had ratified in the middle of the summer holidays.

Bob had been advised that it would be nice for someone in the FAB department to stand for the staff representative on the academic board. Miss Todd had stood as a candidate for staff governor. Jimmy Graham had stood for Student Union secretary and David Fretwork had stood for president. Susan Miller was there as female ethnic minorities' candidate.

As a new head of department and a 'curate', albeit a lay preacher, the Reverend Doctor Henry Gerbil had offered his services as a neutral arbiter. Traditionally the Food and Beauty staff avoided all college activities and so the late haphazard additions to the candidates' list were more or less ignored by the academics and business studies departments. Each member of staff received a numbered piece of paper with their name on it. This they had to sign and present to the receptionist on duty in the foyer of Dronsley College. Perhaps the landslide catering take-over of the Students Union the day before should have served as warning that the catering department was now strangely participating in college affairs. Principal Parable put it down to the wonderful influence of the new departmental head, the Reverend Doctor Henry Gerbils. It was not to be a good year at all for the Parable brothers, in fact. Hector had been instructing a new intake of students as to how the new convection oven worked. There had been problems with the gas supply. As a plumber, the City and Guilds negotiated curriculum expert was capable of demonstrating some expertise in pipes and things. The gas mains should have been off when he negotiated the apparent lack of fuel. Somehow it wasn't and there was a somewhat large bang. Mr Parable's brother lost his eyebrows and got singed hair but was otherwise physically unhurt. He had a nervous disposition, though, and was consequently off sick for a week suffering from shock. Hector was ecstatic.

On the day that Mr Parable's brother was due back someone dropped a thunderflash on top of the newly-arrived car. The principal's brother had been allocated a car park space adjacent to the main building, along with the privileged heads of department. The poor man sat cowering in his car as people gathered round seeking the commotion. The student throng, including the new student union president, David Fretwork, had apparently been unable to find the evidence. The principal's brother had returned home.

The next day had seen someone put Rodney, a very fierce Alsatian, in the brother's car. Rodney was even fiercer than ever at the unexpected incarceration. He had lunged out at Mr Parable's brother, taking a fierce bite at his upraised arm in the process.

On the third day there had been visitors to Mr Parable's

car, which was garaged at the Southern Constellation where he was staying. He had initially stayed with Principal Parable but someone had alleged that he had been doing naughty things with the principal's wife. The cars tyres had been let down and there had been a message 'GO HOME OR ELSE'. It was unfortunate that it was such a wet day. Whilst walking up the college drive, minus car, the poor man had been drenched by a passing car which had gone through a puddle at great speed. The car had looked very much like Hector's car but Hector was supposedly on TA training for two days.

The competency expert was off for a fortnight with flu. He was not exactly in a hurry to return. When he did return it was to be the week of the Dronsley festival of light. Principal Parable had found the new catering head very receptive to the proposals that Dronsley College should participate in raising funds for the new world church sponsorship scheme. The local church was proposing setting up an exchange teacher system in Brazil so that missionaries could educate Amazonian Indians. Hector's second years had proposed a second year banquet on the lines of a Roman feast. An epicurean dinner would be offered to be sold at large profits towards the fund raising. Principal Parable managed to sell quite a few tickets to his friends, although he made sure that he did not pay himself, of course.

Principal Parable was not able to weigh up the new Food and Beauty head. Written references had been excellent but there was something quite mysterious about the reverend doctor's background. The new upsurge in the catering department's political awareness had not been quite so useful as Principal Parable had expected. Whereas Principal Parable had expected to be the manipulator, it seemed that the reverend doctor had influence over the delegates. They seemed to have access to last-minute documents.

It is a common ploy of politicians to keep information and even agenda secret until the last minute so that it is difficult to prepare any substantial case against unpopular measures. Principals can always force things through under 'any other business' by starting off on trivia and spinning this out. Delegates start flagging after a couple of hours, especially if it's time to go home. The attitude by 6.30 p.m. after a 3.30 p.m. start is, 'Let's get it over with and go home'. On the first meeting in which Principal Parable had planned to set up a priority system for coursework assessment type courses without any examinations using competency approaches there had been significant prepared opposition. The registrar, Principal Parable and the principal's secretary were the only ones fully conversant with the picture within the college. The principal's brother was involved as an agent of the department of education, that so-called 'secret garden'. Yet an hour before the academic board there had been a demonstration against competency teaching methods by the Student Union. The students strangely wanted nationally recognized examinations with distinctions and credit passes. At least the catering students and the business studies department students did.

The guests were assembled for the Roman feast. The students were dressed for a Roman orgy. Hector had let the students negotiate the dress, expecting the worst. He had manipulated the competency expert into supervising the selection of banquet theme. He had deliberately given the wrong room number to the principal's brother so that he could prepare the students' responses before the principal's brother arrived.

The principal's brother kept getting the wrong room because he was so often misled. His timetables kept getting lost as well and the students were apparently secretly encouraged to wind him up. He was deliberately misled with false information as the students and staff contrived to act out scenes which resulted in him in turn misleading his brother, the principal. The girls had donned togas made out of sheets and they nearly all wore black bra and pants underneath. The three or four girls not wishing to flaunt so much flesh had been allowed to wear monkish cowls. The boys had on some Roman soldier-type uniforms borrowed from the nearby theatre which had just finished Shakespeare's *Julius Caesar*.

'The costumes are a bit brief, aren't they?' said the chairman of the board of governors.

'If it weren't for causing a scene I would walk out,' said Mrs Ponsonby Smith.

'I shouldn't be thinking what I'm thinking,' said Colonel Prowse, trying not to leer at Stella Pavrotti.

'I thought you chose the theme and costumes,' said the principal quietly to his brother.

'These aren't the same costumes,' said his brother in embarrassment.

'You know how devious the catering department is, I bet Hector Britain or the Reverend Doctor is behind this.'

'May I have a little more wine?' said the Colonel, gazing down Stella's cleavage as she poured.

The banquet began with *gnocchis Romaine*. Even Anton Mosimann has difficulty in making this dish look or taste appetizing. It was somewhat salty as Hector had not been at his best supervising the afternoon kitchen preparations. The competency expert had been here, there and everywhere under Hector's feet until the final minutes before changing to join his brother in the restaurant. Hector was now at the brandy which he had been savouring for the time when the competency man would leave him alone. The saltiness tended to encourage the guests to drink more of the heavily laced Roman wine. Simon Naunder was busy rushing around trying to make a name for himself. Hector was obviously out of the running for the deputy head of the growing Food and Beauty department. Debbie Harris had declined to wear the skimpy female togas and was dressed in one of the long cowls. She had been assigned to look after Mrs Ponsonby Smith because of this. Mr Simon Naunder noted out of the corner of his eye that David Fretwork had disappeared behind a screen with a flask of the Roman wine. David had pulled Stella in after him. Jimmy saw the look and saw Mr Simon Naunder swing round to catch David and Stella behind the screen. Jimmy hastily put out a foot and Mr Simon Naunder fell over him and plunged forward. Unfortunately, as he sought to steady himself he caught Debbie's cowl which was rent asunder to reveal that Debbie was not wearing monastic underwear.

'Disgraceful,' said Mrs Ponsonby Smith.

She would not be calmed down even though it was an accident. She stormed out threatening to bring the matter up at the next board of governors meeting. Her friend Charlotte Wimple, a vicar's wife, went after her.

The event continued with a course of red mullet cooked with the inside left in. There was another farinaceous course with *polenta*. There was roast quail which was exceedingly tough. There were vine leaves stuffed with fig. There were grapes with oysters in brine.

'The worst meal I've ever had here,' said the chairman of the board of governors. 'I would rather have had bangers and mash.'

Privately, the principal had to agree.

'It sounded very nice the way they put it to me,' said the Parable's brother.

Very few of the assembled guests had the temerity to complain out loud. The students were called forward to be thanked, including Debbie tied up with un-Roman safety pins.

The principal was about to launch into a lengthy speech when there was a sound of flutes and in came a heavily-veiled lady. She made her way up to the area behind the principal's place at the head of the u-shaped table. She began a recitation from Homer and the principal's chief guests and himself turned their chairs on one side to watch and listen.

'Splendid, splendid,' said Principal Parable, recalling Cambridge days of Roman History and Greek Classics.

The flutes struck up again and the heavily-veiled figure

began dancing. Mr James Wimple, the curate, was very impressed until suddenly the dancing figure and the music escalated the speed of the dance. She became like a whirling Dervish and as the speed built up, the veils were hastily ripped away.

'Stop it! Stop it!' said the principal who had suddenly realized that this was a Roman type of striptease act. By now the heavily-veiled figure was very skimpily dressed. The figure was now topless and would soon be naked. Mr Simon Naunder thrust the large cake at Jimmy from off the corner table and he hastily draped the tablecloth around the semi-naked figure. The most respectable pillars of the community made known their distaste with comments such as 'Disgraceful' and 'Disgusting' and 'Bad show'.

Two female students offered to escort the 'stripper girl' out of the restaurant but the principal wanted to know who had sent for her.

'Mr Parable,' she said, 'a Mr Archie Parable.'

'I did not hire you, madam,' said the competency expert.

'Oh, yes you did, you organized the costumes here as well,' she said.

'Disgraceful.' 'Disgusting.' 'Bad show.' 'Wouldn't have happened in Elliot's day' were some of the more commonly heard expressions from the outraged people present.

The lady insisted that she had been hired and she had only done what she had been paid for.

'I have been paid or I wouldn't take everything off,' she said.

'There you are, I haven't paid her anything,' said Archie.

'But I have,' said the principal. 'And you gave me the bill for it.'

'Disgraceful.' 'Disgusting.' 'Bad show.' Would not have happened in Elliot's day,' the chorus resumed.

'I shall be raising this at the next governors meeting,' said the chairman.

'I would not have hired a common trollop to disrobe at such a prestigious function,' said the Principal Parable. 'I never want to see you again,' he continued and he turned back to apologize to his guests.

'Who are you calling a trollop?' said the young woman who struggled free from the tablecloth revealing her shapely breasts once more.

As he turned round to face the semi-naked figure approaching he overlooked the cake and his left hand lunged into the middle by accident. The soft icing was left with a large handprint in the middle. The semi-naked woman slapped his face in anger. As he tried to hold her off the soft sugar was spread down her side cloyingly. The dancer removed her last veils to wipe herself down, revealing all that remained to be seen.

'Disgusting,' said the Colonel, leering down nevertheless at the more private parts of the exposed anatomy.

'Cor, look at that,' said Jimmy.

'You keep your eyes away,' said Stella to David.

'It's not my fault,' said Mr Archie Parable, the competency expert.

Mr Archie Parable returned to London two days later. The stripper had arrived at his doorstep soon after his wife had come up suddenly to find out what was going on. She had received an anonymous phone call about philandering with the principal's wife and then the corruption of the Roman orgy. Meanwhile, Principal Parable did not know who to blame for the fiasco of the Roman feast. Hector Britain was, however, a major suspect.

29

INTO THE FUTURE

The scene was the principal's office of Dronsley College of Further Education but it was now called the North Derbyshire University and it wasn't a principal but a dean in charge now. There were two portraits on the wall of the committee room, now called the senate. One was an elderly figure looking across from the right at a younger man looking across from the left. The former was a portrait of Principal Elliot Ness, the latter was a portrait of the dean, the Reverend Doctor Henry Gerbils. These portraits were under discussion. There was a new head of state for the university which embraced the old Fanshawe Secondary School, The Dronsley Grammar School and the Dronsley College of Further Education. The new dean Jamie Britain, was ex-Captain Britain's son and he had been at the university for a year now. The Reverend Doctor Henry Gerbils was one of the board of governors as well as being Jamie's father-in-law.

'I wonder if you would object to my taking the portraits down from the committee room?' said the new dean

'If these portraits are ever removed it will be the end of the university,' said the reverend gentleman. 'Remember what happened to Gibraltar when the Barbary apes were removed.'

'Oh, don't be daft,' said the new dean.

'I'm not daft, Jamie. I'm deadly serious,' said the reverend doctor.

'I got the guidance to run this place out of the goodwill

of old Elliot Ness. There was another so-called principal who took over from me. He took Elliot's place and removed Elliot's portrait. He didn't last long which is why his picture isn't here. I put Elliot's picture back and I helped to build this place to what it is today. Elliot Ness did as much before me. I advise you, if you're staying, of course, to have a portrait done to go in the middle. I'll even pay for it. You can always be young-looking then, like the picture of me.'

In actual fact, the reverend doctor did not look much older than the portrait, even though it had been taken over a quarter of a century before.

'What did happen to the other principal?' asked Jamie. 'My father would not say and nor would my uncle.'

'You put all the computer record systems in, didn't you? But the records seem to be missing for the year when you must have arrived.'

'Computer problems, I suppose,' said the reverend doctor.

'There are some computer records going back well into the 1906s,' pointed out Jamie. 'Didn't you install computerisation here?'

The reverend doctor had indeed installed computer systems into the college but the initiative had been taken by Mr Parable. It was not Mr Parable's complete miscalculation that the new computer system had been combined with the PBX telephone exchange. A certain Reverend Doctor Gerbils had pointed out the advantages of joining up computers with telephone terminals. Mr Archibald Parable had passed the idea on to Mr Parable and this was yet another fiasco which had contributed to the growing psychological pressure on Principal Parable. SEVERAL records had been erased.

Jamie felt the reverend doctor's eyes poring into him. The reverend doctor was fiddling with his fob watch. Jamie began to feel tired but fought against the feeling.

'You should have a portrait done. You ought to have a portrait done.'

Jamie felt a sort of falling sensation.

'Put the portrait in the middle. Put the portrait in the middle. Put your portrait in the middle.'

Jamie's eyes closed. Why did he feel so very very tired?

'You must never move the portraits from the committee room. You must leave the portraits in the committee room.'

'Wake up, Jamie lad. You must be working too hard,' said the reverend doctor. Jamie had never done this before. Why had he dozed off?'

The fob watch was back in the reverend doctor's pocket. What had they been talking about?

'I've been thinking of having a portrait done for the senate room,' said the new dean. 'It would look impressive between you and that Elliot Ness bloke, wouldn't it?'

'My father said that there was a principal in between you and the other chap. What happened to him?' asked the new dean.

Now Jamie remembered what he had been asking before. 'What happened to the principal before you, and don't say that it was Elliot Ness. Who was it anyhow?'

The reverend doctor thought back and smiled. He had suggested that Principal Parable had a year's sabbatical in Brazil with the Festival of Light campaign. The chairman of the board of governors had even seconded the proposal. The vice-principal had come to lean on the reverend doctor's support quite heavily. The vice-principal was only filling in time anyhow. Ex-Principal Elliot Ness had agreed to act *ex officio* as a sort of governor and the holy trinity, as they came to be known, took over the college administration. Principal Parable never returned, nor did his brother who was promoted as head of the Education Ministry's curriculum development organisation.

'I think the curse of Elliot Ness drove him mad,' said the reverend doctor. 'He went to Brazil on sabbatical and never returned.'

'Uncle Hector said that you started here as head of Food and Beauty, you know,' said the new dean. The reverend doctor neither concurred nor demurred from this suggestion. He remained as impassive as the Sphinx.

'It's time for the senate meeting,' said the secretary.

The two educationalists proceeded to the committee room and the dean looked at the two portraits looking down on the assembly.

'I hope you don't mind a portrait of me sitting in the middle,' said Jamie.

'Not at all,' said the reverend doctor. 'Have it done whilst you are still young.'

The board of governors meeting was soon over. It was only 7.30 p.m. 'Let's go and see Hector at the recreation club,' said the reverend doctor.

'I really fancy some bangers and mash. It's the only place left where you can get sausages because of the EC regulations. We must keep it as a private club.'